INSTANT ADULT

A novel
by Dave Hughes

Prickly Pair Publishing
Chandler, Arizona, USA

This book is a work of fiction. All names, characters, places, and incidents are either the product of the author's imagination or are used fictitiously. Any resemblance to actual persons, living or dead, business establishments, events, or locales is purely coincidental.

Other novels in the "Gay Tales for the New Millennium" series:
Instant Adult
Open Books, Closed Sets
If I Seem Quiet…

Watch for two more novels in this series in 2024.

Visit AuthorDaveHughes.com to learn more about Dave and his books. You can subscribe to his newsletter to gain background information and insights into Dave's books and the writing process, and receive advance notice of upcoming book releases (and subscriber early-bird discounts). You will receive Dave's short story, *Cruise Virgins*, free when you subscribe to his bi-weekly newsletter.
If you would like to contact the author, please send an email to dave@authordavehughes.com.

Cover photos:
City skyline: sevenke (licensed from Shutterstock)
Young man: Kseniia Ivanova (licensed from Dreamstime)
Cover design: Dave Hughes

Library of Congress Control Number: 2022912593

ISBN: 978-0-9970017-8-5

Welcome to Los Angeles

Monday, July 23, 2007

Bryan woke up at around 5:30 a.m., as the bus he had been riding for the past 34 hours pulled into the station in Barstow, California. He managed to sleep at least half the time, but not well. He hadn't showered in two days, and he was starving. He managed to grab a small dinner at the Green River, Utah, stop at 7:00 p.m. yesterday. The bus had stopped for an hour in Las Vegas at 2:00 a.m., but he slept through that. The bus would stay in Barstow for half an hour and there was a McDonald's nearby, so Bryan took the opportunity to use the restroom and eat a quick breakfast.

The sun had just started to rise as the bus pulled away and returned to I-15 for the rest of the trip into Los Angeles. The Rocky Mountains he had admired during the ride from Colorado into Utah on Sunday afternoon were now replaced by stark desert wasteland, mostly flat with occasional small mountain peaks in the distance. Not much to look at.

He tried to catch a couple more hours of sleep, but with the daylight streaming into the bus and the anticipation of finally being close to LA, the best he could manage was a couple of brief dozes.

At 7:25 a.m., after a brief stop in San Bernardino, the bus turned onto I-10 for the final sixty miles of its journey to Los Angeles – just in time for Monday morning rush hour traffic. As the bus lurched along in the stop-and-go traffic, Bryan gazed out the window at mile after mile of bland suburbia. The endless nondescript office buildings, shopping centers, fast-food restaurants, billboards, apartments, and houses soon blurred together into an uninspiring suburban mosaic. The occasional graffiti along the freeway walls was not quite the 'Welcome to Los Angeles' sign he might have hoped for. Still, he felt excited that his journey was almost over and a new, possibility-filled chapter of his life was about to begin. Practically everything about the future was unknown, but still, he felt optimistic.

Finally, as the bus approached the I-5 interchange, the bold skyline of downtown LA came into view. It was a stark contrast to the endless tableau of one- and two-story buildings Bryan had seen up to this point.

The bus exited the freeway and turned onto a dirty street in a stark, rough-looking industrial neighborhood. There was scarcely a surface that had not been adorned with gang-themed graffiti. The mostly anonymous businesses were enclosed behind solid block walls topped with barbed wire coils. The few doors and windows that were visible were protected by heavy iron bars. Trash and sleeping homeless people were everywhere.

The LA that Bryan was being introduced to couldn't have been farther from the sunny picture painted by his boyfriend Chris's older brother Tyler, who had spent the last three years attending UCLA. He thought, *Could this be the same city that also contained Beverly Hills, Hollywood, beaches, and Disneyland? In what parallel universe do those exist?* Bryan was expecting a sunny land of milk and honey with endless entertainment and unlimited possibility. What he was seeing was a gritty, dystopian hellscape.

The bus stations Bryan had experienced up to this point were plain, utilitarian places located in the less-traveled, lower-rent back streets of most cities. But at least they were safe. The Los Angeles bus station was surrounded by high fences with security guards at the entrances. Tents lined the sidewalks. It looked like the middle of a combat zone.

Bryan's heart sank. *I traveled 36 hours for this? This is my future?*

He decided to spring for a taxi rather than stand on the street to wait for a bus, then attempt to navigate transfers encumbered by his two suitcases, backpack, and trumpet.

As the taxi headed north on Alameda, the scenery gradually improved. Islands of trees, grass, and shrubs replaced the solid block walls and barbed wire-topped fences. Office buildings with windows replaced the stark warehouse buildings. Graffiti, while still present, was less ubiquitous.

The cab turned onto the 101 freeway. Several miles later, it exited onto Hollywood Boulevard. After several blocks, it turned left onto a side street and dropped Bryan off in front of the Los Angeles LGBT

Youth Project. He gathered his belongings and hauled them through the door.

The receptionist looked up from her computer and smiled at Bryan and his luggage. "Good morning! New in town?"

"Yes, ma'am. I arrived by bus this morning."

"Where are you from?"

Bryan wondered whether he should divulge any information about where he came from, for fear that the receptionist might report him to the police as a missing person. But he felt that this was probably a safe place. "Kansas."

"Welcome to LA. How may we help you?"

"I was told that you might have services available for LGBT youth."

"Yes, we do. You've come to the right place. Why don't you have a seat over there and I'll see who's available to talk with you."

"Do you have a restroom?"

"Yes, down the hallway on your left."

"And would you please keep an eye on my stuff?"

"Sure. Why don't you move it over here behind my desk?"

Bryan carried his suitcases, backpack, and trumpet to the spot the receptionist indicated, then found the restroom. When he returned to the lobby, the receptionist led him to a small office staffed by an intake specialist.

"Hi, I'm Cynthia." She offered her hand, which Bryan shook.

"I'm Bryan. Nice to meet you."

"Have a seat." She motioned toward the guest chair facing her desk and Bryan sat down.

"Melanie mentioned that you just arrived from Kansas."

"Yes, I got in this morning. I've been on a bus for 36 hours."

"Goodness. You must be tired. So, what brings you to LA?"

"Well, basically, I needed to leave home. My parents recently found out I'm gay, and they're not cool with it at all. See, my dad's a pastor at a large church, so they're really religious and conservative. Anyway, I found out that they were going to send me to this camp in Alabama where they try to convert gay kids to be straight, and I really didn't want to go."

Cynthia frowned, but in a caring, empathetic way. "Oh, no. I've heard about those places. I'm sorry you're in this predicament. Do you have a place to stay tonight?"

"Yes. My manager at my last job used to live here, so he contacted a couple of his friends and they're going to let me stay with them, at least for the first week or so."

"Okay, good. So many kids who arrive here have no place to go. We have some beds here, but often there aren't enough and kids end up sleeping on the street."

Bryan was shocked. "Do you have a lot of kids that show up here?"

"All the time. From all over the country. It's tragic how many parents kick their kids out and how many kids come here to escape bad living situations. We have a lot of resources to help homeless kids, but it never seems to be quite enough. What do you need? Food? Clothing? Any medications?"

"Well, I'm starving right now, but I'll be fine after I get something for lunch. Are there restaurants nearby?"

"Yeah, there are all sorts of places. We also have food here, if you can't afford anything."

"Thanks, but I have some money. I closed my bank account back home. I'll be opening a new one here pretty soon. And I brought two suitcases full of clothes and stuff."

"Sounds like you're better off than about 99 percent of the kids who show up here. So how may we help you?"

"My manager suggested that I should change my name and get legally emancipated. He said you might have attorneys who volunteer their services."

"Yes, we do. How old are you?"

"Seventeen."

Cynthia turned to her computer and typed a few things. Then she picked up her phone and dialed a number.

"Hello, Hal? It's Cynthia from the LGBT Youth Project. How are you today?" Pause. "I'm fine, thank you. I have a young man here who just arrived in town and wants to see about changing his name and getting emancipated. Can you help?" Pause. "He's here right now. Let me ask."

Cynthia turned to Bryan. "Are you available at 3:00 this afternoon?"

Bryan replied, "Yeah. I don't have anything else to do."

Cynthia turned back to the phone. "Yes, he'll be here at 3:00. His name is Bryan. Thanks so much, Hal. You're an angel." Pause. "Okay, see you this afternoon. Bye!"

Cynthia jotted down a name and phone number on a notepad, then tore off the sheet and gave it to Bryan. "The attorney's name is Hal Morris. He'll get you all taken care of. How does that sound?"

"That sounds fantastic. I wasn't expecting this to happen so fast."

"Sometimes things work out well."

"Is it okay if I go get something to eat, then hang out here for the afternoon? One of the guys I'm staying with is going to pick me up here at around 5:30, so can I stay here until then?"

"Yes. We created this center so it would be a safe place for young people to hang out. There's some food and bottled water in the kitchen area. There's a library with some books and a few computers if you need them. So, make yourself at home."

"Thank you very much, Cynthia. I appreciate your help."

"My pleasure. I hope things work out well for you. Remember, we're always here if you need anything."

Bryan walked back up the street to Hollywood Boulevard and turned right. He discovered that he was walking on the Hollywood Walk of Fame, with all the stars of famous actors and actresses embedded in the sidewalk. After several blocks, he crossed the street and walked back on the other side. After walking past more stars, he reached the Guinness World Records Museum and the Ripley's Believe It or Not Museum. The Hollywood Wax Museum was across the street. After the long bus ride through hundreds of miles of desolate landscape and the gritty area surrounding the bus station, he was amazed that he was now standing right in the middle of world-famous Hollywood! There was so much for him to discover.

He passed plenty of restaurants of all types, but considering his tired and unshowered condition, he chose the comfort and familiarity of McDonald's. There would be plenty of other occasions to explore all the wondrous new things around him.

After lunch, Bryan walked around Hollywood some more. He returned to the LGBT Youth Project office at 2:30 and waited in the lobby for Hal Morris to arrive.

At a few minutes past 3:00, a 40ish, somewhat short and compact man with wire-rimmed glasses and curly, thinning hair rushed into the lobby. He was smartly dressed in a jacket, open-collar white shirt, stylish jeans, and expensive-looking loafers. He greeted the receptionist, who then pointed in Bryan's direction. Bryan stood up as Mr. Morris approached.

"Bryan? Hal Morris." Hal quickly scanned Bryan, smiled, and shook his hand vigorously. "How are you today?"

"I'm good, thanks. I appreciate you meeting with me on such short notice."

"My pleasure." He turned back to the receptionist. "Is there a room we can use?"

"The small meeting room down the hall on the right should be open."

"Thanks."

Hal led Bryan down the hall to a room with a rectangular table and six chairs. Hal sat in a chair at one end, and Bryan sat in the chair to his right.

"Welcome to Los Angeles. Why did you decide to come here?"

Bryan gave Hal a brief explanation of how his parents found out he was gay, grounded him, forced him to go to counseling, and how he discovered that they were about to send him to a gay conversion therapy camp. He told him about his former boss, Mr. Simonton, and how he had suggested LA and helped Bryan plan his escape.

As Bryan's story progressed, Hal's demeanor shifted from upbeat to concerned and empathetic.

When Bryan finished, Hal asked, "So, how may I help you?"

Bryan replied, "My manager suggested that I should get legally emancipated so I can do things on my own without my parents' involvement. That way, if they find me, they can't force me to go back home. I also want to change my name so it makes it harder for them to find me."

"How old are you?"

"Seventeen."

"And when's your birthday?"

"October 14th."

"Hmm. Well, your boss was correct that becoming emancipated would prevent your parents from being able to force you to come back home. Unfortunately, this process typically takes four to six months. And except in a few rare circumstances, it requires the parents' consent for you to be emancipated. Since you turn eighteen in less than three months, there isn't enough time for the process to work."

"So, what can I do?"

"You'll just have to wait it out."

"And what about changing my name?"

"Unfortunately, while you're still a minor, that requires your parents' consent."

Bryan let out an exasperated sigh and buried his head in his hands. Then he said, "So, I was counting on doing all these things like opening a bank account, getting a job, getting a cell phone, and enrolling in school using my new name. If I do all that stuff with my current name, won't that make it easier for them to find me?"

"Not necessarily. For example, the bank account. A bank's customers aren't searchable on the internet. Same thing with a company's list of employees or the list of kids enrolled at a school. In fact, they go to great lengths to keep that private."

"But can't the FBI get a warrant to get that information?"

"Yeah, but that's like looking for a needle in a haystack. If they don't even know what city you're in, they're not going to get a warrant for every bank, every employer, and every school in the country. And if you opt for an unlisted number, it will be very difficult for them to find your number or your address."

"But if I wait until I turn eighteen to change my name, then I'll have to change it in all those places."

"Oh, well. It will be a hassle, but it can be done. And I'll be happy to help you with the name change."

"Thanks." Bryan thought for a moment. "So, a minute ago you said there were a few circumstances in which I might be able to get emancipated without my parents' involvement. What are those?"

"That would only come into play if you could convince the judge that your parents aren't trying to find you, or if you would be in physical danger if you returned home."

"Well, they've probably called the police, so that's out."

"Besides, to become emancipated, you have to prove that you have a secure place to live – meaning you're not homeless or couch-surfing, a steady job where you earn enough money to cover all your living expenses, and you're going to school. So, it's not like you could do this tomorrow. It will take some time to get all those things in place."

"And I'd have to do all those things with my current name."

"Yep. And speaking of which, do you have a place to stay?"

"For now. My boss knows these two guys who have offered to let me stay with them for a week or two until I can find an apartment or something."

"If I may ask, how much money do you have?"

"About $3,000."

"That's about $3,000 more than most kids have when they arrive here. Still, it won't last very long out here. What are you planning to do for work, especially considering that you have to go to school in September?"

"I was going to try to get a job in a grocery store or something like that. That's what I did back home."

"Well, I have more bad news for you. Apartment prices are a lot higher in LA than they are back in Kansas. I don't see how you could earn enough money with a grocery store job to live in an apartment and buy food and pay bills, unless you found two or three other people to share it with. Besides, once you start school, you can't work as many hours. Renting a room somewhere might be a better option."

"I would do that. I just need a bed and a bathroom."

"So, you're seventeen. You'll be, what, a senior this year?"

"Yes."

"What are your longer-term plans?"

"I want to go to UCLA. That's one of the main reasons I decided to come to Los Angeles. I figured that after living here for a year, I would qualify for in-state tuition. I'm going to try to get a scholarship. I'm a straight-A student, and I figure that since I'll have no support from my parents that might help me qualify."

"I can tell you're pretty smart. What are you planning to major in?"

"Computer science or something like that. I want to be a software engineer or an application developer. I've been the webmaster for my father's church the past couple of years."

Hal paused for a moment as if he was contemplating what to do next. Then he said, "Okay, I might be able to help you. Let me tell you a little bit about me. I own a house a few blocks from UCLA. That's where I went to school. I have four rooms I rent to college students. It's a nice bunch of guys – all gay. It's kind of a safe space if you know what I mean. Anyway, one of the guys who was going to move in next month just told me he lost his scholarship and he's not returning to school, so now I have a room open. I've never rented to a high school kid before, but I'm willing to make an exception in your case since you'll be 18 in three months and you seem pretty well-grounded. The rent is $500 a month. How does that sound so far?"

"Awesome!" Up to this point, Bryan had been feeling more and more pessimistic about his prospects for making it on his own in this big, expensive city. Suddenly, things were looking up again.

"Okay, well, you should come to see the place first. Want to check it out now?"

"Can we be back here by 5:30?"

"What happens at 5:30?"

"That's when one of the guys I'm going to be staying with will be here to pick me up."

Hal glanced at his watch. 3:40. "Yeah, probably. Do you have his number?"

"Yes."

"Okay, let's go. I can call him if we're going to be delayed."

Hal and Bryan walked up to the reception area. Bryan asked the receptionist, "Can you watch my stuff for the next couple of hours?"

"My shift ends soon, but somebody else will be here. It's okay to leave your stuff here."

Hal said, "Why don't you bring your stuff along? If you like the place, you can go ahead and move in. If not, you'll have it with you and you won't have to worry about someone else watching it."

Bryan thought for a second. "Well, okay."

Hal took Bryan's smaller suitcase and trumpet, and Bryan carried his larger suitcase and backpack. Hal led him to a shiny black BMW hardtop convertible. Hal popped the trunk and they managed to fit Bryan's possessions into the trunk with not much room to spare.

Bryan, at 6' 6", had to scrunch a bit to fit into the car. Hal said, "It's a nice summer day, and we'll be driving surface roads. How about if I put the top down?"

Hal drove a couple of blocks south, then turned west onto Sunset Boulevard. For the next nine miles, Bryan was treated to an eye-popping view of some of the better parts of Los Angeles. The first couple miles were regular city blocks, but as they continued into residential areas, the surroundings looked nicer and nicer.

Hal pointed out several landmarks, like The Comedy Store and the Beverly Hills Hotel. They entered a winding section of Sunset Boulevard, and Hal pointed to a bunch of trees on the right. "On the other side of those trees is Michael Jackson's mansion."

Finally, they approached UCLA, where Sunset Boulevard formed the winding northern boundary of the campus. A couple of blocks past the campus, Hal turned into an upscale residential neighborhood, made a couple more turns, then pulled into the driveway of a well-manicured, modern-looking home. He pressed the garage door remote and pulled the car into the garage. The garage was at street level, but the home sat on higher ground, requiring a trek up about twenty steps.

Bryan stood in awe as he surveyed the exterior of the house. It looked more upscale and fashionable than any house he had ever seen in his hometown, Prairie Village.

Hal opened the door and escorted Bryan in. The interior was even more impressive than the exterior. Hal gave him a quick tour, including the available bedroom. It contained a queen-size bed with a colorful bedspread, a computer desk and chair, a dresser, and a small dorm fridge. The closet was about twice as large as the closet in his former bedroom. The view out the window was to the side of the house, so most of what he could see was a tall dense hedge that separated this house from the one next door.

Next Hal led him into the kitchen. It was spacious and modern, with a large stainless-steel refrigerator and a Jenn-air stove. There was a large kitchen island with a row of four stools, and a fancy multi-light fixture hanging above it from the ceiling.

Hal said, "You're on your own for buying food and cooking, although sometimes the guys team up for meals or share leftovers. You can use the fridge in your room for things like sodas or beer – well, not beer for you yet – and some of your food. You can put the rest in here. You can use this freezer, and there's a standalone freezer in the utility room. We use little colored dot stickers so we can tell whose food is whose. We share the condiments, so we don't have five sticks of butter and five bottles of ketchup.

"On Sunday evening, I usually cook dinner for everyone. Nothing fancy, just pizza or chili or hamburgers, something like that. After that, we usually watch a movie or play a game or something. It's the one time each week when everyone's together, kind of like a family night.

"Everyone's in charge of keeping the kitchen and the common areas neat and clean. As long as you do a good job of putting things away and wiping up after yourself, you'll get along with everyone fine. If you see the dishwasher is full, run it. If you see that it's been run, empty it. If the trash can is full, empty it. Everyone's really good about doing their part, so we don't have any issues."

Bryan was already in total disbelief that he could be living here, but then Hal led him out to the backyard. It looked like a tropical oasis. There were tall oleander hedges with pink and white blossoms, a couple of palm trees, and a variety of other lush plants and shrubs. The pool sparkled, and there was a raised deck with a sheet waterfall at one end. There was a hot tub in one corner and an assortment of lounge chairs and outdoor tables with umbrellas. There was a pass-through window from the kitchen to an outdoor serving counter and a tiki bar with a thatch roof.

Bryan was completely awe-struck. "This is unbelievable! I've never seen anything like this!"

"Welcome to Southern California. Lots of houses have pools. As you can see, the backyard is totally private, so the pool and the hot tub are clothing-optional. You do what you feel comfortable with, but you'll probably find that the other guys just go naked. Except for when we have parties – although sometimes those end up being clothing-optional too. The backyard is like everything else – everybody does their part to keep it neat and clean. So, if you come out here and leaves are floating in the pool, grab the skimmer and scoop them out."

"This is amazing!"

"So, are you interested?"

Bryan made some quick calculations in his head. *Once school starts, I should be able to work 25 to 30 hours a week. If I can get $10 an hour, like I was making at Price Cutter back in Kansas, I should be able to clear $800 to $1,000 a month. After rent, that would leave $300 to $500 a month for food and whatever else I need to buy. So, while it might be tight, I can probably make it work. And I have $3,000 I could dip into occasionally if I have to.*

"Absolutely! This is incredible!"

"Alright, then. Welcome to our little gay family." They shook hands. "By the way, the other guys' names are Ricky, Ted, and Darnell. Darnell's gone for a few more weeks; he'll be back in September. Ricky and Ted come and go. Just say hi to them if you see them. If I see them first, I'll let them know about you."

"May I borrow your phone? I need to call the guy who is supposed to pick me up at 5:30 and tell him I won't need to stay with them after all."

Hal handed Bryan his phone, and they walked back inside. Bryan dug out his would-be host's phone number and called him. Then Hal helped Bryan carry his suitcases into his new bedroom.

"Mr. Morris, I can't thank you enough. I'll do everything I can to keep the place clean and get along with everyone else. Thank you, thank you, thank you!!!"

"You're welcome. And call me Hal. None of that Mr. Morris stuff."

"Okay, Hal. And speaking of what to call each other, I've decided that my new name is going to be Ryan Robertson. Even though I can't change it until I turn 18, can I introduce myself to the other guys as Ryan now? That way, they won't have to re-learn my name in a couple of months."

"Yeah, sure. That makes sense. Whatever you want."

"Thanks. Okay, I'm going to go take a shower and unpack now."

"Sounds good. The master suite is at the other end of the house, over there. Just knock on the door if you need anything."

It only took a few minutes for Bryan to empty the contents of his suitcases into the closet and dresser. There were a few towels and washcloths in the closet, so he grabbed one of each and headed into the bathroom to take a shower. Like the rest of the house, the bathroom was beautiful, with a marble walk-in shower and two modern designer sinks.

By the time Bryan had showered and changed into fresh clothes, it was nearly 5:00. He walked across the house to the master suite and knocked on the door.

"Come in."

Bryan took a few steps into the master suite and quickly glanced around. It was a large room – much bigger than his parents' bedroom in his former home. The front portion of the suite, which was probably intended to be a sitting area, served as Hal's home office. He sat at an L-shaped desk, with one side facing toward the door and the other side facing an oversized window that looked out upon the pool. Farther back, a king-size bed was framed by a massive, elegant headboard with mirrors facing the bed and shelves on each side. The room was lavishly appointed with potted plants, a few pieces of artwork, and a variety of photos and nick-nacks. Hal lived well.

"Hi, Hal. Hey, can you point me in the direction of any restaurants or stores or anything? I want to go grab a bite for dinner and pick up a few things."

"Yeah, sure. We're just a couple of blocks from Westwood Village. It's across from the campus. There are all kinds of restaurants and shops, a Target, a couple of grocery stores and drug stores, and just about anything else you can think of. Here, let me jot down the directions. There's a lot of winding roads and turns, but you'll learn it quickly." Hal reached for a notepad, scribbled a few lines, then tore off the sheet and handed it to him. "It's about a 15-minute walk. There's also a couple of old bikes in the garage that previous guys have left behind."

"Thanks! See you later."

Bryan followed the directions Hal had written down. He smiled when he arrived at Gayley Avenue, then followed it into Westwood Village. He passed a hamburger place, but since he had eaten at McDonald's for lunch, he decided to continue. He passed an interesting array of store-front restaurants – a pita place, a deli, a Korean barbecue – but they were all designed primarily for take-out, with very little in the way of seating. He turned and wandered a couple more blocks, finally ending up at what looked like the center of town. There was a pizza place with some sidewalk seating, so he decided upon that.

The pizza was delicious, and Bryan enjoyed sitting at a table on the sidewalk. Since it was summer, there weren't many people. Bryan tried to imagine what this town would look like when it was throbbing with college kids. He remembered Memorial Day at Chris's house, listening to his older brother Tyler talk about all the fun things there were to do here. He looked forward to being part of it.

When he finished, he walked around a bit more. He passed a Target and stopped in to pick up some toiletries and some more underwear, socks, and T-shirts. As he began his return journey, he passed a grocery store called Pure Foods. His hands were already full with bags from Target, so he decided to take them home, then walk back to Pure Foods to pick up some food for the next few days.

When he returned and started roaming around the store, it soon became apparent that this wasn't Price Cutter. The décor was decidedly more upscale. The large produce department practically overflowed with attractively presented fruits and vegetables of every kind, including some he had never seen or heard of. A large deli area offered a vast array of meats, cheeses, and prepared dishes, with displays of wine bottles liberally scattered throughout. Everything in the meat department and baked goods looked appealing and delicious, and was priced accordingly.

It never occurred to Bryan that groceries didn't cost about the same everywhere. *Why are things so much more expensive here? Is this a California thing? How do college students afford this?* Then he realized this store probably serves the residents of his neighborhood more than the students. He wondered where the students shopped.

Bryan picked out some food for breakfast and lunch, a few frozen dinners, and a 12-pack of Dr Pepper, and paid for his purchases. As he passed the customer service desk on the way to the door, he noticed a sign that read, 'Now Hiring!' He stopped at the desk and asked the representative what kind of jobs were available. She gave him an application and told him to come back tomorrow during the day and speak with a manager.

Bryan returned home. He was worn out from carrying the five plastic bags and the 12-pack of Dr Pepper, which had become more cumbersome as the journey progressed. He had been running on adrenalin all day and his energy was flagging quickly. He placed green-colored dot stickers on his frozen entrees and carried them to the freezer in the utility room. He unloaded six cans of Dr Pepper into his room fridge. It was barely 8:00, but he climbed into bed and fell asleep immediately.

Settling In

Tuesday, July 24, 2007

On Tuesday morning, Bryan awakened at around 8:30. He had decided not to set an alarm and to allow himself a few unstructured days to unwind and acclimate himself to his new surroundings. The demands of a job and school would return soon enough. He contemplated lying in bed for a while longer, but he was too excited about the day ahead of him to fall back asleep.

He had slept soundly for twelve hours. His new bed felt so comfortable after two nights of trying to sleep in a bus seat. Now fully rested, he was ready to take on the day. He took a shower and selected his nicest shorts and a polo shirt. Hopefully, that would make a good enough impression at an interview for a grocery store job.

After a quick breakfast, Bryan walked out into a beautiful sunny morning with his completed job application in hand and headed to the Pure Foods store in Westwood.

Bryan approached the customer service desk and asked to speak to a manager. After about 20 minutes, a thirty-something woman wearing a green Pure Foods polo shirt arrived. "Are you here for a job interview?"

"Yes, ma'am. My name's Bryan Bauer." He wondered if he should bring up the topic of his upcoming name change and ask to be called Ryan, but decided against it. He didn't want to introduce anything complicated or suspicious before he secured the job. Besides, that could lead to more questions. And he had no way of knowing whether this woman might turn him in to the police if she discovered he was a runaway.

"I'm Veronica Masters." She glanced around. "Let's go back to my office."

Ms. Masters led Bryan through a staff-only door into a small office with a desk covered in papers. It was much like the office of his former manager, Russ Simonton. For a store that was decidedly more upscale, he was surprised that the manager's office wasn't noticeably nicer.

Ms. Masters scanned Bryan's application, then said, "Hmmm… so you were working at a grocery store in Prairie Village, Kansas until… just this past Friday?"

"Yes, ma'am. I moved here over the weekend."

"What did you do at your last job?"

"Mostly restocking. I helped out at the registers whenever it got busy. And whenever I had a few free minutes, I would go up and down the aisles and look for items that had been misplaced and put them back where they belong, and pull products up to the front of the shelves, just to keep everything looking nice."

"That's good. Keeping the store looking nice is important."

"Yeah, I guess I have an eye for that sort of thing. I like seeing things neat and organized."

"So, what would you say are your best qualities?"

"I'm motivated and I can work well without much supervision. I can look around and see what needs to be done, and do it without being told. And I'm flexible – I'm willing to do whatever you need."

"And what would you say are your weaknesses?"

Bryan took a moment to ponder that question. Neither Mr. Simonton nor Mr. Rudolph from the year before had asked him that, and his dad never interviewed him for the work he did at the church. It seemed like a dumb question, but he had to come up with something.

"I don't know. I'm kind of quiet and shy. I mean, I get along well with people and I like to help customers, but I'm probably better doing stuff like stocking shelves than facing customers all the time."

Ms. Masters jotted notes while he talked. She didn't make much eye contact. She remained expressionless, so Bryan couldn't tell how he was doing so far. Finally, she looked up and said, "What hours would you be available to work?"

"For now, I can work any time you want. I'd love to get as many hours as possible before school starts. Once school starts, then I can work from 4:00 on, and any time on Saturday and Sunday."

Ms. Masters paused for a moment, then looked up at him. "Do you have any questions for me?"

"I don't think so. I'm pretty familiar with working in a grocery store."

"Would you mind if I contacted your last manager for a reference?"

Bryan felt certain that Mr. Simonton would give him a glowing reference, but he realized he hadn't contacted him since he arrived in town yesterday. "No problem. But I'd like to let him know that you might call. Can you wait until later this afternoon?"

"I'll wait until tomorrow." She scanned his application one last time. "Is this the best number to reach you?"

"Yes, ma'am." Bryan had given her the number of the landline at the house since he didn't have a phone yet.

"Okay, I'll get back to you in the next couple of days. If you don't hear from me, it's okay to call the store and ask." She stood up and extended her hand.

Bryan shook it and said, "Thank you very much for your time. I hope I can join the Pure Foods team!"

Ms. Masters remained expressionless as she ushered Bryan back into the public area of the store. She said goodbye and hurried back to her office.

Bryan left the store and started walking around Westwood Village to discover more of what was there. He had no idea whether he would get the job. Ms. Masters was difficult to read. She seemed frazzled and preoccupied, even at 10:00 in the morning. Maybe she had a lot of other things to deal with. He wasn't sure whether she would be a good boss or not. She didn't seem as friendly and open as Mr. Simonton. He had been polite and enthusiastic, and he felt confident that he had interviewed as well as he could. He couldn't tell how his answer about his weaknesses had been received. Oh, well – there was nothing he could do about it now. He decided to keep his eyes open for other 'now hiring' signs.

Bryan passed a Banktopia branch and stepped in. A young man was sitting at an information desk near the front door, talking to another customer. Bryan waited several feet away. The young man got up and escorted the customer back into some cubicles to meet with someone else. When he returned, Bryan stepped forward.

The young man flashed a friendly smile and said, "Welcome to Banktopia! How may I help you?"

"I'm looking to open an account somewhere, and I'm just kind of checking out my options. Do you have any information you can give me about your checking account plans?"

The young man reached for a pamphlet, opened it up, and showed it to Bryan. "We have three checking account plans: Basic, Preferred, and Deluxe. They're all similar, but they differ on things like the minimum balance required to avoid monthly fees, overdraft protection, foreign ATM charges, and things like that. By the way, I'm Skyler!"

Skyler smiled broadly and extended his hand to Bryan.

Bryan shook it, hesitated for a second, and said, "Bryan. So, how much of a balance would I have to maintain to avoid fees?"

"One thousand dollars. You can also qualify to have the monthly fee waived if you have your paycheck direct deposited and at least one bill auto-paid from the account."

Bryan smiled and took the brochure from Skyler. "Okay, thanks. I'll look it over and perhaps I'll be back."

"You're most certainly welcome. I hope to see you again soon!" It seemed to Bryan that Skyler truly meant that.

Bryan turned and walked out the door. As he held the door open for another customer to enter, he glanced back in. Skyler smiled and waved. Skyler was certainly a ray of sunshine, especially after his dry, soulless encounter with Ms. Masters. Bryan wondered if he was that friendly with everyone.

As Bryan continued his exploration of Westwood Village, he considered the terms of the checking account plans. He assumed that he would be able to have his paychecks from Pure Foods automatically deposited, assuming he got the job. He guessed that most other employers probably did that too. But what about a bill he could set up for auto-pay? He didn't have any bills; he would just be paying Hal $500 a month.

At the next intersection, he turned right and found himself in front of a phone store. Of course! He needed to get a mobile phone – hopefully one of the new iPhones – and he would need a monthly plan. He could have that auto-paid!

He stepped into the store and looked around for some information about their plans and the phones they offered. A young lady named Courtney approached him. "May I help you?"

"Yeah, I'm interested in getting an iPhone!"

"You and the rest of the world. We're looking at about five weeks now. But it could change. Would you like to sign up for the waiting list?"

"You mean you don't have them in stock?"

Courtney looked at him like he had just arrived from another planet. "Are you kidding? We sold out our initial shipment in about two hours. People were lined up for blocks. Whenever we get a new shipment in, they go to the people on the waiting list. You want me to add you to the list?"

Crap. Bryan needed a phone now.

"How much are they?"

"$499 for 4 gigabytes, $599 for 8 gigabytes. And you're required to sign up for a 2-year service agreement, which starts at $59.99 a month and goes up to $99.99, depending on how many minutes you want."

Holy shit. Bryan had no idea it would be this expensive. He saw his dream of being among the first people to own a new iPhone evaporate before his eyes.

"Hmmm… Okay. So let me ask you another question. I have a Nokia phone now. Can I get a new SIM card for it? And how much would that plan cost?"

"Yeah, we can do that. The most basic plan is $39.99 a month for up to 450 minutes."

Bryan did some quick math in his head. That was just 15 minutes a day. "How much if you go over that?"

"Each block of 50 minutes is another $2.50."

"So, if I go over by 51 minutes, I'll get charged $5.00."

"That's right."

"How about texting?"

"You can either pay 15 cents per text or get unlimited texting each month for $20."

Bryan did some more math. The break-even would be 133 texts. That's only four per day. Once he started making friends, he could be texting a lot more than that. Probably better to go with the $20 for unlimited texting. But that meant having a cell phone was going to cost $60 a month. Wow. But he needed to have one.

"Okay, thanks for all the info. Let me think about it."

Courtney nodded and headed off in search of her next customer – one who might actually buy something and earn her a commission.

Bryan headed home. It was almost lunchtime, so he paid attention to the small storefront restaurants he was passing. Most of them offered only a few seats along the windows, so he assumed most of the customers got takeout. He passed a place called My Gyro which offered Mediterranean food. He stepped in and scanned the menu board on the wall above the counter. It offered food with odd names like shawarma, wowshi, koftah, falafel, tzatziki – all food he had never heard of. But in the spirit of adventure and discovery, he decided to give it a try.

Ricky

Tuesday, July 24, 2007

When Bryan arrived back home, he set the brochures down on his desk and opened his laptop. He planned to spend the next hour or so researching and comparing the other banks in the area. Then he would turn his attention to the plans offered by each of the major cell phone providers.

Then he remembered he needed to contact Russ Simonton to let him know that Veronica Masters might call him and ask for a reference. He got up and walked to Hal's room to ask if he could make a long-distance call on the landline without incurring a charge, or if he could borrow Hal's phone. He knocked on the door. Hal wasn't there.

He wondered whether any of his housemates were home. He hadn't met any of them yet. He didn't know which housemate lived in which room, so he knocked on each of the other doors in his end of the house. No answer.

Bryan decided to hang out in his room for a while and wait for someone to come home. If necessary, he could make the call on the landline and pay Hal back later.

He started up his laptop and opened a map of Westwood Village. He tried to retrace all the places he had wandered so far. The streets in the village ran in all directions like a haphazard web, while the streets in his residential neighborhood wandered and curved all over the place. It was a wonder he didn't get lost. It was a far cry from the predictable north-south and east-west grid of the Kansas suburbs from which he had escaped.

He zoomed in and scanned the village for banks, then opened up a new window for each of them. He had just started comparing Banktopia with one of its competitors when he heard the front door open. A male voice was engaged in spirited banter with no one else.

Bryan walked into the living room. A handsome, well-built young man with light brown skin and thick, jet-black hair was heading into the kitchen. Bryan could see the phone earpiece sticking out of his ear. The young man almost disappeared into the kitchen when he caught sight of Bryan in his peripheral vision and stopped. "Hang on a sec," he said to his phone.

He took a couple of steps back into the living room, squared his shoulders, and glared at Bryan. "Would you mind telling me what you're doing in this house?"

Bryan suddenly realized that if he was perceived as an intruder, he could be shot.

"Oh, uh, I live here. I moved in yesterday afternoon."

For a tense moment, the other guy stared at Bryan, sizing him up. Despite Bryan's height advantage, he was of slight build and this guy was obviously stronger than him.

"My name's Ryan." Bryan reached out his hand.

The other guy relaxed a bit and decided that Bryan was probably telling the truth and wasn't a burglar. "Ricky." He shook Bryan's hand. "Sorry. I haven't seen Hal since yesterday morning. I didn't know he had found a new guy already."

"Yeah, it came about kinda suddenly."

"I'll say. He just found out last Friday that Tyler wasn't going to be able to live here, and now he's found a replacement already. Anyway, welcome. And sorry about that."

"No problem. I can tell already I'm going to love living here. Hey… do you know if I can make a long-distance call on the landline?"

Ricky looked puzzled, like he didn't understand why anyone would even ask. "I don't see why not."

"I mean, I don't want Hal to get charged."

"I don't know what kind of plan he's on. I don't even know why he still has it – everyone uses their cell phone. Anyway, go ahead. He won't care."

"Okay, thanks. I don't have a cell phone yet. So, hey, after I make my call, can I talk to you for a sec?"

"Sure. I'll be in my room."

Bryan returned to his room, found the paper with Russ Simonton's number, then went into the kitchen to place the call. After three rings, Russ picked up. "Russ here."

"Hi, Russ! It's Bryan." Bryan suddenly wondered whether Ricky could hear him talking. He had just introduced himself as Ryan, now he was calling himself Bryan. Oh well, they sound almost the same.

"Bryan! Great to hear from you. So, I guess you made it to LA okay."

"Yeah. The bus ride was … an adventure. Anyway, I don't know if you've heard from Robert or Trevor, but I ended up finding a place to stay right away, so I didn't need to stay with them."

"Yeah, they mentioned that."

"I hope that wasn't rude or anything."

"Nah, they understood. So, tell me about your new place."

"Oh, man, it's unbelievable! I mean, seriously. It's this real modern place with all kinds of nice furniture, and it's in a beautiful, rich neighborhood. And the guy who owns it rents out four rooms to college students. Well, and now me. I guess some guy had to drop out, so he had a room available. And it's only $500 a month! Oh, and you should see the backyard! There's a pool and all these beautiful trees and plants, and there's this bar with a thatch roof… it's like a resort back there."

"Wow… sounds like you lucked out."

"I did. It's almost too good to be true. Oh, and get this: it's just a few blocks from UCLA! I mean, I can walk there in fifteen minutes. And they have a couple of bikes here too."

"Do the others know you're gay yet?"

"Oh, they're all gay. So's the guy who owns it. I met one of them just now. I haven't met the other two yet. After I got here yesterday in the late afternoon, I just went out and got something to eat, bought a few things, then came back and crashed. I slept for like twelve hours. Anyway, I just applied for a job at a grocery store here. It's called Pure Foods."

"Oh, yeah, I went to a couple of them when I lived out there. Pretty upscale – and expensive."

"I'll say. I can't believe how much stuff costs out here. I guess I just assumed that stuff costs the same everywhere."

"Nope. That place is pretty high-end. The stuff like meat and produce is higher quality, but you sure pay for it. There are regular grocery stores, too. Fred's is a popular chain. They'll be a lot more reasonable. Ask your housemates where they shop."

"I will. Anyway, the manager of this place asked if she could call you for a reference."

"Of course."

"Yeah, I thought so, but I wanted to let you know. Her name is Veronica Masters. So anyway, how are things at the store?"

"Oh, pretty much the same – minus you."

"Did the police come and question you?" Bryan suddenly remembered that maybe Ricky could hear his end of the conversation.

"No, which kind of surprises me. But then, it's only been three days. But don't worry about that."

"Okay, well I should probably get off the phone. I'm calling from the landline in the house. I'm going to get a phone later today or tomorrow. I'll send you an email with my new number and stuff."

"Okay, and let me know if you get the job. I'll put in a good word for you."

"Thanks, I really appreciate it. And thanks for everything you've done for me."

"My pleasure. Take care and stay in touch."

"Okay. And say hi to Frank for me."

"I will. Bye."

Bryan hung up and then walked over to Ricky's room and knocked.

"Come in."

The furniture in Ricky's room was pretty much the same as Bryan's, but the similarity ended there. There was a weight bench with a barbell and several free weights lying around on the floor. There were two posters of Latina singers taped to the walls as well as a calendar with a picture of a muscular naked man sporting a large erection. Clothes and a wide variety of other possessions were strewn all over the place.

Bryan took a couple of tentative steps inside. "Hey, uh…"

"Yeah, I'm kind of a slob." Ricky smiled.

Bryan smiled back. "Hey, it's your room. Anyway, I was wondering… where do you go to get your groceries?"

"Fred's, usually. There's one in Westwood. Or maybe Food-o-Rama if I'm driving past one."

"Do they have Price Cutter out here?"

"What's that?"

"They have those back home – er, where I used to live. I worked there." Bryan made a mental note: stop calling Kansas 'home.' It's not home anymore.

"Nah, I don't think so."

"Anyway, I went into this place called Pure Foods yesterday, just 'cause it was the first place I found–"

"You mean Pure Rip-off. That's the rich people store."

"Yeah, I noticed. Anyway, I applied for a job there."

"Good luck. At least you know they'll have money to pay you."

"So, where is Fred's?"

"Just a couple blocks farther down on Weyburn."

"Okay. And who do you use for your cell phone service?"

"Horizon. But Marathon's pretty good too. It probably doesn't matter much. It's not like you have to worry about lack of coverage around here."

"And how about banking?"

"I use Americabank."

"Do they have a good plan that doesn't have fees?"

Ricky shrugged. "I don't know. I never pay any attention. I guess maybe I should."

"Okay, thanks."

"No problem. So, where are you from?"

"Kansas."

"Whereabouts?"

"Just outside of Kansas City."

"Ah. I think the guy who was going to live here was from somewhere around there. Or maybe it was Nebraska. Something like that. You gonna be a freshman?"

"No, actually, I'm going to be a senior in high school. I want to go to UCLA next year, though."

Ricky looked puzzled. Why would someone come out here to go to high school? He decided not to ask. Instead, he said, "You're in high school? Man... I know Hal likes his college boys, but he really robbed the cradle this time!"

Bryan was stunned. *Is it possible that Hal could be ... no, he can't be. Hal didn't seem creepy and he hadn't said or done anything inappropriate ... yet. But how can I really know? Was that why he offered me a place to stay so quickly? And to think, he volunteers for the LGBT Youth Project! I wonder if they know?*

"Uh... Is there something I should know about Hal?"

Ricky saw the shocked look on Bryan's face and paused for a second. "Oh! No, no! I didn't mean it that way at all. Oh god, no. Hal's a great guy. I think there's a part of him that wishes he could be in college forever, but no, he's not a perv or anything like that. He's harmless."

There was a brief gap in the conversation. Bryan decided to excuse himself before Ricky started asking more questions.

"Well, hey, thanks for all the info. And nice to meet you."

"Sure, no problem."

Bryan backed out the door and closed it softly. He returned to his room and resumed his research on the local banks and cell phone carriers. He discovered that the new iPhones were only being offered by one carrier – the one he had visited – so there would no iPhone for him in the foreseeable future.

He decided that Banktopia would do fine. He went through his drawers and retrieved the cash that he had stashed in various places among his clothes. He pulled $200 aside and stashed it back in a drawer, then placed the rest inside his backpack. He found his Nokia phone and added it to his backpack. Then he set off on foot for Banktopia.

Skyler

Tuesday, July 24, 2007

When Bryan entered Banktopia, a young lady in her mid-20s was sitting at the welcome desk. Aside from a couple of people at the teller windows, there were no other customers in the bank. When she looked up and saw Bryan approaching, she formed a half-smile that reflected both an obligation to be cheerful and boredom. "Welcome to Banktopia. How may I help you?"

"Hi. I'd like to open a checking account."

As soon as Bryan spoke, Skyler's grinning face popped up from behind one of the cubicle walls. Skyler scurried from his cubicle up to the welcome desk. "Oh, hi! Glad you came back!" He turned to the woman at the desk and said, "I spoke with this gentleman when he was here this morning." Turning to Bryan, he said, "I'd be happy to help you. Right this way, please."

As Skyler turned back toward his cubicle, he and the woman exchanged glances. Bryan couldn't quite see Skyler's face, but the woman's face said, 'Uh-huh. You go, gurrrl.'

As Bryan followed Skyler back to his office, he couldn't help but notice Skyler's slender, compact physique. He wasn't muscled, but he didn't have an ounce of extra body fat. His torso gradually tapered from his broad shoulders to his slim waist, and his firm, round buns were appealingly emphasized by his perfectly-fitting trousers.

Once they reached Skyler's cubicle, Skyler sat down near the edge of his seat with impeccable posture and a perky smile and asked, "Did you have a chance to look over the brochure?" Bryan nodded. "Which plan did you decide upon?"

"I think the Basic is all I'm going to need, at least for the time being."

Skyler nodded slightly to signal that, of course, Bryan had made the right decision. "Sure. If you're only going to be depositing money and using your debit card to pay for things, that should be all you need. You can always switch to a different plan if your needs change in the future. May I see your photo ID?"

Bryan retrieved his Kansas driver's license from his wallet and handed it to Skyler. He hesitated for a second, then leaned in and spoke softly. "So, uh… I'm planning to change my name in a couple of months. Would it be possible to create this account using my new name?"

Skyler studied him for a moment, then said, "No, we're not allowed to create accounts for fictitious names, which is what this would be until your name change becomes official. I have to use the name I see on your government-issued photo ID."

Bryan's eyes dropped.

Skyler said, "But once you have a court order, just bring it in and it will be no problem to change the name on your account at that point."

"Okay."

Skyler returned his attention to Bryan's driver's license. "Is this your current address?"

"No, I just moved here a couple of days ago. Let me give you the address where I'm living now."

"You can do either, but if you're just here for school you might want to use your parents' address. You might be living in a different place each year."

"No, I want to use my new address." He told Skyler his new address and Skyler typed it into his computer.

"And… may I have your Social Security number?"

Luckily, Bryan had remembered to bring his Social Security card with him. He was thankful that Russ Simonton had suggested that he take it when he left home and that he was able to find it. This process would probably have ground to a halt otherwise.

"Now, who would you like to list for your POD?"

"What's that?"

"Payable on death. If something unfortunate were to happen to you, that's who would get your money."

"Do I have to list someone?"

"You don't have to, but it's a good idea. Otherwise, it will go into an unclaimed funds account with the state and someone would have to file a bunch of paperwork to claim it. A lot of times, that money is never claimed."

Bryan looked perplexed. He didn't want to leave it to his parents, although it really wouldn't matter after he was dead.

Skyler sensed his uncertainty and said, "You can always change it later." He smiled in an attempt to reassure and calm Bryan, and to keep the process on track.

"Can I leave it to a minor?"

Skyler thought for a moment. "I don't see why not."

"Okay. Brandon Bauer. He's my younger brother."

"And what's his address?"

"That's the one on my driver's license."

Skyler turned to his computer and typed a bit more. He seemed confident in his ability to execute this entire process flawlessly. His enthusiasm and dedication to his task made it seem like he was experiencing fulfillment by doing this work – almost like he was answering his life's calling.

Skyler turned back to Bryan and smiled. "Alrighty, then. How much money would you like to deposit?"

"$2,400."

"Will that be in the form of a personal check or cashier's check?"

"I have cash."

Skyler hesitated again. He wondered why this guy was carrying around so much cash, but he knew he shouldn't ask. Cash was still legal tender, after all.

"I assume you'll want a debit card. Would you like me to order some checks?"

"Do people even write checks anymore?"

"Not often, but it does come in handy now and then. The first batch comes free with the new account."

"Okay, sure. Why not?"

"Alrighty, then. Please wait here for a moment." Skyler got up, left his cubicle, and returned a moment later with a nice-looking glossy folder. He opened it, retrieved a couple of items, and spent the next three minutes silently typing more information into his computer. Bryan wondered what all the typing was for. As he watched Skyler hard at work, he had to frequently remind himself to glance around at other things so Skyler wouldn't sense that he was staring at him. Skyler was so focused on providing all the information his computer screen was demanding, he probably wouldn't notice anyway.

Bryan wondered what his story was. *Is he a student at UCLA and this is a part-time job? Is he even going to college? Is this his chosen career path, and he'll work here for years to come, rising up the ranks of bank management? What's he like outside of work? Is he always this perky and friendly? What else is going on in his life? Is he single or does he have someone special? Is he even gay?*

Skyler finished typing and turned back to Bryan. "Would you like to apply for a credit card?"

"Really? Would I even qualify?"

"Let's see." Skyler typed Bryan's Social Security number into his computer, waited a few seconds, and said, "Yes, you probably would. You don't have much credit history, but there's nothing bad on your record. You've never had an overdraft. You've had a pretty good income over the past couple of years for a student. You won't get a very high credit limit, but that will get raised as you earn more money, assuming your credit score stays high."

Getting a credit card hadn't even been on Bryan's radar. But maybe it would be a good idea, now that he was on his own and on the verge of adulthood. "How much does it cost?"

"If you pay the bill in full each month when it's due, it doesn't cost anything. But if you don't pay your bill in full, then you start getting charged interest. And that can add up quickly."

Bryan sat silently, weighing the pros and cons in his mind.

Skyler said, "You don't have to decide right now. If you're unsure, you probably shouldn't. You can come back any time." Bryan sensed that Skyler hoped he would. No, he was probably just imagining that.

"Is there any penalty if I have it but don't use it?"

"Not at this point. If you started applying for lots of credit cards, that wouldn't look good."

"Alright, then. What the heck. Sign me up!"

"Okay. So, what is your monthly income?"

"Well, that's a bit tricky. I applied for a job at Pure Foods yesterday, but I don't know whether I'm going to get it. But if I don't, I'll get a job someplace else. At my last job, I made around $1,600 a month. But once school starts, it will probably go down to around $1,000 a month."

Skyler typed in $1,600. Then he typed in some more stuff, then finally pressed the Enter key to submit the application. Skyler swiveled his chair away from his computer screen to face Bryan directly. He picked up the folder he had been working from, turned it 180 degrees so it was facing Bryan, and opened it. He smiled, and his level of enthusiasm kicked up another notch. Bryan sat up in his chair and leaned forward slightly.

"Welcome to Banktopia! This is your new customer welcome packet. Here are a few starter checks in case you need them before your regular checks arrive in the mail. Here's a temporary debit card. Your permanent one will arrive in a few days. Make sure you sign it on the back. This booklet tells you all about your new account, along with the various features and benefits. This sheet over here steps you through how to get started with accessing your account online. There's also a phone app you can download, and it tells you all about that."

Skyler glanced back at his computer screen and smiled. He pressed a few keys, and his printer woke up and sprang into action. The instant the second piece of paper completed its emergence from the slot, Skyler snatched them and placed them in front of Bryan. He looked him in the eyes and smiled. "Congratulations! You have been approved. This is your credit card number. Your card should arrive within a few days, but if you need to charge something before then, you can show this to the clerk and they can manually enter the number. The terms are spelled out in the fine print. You should probably look it over to familiarize yourself with them."

Skyler tucked the papers with the credit card information into one side of the folder. He reached for one of his business cards and pressed the corners into the four little diagonal slits that had been cut in the folder flap for that purpose. "Here's my card. Please feel free to call me or stop in any time." He made eye contact and smiled. Bryan could tell that he meant it.

Skyler closed the folder and extended it to Bryan. "Congratulations! And thanks again for choosing Banktopia for your personal banking needs."

Bryan assumed everything that had taken place up to this point was part of Skyler's memorized script for opening an account with every new customer. He had no way of knowing whether Skyler always displayed this level of vivacious enthusiasm, but while it occasionally seemed contrived, mostly it was endearing. If only everyone could be so happy at their job.

Skyler asked, "Do you have any questions?"

Bryan assumed this was a rhetorical question which really meant, 'We're finished. You may leave now.' He said, "No, I don't think so," and started to get up from his chair.

Skyler lowered his voice slightly. "Well, I have one."

This unexpected, off-script question caught Bryan by surprise. He sat back down.

"I'm about due for a break. You wanna go grab a coffee at the place across the street?"

"Well, I don't drink coffee, but–"

"They have other drinks. Their iced green tea is delicious."

Bryan smiled. "Okay, sure." Why not?

"Good. So why don't you head over there now, and I'll meet you there in a few minutes."

Bryan nodded and stood up. Skyler led him to the edge of the cubicles and gave him a subtle nod that said, 'see you soon.'

Bryan left the bank, walked across the street, and waited on the sidewalk. A few minutes later, Skyler arrived and led him inside.

A slender, 20ish girl with pink-tipped jet-black hair and numerous piercings around her face spotted Skyler and asked, "the usual?"

Skyler replied, "Yes." He turned to Bryan. "And what would you like?"

"I dunno… that iced green tea sounds good."

Skyler turned back to the clerk. "And a Trenta iced green tea."

Bryan reached for his wallet and whispered to Skyler, "What's Trenta?"

"Extra-large. Don't worry, it's on me."

"Not literally, I hope."

Skyler looked puzzled.

"I'll try not to be a klutz and spill it on you."

Skyler got it but wasn't particularly amused.

A minute later, they were seated at a small high-top table next to the window. Bryan eyed Skyler's drink – a thick, creamy, light brown blend with brown specks, topped with whipped cream and chocolate drizzle – and asked, "What's that?"

"A double-chocolate cookie crumb Frappuccino."

Skyler hopped off his high seat and returned a few seconds later with a straw. "Wanna try it?"

Since Skyler had already made the effort to procure a straw, Bryan felt he should oblige. "Sure."

Skyler shoved the straw down through the crème and pushed the drink across the table to Bryan. He took a sip. It tasted as rich and sweet as it looked. The initial impression on his tongue was chocolate and sugar, but it finished with the taste of coffee which Bryan wasn't accustomed to.

"Wow – that's pretty good." It wasn't in the same league as a slushie from Slush Fun, but it was okay and he wanted to be agreeable.

"Yeah, it's a nice little mid-afternoon treat. The caffeine and sugar rush gives me a lift so I can make it through the rest of the day."

Bryan felt he should reciprocate and asked, "Would you like a taste of mine?"

"No thanks. I've had it before. I guess I'm more of a coffee person."

"I know what you mean about the sugar buzz. Back in Kansas, we had this place called Slush Fun. It wasn't fancy like this, it was just a drive-in. But they have these drinks called slushies with all kinds of flavors. My best friend and I used to hang out there all the time. We'd sit in the car and talk about whatever."

"Yeah, we have those out here too." The look on his face said, 'you actually went there?'

"This iced green tea is good. Thanks! You didn't have to pay for it."

"My pleasure. But, hey. Speaking of Kansas, tell me a little bit about Bryan Bauer. What brings you from the amber waves of grain to the throbbing metropolis of Los Angeles?"

Bryan was feeling cautiously adventurous up to this point, but Skyler's inquiry prompted a wave of apprehension. *How much should I say? How can I explain my circumstances in a way that would seem reasonable and believable without raising more uncomfortable questions? I've already given him a lot of information. On the one hand, he seems nice, and I need to start making friends here. On the other hand, I need to be careful about how much I tell other people.*

"Well…" Bryan took another sip of his iced tea. *Stay calm. Don't let him see that you're nervous. He's probably not going to turn you in.* "I wouldn't quite say I came from wheat fields. I'm from the suburbs of Kansas City, on the Kansas side. But yeah, a lot of Kansas is flat farmland. Anyway, I'm hoping to go to UCLA, so I came out here to establish residence so I could qualify for in-state tuition."

"So, you're not actually going to UCLA? You just think you might go?"

Bryan forced a nervous smile. "I'm going to be a senior in high school this year."

Skyler looked surprised. Apparently, he hadn't paid attention to Bryan's birthdate on his driver's license or done the math. He assumed he was here for college.

"So, your family picked up and moved out here just so you could get in-state tuition?"

Uh-oh. Here goes. "Well, no. I'm the only one who moved out here. I'm staying with friends."

Questions were swirling inside Skyler's head. "So, you're willing to live apart from your family for a year and be out here on your own, just to get in-state tuition to a school you don't even know you're going to be attending yet?"

"Well, I'd be living on my own starting next year anyway."

"True."

Skyler pondered what he should, or should not, ask next. Bryan wondered how he could shift the conversation to another topic – *any* other topic. He could turn the tables and ask Skyler to say more about himself. Before he could open his mouth, Skyler decided to ask the question that had been on his mind since the beginning of their meeting at the bank. "So, I'm just curious. It's none of my business, so you don't have to answer. But I can't help wondering why you are going to change your name."

Bryan was taken aback by Skyler's boldness and nosiness. He quickly weighed the pros and cons of telling him the full story and decided not to.

"I'd rather have a different name."

There was a moment of awkward silence.

Skyler said, "Well, okay."

Bryan said, "Maybe I'll tell you more another time. But enough about me. Tell me a little bit about you."

"I don't know… there's not much to tell. I live in Van Nuys, about ten miles north of here. I still live with my folks. I went to Los Angeles Valley College, a community college a couple of miles away from my house. I got an AA in Business Administration, majoring in Banking and Finance. So, that got me in the door at Banktopia. Now I'm just working, trying to save up some money, and trying to figure out what comes next – whether I want to go back to school to get another degree or focus more on getting out on my own."

"Have you lived here all your life?"

"We moved here from Wisconsin when I was about five. So yeah, almost all my life." Skyler glanced at his watch. "Oh, shit. I should've been back five minutes ago."

"You wanna have dinner or something?"

Skyler thought for a second. "I can't tonight. But yeah, let's do that sometime. Give me a call at work. You have my number. Or shoot me an email."

"Okay. And thanks again for the iced tea."

Skyler nodded and rushed off.

Bryan watched out the window as Skyler hurried across the street and disappeared into the bank. He wasn't sure whether he had just been blown off or whether Skyler really wanted to get together for dinner another time. He decided to wait a couple of days, then send him an email.

Bryan thought some more about what had just happened. *Was that a date? It seemed too short and spontaneous to be a date, but it kind of was. What about Chris and me? We constantly hung out together as best friends, but those times didn't qualify as dates. But during the last few weeks, when we both figured out that we're gay and things got physical, then obviously we were boyfriends. But when did the actual transition from friends to boyfriends occur? Maybe it was that night in the motel room. There near the end, whenever we hung out together, were those dates?*

Aside from time spent with Chris, if those were in fact dates, Bryan had never dated anyone before. He had never asked anyone out on a date or been asked. He had always assumed that dating was something boys do with girls. Do two guys even date? It seemed like they would, but Bryan had never thought about any of this before. It was all so foreign and complicated. Maybe there was an instruction manual – *How to Be Gay* or *What Gay Guys Do*, or something like that.

Bryan suddenly realized something else. *I just assumed Skyler is gay, but is he? Neither of us specifically said 'I'm gay.' Is this just wishful thinking? Am I making assumptions based on stereotypes or hopes? Is Skyler this friendly and perky with everyone? Did he invite me along on his break because he wanted company or he just wants to become regular friends? Or did he want to pump me for information about why I wanted to change my name because it related to how I wanted to open my account and it seemed suspicious?*

If he's not gay, maybe that's why he blew off my suggestion for dinner and scurried away so quickly. On the other hand, he did say I could call or email him.

Bryan shifted his focus to the day's agenda. His next stop would be the phone store where he would buy a new SIM card for his current phone and sign up for a plan. He finished his iced tea, walked out of the coffee shop, and tried to remember which way the store was.

Mrs. Rodriguez

Wednesday, July 25, 2007

On Wednesday morning, after showering and eating breakfast, Bryan logged onto his computer to determine which school district he was in. He learned that he would go to Westwood High School, which was about two and a quarter miles away and on the other side of the freeway. It was too far to walk, but doable by bike. Fortunately, Hal said there were a couple of bikes in the garage that guys who previously lived there had left behind.

He pulled up MapQuest and plotted the best route to get there. He jotted down the directions and put the slip of paper in his pocket. Then he gathered up his report cards from his previous years of school, put them in his backpack, and took off on one of the bikes.

After pedaling about 20 minutes, he arrived. The school occupied a large city block and was surrounded by a high wrought-iron fence. Everything in this neighborhood was crammed together much more densely than the homes and schools he was accustomed to in Prairie Village, Kansas. Newer buildings had been added to the campus over the years, but the main building looked like it had been there for decades. It was a generic, utilitarian two-story brick building with large framed windows that also looked ancient. A shrubbery-lined walkway led from the street corner to what Bryan assumed was the main entrance. There wasn't a bike rack in sight, so he chained his bike to a lamp post and ventured inside.

He found the office easily. A receptionist turned away from her computer and said, "Hello. May I help you?"

"Hi. Yes, I'd like to speak to someone about enrolling for the coming school year."

Her smile changed to a neutral expression and she said, "Your parents can take care of that online, although the deadline for many of the advanced programs has already passed."

Good grief. Yet another disappointment. "I just moved here a couple of days ago, and… well, my parents aren't really in the picture. I'm kind of on my own. Is there someone I could talk to about my situation and maybe ask a few questions?"

The receptionist gave him a curious look and got up from her chair. "Wait right here for a moment, and I'll see if someone's available."

About twenty seconds later, the receptionist returned along with an older lady who approached Bryan with her hand outstretched. "I'm Mrs. Rodriguez, the Principal. Please come into my office."

"I'm Bryan Bauer." He shook her hand. Her warm smile and motherly charm immediately put him at ease.

After Mrs. Rodriguez sat down at her desk and Bryan sat down in a guest chair, she asked, "How may I help you?"

"Well, I just moved here a couple of days ago. I'm heading into my senior year, and I need to enroll and sign up for classes. I started to enroll online, but I'm in kind of a unique situation, so I thought it might be easier to come in and talk to someone. Plus, I have some questions."

Mrs. Rodriguez nodded and waited for him to continue.

"So, the online form has fields for things like the parents' names and contact information. I know in most situations it would be the parents who fill out the form. But, well… I'm not living with my parents. I kinda had to leave home to get away from… well… an uncomfortable situation. So, I'm pretty much on my own. Of course, I want to go to school. Is it possible for me to enroll myself without my parents being involved?"

Mrs. Rodriguez's friendly demeanor changed to one of curiosity and concern.

"First of all, the most important thing is for you to be in school. We'll take whatever steps we need to take to ensure that you attend school. But it's also important that you're safe and that your basic needs are being met. Are you currently experiencing homelessness?"

"No, I have a place to stay. I've rented a room in a house near campus."

"How are you planning to pay for it and feed yourself?"

"I have some money saved up, and I'm applying for a part-time job.

I'm pretty sure I'll be able to afford it."

"Do your parents know where you are right now?"

"No." Bryan was starting to get concerned. Would she turn him in?

"So, about your situation at home. Did you feel that you were in danger? Were you being beaten or abused?"

Bryan grew nervous. *How much should I tell this woman I just met? She seems nice, and she seems like she cares. But what might she be required to do?*

"No, I wasn't being physically beaten or abused. But let's just say that if I stayed, or if I was forced to go back, something very bad would happen to me."

Mrs. Rodriguez looked puzzled, but she sensed that she shouldn't push too hard.

"We have access to resources that can provide various forms of assistance if you need it."

"Thank you, but I don't need any resources. I'm okay. I just need to sign up for school. And I need to not have my parents find out where I am, 'cause then I would get sent back. I don't want to go back there under any circumstances."

"Okay, I understand. So, what are your plans? Do you intend to go to college? Are you more interested in vocational training? What do you plan to do after you graduate?"

"Definitely college. I'm hoping to go to UCLA. That's one of the reasons I came out here. I want to become a software engineer or an application developer – something like that."

"What kind of grades did you get at your last school?"

"I was a straight-A student. I got one or two Bs, but almost all As. I have my final report cards for all my previous years of school."

"Good. That will be helpful."

It occurred to Bryan that those report cards had the name of his last school on them. Shit.

"So, if you have advanced placement courses, I'd like to try to get into those if I can."

"Okay, I'll see what we can do. And are there any electives you want to take?"

"Yes. If it's possible, I'd like to be in band. I play the trumpet. I was first chair at my last school. I was in marching band, wind ensemble, and jazz ensemble. Do you have those here?"

"Yes, we do. For a while, back in the 90s, we had to discontinue our music programs due to a lack of funding. They cut music in the elementary and middle schools, so we didn't get many kids coming up who played instruments. But thankfully that situation has turned around and we can offer those programs again. We're still sort of rebuilding, but our band director is doing a wonderful job and it gets better every year."

"That sounds great. I don't plan to major in music, but music is very important to me – especially jazz. I don't really care about how good they are, I just want to be able to play. And, at my last school, most of my friends were other band kids. So, how do I sign up?"

"I'll put you in touch with the band director. I think band camp is going to be starting in a week or two. But let's get you enrolled first."

Mrs. Rodriguez turned to her computer. "I can go through all the forms with you. We'll figure out what information to provide as we go along."

Bryan was feeling much better about this. Mrs. Rodriguez seemed like a very nice lady, and he was starting to feel like he could trust her.

"Okay, so before we get too far into this, I have a question. I'm going to turn 18 in October. As soon as I do, I'm planning to change my name. Can we put my new name into the system now?"

Mrs. Rodriguez thought about that. She wanted to ask more questions but decided not to. "Probably not, but let me check." She spent a few minutes searching on the school system's website and reading relevant pages. Then she picked up the phone and called someone at the school system's main office. Finally, she hung up the phone and turned back to Bryan. "No, I'm sorry, I have to enter your legal name into the system. But when your name change goes through, bring in the court order and we can change it for you at that time."

"Yeah, I kinda figured that would be the case, but I thought I'd ask anyway."

"Besides, your report cards have your current name on them."

"Okay, but… do you think it would be possible to have my teachers start calling me Ryan, like it's my nickname, even if my current name is in the system? That way, nobody has to re-learn what to call me in a couple of months, and it will avoid a lot of questions I'd rather not have to deal with."

"Yes, I see nothing wrong with that. Once we decide upon which classes you'll take, I'll send a note to your teachers. It would help if you went up to each of them on the first day of classes to remind them."

They finished going through all the forms and choosing the classes Bryan would take. Finally, Mrs. Rodriguez asked, "Do you have any other questions?"

He did. He had been debating whether to ask, but he felt good about Mrs. Rodriguez, so he decided to take a chance.

"Yeah, there is one more thing." Bryan took a deep breath. "What's it like for gay kids here? Are the other kids pretty cool with it, or have there been problems? Or do you even know if there are any gay kids here?"

Mrs. Rodriguez smiled. Her comforting demeanor reassured Bryan. "We celebrate all kinds of diversity at our school. You'll notice right away that our students come from a wide variety of backgrounds. We have a large number of Latino students, as well as African-Americans, Asian-Americans, and people of European descent. We teach acceptance of others who are different, and that includes different religions, different socio-economic backgrounds, different orientations, and different physical abilities. We have a GSA group led by one of our faculty members, Mr. Perez. You might want to check that out."

"GSA?"

"Gay-Straight Alliance. Some of the kids in the group identify as LGBT, and others are there to be supportive of their friends. I'm sure some of the kids are still trying to figure it out. But in any case, we strive to make this a welcoming place for everybody. Now, I can't guarantee you that you won't have any problems. Kids are kids, and sometimes they tease each other and say things they shouldn't say. They may not realize how much it hurts others. But we're in school to learn, and that includes learning about differences and acceptance. If you have any problems, you can always talk to me or Mr. Perez, or anyone in this office."

"Thank you, Mrs. Rodriguez. That makes me feel a lot better. And thank you for being so helpful, and for understanding my situation."

Mrs. Rodriguez didn't fully understand his situation, but she had put some of the pieces together. She stood up and smiled. "My pleasure. And welcome to Westwood High School. I think you'll be happy here. And my door is always open if you need anything."

Bryan unchained his bike and retraced the route he had taken to reach the school. Most of the route wasn't bike-friendly, and he was concerned about his safety, particularly in heavier traffic. When he reached home it was almost noon, so he nuked one of his frozen meals, ate it in the kitchen, then returned to his room.

After about a half-hour, he heard the phone in the kitchen ring. He didn't think much of it at first, but after the second ring, he decided he should go answer it. He opened his bedroom door and started to walk toward the kitchen when he heard Ricky pick up the phone. Ricky affected a dull, monotone voice and said, "Mort's Mortuary. You kill 'em, we chill 'em."

What the...?

"No, there's no one with that name here. ... No problem. Bye." Ricky hung up the phone.

By this time, Bryan had entered the kitchen. "What was that all about?"

"Wrong number. Some lady was looking for Bryan Brower or something like that."

Bryan nearly exploded, but then he realized that Ricky knew him as Ryan. He didn't know that Bryan was still his real name.

"Did she say where she was calling from?"

"No, why? Were you expecting a call?"

"Yes! From the place where I applied for a job yesterday!"

"Oh, sorry."

"And what was that about Mort's Mortuary?"

Ricky chuckled. "We never get important calls on that phone. We all have cell phones. Whenever calls come in on that line, it's either a sales call or a robocall or some kind of scam. So I like to have a little fun with them, just to throw them off-guard so maybe they'll take this number off their list. I've got a whole bunch of 'em. Wanna hear some of them?"

"No. And I don't have a cell phone yet, so if a call comes in it might be for me."

"Okay."

"Do you know if there's a phone book around here?"

"I dunno. But if you want to call the number that just called here, dial star-69."

"Oh, okay. Thanks!"

Ricky smiled and went back to his room.

Bryan dialed star-69. After a couple of rings, someone picked up. "Pure Foods. May I help you?"

"May I speak to Veronica Masters, please?"

"Just a moment, please." The voice placed Bryan on hold, where he was subjected to an overly enthusiastic recording pitching Pure Foods' commitment to sustainable, organic produce. After 15 seconds, it was mercifully cut off by a click and a woman's voice. "Veronica Masters."

"Hello, Ms. Masters, this is Bryan Bauer. I interviewed with you yesterday."

"Yes. I just tried calling you, but I guess I dialed the wrong number. Anyway, I was calling to offer you the job if you're still interested."

"Yes! I am definitely still interested! When would you like me to start?"

"Can you come in tomorrow morning at 9:00?"

"You bet!"

"Good. I'll have some paperwork for you to fill out, we'll go over some policies and procedures, then I'll take you around and introduce you to some people. Then we'll put you to work."

"Sounds great. Should I bring anything?"

"Your bank account information if you want to set up direct deposit. Other than that, I can't think of anything. Most of the information we need is on your application."

"Thank you, Ms. Masters. I'll see you at 9:00 tomorrow. I'm looking forward to getting started!"

"Okay. Bye."

Family Night

Sunday, July 29, 2007

At around 4:00 on Sunday afternoon, Hal knocked on Bryan's door. Bryan almost didn't hear him. He pulled his headphones off his ears and said, "Come in."

Hal took a couple of steps into the room. "Hey, don't forget that it's Sunday, so we're having dinner together at around 6:00."

"Yeah, I'm looking forward to it!"

"I'm making pizza. What toppings do you like? Or more to the point, is there anything you don't like?"

"I like everything. The more, the better. Even anchovies. So yeah, whatever you make will be fine."

"Cool. Any food allergies?"

"Nope."

"Good. Oh, and I'm going to ask everyone to share a bit about themselves, so you can get to know everyone a little better and they can get to know you. So, just a heads-up."

"Okay, thanks for letting me know."

Hal left the room and closed the door.

Bryan wondered how much he should share about the recent events which led him to Los Angeles. He was unfailingly honest by nature, but he figured he should be discreet about sharing certain specific information. Should he tell them his real name? Or that he ran away and the police are probably looking for him? Should he even say exactly where he came from? Surely, his new housemates would be sympathetic to his situation and they wouldn't report him to the police as a missing person. He wanted to be able to form open, trusting relationships with his new friends, but he needed to be careful – at least until he turned 18.

***

Bryan emerged from his room shortly before 6:00 with a can of Dr

Pepper in hand. Hal and Ricky were in the kitchen and Ted was setting the table. Hal had just removed two homemade pizzas from the oven and was slicing them with a roller-cutter. They looked fantastic.

Hal offered Bryan a beer, and he decided to try it. He made a quick trip back to his room to return the Dr Pepper to his fridge.

After everyone sat down and served themselves a couple of slices, Hal raised his beer and said, "A toast – to the newest member of our family, Ryan." Everyone clinked their bottles with each other and took a sip. Bryan didn't care for it, but he decided to be gracious and drink it anyway.

Hal continued. "I thought it might be a nice idea for each of us to say a little bit about ourselves so that Ryan can feel a little more at home. I'll start."

Hal took another bite of his pizza and a swig of beer.

"I grew up in Encino, not too far north of here. My parents disowned me and kicked me out when they found out I was gay. I was able to couch-surf with my friends for a little while. But I found out that you can overstay your welcome quickly, so that was just a short-term solution. Back then, the LGBT Youth Project existed, but it was much smaller and didn't have nearly the resources it has today. But they were able to help me out a little. That's why I volunteer and contribute money to them – so I can help make it better for young people who are getting kicked out of their homes now.

"I did my undergrad at UCLA in the mid-80s, then went to their law school. I loved UCLA then, and I still do today. But it was rough for me to make it through college on my own, so I wanted to do something to help other guys who find themselves in a tight financial situation. I wanted to live close to UCLA and I also wanted to offer a place to stay for gay college students, especially if they've been kicked out by their families or harassed in the dorms. So, I bought this house in, hmmm… I guess it was 1995. So, it's been twelve years! Hard to believe it's been that long. And of course, getting to live with several hot young college guys isn't too bad either. Ricky, how about you?"

Ricky finished chewing the bite of pizza he had just put in his mouth, then began.

"I'm Ricky Montez. It's short for Enrique. I'm a sophomore, although I'm taking a break for now, until I can figure out what I want to be when I grow up."

Ted interjected, "Dude, you're trying to figure out how you can keep from growing up!"

Ricky laughed. "And what's wrong with that? Anyway, so I'm working and trying to save up some money, and trying to have a good time while I figure things out."

Bryan asked, "Where are you from?"

"El Paso. My family knows I'm gay and they're kind of okay with it, but it's kind of like 'we just won't talk about it,' you know? I go back for a visit once in a while, like for Thanksgiving or Christmas. I mean, I love my family and I want to stay in touch with them, but I don't fit in there anymore. Besides, my dad's an alcoholic, so it's not always pleasant to be around him. And they're always just kind of struggling to get by. So, I'm better off here where I can be myself and live my life the way I want."

Ted said, "Well, I guess I'm next. I'm Ted Purcell. I'm from Allentown, Pennsylvania. Like Ricky, I don't belong there anymore. My mom and dad split up when I was ten. Mom realized she was a lesbian when she fell in love with one of the other women in the neighborhood. When they were getting their divorce, the judge gave Dad full custody of me because, you know, she was a lesbian and the judge was a homophobe. I think my dad had the better attorney. So Mom and her partner moved to Northampton, Massachusetts. I guess a lot of lesbians live there and it's much more liberal and tolerant. Anyway, besides Dad losing his wife, he lost his job when the steel mills started closing down. If you've heard that Billy Joel song about Allentown, it pretty much hits the nail on the head. So anyway, he started drinking a lot and he was kind of an asshole to be around. When I started figuring out that I was gay, I knew there was no way I could tell him. I started working out at the gym, both to build myself up and just to get out of the house, you know? And I could tell that some of the other guys at the gym were probably gay, so it was good to see some other people like me.

"After I got out of high school, he had no money to send me to college and I wanted to get the hell out of there, so I joined the Marines. Dad was all for that. I think he suspected that I was gay, and he thought the Marines would make a man out of me – a straight man, that is. Plus, I think he was glad to have me gone. That was in 2000. Little did I know that 9/11 would happen the next year and I would get sent to Afghanistan. Fortunately, I made it back. Some of my buddies didn't. Anyway, I ended up at Camp Pendleton, which is halfway between here and San Diego. I didn't want to re-enlist, so I got out and started going to UCLA. The GI Bill pays for my tuition and, thanks to Hal, I can live here affordably, so that all worked out. I'm heading into my senior year, majoring in Accounting. I'm applying to get into the Anderson School of Business and get a Masters in International Business. So if I get accepted, I'll be here a couple more years."

Bryan asked, "Do you have any contact with your mother now?"

"Yeah, we're on good terms. When I turned 18, I could have moved up there and lived with her and her partner. I visited, and we all got along okay, but I could tell they have their own life together now. They're raising two younger kids they've adopted. So, suddenly having an 18-year-old son living with them wasn't going to work out. Obviously, they don't have any problem with me being gay. But we're in touch and I call her once in a while, like on Christmas. I send a card for her birthday and Mother's Day, but we're not close."

Hal said, "And then there's Darnell. He'll be back around the beginning of September. He's out there touring the country – the world, actually – as his alter-ego, the fabulous Miss Whitney Austin."

Bryan said, "So he's a drag queen?"

Ricky replied, "Mmm-hmmm. And not just your run-of-the-mill lip-synching drag queen. That girl can *sing!*"

Ted said, "She's amazing. Her routine is part singing, part comedy routine, part social commentary."

Ricky added, "and *all* fabulous! She's pretty fabulous when she's not in drag, too."

Hal said, "She's been performing in Provincetown most of the summer. In a couple of weeks, she'll fly to Europe to perform on a gay Mediterranean cruise."

Bryan's eyes popped open. "They have gay cruises?"

Hal replied, "Yeah. There are six or eight every year. They go to the Mediterranean, the Caribbean, and a bunch of other places."

Ricky said, "I don't know. I mean, I love gay men and everything, but two thousand queens on a ship? I don't know if I could handle that."

Ted said, "Oh, please! If anyone can handle two thousand gay men, it would be you. You wouldn't be able to stay off your back long enough to hit the buffet!"

"Uh-uh, now, don't you be hatin' on my generosity and my sexual popularity. You could stand to get laid now and then. Might lighten your ass up a little."

Ted smiled and shrugged. "Yeah, you're probably right."

"Oh, I know I'm right. What good is having that perfect body if you never share it with anyone? You need to spend less time in the gym and more time in someone's bedroom."

Ted didn't appear to be the least bit ruffled by that exchange, but Bryan looked shocked and a bit uncomfortable. Banter of this nature was completely foreign to him. *Is this how these guys talk to each other all the time? I'm going to have to learn a whole new set of conversational skills to fit in here.*

Ricky noticed his discomfort and said, "Oh, honey, don't mind us. We carry on like this all the time. It's all in fun. Nobody means any harm. We're all different, but we're a family. So now, tell us about you."

Bryan smiled. He was moved by how open and honest his housemates had been with him. He decided it would be okay to share more of the circumstances surrounding his sudden move from Kansas to California.

"Okay, so where to begin? Let's see… I'm from Kansas City – actually, one of the suburbs on the Kansas side. I'm going to be a senior at Westwood High School, over on the other side of the 405. Then I hope I can go to UCLA. I love music, especially jazz, and I play the trumpet. Don't worry, I have a mute to muffle the sound, so my practicing shouldn't bother you. Let me know if it does. I also ran on the track team for the last couple of years at my last high school.

"Anyway, my father – or I should say, my ex-father – is the pastor at a very large, very conservative church. He found out I was gay about a month ago, and he pretty much crapped his pants. He grounded me, took away my phone, and said I could never see my boyfriend again. And they were going to take me out of the public high school, where I had all my friends and band and track, and send me to this little Christian high school. Then they tried sending me to this so-called counselor. He wasn't a real psychologist or psychiatrist or anything like that, he was this creepy dude with a Ph.D. in Theology. He thought that if I just prayed every day God would cure me of being gay. So, after about three weeks I told them I wasn't going to see him anymore. Then my dad and this counselor made plans to send me to this place in Alabama where they try to perform some kind of gay conversion therapy on kids. Luckily, I found out about it the day before they were going to take me there, and I ran away. I just threw a bunch of my stuff in a couple of suitcases and got on the next bus heading to LA. I showed up at the LGBT Youth Project this past Monday morning and they hooked me up with Hal. And thankfully, Hal had a room available. So here I am!"

Hal already knew the story, but Ted and Ricky were stunned. Ricky said, "So, do your parents know you're here?"

"Nope. And I hope they never find out. I don't even consider them my parents anymore. I mean, who would do that to their own kid? I guess you could say I have disowned my parents. Anyway, just so you know, Ryan isn't actually my name – yet. My real name is Bryan. When I turn 18 in a couple of months, Hal's going to help me get my name changed. But I figured it would be easier for you to start calling me Ryan now."

Ted asked, "Do you have any brothers or sisters?"

"Yeah, I have a younger brother named Brandon. What sucks the most is that I had to run away from him, too. I love him a lot. Since my dad was always so wrapped up in what was going on at his church, he never had much time for us. So, Brandon and I were really close. I played with him and talked to him to kinda make up for what he wasn't getting from Dad."

Hal asked, "How did they find out you're gay?"

"Well, I had a boyfriend named Chris. We were hoping we'd get to go to college together and then spend the rest of our lives together. But one Friday night he and I were hanging out together, and we decided to park the car in this out-of-the-way place where, like, nobody should have seen us. Anyway, this cop came by and caught us kissing. He couldn't really give us a ticket for kissing. But as it turns out, he goes to my dad's church, so he told my dad that he caught Chris and me making out in the car."

Hal said, "That was shitty. He shouldn't have been able to do that."

"Yeah, well, he did. And I guess we were lucky that he didn't catch us doing more than kissing, 'cause then we could have been arrested. But anyway, Dad found out, so that's bad enough."

Ricky said, "Wow, that really sucks. Like suddenly, you're out on your own."

"Yeah. It was only four hours between the time I found out they were about to send me to that place in Alabama and when I left home for the last time. The worst part is that I can't see my brother or my boyfriend anymore, or my friends at school. I'm kind of shy, so I'm not good at making new friends. But I guess I'm going to have to. I hope maybe Chris and I can still go to college together, but I can't even let him know where I am, at least not for a while. And someday when Brandon is grown up and out on his own, I hope I can get back in touch with him. But until then, I'm all alone."

Ted said, "No, you're not. You have us. We're your family now. If you ever need to talk or you have any questions about anything, I'm always here for you. And I know the other guys are, too." Ricky and Hal both nodded.

"Thanks. That means a lot to me. And as much as that all sucks, I'm also very thankful. I'm thankful that I found out about their plot to send me to that place. It looked like hell on earth. I'm thankful that I've saved up some money from my jobs, and I have a new job at Pure Foods. And I am so thankful to be here. This house is amazing! And you guys have been so nice to me. I feel like I'm safe and I have a home. And I'm thankful that I don't have to hide being gay anymore. It's like, I was constantly scared that my parents would find out, and that wasn't fair to my boyfriend Chris. He tried so hard to pull me out of the closet and I let him down a lot. But that's the way it was."

By this time, they had finished dinner, so everyone stood up. Ted turned to Bryan and said, "C'mere." Ted gave Bryan a firm, friendly hug. "Wow. You've been through a lot." Ricky and Hal hugged Bryan, too. It was just what he needed at that moment.

Then everyone pitched in to clear the table, load the dishwasher, and clean up the kitchen. When they were done, Hal said, "So, what'll it be tonight? A movie, a game, or something else?"

Bryan asked, "What games do you have?"

Hal said, "Here, let me show you." He led Bryan to a closet near the family room. Bryan scanned the twenty or so games in the closet – some familiar and some not. Then he spotted a long, slender black box. He recognized it from that evening at Chris's house a month ago when they played it.

Bryan said, "That one," and pointed to The Big Black Deck.

Hal smiled and pulled it off the shelf. "Okay. Well, we'll certainly know a lot more about each other after this evening."

The four guys sat down at the kitchen table and unpacked the game. Hal asked, "Have you played this before?"

"Yeah, kind of. About a month ago I was over at my boyfriend's house, and his parents and his older brother were gone, so it was just the two of us. His parents played this game with several friends of theirs, which kind of blew my mind. I mean, I could never imagine my parents playing this. Anyway, since it was just the two of us, we couldn't play it like you're supposed to. But we read questions and picked answer cards and read them to each other. So, yeah, I know what the game's about. It will be fun to play it for real."

They each drew six answer cards and started playing. One of the cards Bryan drew was:

A huge hard cock

The beer Bryan drank at dinner had him feeling relaxed and a little less inhibited. He said, "Ha. I got one of the same cards I got when Chris and I played. And after we played for a little bit, we went upstairs in his bedroom, and uh… well, let's just say we got to know each other a bit better."

The other three all shot glances at each other. Bryan didn't notice.

Running Buddies
Monday, July 30, 2007

On Monday morning, Bryan woke up at around 7:45. After lying in bed for another 15 minutes, he decided he wasn't going to fall asleep again so he might as well get up. He stepped into his shorts and headed for the bathroom.

As he was walking down the hall, Ted's door opened and Ted emerged wearing running shorts, shoes, and a tank top.

Bryan said, "Good morning! Heading out for a run?"

"Yeah, I like to try to get out before it gets too hot."

"Mind if I join you? I can be ready in five minutes."

Ted paused for a moment. He was accustomed to running by himself so he could have complete freedom to run wherever he felt like going, at a speed that pushed his limits, and for as long or short as he wanted. But there wasn't a good reason to say no and he didn't want to appear stand-offish to the new guy, so he said, "Yeah, sure. I'll wait for you by the front door."

Bryan stepped into the bathroom long enough to pee. He returned to his room and put on his running gear, then met Ted at the front door. "Thanks for waiting."

"Sure. Where do you want to go?"

"I'll follow you. I don't know the area very well yet."

"Okay, well let's go over to the track at Drake Stadium on campus." Much of the area around UCLA was hilly and Ted didn't know what Bryan was capable of, so a flat track was probably the best choice. They could go for as long or as short as Bryan could handle.

"Sounds good. You lead the way. You go at your pace. I can probably keep up."

Once they got started, Bryan said, "Thanks for letting me come along. I think I mentioned last night that I was on the track team at my old high school. My boyfriend Chris was on the team too, and we used to run together all the time."

"Oh yeah, that's right. So, I guess I'm going to have to try to keep up with you!"

"I'm sure we can find a pace that's good for both of us. This works for me."

They zigzagged through several blocks of residential streets to get to Gayley Avenue, which led them into the campus. Bryan said, "I think it's funny that they have a street named Gayley."

Ted smiled. "Yeah. The novelty wears off pretty quickly. You'll get used to it."

They ran along the campus walkways, through De Neve Plaza, to Bruin Walk, and then to Drake Stadium. Once they were inside the stadium, Ted removed his tank top and laid it on the ground just off the edge of the track, along with his water bottle. Bryan was expecting to run with his shirt on like he always did at home, but decided to follow Ted's example. There was no one else at the track, and the sight of college guys running shirtless was probably commonplace.

For a few seconds, Bryan stood motionless as he gazed at Ted's nearly-naked body. Bryan guessed he was about 6'2" tall. He had a light complexion and short, neatly-groomed orange-brown hair. His pecs were perfectly defined, thanks to countless hours at the gym over many years. His stomach was a tight, flat six-pack. His chest was hairless, but a narrow dark orange treasure trail led from his navel down into his shorts. *I wonder if his chest is naturally hairless or if he shaved it.*

Ted's voice yanked Bryan back into the present moment. "Ready?" Ted started running down the track. Bryan felt a brief wave of embarrassment. *Did Ted notice I was ogling him? Was it a little too obvious?*

Bryan purposely lagged a couple of steps behind so he could behold Ted's perfectly chiseled V-shaped torso from the rear. He admired Ted's broad, bold shoulders and solid, muscular triceps as they swung forward and backward in synch with his steps. Inside his thin silky shorts, his firm round buns shifted up and down as his lean, powerful legs gracefully propelled him forward at a good six-minute-mile pace. After about twenty steps, Bryan sped up until he pulled alongside Ted.

They ran side-by-side without saying much. For the first time, Bryan felt inadequate about his physique. He had always been skinny as a kid. Since taking up running his sophomore year, he had obtained some definition in the form of tight, sinewy legs and firm butt cheeks. He had no trouble burning off the calories from the slushies and junk food he and Chris regularly consumed at Slush Fun, and the occasional overloaded pizza or double-meat pulled pork sandwiches that were staples of his teenage diet. But he had never lifted a weight in his life. His torso and arms, while free of excess body fat, showed no definition whatsoever. He wasn't even interested in lifting weights, but now that he could see what it did for Ted, he wondered if it might be worthwhile.

After eight laps, Ted decelerated and headed for his shirt and water bottle. "Let's take a break for a moment, okay?" He picked up the shirt and wiped the sweat off his face. His chest gleamed with perspiration which somehow made it all the more delectable. *I'd like to lick every drop of sweat off his body.*

Ted said, "Looks like you're holding up well!"

Bryan said, "Yeah, you're setting a good pace. Feels great!"

"Are you planning to join the track team at your new school?"

"Probably not. I need to work as many hours as I can get. It's going to be challenging to be in marching band 'cause of my job."

"Yeah, I'll bet. Plus, you'll have homework."

"Besides, track was fun because I got to do it with Chris. We didn't fit in that well with the other guys on the team. Without him, it might not be as much fun."

"Well, you'll probably make some new friends. You can wait and see what comes along."

They started running again. Ted asked, "What events did you compete in?"

"I did the hurdles, both the 100 meters and the 300 meters, plus the long jump, and I was part of the 4x440 relay."

"Since you're so tall, I'll bet that made the hurdles easier for you."

"Yeah, that's actually how I got onto the team in the first place. I never even thought about running on the track team, or being on any kind of sports team, for that matter. But when I was in gym class my freshman year, we spent several weeks on track and field in the spring. The gym teacher told the track coach that I did well with the hurdles because I'm so tall, and he asked me to be on the team. Plus, because I have long legs, that helped me run faster, too."

They ran for a couple of minutes in silence. So much had happened in the past couple of months that Bryan rarely thought about the track team.

"We went to the state championship track meet a couple of months ago, and I finished first in the 300-meter hurdles."

"Wow! That's pretty impressive! I'm running with a state champion! I'll try to keep up."

"Well, it was Kansas, not California. But still."

"How did you do in your other events?"

"I finished fourth in the 100-meter hurdles and our relay team finished third in the 4x440 relay. I really should have won both of those, too, but I didn't get much sleep the night before, so I wasn't at my best. We were leading in the relay until I dropped the baton at the hand-off. That was a disaster. We were lucky we got third."

"Still, that's nothing to be ashamed of."

"Yeah, I guess so. There's more to the story. Maybe another time. Were you in any sports?"

"I wasn't a very athletic kid. I tried wrestling one year. I liked it and did okay at it, but I wasn't great. I had to wear two jockstraps to keep from getting a hard-on, and there were times I could have used three. So, I figured it would be better for me to quit than have the other guys figure out I was gay." He paused. "They probably figured it out anyway."

After another couple of laps, Bryan said, "So, you started lifting weights in high school?"

"Yeah. I didn't want to be a skinny little wimp. I figured it might discourage guys from beating me up if they found out I was gay."

"I think some of the guys on the track team figured out that Chris and I were gay. But I never thought I'd get beat up. Picked on sometimes, but not beat up."

"Yeah, there were some rough kids at our school. But I have to say, lifting weights also built up my self-esteem, which I needed."

"How long did it take you to look like you look now?"

"A couple of years. By the time I went into the Marines, I was in great shape. That really helped me make it through Basic. The bases all have gyms, but when I was deployed to Afghanistan I had to get by with push-ups, sit-ups, and running. Here, I can go to the gym on campus whenever I want."

"Well, all your hard work has paid off. You really look great."

"Thanks. Yeah, I'm pretty happy with my body. I don't want to get all bulked up like the Hulk or something, I just want some nice definition."

After they ran a few more laps around the track they headed home. As they climbed the steps to the front door, Bryan said, "you want to jump in the pool and cool off?"

Ted unlocked the door and stepped inside. "Nah, I think I'll just take a cold shower. I don't want to get all my sweat in the pool."

"Yeah, I guess there's that."

"Do you need to go first?"

"Let me just rinse off, then I'm going to get in the pool."

"Okay, cool. Hey, I enjoyed that. I go running at 8:00 most days, so anytime you want to join me..."

"Yeah, I will. Thanks!"

Bryan took a two-minute shower to rinse off his sweat. He hadn't packed a swimsuit, but Hal said the other guys didn't wear them anyway. Bryan had never skinny-dipped before. In fact, to the best of his recollection, he had never been naked outdoors. No one else was around, so why not? His life these days was full of new experiences.

He wrapped a towel around his waist, grabbed a can of Dr Pepper from his fridge, and headed out to the pool. He selected one of the inflatable rafts stacked by the edge of the patio and jumped in. The water was a bit on the cool side, but after that run, it felt good. Bryan hoped Ted would change his mind and join him, but no such luck. He longed to discover whether the rest of Ted's physique was as magnificent as everything he had just seen, but that would have to wait for another day.

After he got acclimated to the water, he climbed onto the raft and relaxed. The gentle current of the pool jets propelled him slowly around the pool.

As the raft gradually rotated, Bryan gazed at the amazing house – his new home. He admired the oleanders, the palm trees, and the clear blue sky. He closed his eyes and savored the light breeze blowing across his face and body, and the feel of the cool water his feet were dangling in.

Over the past five weeks, he had dealt with a lot of shit. It was difficult to leave everything he had ever known – his family, his friends, his house, his school, his neighborhood – with only a couple of suitcases full of possessions. It hurt to realize that his father could be so dogmatic, stubborn, self-centered, and cruel that he would subject his son to such humiliating treatment and try to send him away to a gay conversion torture camp. It was disappointing that his mother would go along with it, even though he felt in his heart that she didn't want to.

Most of all, it was painful to leave behind his precious younger brother Brandon, whom he loved so much. He felt bad about not being able to say goodbye and leaving Brandon to deal with his parents – and life – on his own.

And then there was Chris, who had tried so hard to help him come to terms with being gay, and who he finally realized he loved. He regretted that he wasn't able to be the boyfriend Chris wanted and deserved, and that they had parted on bad terms. Maybe, someday, they could have a future together. Maybe.

But yet, he was filled with gratitude. Gratitude for Russ Simonton, who supported him through his crisis and helped him plan his escape, and who was his first role model as a happy, self-accepting, partnered gay man. Gratitude for the friendly, helpful people at the Los Angeles LGBT Youth Project, and that such a facility exists. Gratitude for Hal Morris, who had offered him a place in this wonderful home, and who would serve as his legal counsel. Gratitude for his new job, his new school, and his new city.

The past was the past. Bryan was filled with hope and optimism for all that lay ahead.

In the master suite, Hal had just finished taking a shower and getting dressed. As he emerged from his walk-in closet and crossed the room to his desk to turn his computer on, he glanced out the window. He noticed Bryan floating naked on a raft in the pool. Bryan was facing away, and Hal's gaze was instinctively drawn to his midsection. He could see the base of his cock amidst the cluster of light-brown pubic hair, but the rest was hidden from view between his legs. He took a few steps back away from the window so he would be less noticeable if Bryan should glance in his direction.

As the raft slowly rotated in the current of the water, more came into view. Bryan was relaxing with his eyes closed. After a minute, his feet were pointed toward the window and Hal was treated to a direct view. He almost couldn't believe his eyes. Over the past two decades, he had pretty much seen it all. But he had rarely seen anything quite as remarkable on such an adorable young man.

One Last Detail

Monday, July 30, 2007

After floating in the pool for half an hour, Bryan went back inside and put some clothes on. Then he headed into the kitchen and made himself two slices of toast to tide him over until lunchtime.

When he returned to his room, he remembered there was still one loose end he needed to tie up before he could close the previous chapter of his life.

He sat down at the computer desk and turned on his laptop. He logged into the web hosting account for the Eternal Savior Christian Church of Prairie Village, Kansas, to complete his final task as webmaster for the church's website.

He opened the Resources page he had created two weeks ago at his father's command. It contained links to all the presentation notes and supporting documents from the anti-gay Rescued Through Love conference the church held on July 14. He deleted all the content on the page and all the linked documents.

In its place, he added a link to the Kansas City chapter of the Parents Support Network – the group that provides support to parents and families of LGBT children. He found an informative article about what the Bible says and does not say about homosexuality and added a link to that. He created a list of gay-friendly churches in the Kansas City area, as well as the LGBT community center and the Pathways youth group.

Once he was satisfied that he had created a positive, affirming Resources page for people who were coming out as LGBT and their parents and families, he published it. Then he navigated to the Users section. He downgraded the privileges of his father's account and the accounts of a couple of other people who had access to the website, so that nobody else could add, edit, or delete web pages. Then he navigated to the Account Profile and changed the login password for the web hosting account. He logged out for the last time.

Just for grins, he searched for the website of Prairie Village Post, his former city's local newspaper. It was a small, tabloid-sized paper that was published bi-weekly and tossed onto every resident's driveway whether they wanted it or not. His disappearance was front-page news.

Local Pastor's Son Missing
Friday, July 27, 2007

Bryan Bauer, a student at Prairie Village High School, was reported missing on Sunday, July 22. He is the son of Rev. Brad Bauer, pastor of Eternal Savior Christian Church, and his wife Brenda. Bauer, 17, was last seen at approximately 1:00 p.m. on Saturday, July 21. Police are investigating the matter but have uncovered no clues as to his whereabouts.

In a statement to the Prairie Village Post, Rev. Bauer claimed, "We have reason to suspect he has been kidnapped by a homosexual organization known for abducting, recruiting, and exploiting children. There is no other explanation for why he would suddenly disappear without warning." When asked, Rev. Bauer confirmed that no ransom note or other communication from any such organization has been received.

Bryan laughed out loud when he read his father's statement. It sounded exactly like something he'd say. He continued reading.

Police detective Susan Wagner noted that there were no signs of a struggle or forced entry at the Bauer home. She stated that Bryan "appears to have left voluntarily, with two suitcases and a small assortment of personal possessions. We are closely coordinating our efforts with the Kansas Bureau of Investigation and the National Center for Missing and Exploited Children. A nationwide missing child campaign is being launched."

Bauer resigned from his job at Price Cutter grocery store on Saturday. No reason for his resignation was reported.

Detective Wagner believes that Bauer is no longer in the Prairie Village area. Police have no leads at this time. Any tips or information regarding Bryan Bauer's whereabouts should be directed to Detective Susan Wagner at the Prairie Village Police Department, 555-PVPD.

The article was accompanied by a grainy, low-resolution photo of Bryan that was taken at a church event three years ago. His face had been cropped from a larger picture. Was that the best they could come up with? Bryan was glad he had removed the more recent, professionally photographed pictures of him from their second-story hallway.

He shut off his laptop.

The New Kid at Band Camp
Monday, August 6, 2007

Bryan arrived at the football field behind Westwood High School at 7:45 a.m. He saw a man who was probably the band director standing on the other side of the football field carrying a clipboard. A megaphone sat on the ground next to his feet. Bryan knew from his email exchanges with the director that his name was Mr. Scales. He recalled the time earlier in the summer when he and Chris were sitting in Chris' car at Slush Fun coming up with names for people that matched their occupations – like an optometrist named Anita Seymour and an undertaker named Doug Graves. When Chris came up with the gynecologist named Harry Beaver, they were both reduced to helpless laughter. Bryan had to stop himself from cracking up just thinking about it. Mr. Scales was a perfect name for a band director. He wished he had thought of it a few weeks ago with Chris. He wondered what Mr. Scales' first name was. If he served in the military and achieved a high rank, he would be Major Scales. That made Bryan chuckle out loud. Several nearby kids stopped talking amongst themselves and looked over at the tall new kid who was standing by himself laughing at something. After giving Bryan quizzical looks, they returned to their conversation. *Great*, Bryan thought. *Right off the bat, they're going to think I'm a weirdo.*

Bryan shook it off and trotted across the field to meet the band director. "Mr. Scales? Hi. I'm Ryan. I know it says Bryan Bauer on your list, but I prefer to go by Ryan if that's okay."

"Yeah, sure. Nice to meet you, Ryan. Which trumpet part did you play at your last school?"

"First. I was first chair in the wind ensemble and the jazz ensemble."

"Well, we don't have chairs in the marching band, but I'll put you on the first trumpet part. When wind ensemble and jazz ensemble start at the beginning of the school year, I'll audition everyone and determine who sits where. But for now, see that girl over there standing next to the plastic bins? Her name is Crystal. She's our librarian. Go over and ask her to put together a flip folder with first trumpet parts for you."

"Okay, thanks!"

"Oh, and Ryan? How's your 8-to-5?"

"Really good, sir. I was the right guide in marching band last year because I'm so tall."

"That's just what I was thinking. I'll put you there again if you don't mind."

"Sure, that would be great." At least the kids would notice him.

Bryan trotted over to Crystal, the librarian. He hoped her last name wasn't Meth. He had to stop himself from laughing again. He really needed to stop doing this, but he couldn't help it.

Once he had his folder, he looked around at all the other kids. There was a lot more diversity among the students, as Mrs. Rodriguez said there would be. He guessed that the largest plurality of kids was Latino. There were also Black kids and Asian kids. He guessed that 10 or 15 percent of the kids were White. This wasn't a problem, but it was completely different from what he was used to at Prairie Village High School, where practically everyone was White. Bryan wondered how he would fit in. Kids are just kids, right? Or did the kids from other backgrounds relate to each other differently? Regardless, he would try to be nice to everyone.

Unfortunately, no cute guy with wavy dark brown hair blowing in the breeze came up and introduced himself, as Chris had done three years ago on their first day of band camp as freshmen. Bryan wondered, *Are any of the other kids gay? How will these kids treat a gay guy if they find out? Surely, in a group of 60 or so kids, there must be at least a few who are gay.*

Mr. Scales blew his whistle. He picked up his megaphone and instructed the kids to gather at one end of the field. He formed the band into four rows, with about 16 kids in each row. The drum major, a handsome young man named Jordan, positioned himself at one end of the front row. He worked his way across the row, spacing the kids at two-step intervals. Mr. Scales placed the trumpets along the right side of the front row, and he placed Bryan on the end.

After everyone was assigned a spot and had been properly spaced, Mr. Scales spoke into the megaphone. "Okay, kids. Now, this will be a review for the upperclassmen – and women – but for the freshmen, we march what's called 8-to-5. That's eight steps every five yards. That way, it fits with the music and it keeps us in perfect alignment. Our goal for today is to get used to taking 22-and-a-half-inch steps, so every eight steps, the ball of your right foot should hit a yard line. The other thing you need to do is look right and make sure you're not ahead of or behind the person to your right." Mr. Scales trotted over to the right end of the front line. "Everybody, I'd like you to meet Ryan. He's a senior. He moved here over the summer. He's had a lot of marching band experience at his previous school and he's tall, so I've asked him to be the right guide. So everyone else in the front line can look to the right and align themselves with Ryan. Those of you in the second, third, and fourth rows will also guide right to the person who's at the end of your row. And each of you guys on the end are responsible for staying exactly five yards behind the person in front of you. Any questions?"

Nobody had any questions.

"Okay, let's try it out. Jordan will give you one long blast and four short blasts on his whistle. Those four short blasts are the speed you're going to march. Megan will give you snare drum taps to keep you in time. Okay, five yards forward. Jordan?"

Jordan blew one long blast and four short blasts on his whistle. Some of the kids took off promptly, while others were slow off the line. Not everyone started on their left foot. It was easy to spot the freshmen, but some of the upperclassmen seemed to have trouble marching a good 8-to-5. This could be a long two weeks. Bryan decided he would just roll with it and do his best and enjoy the experience for what it was. Not every band could be as good as the Prairie Village Marching Panthers, after all.

After several trips up and down the field, Mr. Scales taught the band left turns, right turns, and to-the-rears, or TTRs as he called them. He led them through several sequences of maneuvers, increasing the complexity a little bit each time.

The band took a break at 9:30. Bryan tried to introduce himself to anyone whose attention he could get, but many of the kids were rushing off to go to the bathroom or retrieve their water bottles. Many of them clustered into groups of friends from previous years, eager to catch up with each other.

After the break, Mr. Scales told the kids to pick up their instruments and cluster in groups according to their instruments. They played some tuning notes and scales, then ran through the school fight song, "The Star-Spangled Banner," and the songs that would become part of the band's halftime show.

Bryan was thankful he had found some time to practice his trumpet since arriving in Los Angeles. He guessed that some of the kids around him were playing their instruments for the first time since the end of the last school year. Either that or they weren't very good. Bryan decided to play softer so it wouldn't seem like he was trying to show up the other kids. He just wanted to fit in.

After the morning sessions, the kids scattered for lunch. Some headed to fast-food restaurants on Wilshire Boulevard a few blocks away, while others went home for lunch. Bryan brought a couple of sandwiches, a bag of chips, an apple, and a bottle of water. He ended up eating his lunch by himself, sitting under a tree.

In the afternoon, the band took its first shot at marching while playing. It was pretty ragged, but Bryan reminded himself that this was just the first day and the band would probably be much better after two weeks of all-day rehearsals.

***

By the end of the two weeks, the band had improved considerably. They were able to execute complete run-throughs of the pre-game and halftime shows, playing while marching. Some of the finer points still needed work, like good alignment and holding instruments at a uniform angle. But it was getting better and the band would be presentable at the first football game.

Bryan hadn't made any real friends yet, but he was on a 'saying hi' level of rapport with the other trumpeters. During idle moments, he scanned the band looking for guys who might be gay. Being newly out himself, he didn't know what to look for. He focused on the good-looking ones, but he knew that just because a guy is hot doesn't mean he's gay.

Jordan, the drum major, was probably the cutest guy there. Bryan liked the confidence he exuded in his role of leading the band on the field. But in some ways, Jordan reminded him of Rocket Crockett, the star of the football and track teams at his last high school. Jordan seemed to be the social leader of the group – at least for the junior and senior guys. Bryan hoped Jordan wouldn't turn out to be a jerk who teased him, like Rocket.

The Truth About Ricky

Thursday, August 16, 2007

Bryan arrived home from band camp on Thursday at 4:00. As he turned the corner onto his street, he noticed the street was packed with cars. There were a couple of solid-panel vans in front of his house.

As he climbed the stairs and approached the front door, he could tell the gathering was taking place at his house. Then he remembered that last Sunday at Family Night, Hal said something about someone coming to shoot some kind of video at the pool. He didn't think anything of it at the time.

When he walked in, he could tell there were a lot of people in the backyard. He stepped into the kitchen, where an assortment of food and drinks was spread out across the kitchen island and the table. He eyed a platter of deli sandwiches and a plate of brownies and wondered if it would be okay if he took one of each. There seemed to be plenty of food.

He stepped closer to the sliding glass door to get a look at what was going on. In and around the pool, there were about a dozen good-looking, well-built, naked men, clustered in several groups of three or four. As he watched for a few seconds, it became clear – there was an orgy taking place. He didn't have a clear view, but a guy in the center of one of the clusters looked a lot like Ricky. And several men with video cameras were capturing it all.

Hal entered the kitchen and said, "Uh, Ryan… would you please move away from the sliding door? You could be caught on camera."

Bryan quickly retreated out of view of the pool and the cameras. Then he asked Hal, "What's going on? Is that what it looks like?"

Hal answered, "Yeah. They're shooting an orgy scene for a porn video. I let them use my pool for a shoot now and then. It brings in some extra cash. I mentioned it at dinner last Sunday."

"I remember you saying something about a video shoot taking place. I guess I didn't realize it would be *that* kind of video. And… is that Ricky out there?"

"Sure is."

"Oh. Okay. So… how much longer do you think it will be going on?"

"Probably another hour or so, maybe less. They're going to lose daylight pretty soon, and more of the backyard will be in shadow."

"Okay, thanks. Oh, and would it be okay if I swiped a sandwich?"

"Yeah, sure. They always order too much, and there's always a lot left over." Hal turned and went back to his master suite.

Bryan grabbed a sandwich and a brownie and headed for his bedroom. He took a quick shower and changed into his Pure Foods shirt.

***

At 4:45, when Bryan emerged from his room to head for work, he heard a lot of voices in the kitchen. He could tell that there was a parade of guys going in and out of the bathroom.

When he returned home after 10:00, everything was quiet and back to normal. There was no evidence that anything unusual had taken place earlier in the day. He walked into the kitchen. The remaining food had been consolidated onto a few plates for the house residents to eat or throw away. Bryan grabbed a paper plate, loaded it with some veggies and a deli sandwich, and carried it over to the table. Sadly, the brownies were gone.

As he was eating, Ricky came in, wearing gym shorts and a T-shirt. He helped himself to some food and sat down across from Bryan. He seemed perfectly at ease, as if being fucked by several guys in front of video cameras was a normal occurrence, all in a day's work.

Bryan suddenly felt awkward. He had no idea what he should say to someone he had seen having sex, and who stars in pornographic movies. He was pretty sure Ricky hadn't noticed him looking out at the action; he was too preoccupied.

Ricky broke the ice. "Hey, how's it going?"

Bryan replied, "Pretty good. Just a typical day at work. And you?"

"Same here."

This was a typical day at work for Ricky?

Bryan said, "Looks like you had a hard day. You must be exhausted."

It took Ricky a few seconds, but he figured out that Bryan had discovered what happened that afternoon. "Yeah, it was *hard* alright."

They ate a couple more bites of food in silence.

Bryan said, "So, do you do that often?"

"You mean, do porn? Yeah… probably two to four times a month."

Bryan wasn't sure whether it was appropriate to discuss this topic. He had no idea what the social protocol for a situation like this was.

"So, if you don't mind me asking, why?"

Ricky smirked as if the answer to this question should be obvious. "I do it for the money – same as anybody else."

"Well, I suppose you could do it for the sex."

"I don't need to do it for sex. I can find plenty of that on my own. I need the money."

Bryan pondered the new information he was receiving. He had so many questions, but he wasn't sure he should ask any of them.

"So, do you mind if I ask you a few questions? If you'd rather not, no problem. I'm kinda new to all this stuff."

"Sure, I don't mind. Shoot. … Well, not literally."

That took Bryan a second, then he figured it out. "Okay. So, how long have you been doing this?"

"A couple of years."

"Do you always do it here?"

Ricky smiled. "Oh, no. This is only like the second time I've done a scene here. We usually do it in a studio, where they can control the sound and the lighting and all that stuff. Or sometimes on location in other places."

"You mean they have studios where they make porn movies?"

"Yeah. There's probably more porn made in the San Fernando Valley than anywhere else in the world."

"Really???"

"Yeah. It's a huge business."

"Does it pay very well?"

"Yeah. I usually make two or three thousand bucks for a scene. It depends on a lot of things, like what they want you to do and how well known you are. 'Cause if you're well known that'll help them sell movies. Group scenes, like we did today, usually pay less, because they have more people to pay. But I took on five guys today, so I made out pretty well anyway."

"So… and I know this is really personal, but… are you usually on the receiving end?"

"Oh, yeah, I'm a total bottom, at least in the business. My dick's not all that great, but my ass is. But I've got good looks and a nice body, so I do pretty well."

"How do you like doing it?"

"It's a job. I mean, some scenes are better than others. Now and then I get paired up with a totally hot guy who really knows what he's doing. We just kind of click, and then it's like, 'I'm getting paid to do this?' But most of the time, you're just going through the motions. They tell you who you're going to do it with and what you're going to do and how you're going to do it. A lot of times it's not what – or who – you would choose to do on your own. But you have to act like you're really into the guy and whatever you're doing with him. At the end of the day, it's just a job."

"So, how did you get started?"

"I auditioned. I met a guy at a bar who was in the business. He introduced me to a producer he worked with. I sent him some photos, and he had me come in to do a scene with someone. Obviously, he liked what he saw, and I've been getting work ever since."

"With that one producer?"

"At first, but then others. You get to know other people in the business. You build a network just like anything else. That's how I met Hal and ended up living here. He knows a lot of people in the business through his work."

"Wait a minute. His work? I thought he was an attorney."

"He is. He works in the porn industry."

"They need lawyers to make porn?"

"Of course. You need lawyers to be in almost any kind of business. They have contracts and distribution deals and all kinds of laws to comply with. And they go after a lot of people who try to steal their work."

"People steal porn?"

"Oh god, yes. Nowadays, with the internet, people upload stuff they don't have the rights to all the time."

"Is it even legal to make porn?"

Ricky chuckled. "Wow… you've lived a sheltered life, haven't you?"

"Yeah, I guess. We never talked about this sort of thing in my house. The only time I ever heard about porn was when my dad would preach about how evil it is."

"So, I'm guessing you've never seen porn."

"Actually, I have. There was this party I went to a couple of months ago with the guys on my track team, and one of the guys put a porn video on. I mean, it was men and women, not all guys. We watched a little of it, but then my boyfriend and I left. It wasn't our thing, obviously."

"I know, right? I mean, pussies … ewwwww! At least now you know what you've been spared from."

"Well, I didn't think it was gross or anything, it was just different from what I want. I actually thought it was all kind of silly. It was interesting to see how all the straight guys reacted to it. Anyway, it kinda ruined the party for us so we left."

"Anyway, back to your question. Of course, it's legal. I mean, as long as the performers are over 18. If they use underage people, that's child pornography, and that's seriously wrong. I mean, people go to prison for years if they get caught making, selling, or even possessing that. And obviously, they can't coerce people into doing it – that's rape. But as long as everyone involved is a consenting adult, then yeah, it's perfectly legal. It's covered by the First Amendment."

"Yeah, I guess that makes sense."

"Oh, and you can't sell it to minors or expose them to it, either. The people who sell it have to try to keep it hidden from people who don't want to see it. But nowadays with the internet, it's kind of hard to do that."

Bryan took a few more bites while he rolled all this new information around in his head. Then he said, "You know, it's kind of funny that porn is legal but prostitution is illegal. I mean, in both cases, people are paying other people to have sex."

"Yeah, I never really thought of it like that. Anyway, I think prostitution should be legal. I mean, why not? It's not like anyone's getting hurt."

"And if it was legal, they could tax it."

"Exactly."

Bryan finished his dinner and was about to get up, but there was still one question on his mind. He thought for a moment about how to word it.

"Okay, so can I ask you a more personal question? You don't have to answer if you don't want to."

"Yeah, sure."

"And I don't mean this to be offensive or anything, I'm just curious to know. Do you feel right about doing porn?"

"What do you mean, like do I think it's a sin or something?"

"Yeah, I guess."

"No, I don't think there's anything wrong with it. If I did, I wouldn't do it. I mean look, man, I was brought up Catholic. We had all this sin and guilt stuff drilled into us from the day we were born – hell, probably from the day we were conceived. Oh, and being a homo was like the biggest sin of all – that, and getting an abortion. Never mind all the gay priests who are diddling altar boys and getting away with it. Well, I'm over all that shit."

"Yeah, after what I've been through, I'm totally over the whole organized religion thing too. But I guess what I meant was, like, I only got to have sex with my boyfriend a couple of times before my dad grounded me and I had to run away. But it was the most beautiful, deep, spiritual thing I've ever felt. I mean, yeah, it was fun and it felt great and all that, but I've never felt so connected to another person before in my life. It was a spiritual connection, not just a physical connection. It was pure love. It was the most beautiful thing. But then, you were out there getting banged by guys you probably don't even know. And you're doing it on camera, so you'll never really know who's going to be watching you have sex someday. I guess what I'm saying is, how does that make you feel afterward?"

"Okay, I get what you're asking. So, there's making love and there's having sex. You and your boyfriend were making love. All we're doing is having sex. That's all a lot of people do most of the time. I mean, we can't all be lucky enough to be in love, but people still have desires, right? We're not suffering from any delusions that what we're doing is anything more than a physical act for other people's enjoyment. Sometimes they'll have you and the other guy kiss and cuddle and act all romantic, but it's just acting. Other times, like out there, it's just sex – nothing more. It's not like we're doing it because it feels good, although sometimes on a good gig it does. It's a job. We're doing it to make money."

"You're just putting on a performance."

"Yeah, that's a good way to put it. We're acting out people's fantasies. We're giving them something they can get off to. We're helping them, really. So yeah, I'm okay with it."

"Do you ever wonder what will happen if someone sees you in real life and recognizes you from a movie they watched?"

"Oh, it's happened many times, especially when I go to the bars in WeHo. Most of the time, they're like 'ooo, there's a porn star,' like that somehow elevates you in their mind. Usually, people don't say anything, but I can tell by the way they look at me. Or they might seem a little awkward around me. Or maybe they're afraid to admit they watch porn, but like who cares? Everyone watches porn. Or they don't know what they should say. Like if they come up and say, 'Hey, I loved that DP you did in *Deep Trouble*' and I say 'thanks.' Then where does the conversation go from there?"

"DP?"

"Double penetration. Use your imagination. And yes, I get double pay for doing that. Anyway, then you have the guys who come on to you and want to get together with you just because you're a porn star. Like then they get to check a box off their bucket list or something. So yeah, all that's a pain in the ass, but it comes with the territory. But it pays well, so that makes it worth putting up with the bullshit."

"What about when you go to apply for a job?"

"Well, I'm not going to put it on my resumé. Besides, if the guy who interviews me recognizes me from my movies, do you think he's going to say anything? He's probably in the closet at work anyway. And it's not like I plan to run for president someday. So yeah, I don't really care."

Bryan and Ricky got up from the table. Bryan said, "Thanks for the talk. I hope it wasn't too weird."

"No problem, man. I'm an open book if you haven't figured that out."

The Truth About Ted

Saturday, August 18, 2007

On Saturday morning, Bryan woke up to his alarm at 7:45. He made a quick trip to the bathroom, then returned to his room and put on his running shorts, shirt, and shoes. Then he went into the kitchen and hung out, hoping that Ted would go for his usual run at 8:00.

Right on schedule, Ted emerged from his bedroom and headed for the door. Bryan got up to greet him. "Hey, good morning."

"Good morning."

"Mind if I join you today?"

"Sure, why not?"

They left through the front door and scampered down the steps to the street. Ted asked, "Where to?"

"I don't care. We can go back to the track, or anywhere else you want. I'll follow you."

"Okay, the track it is." They started running toward campus. "Looks like you had this planned."

"Yeah, I kinda wanted to talk to you about a few things. Maybe when we take a break."

They ran in silence through their neighborhood, then across the UCLA campus to the track. Bryan contemplated how he would bring up the topic he wanted to discuss and what he wanted to ask Ted. After two miles, they stopped to drink some water and relax for a few minutes.

Bryan could tell that Ted was waiting for him to start talking about whatever was on his mind, so he began. "Did you happen to notice what was going on around the pool on Thursday?"

"You mean the orgy scene they were shooting?"

Bryan nodded.

"I didn't see any of it if that's what you're asking. I mean, Hal told us it was going to happen last Sunday, so I made other plans for the day."

"Yeah, I heard Hal say there was going to be some kind of video shoot, but I didn't realize what kind of scene they would be shooting. I guess I'm pretty naïve."

"Well, you're new here. I can see why it wouldn't be obvious at first."

"So, do they do that very often?"

"Only two or three times a year. They probably don't want the same pool and the same backyard showing up in movies all the time. Plus, it's kind of a nuisance for the neighbors, with all the cars parked up and down the street."

They each took a swig of water. Ted waited a few moments to see if Bryan was going to ask anything else before they resumed running. Bryan perceived that Ted wasn't very interested in having this conversation but he was willing to do it anyway, so Bryan decided to continue.

"Did you know that Ricky was in it?"

"I'm not surprised."

"I didn't even know he did porn until Thursday, or that Hal worked in the business."

"Yeah, I was kind of surprised that no one has said anything about that at dinner yet. I guess they assumed you'd figure it out sooner or later."

"How do you feel about it?"

"It doesn't bother me. I mean, it's not something I want to do anymore, but what they do is their business. And I don't mind them doing occasional scenes at the house, I just don't want to be there for them. I'd have to stay out of the way anyway."

"Wait a minute. You said you don't want to do it *anymore*. So, does that mean you've done porn too?"

"A little. When I came back from Afghanistan, I was stationed at Camp Pendleton. In Oceanside, which is the town right next to it, there was this dude who would pay guys to come to his house and jerk off in front of his video camera. Then he'd put it on the internet."

"Were there that many gay guys in the Marines?"

"There were plenty. But a lot of those guys were straight. He'd have a couple of beers with them, maybe a joint if they were into it. Then he put on straight porn for them to watch while they jerked off. It's not like they had to have sex with another guy. To them, it was just a way to pick up some extra money."

"And he made money doing that?"

"Oh, hell yes. People ate it up. Lots of gay guys fantasize about Marines. He'd make two or three of those videos every week."

"Couldn't you get in trouble for doing that sort of thing?"

"In theory, yes. But we weren't wearing our uniforms. I mean, he could have been using guys who just looked like they might be Marines. Anyway, I don't know if the higher-ups knew about it or not. If they did, they didn't think it was serious enough to launch an investigation. I don't think anyone ever got caught."

"So, you did that?"

"Yeah, a couple of times."

"But it was just jerking off."

"Well, there were a few times when he'd find guys who really were gay – or at least flexible – and he'd see if he could get them to do more if he paid them more. Some guys let him give them blowjobs. So, I did a couple of scenes with another guy where we went further."

"Wasn't that riskier if you got caught?"

"Yeah, but it was near the end of my enlistment and I knew I wasn't going to re-up, so I didn't really care. Shall we start running again?"

Bryan nodded, and they began running again. He couldn't stop thinking about all the new information he had absorbed since Thursday afternoon. *My housemate Ricky stars in pornographic movies for a living. My landlord is an attorney in the porn industry. Ted, who I really like and up to this point has been an informal mentor, has done porn in the past. My home is occasionally used as a set for porn scenes. What about Darnell? Besides being a drag queen, what else am I going to find out about him?*

He had no way of knowing any of this when he agreed to move into this house three weeks ago. Everything had seemed so perfect – the beautiful home, the idyllic backyard and swimming pool, the upper-class neighborhood, the proximity to UCLA. It all seemed too good to be true. Perhaps it was.

After the past few weeks, Bryan realized there were so many things he didn't know, both about adult life in general and gay life in particular. He now realized how sheltered and naïve he had been back in Kansas. It was difficult for him to come to terms with being gay and falling in love with Chris, but he assumed that once they got out of Kansas they could spend the rest of their lives together. There was so much new terrain to navigate, so much about gay history and sub-culture to learn, and so many reality checks to deal with.

How does all this new knowledge change things? Can I still live here? None of this new information fundamentally changes my situation. I still have a nice place to live. My housemates are still nice and easy to get along with. The tawdry aspects of their lives don't directly impact me. Should it bother me to be surrounded by people in the porn industry? Do I see my housemates differently now, and can I still respect them? Or am I hanging onto moralistic values instilled in me by my parents and their church, which I need to re-evaluate and perhaps discard?

Bryan glanced at Ted, who was running a step or two ahead of him. Ted was running shirtless, as he had the last time they ran together. He was still the same handsome, well-defined, sexy man Bryan had not-so-subtly ogled a couple of weeks ago, but now he seemed a little less desirable. Despite being bathed in glistening perspiration, some of the luster had worn off.

After running several more laps, they paused for a break before heading home. After a few swigs of water, Bryan asked, "So, how did you meet Hal?"

Ted's eye contact with Bryan indicated that he had correctly inferred the underlying meaning of this innocuous-sounding question. He took another swig of water.

"Actually, he posted an ad on a bulletin board for roommates wanted at the LGBT student organization office on campus. I spent the first quarter of my freshman year living in the dorm. I didn't like it and I didn't fit in that well, since I was older than most of the other kids in the dorm. My reality of having been in the Marines was a bit different from their reality of just coming out of high school. So, I was looking for a place to live off-campus that wouldn't cost too much, and Hal's place fit the bill."

"How do you like living there?"

"It works. Obviously, I still live there. If I get accepted into grad school, I plan to keep living there. As you've probably noticed, I keep to myself a lot. I like all the other guys, but we're not really friends. We don't have much in common other than being gay."

They left the track and started running toward home.

As they ran, Ted said, "But to answer the question I think you were asking, yes, I did a few scenes a couple of years ago for people Hal connected me with. But I'm not really into it, and I don't need the money at this point. The GI Bill is paying for my undergrad and I get a housing allowance, so that covers most of my expenses. I can pick up a gig or two if I need a little more money."

Bryan wasn't quite sure what Ted meant by that. He thought of gigs in musical terms, but he didn't think Ted played an instrument or sang. Gig could mean any kind of part-time job or a one-off of some sort. He thought better of asking.

After a moment, Bryan asked, "Will the GI Bill pay for your grad school?"

"Nope. It covers 36 months of full-time enrollment, which is enough to get my undergrad. I've been going year-round so I can finish in three years. I figured, why take summers off and do nothing? But anyway, yeah, I'm going to have to figure out how to pay for that. Maybe I can get a TA job. If not, I'll take some more escort gigs."

Bryan looked confused. He immediately sensed that this would be yet another learning moment about something he had no idea even existed. "Okay, so what's an escort gig?"

They turned the corner onto their street, and Ted slowed down to a walk for the rest of the journey.

"Yeah, sorry. I shouldn't have assumed that you knew about that. It basically means that some guy will hire me to spend time with him for a while. A lot of times, it's guys who come here on business trips and they don't have anything to do in the evening. Or sometimes, it's older guys who are single. They want someone to be with for a while. They're lonely and they don't feel like going out to bars or any of that other stuff."

"And they pay you for that?"

"Yeah. Very well, in fact."

"What do you do?"

"Whatever they want to do. A lot of times, we talk for a while first. It helps break the ice and establish a rapport. Usually, what they're really hungry for is human contact. And that happens on many levels. It helps to be a good listener and a good conversationalist. Wherever they want to take things, I follow. Although I insist that whatever we do has to be safe."

Bryan looked puzzled. "What do you mean?"

"I insist that we use condoms. Sometimes guys want to do it without them."

"Wait a minute. Are you saying you have sex with these guys?"

"That's the point, yes."

"So, they're really paying you to have sex."

"You got it."

They arrived at the house and walked inside. Bryan was speechless. He needed time to process this new information before he asked any more questions – if he even wanted to.

Bryan asked, "You want to get in the shower first?"

"Yeah, thanks."

The Elephant in the Room

Sunday, August 19, 2007

After working eight hours on Saturday, Bryan returned on Sunday to work from 9 to 5. He didn't mind; he wanted to log as many hours as possible before school started tomorrow. After that, he'd have to cut back his hours. And fewer hours meant less money.

He was also glad to have a reason to be out of the house. Everything he had learned about his housemates over the past few days was unsettling. He did his best to remain focused on his tasks at the store, but he couldn't help thinking about his situation at home.

At 5:00, Bryan headed home. He wasn't looking forward to the weekly family dinner. He felt an obligation to his housemates to be there, and there wasn't a graceful way to back out at the last minute.

When Bryan entered the house, he smelled tantalizing wafts of smoke drifting in from the barbeque grill in the backyard. Hal was grilling chicken breasts slathered with hickory smoke barbecue sauce. He headed for his room, where he changed from his work polo shirt and long pants into a T-shirt and shorts. At 6:00, he joined his housemates at the dinner table. He tried to smile and be friendly.

After everyone had passed the potato salad, baked beans, and dinner rolls, the usual what-have-you-been-up-to-this-week conversation started. Hal and Ted didn't have anything unusual to share. Ricky talked about the great party he went to last night, with lots of hot guys and lots of drinking and 'getting lit.' Even though he went home with some guy, he was able to squeeze in a few hours of sleep before hitting brunch and a Sunday afternoon T-dance in WeHo. Rather than being exhausted, he still seemed to be riding a wave of energy.

It was clear to Bryan that Ricky was living a fast-paced, frenetic life of partying and clubbing. He wondered how a seemingly unemployed college drop-out could afford such a lifestyle, but now his source of income was clear.

After Ricky finished, there were a few moments of silence. Then

Hal turned to Bryan and said, "So I know you've been in band camp for two weeks, and school starts tomorrow. How has it been so far? Have you made any friends?"

"Not really. I'm not very good at meeting new people, and most of the kids already know each other from last year. So, I just kind of keep to myself."

"Well, give it time. But don't be afraid to be the one who starts up a conversation."

"Yeah, I know. Tomorrow, there's going to be an informational meeting at lunchtime about all the clubs they have at school. They have a gay-straight club, so I'll probably check that out."

Ted asked, "Have you thought about how 'out' you're going to be at school?"

"Yeah. I'm not going to be obvious with it, like 'Hi, I'm Ryan and I'm gay,' but I'm not going to hide it either. If they find out, they find out. If they don't like me for it, too bad. I wish I could have been out at my last school. That was kind of an issue for me and Chris."

Ricky said, "I hear ya. I spent my whole time in high school trying to hide who I was, and I felt like such an imposter. It just drained my energy. Then they found out anyway. Man, just be you. There will be people who like you for who you are."

Hal said, "There's an expression that says, 'I'd rather be hated for who I am than loved for who I am not.' I learned that when my parents kicked me out."

They ate in silence for a few more minutes. Then Ted asked, "Is there anything else?"

Bryan didn't want to be the one to bring up the elephant in the room, so he reached for something else. "Yeah. Over the next few weeks, they're going to have people from lots of colleges coming to the school to try to recruit people. I know I want to go to UCLA, but I guess I should meet with some of the reps from other schools anyway."

Hal said, "Yeah. You should keep your options open. I mean, you should easily get accepted with your grades, but what if someplace else offers you a better scholarship? Or it just fits your academic needs better?"

"Yeah, I guess. But it's kind of overwhelming that I'm just starting school tomorrow and I'm already having to think about where I'm going to go next year. It's like I have to think beyond my senior year even though it hasn't happened yet. Like this whole year is going to be an afterthought."

Hal said, "In some ways, it takes the pressure off. Think about it – once you know you've been accepted into a college, you don't have to worry so much about your grades this year. I know you'll do the best you can, but since you have to work too, you may not have as much time for homework."

"Yeah, I won't have much time for anything that takes place after school. In the fall, I'll have marching band rehearsals on Monday and Wednesday afternoons and football games on Friday evenings. So that cuts down the number of hours I can work. I can't take on anything else beyond that."

"Still, try to enjoy your senior year as much as you can. Someday, after you're out in the work world, you'll want to have fond memories of your high school and college years."

Bryan thought about that. He had fond memories of his freshman, sophomore, and junior years at Prairie Village High School. His senior year would have been even better, especially given how things had progressed with Chris. All that had been ripped away from him. Would one year at this new school, where the kids seemed so different, be as good?

Neither Bryan nor the rest of the guys said much else during dinner. The food was delicious, so maybe everyone was focused on enjoying their dinner.

After dinner, they cleared the table and put away the leftovers. Then Hal said, "So what are we up for tonight? A board game? A movie?"

Everyone looked at each other, hoping someone else would make a suggestion.

Bryan said, "I need to check out early this evening. Between working a lot of hours and two weeks of band camp, I'm exhausted. I need some time to unwind. I'll probably go to sleep early."

Nobody said anything, but Bryan could tell that this was a mild rejection to Hal and the others. But it's what he needed to do. He retired to his room.

Reality Checks

Sunday, August 19, 2007

At around 10:00, Ted knocked on Bryan's door. "Hey, Ry? It's Ted."

"Come in."

"You doing okay?"

"Not really. I'm pretty bummed. I have a lot on my mind."

"You wanna talk?"

Bryan thought about it for a few seconds. Maybe talking about it would do some good.

"Yeah, okay."

"Want to go out and chill in the pool? It's a beautiful clear night. I like to go out there at night – it's peaceful and relaxing. It really helps clear my mind."

"Okay."

"See you in a couple of minutes." Ted turned to leave.

"Oh, hey."

Ted turned back.

"So… are you going to wear anything or not?"

"I usually don't, but I will if it will make you more comfortable."

"Nah, that's okay. I'll be fine."

Ted left to return to his room.

The prospect of being naked with Ted didn't hold the allure it did a few days ago, which was probably a good thing. At least now he could probably avoid the awkwardness of an unwanted erection.

He removed his clothes and wrapped a towel around his midsection. Then he left his room and headed toward the sliding glass door that led from the kitchen to the backyard.

Ted arrived in the kitchen at the same time. "Want something to drink? Maybe a beer?"

"No, thanks. I don't like it all that much."

"How about a glass of wine? I've got a bottle of white in my fridge."

"Yeah, okay. I'll try that."

Ted went back to his room and returned with a chilled bottle of pinot grigio and two clear plastic wine glasses. He found a corkscrew in one of the kitchen drawers and opened the bottle.

Bryan opened the door and let Ted pass through, then closed the door behind them. Ted set the bottle and glasses down at the edge of the pool. As Ted walked back to the patio to fetch a few pool noodles, Bryan dropped his towel. He sat down on the edge of the pool and lowered himself in. Ted tossed the pool noodles into the pool and dropped his towel. Of course, Bryan couldn't help but see the rest of Ted that he hadn't seen on their runs. It nicely completed the picture of a perfectly muscled, impressively defined, handsome, and very sexy man. It was clear that developing and maintaining a magnificent body had been a high priority for Ted over the past ten years. Yet despite his breathtaking external appearance, he still projected a quiet, introverted, even humble manner. Ted seemed perfectly at ease with being naked in front of his housemate.

Ted poured a few ounces of wine into each of their glasses, only filling them to the widest point, less than half full. Bryan wondered why he didn't just fill them, but he wasn't going to say anything. Ted picked up the glasses and handed one to Bryan. "Cheers!" They tapped their glasses together, although the plastic glasses made a barely audible thud rather than a clink. Bryan raised the glass to his lips and swallowed a full gulp.

Ted smiled. "First time having wine?"

"Yeah."

"Okay, well let me offer you a suggestion for how to best enjoy wine. Wine is meant to be sipped, rather than gulped quickly like water or soda. First, you swirl it in the glass, which will unleash the aroma, or as it's sometimes called, the bouquet." Ted demonstrated. "Then, breathe in the bouquet. That helps prepare your taste buds for the wine. Then you take small sips, and roll it around in your mouth to enjoy the taste some more." Ted took a small sip. "You try it."

Bryan thought, *Isn't this a bit pretentious and sophisticated? After all, we're just two naked guys in a pool, not elegant rich people at some fancy restaurant or cocktail party.* But he didn't want to cause an issue with Ted, so he tried it. To his surprise, the pinot grigio smelled nice. Leaving it in his mouth for a few seconds before he swallowed it made the wine taste pretty good.

It was yet another reminder that he was a naïve, sheltered boy from Kansas who had so much to learn about adult life and the real world.

"How do you like it?"

"It's delicious. Thanks."

"My pleasure. So… what's on your mind?"

"Oh, all kinds of things." Bryan took a moment to gaze at the clear night sky and contemplate what he should and shouldn't say, and how.

Ted allowed a moment of silence to pass, then said, "Now that you know what a den of iniquity this is and you live with a bunch of godless degenerates, are you having second thoughts about living here?"

Bryan smiled. "Nah, it's not that bad. But it has been a bit… eye-opening."

"I'll bet."

"It's like I kinda wish I had been told about all this upfront, y'know?"

"Would it have changed anything?"

"I don't know. It might have. But then, who knows what my alternatives would have been? My boss from my job back home – I mean, in Kansas – had a couple of friends who were going to let me stay with them for a week or two. But I would have had to find something else quickly. And who knows what I would have found? I mean, I don't think I could have found anything for 500 bucks a month. Certainly not someplace as nice as this that's so close to UCLA. So, I have to keep reminding myself that I'm very lucky."

"Yeah, I feel very lucky to live here too. But here's the thing. Just because Ricky does porn, it doesn't mean you have to. Just because I'm an escort, it doesn't mean you have to. And it's not like you have to be best friends with the other guys who live here. I mean, I like them okay and we get along pretty well as housemates. But otherwise, we don't have much in common besides being gay and living under the same roof."

"Yeah. But I guess what I really miss is being part of a family. Now that I look back on it, I see a lot of things about my parents – mostly my dad – that I wish had been different. But at least it was a family. I never realized how important it was to have a few people who were always there."

"Yeah, a lot of times you never really appreciate something until it's gone. So, you were hoping this new bunch of people would be a close-knit family unit just like the one you left behind."

"I hadn't thought about it that way, but that pretty well sums it up." Bryan took another sip of his wine and looked up at the sky some more. "I feel so alone. When I first got here, there was all the excitement of being in this fabulous new place. And I felt good about getting away from being sent to that gay conversion place. Like I finally triumphed over my dad and now I get to live my life my way and he can't do anything about it. And for a while, getting my job, enrolling in school, and learning my way around kept my mind off things. But now it's obvious that everything isn't rosy and things aren't what they seemed to be, and well… I don't know."

"Yeah, life has a way of giving you reality checks, sometimes at the worst possible times. Not that there's ever a good time, I guess." Ted poured some more wine into each of their glasses. "How do you think school is going to be?"

"I don't know. But I just finished two weeks of band camp, and it wasn't all that great. I still feel like such an outsider. I was thinking back to the time when I started my freshman year. Before that, my parents made me go to this little private Christian school. But then I got to go to this big public high school with all these new kids. And I showed up for band camp the first day, and the other kids all knew each other. Even the other freshmen knew each other because they all went to the same middle school. So anyway, I was just standing on the sideline by myself waiting for rehearsal to start, scared about how I would fit in with all these new kids. Then this guy came up and introduced himself to me. It was Chris, who became my best friend. Of course, I didn't even know I was gay back then. Anyway, he introduced me to all his friends, and before long I was part of the group. And of course, it turned out that he's gay too. A couple of months ago, we finally came out to each other. We started talking about our future, like going to college together and stuff. But now that's all gone and I miss him so much. And I keep hoping that some kid at school will come up and say hi and start introducing me to people. That hasn't happened yet, but it's only been two weeks."

"Maybe you need to take the initiative, and just start smiling and saying hi to people. After all, they don't need to meet you – they already have plenty of friends. You're the one who needs to meet people."

"Yeah. I've been trying, but nobody seems very open. For one thing, there's a lot more racial diversity among the kids here. And that's not a bad thing, but it seems like the kids tend to hang out with the people who are like them. And there aren't that many other White kids. This one guy, Jordan, is the drum major, and I tried saying hi to him and he acted like he didn't want to talk to me. Anyway, I'll meet a lot more kids tomorrow when school starts. Maybe some of them will be more friendly. And I plan to check out the gay-straight club."

A few moments of silence passed.

Ted asked, "So, back to things here at home. Now that you know what I do, how does that change things?"

"Well… I have to admit, I see you differently now."

"In what way?"

"I don't know. I guess I didn't imagine that this is the sort of thing you would do. You seemed a bit more… I don't know…"

"Decent? Upstanding? Honorable?"

"Yeah, I guess. I didn't want to say anything that would sound bad, 'cause I don't want to insult you or anything. But yeah, I don't think quite as highly of you, to be honest."

Ted paused. "In a way, I guess that's a good thing. I was starting to get the impression that you were developing an image of me that was a bit too… idealized. I'm not a perfect person – far from it. I have a lot of flaws and a lot of issues I'm dealing with. And I sensed that you were becoming attracted to me, both romantically and physically, and I don't want that."

"Why not? I know you're not perfect – we all have faults. But you don't need to be perfect. I really like you, and yeah, you're pretty hot."

"Well, thanks. But look. You're a real nice guy. You *are* decent, upstanding, and honest. And definitely good-looking. You're probably a much better person than I am. But here are the realities. First, you're what? 17? I'm 25. That's eight years difference. That's kind of a lot. And it violates the half-your-age-plus-seven rule."

"What's that?"

"That means you shouldn't date anyone who is younger than half your age plus seven. So, in our case, half of 25 is 12 and a half, plus seven makes 19 and a half."

"Isn't that pretty arbitrary? I mean, I don't think of you as too old. Age is just a number anyway."

"I think the rule works in most cases. At our ages, eight years is a lot. I've had a lot more life experiences than you have, and a lot of it hasn't been very pleasant. We're at different points in our lives, you know? And another thing, there's kind of an unwritten rule here that we don't get involved or sleep with each other. It avoids a lot of drama if things don't work out. But mostly, I'm not interested in a relationship with anybody at this point. I just want to get through college, get my Masters, and get my career started. Then maybe when I settle down I'll start thinking about a relationship. But for now, I want to stay focused on my education."

Bryan said, "Yeah, I get it. My brother Brandon is eight years younger than me, and we're at totally different places in our lives. It never occurred to me until now that there's as much space between you and me as there is between me and Brandon."

"Yeah. But the older you get; eight years becomes less of a difference. Like there wouldn't be as much difference between me and a 33-year-old. That's why the formula works."

They spent a few minutes in silence. Bryan wondered whether he should ask about the other thing that was on his mind, and if so, how.

He appreciated that Ted was opening up to him and they were establishing a rapport that would allow them to have deeper conversations.

"So, can I ask you a couple of questions about what you do as an escort?"

"Sure."

"Okay. So, you mentioned that you did porn a while back. And now you're an escort. Basically, guys pay you to have sex with them. Isn't that the same as being a prostitute?"

"Well, it's kinda the same and kinda not. I mean, I'm not standing on a street corner hooking up with someone who drives by, then doing a quickie in a motel room or something. It's a bit classier and more discreet than that. I form more of a connection with the person and it's a nicer experience. It's not as tawdry as prostitution."

"But it still sounds like it's just a nicer word for prostitute. And prostitution's illegal. Ricky and I were talking about this a couple of days ago, that being a porn star is legal, but prostitution is illegal."

"Yeah, technically that's true."

"Aren't you worried about getting caught?"

"No, not really. As I said, we're not standing around on street corners where we could get busted by undercover cops."

"So, how do your tricks find you?"

"First of all, they're clients, not tricks. Anyway, there are escort services online. On the websites, it doesn't say anything about sex or what is going to happen when somebody hires an escort. They're just paying for someone to come spend time with them. What happens is up to them. Of course, we all know what the assumption is, but it's never stated."

"Couldn't an undercover cop use an escort service and then bust you when you start having sex?"

"Yeah, I guess, but it never happens. Plus, the client is always the one who initiates it. I never initiate anything."

"But even so, if doing porn is legal and being an escort is illegal, why don't you just do porn?"

"I didn't really care for it. I mean, it's just like being an actor in any other kind of movie. You spend a lot of time waiting around for them to get the lighting and the sound set up. Then you do a bunch of takes from different camera angles. You've got some director telling you exactly what he wants you to do and how he wants to you do it, and all that stuff. You're not being you. You're a fantasy character that might be doing things you wouldn't otherwise do, with people you wouldn't otherwise do it with. It's all mechanical. It's work – it's not enjoyable at all. With escorting, at least I get to know the guy and form some sort of a connection with him. We do what he wants to do, so it's satisfying for him. And it satisfies me to know I've given someone a nice experience."

"Okay, but you're still getting paid for sex. And in a way, you're acting out the fantasy the client wants to have."

"Yeah, I guess. But… how do I say this? It's usually about more than sex. With a lot of my clients, what they really want isn't sex, it's intimacy. It's connection. It's another human being to touch them and listen to them and spend time with them. They just use sex as a way to get that. I mean, sure, sex is fun, and getting off feels great, but deep down that's not what they really need. I usually spend several hours with them. Many of them want to talk. They're lonely. They want someone to tell their stories to; someone to discuss their concerns with; someone to listen. A lot of times, when we're done with the sex, we lay there in bed in each other's arms. I think that might be the best part for them."

"How often do you do this?"

"Right now, several times a month. Maybe once or twice a week. I could work every night if I wanted to, but I don't. I need to study for school and this is bringing in enough money. I don't even have my listing on the website active now. I have enough work with my current clients and the occasional referral."

"You mean you see the same people over and over again?"

"Yeah, I have several regulars who call me every month or two."

"So, what are they like?"

"Well, everyone's different. But if I had to put together a composite of my clients, I'd say most of them are in their forties or fifties. A few are younger or older. They're successful at their jobs but a lot of times they're closeted, so they're single and lonely. I mean, they have friends, but they don't have a place in their life for someone special."

"But still, aren't you kind of taking advantage of their loneliness to make money?"

"How is it taking advantage? They choose to do this. They have plenty of money. What they don't have is human connection. What good is having a lot of money if you're lonely and miserable? If they feel better about themselves after a few hours with me, isn't that worth something?"

"But why don't they just come out and live their lives openly?"

"I don't know. That's not my choice to make, nor would I even suggest that to them. And it's not always that simple. Like I have one client who, let's say, isn't very attractive on a physical basis. But he's actually a nice guy. He's got a curved spine, so he's kind of hunched over to one side, like one shoulder is noticeably higher than the other. He's pretty open about being gay, but he's never been able to find a guy who can get over that initial hurdle of what he looks like. So, he's pretty much given up on ever finding a partner. There's another guy who is part of a very wealthy, conservative family. He's certain that if his parents found out, they'd cut him out of the estate. For me, it wouldn't be worth it. But that's his choice to make."

"Yeah, I can relate to the whole thing about not wanting your family to find out."

"Right. And then I have a couple of clients who come here fairly often on business trips. I meet them in whatever hotel they're staying at. And let me tell you, I've been in some pretty expansive, luxurious places. Anyway, in most cases, I don't know what their situation at home is. I just know that they always look forward to seeing me whenever they come here."

"Do you think they're cheating on their partners?"

"Maybe. Or their wives, probably. But I don't ask. One thing about being an escort is that you have to be very discreet and non-judgmental. That's one reason they're willing to pay a lot. I've escorted for some pretty famous people."

"Like who?"

"I can't tell you. That's the point."

"But, like movie stars? Sports figures? Politicians?"

"Yes. All of the above."

Bryan didn't have any more questions, at least for now. He had enough new information swimming around in his head. After a few minutes, he said, "Well, it's probably time for me to go in. I've got school tomorrow. But thanks for the talk. And the wine."

"Most of it was probably not what you wanted to hear."

"Yeah, but I guess it's better to know the truth."

"Yep. The truth will set you free – but first, it will piss you off."

Bryan gathered up the pool noodles, hoisted them onto the deck. Then he climbed out of the pool and wrapped his towel around his waist. Ted climbed out, donned his towel, and gathered up the wine bottle and glasses. They went back into the kitchen, where Ted carried the wine glasses to the sink.

Bryan started heading for his room, then turned and said, "Good night."

"Good night. Hey…" Ted took a few steps toward Bryan. "Are we okay?"

"Yeah, I guess."

"As I said, I don't want to get romantically or physically involved with you. But you're a nice guy, and I like you. I hope we can still be friends, despite everything you know about me now. And I'm always willing to talk or answer questions."

"Thanks. Maybe you can be kinda like a big brother."

"Yeah, that would work."

"And it would be great if we could hang out now and then, and still go running together sometimes."

Ted nodded. They both smiled. Ted took a couple of steps closer to Bryan and gave him a tight hug. Despite his changed feelings for Ted, Bryan savored the skin-to-skin contact of Ted's firm, slightly moist chest pressed against his, and the comfort of their arms wrapped around each other's backs. Ted gave Bryan a light kiss on the side of his neck, then stepped back. They made eye contact and smiled again. Things would be okay.

School Starts

Monday, August 20, 2007

Bryan's alarm clock went off at 6:30 a.m. He punched the snooze bar twice, but 18 minutes later, he knew he had to get up. School started at 8:00, and he wanted to be sure to be there bright and early. He now regretted staying up until 11:30 talking with Ted and drinking wine in the pool. But the wine had helped him get to sleep and the conversation with Ted was enlightening and had brought them closer.

The first day of classes was a whirlwind of excitement, discovery, and chaos, sprinkled with liberal doses of trepidation. Bryan struggled to navigate the hordes of wandering students, who were either clustered in groups of reunited friends or trying, like him, to find their next classroom. The first day's classes were introductory, including such mundane tasks as distributing textbooks and going over syllabi and course objectives. The real instruction and homework assignments wouldn't begin for another day or two.

Bryan recognized a couple of kids from the marching band in most of his classes. They at least acknowledged him as a familiar face. Thankfully, Mrs. Rodriguez had been able to add Bryan to the Advanced Placement classes for English, Math, and Science. Jordan, the drum major, was in each of those classes. He seemed rather cold toward Bryan for some reason.

The meeting to introduce students to the various clubs at school was being held at one end of the cafeteria. A microphone, a portable speaker, and a few information tables had been set up. Mrs. Rodriguez made a few opening remarks, then introduced each of the faculty sponsors. They, in turn, said a few words about each of their clubs. Mr. Perez introduced the Gay-Straight Alliance, which was received with scattered snickering and derision. It would meet every other Thursday during lunch in a classroom near the cafeteria. Bryan decided that he might also check out the computer club and the debate team to see if either of those seemed interesting.

Band was held during the sixth and final period. During period 6, the Wind Ensemble met to begin learning music for the fall concert. On Mondays and Wednesdays, marching band practice was held after school until 4:30. Bryan learned that Jazz Ensemble met after school on Tuesdays. Having to stay late on Monday, Tuesday, and Wednesday afternoons along with the football games on Friday evenings would make it harder for him to get hours in at Pure Foods. But the music was worth it to him.

When Bryan entered the band room, he saw that Jordan was sitting in the first chair in the trumpet row. A couple of the other trumpeters from the marching band were sitting in the chairs next to him. Many of the kids in the marching band, but there were a few others who were only in the Wind Ensemble. There was an empty chair near the end of the row, so Bryan scooted past the others until he reached it. Bryan sat down, turned to the girl next to him, smiled, and said, "Hi, I'm Bryan."

"I'm Miranda. Are you a freshman?"

"No, I'm a senior. I moved here a few weeks ago."

"Well, welcome to band."

Bryan smiled. He retrieved his trumpet from his case and applied valve oil to his valves. He warmed up by blowing a few long tones, running a couple of scales up and down two octaves, and playing some lip slurs. This was his normal warm-up routine, but Miranda and several other trumpet players glanced over in his direction.

The bell rang and Mr. Scales called the rehearsal to order. He led the band through a B-flat scale and tuned the band by section. Then he said, "On your stands, you should have an audition sheet that's appropriate for your instrument. On it, you'll see that there are three short passages – one is easy, one is medium, and one is difficult. You should choose whichever one you can play well. In other words, it would be better to play the medium piece well than to try to play the difficult piece and do it poorly. You'll be asked to play a scale starting on low concert B-flat and going as high as you can comfortably play. You'll also be given a short piece to sight-read. It should all take about two minutes each, tops. Auditions will be held Wednesday and Thursday. We should be able to get through the whole band in two days. We'll audition all the people in each section on the same day, so everyone gets the same amount of preparation time. Auditions will be blind, that is, you'll be given a number. The three people who will be evaluating you will be behind a screen, so they won't know who is who. I will then tally up their scores and determine who will play which parts in which chairs. Then finally, I will match the names to the numbers. So it should be completely fair and impartial. Are there any questions?"

Connor, one of the trombone players asked, "To whom should we give the envelopes with the unmarked 20s?" Several other students chuckled.

Mr. Scales replied, "You can give them to me. Of course, it won't change your audition results, but I can always use the extra money."

Jordan asked, "When will we get the results?"

"On Friday. Until then, just sit where you are and play the part in front of you. But remember that who's sitting where and playing each part now is temporary. It will probably change on Friday. Okay, now let's play some music! You should have *Holidays on Broadway* on your stand. Let's start with that."

Bryan played this arrangement as a freshman. It was a fairly easy arrangement, but one that was well-received by the audience.

Mr. Scales began conducting. The band sounded horrible. Despite having just tuned, intonation was all over the place. People missed rhythms, and some people were lost by the time the band got to rehearsal letter B. Mr. Scales stopped the band and said, "Okay, remember to look at your key signature. I heard a lot of people missing sharps. Let's try it again." It was only marginally better. Mr. Scales displayed an impressive amount of patience. It was the first day, after all.

The Gay-Straight Alliance: Week 1

Thursday, August 23, 2007

When lunchtime came on Thursday, Bryan stopped by his locker, grabbed the lunch he had packed, and headed to room 226, where the Westwood High School Gay-Straight Alliance was about to hold its first meeting of the new school year.

Fifteen desks near the front of the room had been arranged into a lopsided circle. There were six or seven kids in the room. Bryan assumed that most of them knew each other already. Three girls were chatting with each other and a couple of other kids were just sitting there eating. Bryan picked a desk and focused on unpacking his lunch and eating it.

Mr. Perez, the faculty advisor, was sitting at his desk. Bryan wasn't taking any of his classes, so this was his first introduction to him. He couldn't tell whether Mr. Perez was gay, but he decided it didn't matter. It's not like he would be dating him. As long as Mr. Perez was supportive of gay people, that's all that mattered.

Bryan wondered, *How are gay men supposed to look? How can I tell, just by looking at a guy, whether he's gay? Do gay men have a set of secret signals? Are there mannerisms or ways of talking or dressing that I should look for? For example, Skyler is almost certainly gay – but I didn't know for sure. This is yet another aspect of this whole gay thing I have to try to learn.*

A few minutes passed and several more kids had entered the room. There were now about a dozen kids; eight girls and four boys. Mr. Perez got up from his desk and sat down at one of the remaining desks in the circle. "Good afternoon, everyone. Welcome, and thanks for coming to the first meeting of the Gay-Straight Alliance, or GSA as we usually call it. I know some of you may be a little nervous about being here, but let me assure you, you're welcome. We are here to support each other. This is a safe space. With that in mind, I'd like us to agree right up front that whatever discussions happen in this room stay in this room. And we should also be mindful of the fact that some of us are straight allies and some of those who are LGBT may not be out. So, we should honor each other's privacy. Do we all agree?"

Everyone nodded.

"Okay. Let's start with introductions. Please tell us your name – first name only is okay if you prefer – what year you are, and something interesting about yourself. If you would like to share whether you identify as lesbian, gay, bisexual, transgender, straight, or questioning, you may. But you don't have to share that if you don't want to. I'll start. I'm Mr. Perez. I teach history and sociology. I'm fascinated by the way various types of people fit into and contribute to society, their particular issues and challenges, and how societies deal with people who are different. Of course, that includes members of the LGBT community, along with many others. Also, my brother is gay. So, I have some visibility into his challenges and struggles, as well as the culture of the LGBT community. I want to do whatever I can to make the world a more accepting place for him and all of you." He turned to the girl sitting to his right. "Monique, would you please go next?"

The kids took turns introducing themselves in sequence, working their way around the circle. Several of the girls said they were here because they have gay friends and they were 'straight allies.' They didn't mention whether any of their gay friends were among those in the room. The other kids didn't mention anything about their orientation.

The girl sitting next to Bryan was an African-American girl who had a rainbow flag patch sewn onto her backpack and an Obama 'hope and change' sticker affixed in the center. When it was her turn, she stated, "My name is LaTanya Sheridan. I'm a junior, and an out and proud lesbian. Outside of school, I like to write poetry and play percussion. My father has a collection of percussion instruments from around the world, and he leads drum circles."

Mr. Perez said, "That's interesting. Where does he play?"

"All over the place. He has a regular ensemble that plays at festivals and events around town. Sometimes he's invited to lead drum circles at spirituality retreats, and sometimes companies hire him to do team building events."

"Fascinating! Thank you for sharing. Next?"

Bryan said, "Hi, everyone. I'm Ryan Robertson. I'm a senior. I'm new this year; I moved here over the summer. I play the trumpet. I'm in the marching band, and I'm looking forward to playing at the football games. And I love jazz, so I'm looking forward to the jazz ensemble starting up. I'm gay, and I thought I'd check out this group so I can hopefully make a few new friends."

The remaining two kids introduced themselves. Then Mr. Perez said, "Okay, now that we all know each other, does anyone have any questions?"

Bryan asked, "So, as I mentioned, I'm new here. How easy is it to be out here? I mean, how cool are most kids with the gay thing?"

Everyone looked at each other to see if someone else would speak first. After a few seconds, one of the girls, Allyson, said, "Well, I'm here as a straight ally. I know a few of my friends are gay, but they're not quite ready to be out yet."

A small, slender Vietnamese boy named Mike Nguyen, who Bryan recognized from a couple of his advanced placement classes, said, "I haven't told anyone. Although I think some kids might suspect, 'cause I don't have a girlfriend or anything."

Monique said, "I don't know. It's like, this school is pretty diverse, so people are used to being around people who are different from them. And it's pretty liberal, politically speaking. So, I think most kids know that they're supposed to be tolerant and accepting of gay people. But since so few people are out, they don't have to deal with it much."

LaTanya said, "As I said, I'm totally out. I'm through with trying to hide who I am. I just put myself out there, and either people like me or they don't. That's their business. If they've got a problem with it, that's just what it is – their problem. So yeah, I don't have that many friends, but that's okay. I know the friends I have are real. They like me for who I am. That's all I need. I'm not going to act like someone I'm not just so I can get more people to like me. I ain't got time for that."

Bryan asked, "Do you feel safe? Do people tease you or anything?"

"Oh, once in a while I hear some comment behind my back, or I hear someone call me LezTanya or something like that. But I just let it slide right off. I figure it doesn't make me look bad, it makes them look bad."

Bryan admired LaTanya's strength and no-bullshit honesty. He decided he wanted to become one of her real friends.

Another girl named Amber, presumably one of the straight allies, said, "I'm totally cool with lesbians and gays, or I wouldn't be here. But I guess I don't understand why it has to be a big deal about whether you're out or not. I mean, it's like if you're gay or lesbian – so what? Why should you have to make a big announcement? And like, for the rest of us, we know there are some kids here who are probably gay. Like, it shouldn't even be an issue."

Mr. Perez said, "I think, in an ideal world, you're right – it shouldn't be an issue. But let me add a little bit of historical perspective. Some of you may have heard of Harvey Milk. He was the first openly gay person to serve on the San Francisco Board of Supervisors. He served only eleven months in office before he was assassinated, along with the mayor, George Moscone. That was in 1978. Back then, LGBT people had no rights at all, and they had to stay closeted so they wouldn't be fired from their jobs or denied housing or anything like that. Back then, cities and states were routinely passing laws that discriminated against gays and lesbians. Harvey Milk famously said that if people would just come out to their friends and families, all that would change, because people would be less likely to support laws that harmed their loved ones. See, back then, gays and lesbians were so hidden that nobody thought they knew one. Harvey Milk knew that visibility was the key to gaining equal rights."

Amber said, "Okay, I get all that. But it's not like we're voting for people's rights here at high school. What does all that have to do with us here?"

Mr. Perez said, "Let's bring what Harvey Milk said into the present. In 2004 and 2006 a lot of states put constitutional amendments on the ballots which would prohibit same-sex marriage. They passed in every state except Arizona – sometimes overwhelmingly. I'll bet a lot of people who voted in favor of those amendments didn't know they had someone in their family or their circle of friends who would be harmed. You guys will be 18 and eligible to vote soon. And who knows? We may have an anti-marriage equality amendment on the ballot here. Do you think you, and some of the other kids here, might vote differently if you knew some of your friends are LGBT?"

LaTanya said, "It's like LGBT is the invisible minority. People can look at me and see that I'm Black and I'm a woman. But they won't know I'm a lesbian unless I tell them."

Amber replied, "Okay, so you're a lesbian. That's cool and everything, but why should it even be an issue? I mean, isn't it kind of personal?"

Bryan said, "On the other hand, why should we have to hide? Before I was outed to my parents back in June, I had a boyfriend. I felt like I had to hide the fact that I was gay and he was my boyfriend, and that didn't seem fair. See, if you're straight and you're dating some guy, you can just say, 'This is my boyfriend,' and nobody thinks twice about it."

Allyson said, "Why can't you just say, 'This is my boyfriend?' I'd be down with that."

"Well, that's great. But how can I even find a boyfriend if I have no way of knowing who any of the other gay guys are? Like, if I let some guy know I'm interested in him and he's not gay, I could get punched out. I don't know about here, but at my last high school, gays and lesbians were totally invisible. I'll bet if you asked, a lot of kids would say there weren't any gay or lesbian kids at our high school. I had no idea whether I'd get beat up or made fun of or ostracized or what."

Mike said, "It's pretty much the same here."

Monique said, "I'll bet most of the kids here would be okay with it. I mean, I never hear people telling homophobic jokes or anything like that."

Mike said, "Maybe they would be. Maybe we're imagining a problem that doesn't exist. But we don't know. And if you don't know, it's scary."

Bryan said, "Yeah, that's kind of why I brought this whole thing up.

I'd like to be open about being gay, but how's that going to go over? Maybe everyone will be like that's cool and no big deal, or maybe I'll get picked on and beat up. I have no way of knowing."

Mike said, "It's like you have to make a big deal about it in order for people to realize that it's really no big deal."

LaTanya added, "Yeah. You have to put it out there and let people see it and deal with it, then we can move on."

Monique said, "Okay, so how do we get from here to there? How do we create an environment where LGBT people feel it's safe to come out? How can those of us who are straight and supportive let other people know that?"

Mr. Perez said, "That's a really good question, and maybe that needs to be our project for this semester. We're almost out of time, but think about it and try to come up with some ideas. We can continue this discussion at our next meeting. In the meantime, keep in mind that October 11th is National Coming Out Day and October is Gay and Lesbian History Month. Maybe we can come up with something to do for either or both of those. I can ask Mrs. Rodriguez if we can reserve the student activities bulletin board for a week if we decide to go that route."

The bell rang, and everyone got up to go to their next class. Mike timed his exit so he'd be walking out the door along with Bryan. He said, "Hey, I heard you say you were interested in the jazz ensemble. I play piano, and I auditioned for it. The guy who played piano last year graduated, so I hope I get in."

"I hope so too! And I'm happy to know someone else who likes jazz. We should hang out sometime and listen to tunes."

"Cool. Well, I'll see you in Chemistry later."

***

The next day, when Bryan entered the cafeteria for lunch, he spotted LaTanya sitting at the far end by herself. He walked up and asked, "May I join you?"

"Sure, have a seat."

"Hey, I admire you for being so up-front about being a lesbian. I hope I can be just as open about being gay."

"Well, that's up to you. That's a choice you make for yourself. No one can force you to stay in the closet. I tried that at first, and I'm here to tell you being out is so much easier than being closeted."

"Is it really?"

"Yeah. It's like a giant weight gets lifted off your shoulders. Hiding takes so much energy. It's much easier to just be yourself. You're more authentic. Like I said yesterday, people will either like you or they won't, and that's up to them. There's nothing you can do about that."

"I figure since I don't have any friends here yet, it's not like I'm going to lose any."

"That's right. And besides, if you had people you thought were your friends, and then they stop being your friends when they find out you're gay, they weren't really your friends in the first place. Or at least they're not the kind of friends you want to have."

"Yeah, but I'm still trying to figure out how to go about it. It's like it would be weird to just walk up to people and say, 'Hi, I'm Ryan and I'm gay.' I mean, how do you bring it up?"

"A lot of times, I don't have to tell people. I show them. Like that rainbow patch I have on my backpack? That lets people know without me having to say anything. Or sometimes I wear T-shirts that say something that lets people know. For a lot of people, it may be awkward for them to talk about it. But if they can see it and they don't have to deal with it directly, they're okay with it."

"But isn't the whole point that we should be able to talk about it?"

"Yeah, but some people aren't ready for that yet. Baby steps. And besides, I don't want to keep talking about it over and over. I just want to go about my day, you know? And if we say it should be no big deal, that helps me send the message without making it a big deal."

Bryan thought back to that day in early June when Chris had taken him to the gay pride festival in Kansas City. A vendor was selling all kinds of gay-themed T-shirts and other rainbow-colored accessories. At the time, Bryan wanted no part of identifying as gay or being part of a gay community. Now he saw the point.

"So, where do you get that stuff?"

"There are a couple of shops in WeHo that sell all kinds of rainbow stuff."

Bryan wondered, *How long it would take to get to WeHo on my bike? Will it be safe? And when will I ever have time? Maybe I could get one of the guys to drive me there someday.*

The conversation had stalled, so Bryan asked, "So, are you out to your parents?"

"Yeah. I told them when I was around 14 or 15. They weren't surprised, 'cause like I've kind of known my entire life. I've never been interested in boys, except maybe to play sports with them. And I was never into dolls and all that girly shit. I've always known I was different, and I just decided at one point that I was okay with that and I'm just gonna be who I am."

"How did they deal with it?"

"It was kind of rough at first. See, they've got this religion thing goin' on. They're with the God Squad. So at first, they were all like, 'this is a sin and you need to pray about it.' But I said, 'This is the way God created me, and I'm beautiful just the way I am. And if I try to be something I'm not, then I'm sayin' God made some kind of mistake when he made me.' And they kept sayin' Jesus this and Jesus that, and finally, I told them to go find someplace in the Bible where Jesus said anything about being gay. And they couldn't, 'cause it ain't there. And then I said, what about that commandment that says 'thou shalt not bear false witness against thy neighbor,' or in other words, 'thou shalt not lie.' I told them I'm not going to lie about who I am. So they thought about all that for a while, and since then they're okay with it. I mean, they probably still wish I was straight, and they're never gonna be marching down the street in the pride parade with the other parents of lesbians and gays. But they love me and they say they're still proud of me, so we're okay."

"That's great. I wish my folks had been open to reason like that."

Bryan recounted the story of how his parents found out, what they planned to do to him, and how he ended up in LA.

"You mean you're out here all by yourself?"

"Uh-huh. Well, not really. I have a room in this house with several other gay guys near campus. They're real nice, and they're kind of like a family to me."

"Do your parents know where you are?"

"Nope. And I hope they never find out. I never want to go back there. As far as I'm concerned, I don't have parents anymore."

"Wow. That's really intense."

"Yeah, it's been kind of rough, but I'm getting by pretty well."

"So, hey. You were talking about the jazz ensemble. Do you know if they have a percussionist?"

"I don't know, but I can ask Mr. Scales. I think it would be cool to have a percussionist in the band."

"Yeah, well I can bring my own equipment if I have to."

"Okay, I'll let him know that."

First Chair
Friday, August 24, 2007

When Bryan entered the band room on Friday, he saw students clustered around several sheets of paper that were taped to the front wall. Everyone was checking out where they had placed as a result of their auditions.

Bryan joined the throng. After about ten seconds, he got close enough to see that he was listed as the first chair in the trumpet section. He smiled. After hearing the other trumpeters in marching band, he wasn't surprised. Since Jordan was the drum major, Bryan wasn't sure how well he played. He turned and headed toward the trumpet row. Jordan was sitting in first chair, as he had all week.

Bryan approached Jordan, who barely acknowledged him and continued to warm up. "Um… according to the audition results, I believe I should be sitting there."

Jordan stopped his warm-up routine and frowned at Bryan. He grudgingly scooted over to the next chair and pulled his case and his mutes over to his new seat. He resumed his warm-ups without saying anything to Bryan.

***

The same scenario occurred on Tuesday at the first jazz ensemble rehearsal. Bryan walked into the band room and saw that Jordan had already arrived and claimed first chair. Mr. Scales had posted a sheet of paper on the wall with the chair assignments for the jazz ensemble. Once again, Bryan was first chair.

Mr. Scales was sorting music on a table and had his back turned to the musicians entering the room. Bryan asked, "Mr. Scales, do you set up your band with the leads in the middle – second, first, third, fourth – or in order – first, second, third, fourth?"

"Leads in the middle." Mr. Scales turned and looked at the seats and saw Jordan sitting in first chair. He let out a barely audible sigh. "Um, kids? As you're getting set up, remember that the first chair players in the trumpets and trombones sit one seat in from the left. It should be second, first, third, fourth. Saxes should be tenor 1, alto 2, alto 1, tenor 2, bari." He looked straight at Jordan. Jordan scooted over.

Jordan and Julio, the third-chair trumpeter, rarely said anything to Bryan during the rehearsal. They cracked jokes and made snarky comments to each other by leaning backward or forward to talk around Bryan.

Bryan tried to be nice to them and smile. Hopefully, as they got to know each other, they could all be friends.

***

After rehearsal, Bryan held back and waited until the other kids had left. Then he approached Mr. Scales and asked, "May I talk with you for a moment?"

"Sure. I've been meaning to ask you how band is going for you so far."

"Well, it's pretty good, mostly. I'm not making many friends yet, but I figure it just takes time. I know they already have their friends from last year, and I'm the new guy. And I'm kinda shy. But I'm enjoying the music."

"Good. So, what's on your mind?"

"Well, a couple of things. First, have you thought about having a percussionist in the jazz ensemble? I've met a girl who plays. Her dad has percussion instruments from all over the world and leads a percussion ensemble. She has her own instruments she can bring if the school doesn't have them."

"I'd be open to that idea. A percussionist would add a lot to the band. Tell her to come talk with me and we can set up a time for her to come in and audition. What's her name?"

"LaTanya Sheridan."

"Okay, well I look forward to meeting her – and hearing her. Now, was there something else?"

"Yeah. I'm grateful that you put me in first chair, but–"

"You earned it. I didn't give it to you. You're a very fine player."

"Thanks. But anyway, I get the feeling that Jordan thinks he should be in first chair. It seems like it's really important to him. He's treating me like I'm invading his territory or something."

"I could sense there was a little tension in the room. And yes, he probably feels like he belongs in first chair and he's entitled to it. He was first chair last year as a junior, so he probably sees it as a setback that he didn't get it again this year. But he's going to have to learn how to deal with it. That's life. And you are the better player."

"Okay, but… well… he's being really cold to me, like he never looks at me or talks to me. It's pretty uncomfortable. Maybe it would be easier to let him have it if it means there would be less tension and we would get along better."

"No. He needs to learn how to deal with situations like this. After he gets out into the world, he's not going to have everything handed to him. There will be people who do better than him. And besides, that wouldn't be fair to you."

"Yeah, but I guess it's not as important to me as it is to him. And if it means there would be less awkwardness and tension–"

Mr. Scales was shaking his head. "Look. I know you're new and you haven't made many friends yet, and you want people to like you. I understand that. But if he likes you if he gets to play first chair but he doesn't like you if he doesn't, well… that's not much of a basis for friendship, is it?"

"No, I guess not."

"You earned it. You deserve it. He'll just have to learn how to deal with it. Life will go on."

"Yeah, okay. Thank you."

"You're welcome. Have a good evening. Oh, and Ryan? I'm really glad you're here."

Bryan smiled, then turned and left. The music program here wasn't as good as the one back in Prairie Village, but Mr. Scales was a nice man and a good director. He was doing his best with what he had to work with.

The Gay-Straight Alliance: Week 2
Thursday, September 6, 2007

When the GSA met for their second meeting, Mr. Perez began the meeting by asking, "How is everybody? How's school been so far?"

Several of the kids mumbled, "okay" or "fine."

Bryan said, "I'm really glad I joined. I'm already getting to know LaTanya and Mike, and it's nice to see a few familiar faces in the hallways and my classes. I feel like I'm starting to fit in a little bit."

Mr. Perez replied, "That's great. That's one of the main reasons we have student organizations. So, have any of you thought about our discussion last week? Do you have any ideas for what we can do to let kids know that this is a safe place for LGBT kids?"

Nobody jumped in right away, like they were waiting to see if someone else would say something first. Then Monique said, "You mentioned October was LGBT History Month. Like, I didn't even know that was a thing. But if we could get approval to use the student bulletin board, we could put up a display of famous LGBT people in history."

Bryan said, "Like who? I know I haven't been out very long, but I have no idea who any historical LGBT people are. That sure wasn't taught at my last school."

Allyson said, "Well, there was that Harvey Milk guy Mr. Perez talked about at our last meeting. There have to be others."

Mr. Perez said, "There are. I'm sure we can do some research on the internet and identify some of them. If we decide to go this route, then each of us can do some research and come to the next meeting with a suggestion for someone to feature on the bulletin board."

LaTanya said, "That's all well and good, but how's that going to help with making this a safer place? I bet most people will just walk right past the bulletin board, especially when they see what it's about. Nobody's going to stop and look at it."

Mike said, "I can see where it might have value. It would say that LGBT people have made important contributions to the world, especially while being discriminated against."

LaTanya said, "I'm not against doing it. I just don't think it's going to do anything to help make this a safer place to be out as a queer person."

Bryan said, "When LaTanya and I were having lunch a couple of weeks ago, she said she has that rainbow flag on her backpack to let other people know she's a lesbian. I want to get one of those too, but I haven't had a chance to get to a store that sells them."

Allyson said, "Yeah, well that's great for you guys who are actually gay or lesbian and willing to be out. I'm willing to say I support your community, but I'm not a lesbian. I mean, isn't the rainbow flag only for people who are actually LGBT?"

Amber said, "What we need is another symbol that says, 'I'm a straight friend' or something that includes both LGBT people and their supporters."

Mr. Perez said, "I read recently that some major corporations in the US have come up with a symbol for that. It's a pink triangle with a green circle around it. They pass out little magnets with that symbol, and people can put it somewhere in their office where it's visible. That way LGBT people know that person is accepting."

Mike said, "It's a nice idea, but how will anyone know what a pink triangle in a green circle means? I don't even know what that means. And we don't have offices."

Mr. Perez said, "Well, the pink triangle was a symbol the Nazis used to identify homosexuals when they sent them to the concentration camps. Not many people are aware that homosexuals were also rounded up and sent to concentration camps and killed. It wasn't only the Jews."

Monique said, "Wow, that's a buzzkill."

Amber said, "Yeah. Why would anybody want to display something or label themselves with an image that was used to kill people?"

Mr. Perez said, "I understand that. But over the years, the gay community used that symbol to identify themselves. It's like they reclaimed it and redefined what the symbol meant. Anyway, the pink triangle isn't used much anymore now that we have the rainbow."

Mike said, "Still… regardless of whether we use that or we come up with something else, how are we going to let people know what it means? How are we going to get them to want to have one?"

Allyson said, "Maybe we could get an article published in the student newspaper that talks about why we're doing this and what the symbol means. Then we could set up a table outside the cafeteria at lunchtime and give them out."

Monique said, "That's a great idea. But where would people put little magnets? On their lockers? That wouldn't work unless you know whose locker is whose."

Mike said, "But if you walked around the halls and you saw a bunch of those magnets on the lockers, you'd get the message that at least some people here support LGBT people."

LaTanya said, "Yeah, until some homophobe comes along and takes them all off."

Bryan said, "Let's get back to the idea of the rainbow patch on LaTanya's backpack. We could make it a sticker that people put on their backpacks, like her Obama sticker. Or they could put it on their notebooks."

Allyson said, "Or maybe little round buttons they can pin on their clothes like some people do for elections."

Mr. Perez said, "I like where this is going. But if you don't like the pink triangle, what other symbol could we create?"

Bryan said, "Maybe a rainbow flag inside a green circle."

LaTanya said, "Or the Human Rights Campaign has this symbol that's a gold equal sign on a dark blue background."

Bryan said, "Maybe the equal sign inside a green circle."

Mike said, "Yeah, but I don't think enough people will pick up on the green circle. I mean, we all know what a red circle with a slash through it means, but the green circle's not so obvious."

Monique said, "Yeah, well no matter what we pick, we're going to have to explain what the symbol means. If we can get an article in the student newspaper, that will help a lot."

Bryan said, "And it would be great if we can get a lot of the teachers to display the symbol in their classroom. And also Mrs. Rodriguez and the guidance counselors."

Mr. Perez said, "I could probably get most of the teachers on board with that, and certainly Mrs. Rodriguez. In the meantime, we've come up with several ideas so far: a bulletin board display of famous LGBT people, a symbol that people can display to show that they're supportive of LGBT people, and an article in the newspaper. Although the last two sort of go hand-in-hand since the article will explain what the symbol is about. Any thoughts about which one we should do?"

Bryan said, "Why not do them all? I think they all have value."

Allyson said, "We could divide up into teams."

Mr. Perez said, "Well, okay. If we can commit the time and energy to do them all, I'm fine with that. So, I'd like to give each of you a homework assignment. First, I'd like you to do some research and come to the next meeting with at least one famous LGBT person who you think should be included on our bulletin board. Find a picture of them and give us a short description of why they're noteworthy. Second, come up with a drawing of a symbol we can use for our supportive friends sticker. It doesn't have to be anything fancy. In fact, simpler is better. A sketch will be fine. Will you all do that before our next meeting in two weeks?"

Everyone said yes or nodded.

Darnell Makes His Entrance

Sunday, September 9, 2007

Darnell arrived home late Saturday evening. Hal picked him up from the airport. During the drive home, Hal mentioned that Tyler had to drop out of school when he lost his scholarship, and a new guy named Ryan moved in a few weeks ago.

Darnell was exhausted. The flight from Athens to Los Angeles had taken 20 hours, including a 4-hour layover in Newark. He had crossed nine time zones, making it a 33-hour day. He hauled his luggage into his room and went straight to bed. Everything could wait until tomorrow.

On Sunday, he slept until almost noon. He spent the afternoon unpacking, doing laundry, and catching up on his email. By the time the weekly family dinner commenced at 6:00, Darnell was caught up and refreshed. He was ready to regale his housemates with tales of his travels and his performances as Whitney Austin in Provincetown and on the all-gay Mediterranean cruise.

Hal had prepared a large crockpot of chili and home-baked jalapeno cornbread. Hal, Ricky, Ted, and Bryan had just served themselves and sat down at the dining room table when Darnell made his fashionably-late grand entrance.

"Brothers, I have returned from my world travels! I bring you greetings from P-town, the gay vacation capital of the world, and Greece, the birthplace of gay civilization!"

Darnell was wearing a gold-on-black T-shirt with a drawing that depicted ancient Greek men doing scandalous things with one another. Above the drawing, it read, "When in Greece" and below the drawing, "Do as the Greeks do."

A celebratory mood swept over the room. Everyone rose from the table. Ricky and Ted each gave Darnell a warm embrace. Then Darnell turned his attention to Bryan. "Oh myyy… who have we here?" Darnell scanned Bryan from head to toe. He turned to Hal and said, "I approve.

He can stay."

Bryan smiled and extended his hand. "I'm Ryan."

"Oh, honey, we don't shake hands around here." Darnell stepped forward and gave Bryan a nice hug.

Hal said to Darnell, "Help yourself to some chili and cornbread, then tell us all about your adventures."

Darnell sashayed over to the crockpot, lifted the lid, and fanned the aroma toward his face. "Mmmm…Mmmm! Just like my mama used to make!"

"I made it just for the occasion."

Darnell served himself and joined the others at the table. "Alright, so… Where to begin? Well, first of all, let me tell you that P-town is *Faaaaaaabulous!*" His voice raised at least an octave. "People think San Francisco and WeHo are gay? Oh, honey. Commercial Street is gayer than Castro Street and Santa Monica Boulevard put together. There are rainbow streamers strung across the street. There are all kinds of gay shops and restaurants for blocks and blocks. And men? I'm here to tell you, it is an all-you-can-eat buffet of hot, steaming manhood!"

Ricky asked, "So, did you get some?"

Darnell feigned a look of shock. "Oh no, you didn't. A lady never speaks of such things."

Hal and Ted almost spit out their chili.

"*Of course* I got some, you fool. Who're you talking to? Good lord, you can't be in P-town eight hours without getting some, let alone eight weeks! I mean, there's the Dick Dock, the nude beach… And every night between midnight and 2:00 a.m., the street in front of this hippie-ish pizza place in the center of town turns into an open-air meat market. And gurrrl, if you can't find toppings there, I don't think I can help you."

Everyone snickered.

Ted asked, "Yeah, but after midnight, aren't you getting, shall we say, the leftovers?"

"Oh, no! At midnight, it's just getting started."

Bryan said, "Wait a minute. You said there was a nude beach?"

"Dicks and butts as far as the eye can see. Tan lines are sooo last millennium – at least that's what I've been told. That's a white people problem."

Bryan asked, "So, are there any straight people there?"

Darnell laughed. "Oh, that's the best part. Once in a while, you see some young straight couple pushing a stroller. And they look soooo bewildered, like they didn't read the brochure close enough. The women look scared, like somehow their babies might turn out gay. What they oughta be worried about are their husbands. They always look a bit too curious."

The other guys chuckled.

"But yes. And let me tell you, you have no idea how good it feels to finally be someplace where you're the majority; where everyone else is like you."

Hal asked, "How did your show do?"

"Oh, honey, they *loved* Whitney! I sold out almost every night. They're already talking about having me back next year. Between that and the cruise, I got over five hundred new followers on my Facebook page!"

Ted said, "So, tell us more about the cruise. What was that like?"

"Well, before we even get started on the cruise, we need to talk about Barcelona. Or, as they pronounce it in Catalan, Bar*the*lona. I kid you not, they say it with a lisp! But anyway, Barthelona. Oh. My. GOD. I could *sooo* move there tomorrow! The art, the food, the architecture… Some of the buildings were designed by this guy named Antoni Gaudi. And let me tell you, he must have been the biggest queen that ever lived. His buildings are all curvy and shit. I mean, they look all whimsical, but it's cute, you know? But his greatest work, the crème de la crème, is La Sagrada Familia. It's this *HUUUGE* basilica in the middle of town. It's massive! He must have been the biggest size queen. And get this… they started building it in 1882, and it still isn't finished! They don't think it will be done until 2026. We got to go on a tour inside, and it is so totally over the top. There's so much big fabulous everywhere you look!

"The only thing more magnificent than the architecture is the men! Who knew Spanish men were so hot? And they are on full display down at Sitges. It's this beach town south of Barthelona. You get there by train. Oh, and that's another thing about Barthelona. You can walk or take the subway anywhere you want to go. You could easily live there without a car. But anyway, back to Sitges, bitches. It was as gay as P-town, if not more. And the beach? Packed solid with hot bodies in thongs."

Ricky asked, "You mean it wasn't a nude beach?"

"No, not there. But there are other nude beaches around the Mediterranean. The Europeans are a lot less hung up about that sort of thing. But anyway, on to the cruise. Oh my god! It was so incredible! I mean, have any of y'all ever been on a cruise before?"

Everyone shook their heads.

"Well, first of all, if you have this image in your head of a bunch of retired old white people – or should I just say 'tired' – and formal dinners where everyone wears tuxes and gowns, well you can forget all that shit. When the gays take over the ship, everything gets fabulous!"

Bryan asked, "You mean there were nothing but gay people on this cruise?"

"Well, there was the staff. But aside from them, yes! Over 2,000 of us. They have all these dance parties, and people get dressed up in outfits you would not believe! Like they have a disco T-dance, and everyone wears stuff like they wore to the discos in the 70s, just more fabulous. And there was an 80s party, and a white party, and five or six other theme parties."

Hal asked, "How do people pack all that stuff?"

"Oh, honey, some of those queens came with four suitcases!"

Ted said, "I don't know. I'm not sure I would like that. I mean, I love gay men one at a time. I like gay men in small groups. But 2,000 gay men swishing and prancing all over a ship? That would be gay overload, at least for me."

"Well, it's not like everyone's waving rainbow flags all over the place. I mean, we had shore excursions at each of the ports we stopped at, delicious food in the restaurants, and great entertainers in the evening – including the fabulous Whitney Austin, I might add. And there are times when you can just hang out by the pool and talk to people. I made so many new friends! But anyway, being on a gay cruise was a lot like being in P-town or Sitges. It's nice to walk around and be surrounded by your people, you know? Like, gay couples could hold hands and nobody batted an eye."

Ricky said, "I heard gay cruises are just big floating orgies."

"Well, then why aren't *you* on them? Gurrrl, you could set up your sling on Deck 14 and let the party come to you. Or come in you, as the case may be."

Bryan said, "Dare I ask? What's Deck 14?"

"Well, the pool is on Deck 12. Then there's Deck 13, where there are more deck chairs overlooking the pool. But up near the front of the ship, you can go up to Deck 14, which, on a straight cruise, is where women can sunbathe topless. But on a gay cruise… well, I wouldn't know anything about that, but I've heard stories."

Hal said, "I'll bet. Anyway, how did your show go?"

"Fabulous! They *loved* Whitney Austin. And the event producer has already talked to me about booking me again."

Everyone had finished dinner at this point, so they cleared the table and moved into the family room. Darnell hooked his laptop up to the TV and showed pictures from his entire trip, including Provincetown, Barcelona, Ibiza, Florence, Rome, Pompeii, Mykonos, Santorini, all the costume dances on the ship, and finally, Athens.

Bryan was amazed. He had no idea that gay cruises and gay vacation spots even existed. It was yet another reminder of how much he didn't know about the nationwide and worldwide gay community he was now becoming a part of. There was so much to explore and experience! Most of all, he was feeling better and better about being gay.

Bryan wasn't quite sure what to make of Darnell. He thought back to that Saturday in June when Chris had taken him to the gay pride festival in Kansas City. He saw a few campy, swishy guys and a couple of drag queens from a distance, but back then he couldn't relate to any of that. But now he was experiencing a flamboyant, effusive, unapologetically gay Black man up close. He marveled at how Darnell took control of the room simply by entering it. During the three months since Bryan began self-identifying as gay, he had never met anyone quite so… so… *gay*. No, Darnell wasn't just gay, he was *fabulous*. And while so much about him was enigmatic and almost overwhelming, he was undeniably fascinating. Whatever else Bryan thought of Darnell, he knew one thing: he liked him.

Darnell's Story
Wednesday, September 12, 2007

Bryan arrived home from marching band practice at about ten minutes to six, tired and hot from the outdoor rehearsal and the bike ride. But he was happy to have a musical outlet and a group to be part of. As he passed the kitchen on his way to his room, he saw Darnell standing in front of the microwave while it heated his dinner.

Bryan stepped into the kitchen. "Hey, mind if I join you in a few minutes?"

"It would be my pleasure."

Bryan dropped his stuff off in his room, then visited the bathroom long enough to do a quick scrub of his face and armpits so he hopefully wouldn't stink up Darnell's dining experience. Then he returned to the kitchen, put his frozen dinner in the microwave, and sat down at the table across from Darnell.

Darnell initiated the conversation. "So, where did you just rush in from, all hot and sweaty?"

"Marching band practice."

"What instrument do you play?"

"Trumpet. But don't worry… I have a practice mute, so when I practice you probably won't hear it."

"It won't bother me, as long as it's not midnight. My daddy always used to listen to guys like Miles Davis and Freddie Hubbard. So, I grew up hearing the trumpet. You ever heard of those guys?"

"Oh god, yes! I've got a few Miles Davis CDs. We played Milestones in my high school jazz ensemble last year. I need to check out Freddie Hubbard some more."

"So, you're into jazz."

"Yeah, it's my favorite kind of music. I'm pretty obsessed with it, actually."

"Well, you can find lots of good jazz happening out here. This is the place. Here, and New York."

"Do you like jazz too?"

"I can appreciate it. It's not my first choice, but it's cool. As I said, my daddy played it a lot when I was growing up."

"What do you like?"

"Divas. I love strong women with big, powerful voices. That's what my mama played. Diana Ross. Chaka Khan. Whitney Houston, obviously. She's my idol, my inspiration."

"How about Ella?"

"Oh my god… There will never be another Ella. She was the greatest. I'd sing her songs, but her music doesn't really reach people today, sadly."

"How about Dianne Reeves? Or Diane Schuur?"

"I've heard of them…"

"If you love Ella, you'll love them. They're two of the greatest jazz singers today."

"I'll have to check them out. Again, I don't know if they'd go well in my act."

"I've got a couple of their CDs you can borrow if you want. Anyway, even if you can't use them in your act, you can still enjoy them."

The microwave dinged. Bryan got up to retrieve his dinner. He was happy that they seemed to be finding common ground.

After he sat down with his dinner, Bryan asked, "So, tell me about your act. What songs do you sing? And what led you to do drag?"

"I've always loved singing. I used to sing along with the music my mama played. Before my voice changed, I could match every note those women sang. And I captured every nuance. I wanted to sing just like them. I wanted to *be* them. Anyway, as my voice changed, I kept hitting those high notes. It's like I had to learn good breath support and figure out how I could still hit them. And as it turned out, I'm a tenor anyway, so my voice never got that deep. I started doing drag because I figured if I could still sing like a woman, then if I dressed like a woman I could perform for people and live out my fantasy of being a diva. You see, I don't approach drag like it's a caricature of a woman for people's amusement, like it's some kind of joke. I mean, it's okay if other people want to do that – that's their business. It's not my place to criticize other people's art or their form of expression. But for me, I do it as a tribute to them, out of respect."

"What do your parents think of you doing drag?"

"Well, I think my mama figured out who I was long before I did. I mean, she could just look at me singing along with those women and see that. My daddy probably figured it out too, but he just couldn't deal with it. I wanted to take piano lessons, but my daddy wouldn't allow it. That was just too girly for him. He was always trying to get me to play sports and be all rough and tough, like that was gonna stop me from turning out gay. But you can see how that turned out."

"That's funny… my mom made me take piano lessons for two years when I was in third and fourth grade. At the time, I hated it. I hated being forced to do something. I wasn't any good at sports and let's just say I wasn't the most masculine kid out there, so having to be inside practicing my piano lessons did nothing to help my image."

"Oh, I hear that. But I guess I learned at some point along the way not to care about what the other kids thought. I figured sooner or later they were going to find out about me and they probably wouldn't like me, so I just decided I was going to be myself and like myself. If anybody else liked me, great, and if not, well then so be it. That's why I always end my show with 'The Greatest Love of All.' It has so many positive messages in it. And that song made it possible for me to love myself."

"It's funny… you wanted to take piano lessons but couldn't, and I didn't want to take piano lessons but I was forced to and I hated it. But actually, I loved the music itself. And as soon as I started playing trumpet, I was thankful that I had those piano lessons. I already knew how to read music and count rhythms and all that, so I could focus on learning the trumpet. And playing the piano taught me about chords and harmony, so that helped me learn how to improvise. But anyway, tell me more about your act. What else do you do?"

"Today, my act is a mix of music and comedy and storytelling. I talk a little bit about my background and my challenges – not so much to talk about me, but to encourage people to overcome their struggles. I try to be not just entertaining, but also inspirational. I want people to leave my show feeling better about themselves. I want them to feel a little more hopeful about whatever it is they're going through."

"Wow… that's wonderful. I hope I get to see you perform sometime soon."

"I hope so too, dear."

"So, now that you're grown up and you're openly gay and you've become successful as Whitney Austin, are your parents cool with it now? And do you have any siblings?"

"I have a younger sister. She's going to Spelman College in Atlanta. She and I have always been tight. She and my mom are my two biggest fans. As for my dad… well, we've reached a place of acceptance with each other, and that's fine. That's probably as good as it's going to get. It took him a while to come around. So, let me give you a little background. I'm from Macon, Georgia. My folks still live there. Anyway, one time one of his friends happened to be driving by this gay bar right when I was coming out. I was just out of high school, so I was underage, too. He told my daddy that he saw me coming out of that bar with another guy's arm around me – a white guy, no less. So anyway, the next day I was at home taking a nap in my room when I was jostled out of my sleep. I opened my eyes, and I was looking straight down the barrel of a shotgun. My daddy was standing there, and he said, 'You want to tell me about your problem?' And I said, 'My problem is that my own father would apparently rather spend the rest of his life in prison for murdering his only son than accept him for who he is.'"

Bryan's eyes were wide open with shock.

"I figured, what have I got to lose? Either I call his bluff and we have a conversation about it, or he shoots me, and then it's all over anyway. And it would serve him right if he shot me, and then some big burly dude in prison made him his bitch."

"So, what happened?"

"He put his gun down and we talked. I tried to tell him that this is the way I am, and this is how it's gonna be. I've got to be true to myself. He started in with all this 'I didn't raise you to be a fairy' bullshit, and I said, 'That's right, you didn't. But I turned out like this anyway. So, do you love me unconditionally or not? 'Cause I'm gay either way.' And he didn't have an answer for that. He just walked out of the room."

"Wow. That was intense."

"Yeah, it sure was. But then a couple of days later, he came to my room and said he wanted to talk some more. He apologized for the gun thing and told me he loved me unconditionally. Then he said he wasn't going to kick me out or anything, but he said, 'Son, Macon is no place for people like you. You'll never be accepted here and you may not even be safe. Your type needs to be in some big city where there are other people like you and folks aren't so prejudiced.' And he was right. Then he offered to buy me a bus ticket to anywhere I wanted to go, and so here I am."

"I'm glad he came around so quickly. My parents sure didn't."

"Well, he wasn't happy about it. But he figured out that he couldn't do anything about it, and he'd better learn to deal with it if he still wanted me in his life. He probably did it as much for my mama and my sister as for him. It was kind of sad. He kinda looked defeated, like he had to give up on the idea of having a real son. But anyway, he did the right thing even though it was hard for him, and I appreciate him for that."

"So, do you have much contact with him today?"

"A little. I talk a lot more with my mama and my sister. I go home for Thanksgiving or Christmas sometimes. But there's more to the story. As I was getting ready to leave for the bus station, he says, 'I still can't wrap my head around this gay thing. Just tell me this. How can you put your dick in another man's shit?'"

Bryan couldn't imagine his father ever saying something like that.

"And I looked him right in the eye and said, 'I don't. I let him put his dick in mine.'"

"You *didn't*."

"Oh yes, I did. That shut him up, too. Anyway, I use that little bit in my act. It gets the crowd every time. Then there was this time last summer – not this past summer, but a year ago – I did some shows here and there around the country, and I had a gig in Atlanta. I knew my sister was gonna be there, but I didn't know until I was in the lobby afterward that my mama and daddy had come up from Macon to see the show. I never in a million years thought my daddy would ever see a drag show, but there he was. And suddenly I realized that he had heard me use that bit in my routine, and I just wanted to crawl into a little hole and disappear. But you know, he said it, right? It was true. And as I like to say, the truth will set you free – but first, it will piss you off."

Bryan chuckled. "That's a good one."

"But that's not what got to him. See, I always close my show by singing 'The Greatest Love of All.' Now, most people associate that song with Whitney Houston. And yes, it was a big hit for her, but she wasn't the first person who sang it. That was George Benson on his *Weekend in LA* album back in the late 70s. Now remember, my daddy likes jazz, so he's all into George Benson and Grover Washington, Jr. and the Crusaders and all those guys that were popular when he was growing up in the 70s. So, he loved that song and what it said about loving yourself and how the children are our future and all that. When he heard me singing it, it moved him to tears. So, we talked, and you know what he said? He said he was proud of me. And I could tell he meant it. Man, you could have pushed me over with my feather boa. I never thought I would hear those words come from his lips. And he told me he realized that I needed to love myself and live my life the way I want to, and that's what I was doing. So, ever since then, things have been okay between us."

"All because of a song!"

"That's right. That's the healing power of music."

"Wow… that's a pretty incredible story."

"Yeah. So, I understand you have a story to tell, too."

"Yeah, although it doesn't involve having a gun pointed at me. Anyway, so my dad's the head pastor at this huge mega-church in Kansas, where I come from."

"Oh, lordy... I can see where this is going."

"Yep." Bryan told his story to Darnell, up through arriving in Los Angeles on a bus.

Darnell said, "So, you and I have that in common – we both got here on a bus. So how did you end up here?"

"Total coincidence and good luck. I mean, someone up there was looking out for me. See, my boss at the grocery store where I worked is also gay, and he and his husband used to live out here. So, he told me to go to the LGBT Youth Project as soon as I got out here. He said they have lawyers who help with things like changing your name and getting emancipated from your parents. So, they connected me with Hal. And I guess some guy named Tyler was going to live here but then he couldn't, so he had an empty room. And so here I am!"

"So now you're out here on your own, and you're how old?"

"Seventeen. I'll be 18 next month. I'm a senior in high school."

"Man, that must be brutal. How're you holding up?"

"Mostly okay. The guys here have been really nice. I got a job right away, and I started school a couple of weeks ago. I had band camp for two weeks before that, so I'm getting settled in."

"Do you ever feel homesick?"

"Not for the place itself, or Kansas, for that matter. I mean, this house is amazing and everything out here is new and exciting, so all that's great. But I really miss my little brother. We were really close. And my boyfriend. I mean, we had just figured out that we were gay like three months ago. But he was already my best friend so we just kinda transitioned into being a couple. But I had to keep it a secret from my parents, you know? We were talking about going to college together here at UCLA. Who knows? Maybe he'll end up here."

"Are you in touch with him?"

"No. I can't let anybody know where I am. As long as I'm a minor, if they find me, they can take me back to Kansas. Then who knows what my parents would do? Probably try to send me to that place in Alabama again."

"Ooo... we're harboring a fugitive!"

"Yeah, I guess you are. It's not like I've committed a crime or anything, but yeah, I've got to fly under the radar for at least a few more weeks, until I turn 18."

"So did you get emancipated and get your name changed?"

"No. Turns out it takes like four to six months to get emancipated, and I would still need my parents' consent. So, I just have to wait it out until I turn 18 next month. Actually, Ryan is going to be my new name. But I'm introducing myself to everybody as Ryan now, so everyone doesn't have to re-learn what to call me. Plus, it kinda helps keep me undercover."

"But after you turn 18, it isn't going to matter whether they find out where you are or not. You'll be an adult and they won't have any more power over you."

"That's right."

"So why bother changing your name?"

"I want to. See, my father is pretty well known around town. And he has these big dreams of becoming a nationally-known televangelist, like doing speaking tours and all that. He got a book deal right before I left. So I don't want to be associated with him. My whole life, I've been identified as his son. It's like I'm not my own person, I'm his son. In fact, there was this jerk at my last school who kept calling me 'PK,' for Preacher's Kid. I hated it. And he was popular, so some of the other guys started calling me that, too. And besides, once my parents found out I was gay, my dad kept saying all this shit about 'No son of mine is going to be a homosexual.' So I figured, if he doesn't want to have a son who's a homosexual, he won't have one."

Darnell furrowed his eyebrows. "Sounds like someone has some anger management issues."

Bryan thought about that for a moment. "Yeah, I guess you could say I'm angry. But I think I have something to be angry about."

"Well, you do. But let me tell you something, sugar. You can be as angry and bitter as you want, but none of that's going to hurt them. It's only going to hurt you. It's going to gnaw away at you every day and keep you from being happy."

"So what am I supposed to do?"

"Well, for one thing, keep doing what you're doing. Create a new life for yourself on your terms. You're doing a great job of taking responsibility for yourself – getting a job, enrolling yourself in school, and all that. I admire you for that. But you have to let go of the hurt. Just leave it in the past. Leave it in Kansas. 'Cause if you keep carrying it around with you, you're going to suffer. And it's self-inflicted suffering. You have to decide that you aren't going to let them have that kind of power over you anymore."

"Easier said than done."

"Oh, I know it is. I've been there myself. Been there, done that, have the therapy bills to show for it. But you've got to put it behind you and move on. You know what they say, 'Living well is the best revenge.'"

Bryan smiled. He was living pretty well already. "Yeah, I guess you're right." He wasn't totally sure, but he was ready to end this conversation.

"Trust me on this one, honey."

Bryan stood up. "Thanks for all the talk. And thanks for opening up to me."

"The pleasure was all mine. And don't worry, things are gonna turn out fine."

They hugged, and Bryan went back to his room.

National Coming Out Day
Thursday, October 11, 2007

After weeks of planning and preparation by the Gay-Straight Alliance, National Coming Out Day had arrived. As lunchtime approached, Bryan grew apprehensive. He and several other members of the GSA would be staffing an information table in the hallway outside the cafeteria. The school newspaper had run an article explaining their new "I'm an LGBT Ally" campaign, and they hoped a lot of kids and teachers would stop by the table to pick up the stickers they had printed, and perhaps engage in some conversation.

When Bryan started this school year, he decided he wasn't going to hide the fact that he was gay. But up to this point, the only kids who knew for sure were the other kids in the GSA. Today, when he staffed the table, he would be officially out to the entire student body. Of course, kids had no way to know for sure whether he was gay or a straight ally, but either way, he was putting himself out there. It would be interesting to see how he was treated by the other kids after today.

The GSA members who were going to staff the table were given permission to leave their third period classes 20 minutes early to set up their table and put up the signs they had printed. Between second and third period, Bryan stopped by Mr. Perez's room and picked up the Ally stickers.

When he arrived at the table, no one else was there. A couple of minutes later, LaTanya arrived. "Hey, LaTanya. You all ready to spread some tolerance and acceptance?"

"I hope. We'll see. I wonder where the others are."

"I'm sure they'll be here in a couple of minutes."

LaTanya brought a large bag of rainbow-colored Skittles and started pouring them into small plastic cups – the kind fast-food restaurants provide for the ketchup pump. Mr. Perez had suggested that people might be more inclined to approach the table if there was food or candy. Hopefully, he would be right – but if not, there would be plenty to divide among the volunteers. Bryan taped the posters up on the wall behind the table.

The bell rang, signaling the end of the third period. LaTanya and Bryan were still the only GSA members at the table, but Bryan felt sure that several of the others would join them as soon as they could make their way there.

Students poured into the cafeteria, passing the GSA table with barely a glance. LaTanya and Bryan looked at each other. Bryan said, "Everybody just wants to get a good place in line. We'll probably get more people on their way out when they're not in such a hurry."

"Maybe. I wonder where the others are."

Bryan and LaTanya stayed on their feet as the rush of students entered the cafeteria. Once the traffic had slowed to a trickle, they sat down. Bryan got out the lunch he brought from home. "You wanna go get something from the cafeteria?"

"You think you can handle the masses on your own?"

"I think I got this."

"Be right back."

Bryan and LaTanya sat at the table by themselves for the rest of the lunch period. As students started leaving the cafeteria, some at least glanced at the table as they walked past. Nobody stopped to talk or pick up an Ally sticker, or even grab a little cup of Skittles.

***

The next morning, when Bryan turned the corner of the main hallway, he saw a cluster of people gathered around the student bulletin board. The GSA members had come in early on Monday morning to put up their display of famous LGBT people. All week, most people walked past and ignored it, just as LaTanya had predicted. But for some reason, there was now a crowd gathered around it.

As Bryan approached, he could see that the display had been defaced. Someone had scrawled 'FAG' or 'DYKE' across each of the pictures with a thick black marker. They had stapled pieces of paper onto the bulletin board with messages such as 'God Hates Fags,' 'AIDS Cures Homos,' and 'No Queers Here.' Mr. Sanchez, the head custodian, had started to remove the display, but LaTanya was arguing with him to leave it in place. Bryan weaved through the group until he reached the front.

Mr. Sanchez said, "I'm just doin' what Mrs. Rodriguez told me to do."

LaTanya replied, "Well, I belong to the group that put this up. This is our display, and I'm telling you to stop."

"You're not my boss. Mrs. Rodriguez is my boss."

"This is not your display, it's my group's display."

Once Bryan figured out what was going on, he said, "Okay, just hold on for a few minutes. Let me go get Mrs. Rodriguez."

Bryan worked his way back through the crowd and ran into the office. He rushed past the receptionist and headed straight to the principal's office. "Hi, Mrs. Rodriguez. I'm sorry to interrupt, but would you please come out into the hallway? We have an issue that needs your attention."

"You mean the bulletin board? Yes, I saw it. I've asked Mr. Sanchez to take it down."

"That's the issue. We don't want it taken down."

Mrs. Rodriguez was stunned. Why would anyone want a display that had been desecrated with hateful speech to remain up? She slowly got up from her chair, then followed Bryan back out into the hall. The students parted, creating a pathway for her and Bryan to walk up to the front.

Mr. Sanchez said, "This student is telling me it's her display, and not to take it down."

Mrs. Rodriguez turned to LaTanya and said, "We have to remove this. We can't have this kind of bigotry and hatred on display for everyone to see."

"Why not? This is the kind of bigotry and hatred we have to deal with all the time."

"Right. And leaving it up only spreads the bigotry and hatred even more."

"Okay, so look. This is LGBT History Month, right? So having these famous LGBT people up here is nice and everything, but let me tell you a little bit more about our history. LGBT people have been beaten up, killed, fired from jobs, and cut off from their families, all because of this kind of hatred and homophobia. This is what it's like to be queer. This is what we have to live with. So this happened, and your answer is to brush it aside and hide it. Just sweep it under the rug and pretend it never happened. Yeah, well you're giving whoever did this exactly what they want. They want to harass us so we stay afraid and invisible. They want to keep us silent while they spew their hatred all over the place. And they won't suffer any consequences for it because somebody will always come along and clean up after them. Look, if you want to do something about homophobia, you've got to start by acknowledging that it exists. You've got to let people see the hatred, not hide it from them. You can't just pretend that we live in a world where everything is peachy and everybody loves everybody. *This* is the world we live in as gay people. *This* is the kind of shit we have to put up with all the time. So if you want to do something about homophobia, you've got to put it out there and make people deal with it. Show it to them! Let them see what it's like for us. Then we can have a conversation about it and start to change things."

For a few seconds, there was dead silence among the forty or so people who had gathered. Then someone started to clap. Then a few more started clapping. Before long, most of the kids present were clapping.

"Well, alright, then," Mrs. Rodriguez said. "The display can stay."

LaTanya walked over to Mr. Sanchez and held out her hand. He gave her everything he had already taken down. She said, "I'll put it back up."

The first period bell rang, and the kids who had gathered around the defaced display scurried to their classrooms.

***

Several times throughout the day, Bryan re-routed his usual journeys between classes to pass by the display in the main hallway. Each time, he saw kids who had stopped to gawk at the display. Some took pictures on their phones.

In his calculus class that afternoon, a girl he barely knew came over to his desk before class started and asked, "Do you have any more of those stickers you were giving out yesterday?"

"Not on me, but I can get you one."

"Thanks."

A couple of other kids who were sitting nearby heard that exchange and said, "Can I have one, too?"

***

After his last class, Bryan stopped by Mr. Perez's room. "Hi, Mr. Perez. May I have a few of those Ally stickers? I had several kids ask me for one today."

"Sure. And the faculty advisors for the drama club and the Asian Students Association asked me for some for their members."

"I wonder why people didn't pick them up at the table yesterday if they wanted one."

"Well, maybe some people were afraid to be seen walking up to the table. But I suspect it has more to do with what happened to the bulletin board today."

LaTanya was right. The conversation had started.

18

Sunday, October 14, 2007

Bryan had to work all day on his 18th birthday. He would have preferred to take the day off to do something fun, like go to Disneyland, but he didn't have that luxury. He needed to work as many hours as possible to stay afloat. As he had discovered over the past three months, it cost a lot more to live on his own than he had estimated. He was gradually depleting his $3,000 savings. He needed to be increasing his savings, not decreasing them, to afford college.

After his shift ended at 3:00, he pedaled home. He'd have almost three hours to get some homework and practicing done before the weekly family night dinner at 6:00.

***

In Prairie Village, Kansas, the three remaining members of the Bauer family sat down to dinner. Brenda had prepared spaghetti and meatballs, which was Bryan's favorite dinner while he was growing up. As she sat down to eat with her husband, Brad, and her son, Brandon, she realized that selecting this meal in remembrance of her vanished son was a mistake. She was becoming more depressed by the minute.

Brandon felt the same way. He thought about Bryan often. He hoped that someday Bryan would come walking through the door and everything would somehow return to normal again. He remembered that today was Bryan's 18th birthday and created a hand-drawn birthday card for him, as he had in past years. Maybe someday he would be able to give it to him.

Brad seemed to be in a good mood, although he couldn't help but notice that his wife and son were not. "I heard from my ghostwriter. He says he should have the draft of my first book ready for my review tomorrow!"

Brenda muttered, "That's nice, dear."

He turned to his son, who was half-heartedly poking at his food rather than devouring it as usual. "How was Sunday School today? What did you learn about?"

"It was okay. They talked about the story of the prodigal son."

How appropriate, Brenda thought.

A few moments of silence passed.

Brad asked Brenda, "What's the matter, honey? Did you remember to take your Prozac this morning?"

She glared at him. "Yes, and I took another half-dose this afternoon. It hasn't helped."

Maybe what she really needs is Midol, Brad thought. But he knew he couldn't say that out loud.

"So, what's eating at you?"

"Do you know what today is?"

"Yes, of course. It's Sunday."

"Do you know what *date* this is?"

Why is she asking me this? Just look on the damn calendar. "Well… it's October 14."

"And is there anything you can think of that might be significant about this date?"

Why is she so angry? "Honey, I don't feel like playing guessing games. Just tell me."

Brenda slammed her fork down onto the table. "It's our son's 18th birthday, you self-centered idiot!"

"Well, okay, fine. But it's not like he's here and we can celebrate it with him. He's the one who ran away from home!"

Brenda stood up, knocking her chair over backward behind her. She picked up her plate of spaghetti and threw it at him. She scored a direct hit, right to the center of his face. The plate crashed to the floor and broke into dozens of pieces. The spaghetti noodles and pasta sauce started falling off his face and sloshing down onto his shirt. She turned and stormed upstairs to the master bedroom, slammed the door, and locked it.

Brandon's first impulse was to bust out laughing at the sight of his father covered in spaghetti and sauce, but he knew he shouldn't. If it had been a scene in a Saturday morning cartoon, it would have been hilarious. But this was real life, and it was anything but hilarious. On the one hand, his father deserved that. On the other hand, he hated to see his mother so upset. It tore him up to see his parents fighting, which they never did before Bryan left. Most of all, the pain of Bryan's absence jabbed at him like a knife. He had been gone for three months, and it wasn't getting any easier. Especially not today.

Brandon didn't want the rest of his dinner, and he didn't want to be around his father. Besides, if he remained at the table it would only prolong his father's humiliation. He got up and ran to his room. Brad sat there stunned and speechless.

***

At around 5:40, Hal knocked on Bryan's door.

"Come in."

"Happy birthday!"

"Thanks!"

"How do you like your steak done?"

Steak? Hal was serving steak? Except for a few visits to Western Corral back in Kansas, Bryan had never had steak. And he suspected there was probably more to a real steak than the cheap cuts of overly-tenderized meat served at Western Corral. "I dunno... medium?"

"Medium it is. It should be ready at 6:00."

Wow, thought Bryan. *This is a step up from their usual family night fare of simple comfort food.*

Bryan entered the dining room at 5:55. The table was elegantly adorned with a crisp white table cloth and red cloth napkins. Ted entered from the kitchen carrying a steaming bowl of homemade mashed potatoes and a basket of freshly-baked buttery garlic bread. There was a side salad to the left of each place setting and a wine glass above and to the right. Darnell, Ricky, and Hal entered from the back patio carrying the dinner plates, each with a sizzling steak fresh from the grill. Hal walked into the kitchen and returned with a freshly uncorked bottle of Malbec, which he poured into each glass.

Everyone sat down and Hal raised his glass. "A toast – to our new adult!" Everyone clinked their glasses and took a sip. Bryan had tried white wine with Ted in the pool a few weeks earlier, but this was his first taste of red. At first, he wasn't impressed, but after a few bites of steak, it began to grow on him. When Hal opened another bottle and offered everyone seconds, he gladly accepted.

After they finished the main course and cleared the table, Ricky brought out five small dessert plates, and Darnell followed with a festively decorated birthday cake with 18 lit candles. A six-color rainbow made of colored icing arched across the top, and 'Happy Birthday Ryan' was written in elegant cursive. Darnell led the others in singing a fabulous rendition of 'Happy Birthday.'

Bryan quickly pondered what he should wish for – a cute, hunky boyfriend or a winning lottery ticket. Then he thought of Chris and wished that someday they would be together again. He took a deep breath and easily extinguished all the candles.

After they had cut the cake and started eating it, Bryan said, "Guys, thank you for making this such a special birthday. Hal, the steak was delicious. Your dinners are always good, but you really outdid yourself this time."

"My pleasure. I figured that you becoming an adult is a special occasion that merits a celebration, so why not?"

"Well, you guys have certainly made me feel special. Seriously, I'm really lucky and thankful to be able to live here and have you guys for friends."

"And tomorrow morning, following our 10:00 appointment at the courthouse downtown, you will officially be Ryan Brandon Robertson!"

"That's the best birthday present I could ask for." *Well, that and Chris.*

Darnell had a curious look on his face, like he had just connected a few dots. "Wait a minute. Where did you say you were from?"

"Prairie Village, Kansas."

"Hmmm… Are you related to Tyler Robertson?"

Oh, shit, Bryan thought. He tried not to show any reaction. "No. Robertson is my new last name, not my name up to this point."

"Oh yeah, that's right."

"Why? Who is Tyler Robertson?"

"He's the guy that was supposed to live here this year, but he had to drop out because he lost his scholarship."

Ted said, "I wonder why."

Hal replied, "He couldn't keep his grades up high enough. If your average drops below a C, they'll cut you off."

"Probably spent too much time hangin' out with Mr. Party Boy," Darnell said as he shot a glance at Ricky.

Ted said, "Have any of you kept in touch with him?"

Darnell said, "Yeah. We're friends on Facebook."

Ricky said, "Same here."

Ted asked, "What's he doing now?"

Darnell replied, "He's finishing his senior year at Kansas, where he can get in-state tuition."

This was a revelation to Bryan. *I've heard my housemates refer to the guy who was supposed to live here as Tyler, but I never imagined it would be Chris's older brother. Does this mean Tyler is gay? He must be. I don't think Hal would invite a straight guy to live here. Should I ask? I'd better not. It might seem like a strange thing to ask about someone I supposedly don't know. It doesn't matter anyway. I'm not in touch with Chris, because I don't want anybody from Kansas to know where I am now. And it's not my place to out Tyler to his brother – especially if I'm not sure he's gay.*

Then Bryan thought of something else.

"Guys… Since you're friends with this guy on Facebook, I'd appreciate it if you wouldn't mention that I'm living here."

Darnell seemed puzzled. "Why? If you don't know each other, what difference does it make?"

Bryan had to think fast. *Darnell's original question was, 'Are you related to Tyler Robertson?' and I'm not. But he knows me. Of course, he doesn't know me by my new name. I shouldn't have said anything. But I did.*

"Well, uh, I know that news about my disappearance made it into the local papers, so he could put two and two together and figure out that it's me."

"Yeah, I guess. But so what if he does?"

"It might get back to my family, and I don't want them to find out where I am. I don't know who he knows. For all I know, he might go to my dad's church."

Ricky laughed and said, "Tyler? Go to church? Oh, I don't think so."

"Well, my dad is pretty well-known around town. I don't know, maybe I'm being paranoid, but–"

Darnell interrupted, "Yes, I think you might be. But in any case, we won't tell him."

"Thanks. I appreciate it."

Everyone sensed that this topic was now finished. The mood in the room was a little awkward. Everyone got up and cleared the table. Hal said, "Just leave the table cloth and the napkins. I'll wash them later. So… what shall we do this evening? Games or a movie? Ryan, it's your birthday, why don't you decide?"

"I'm kinda more in the mood for a movie."

"Okay. Go pick one out."

Bryan looked over the many titles in the bookcase filled with DVDs. Most of them were just titles – he had no idea what they were about. "Okay, help me out here. What's a gay classic that every gay man should see? I've already seen *Brokeback Mountain* and *Priscilla, Queen of the Desert*. What else is there?"

Darnell walked over and scanned the shelves. "*The Bird Cage*." He pulled the DVD case off the shelf. "It's an American remake of a French classic, *La Cage Aux Folles*. It stars Robin Williams and Nathan Lane playing a gay couple. It's a hoot."

Ricky said, "It figures you'd pick a movie about drag queens."

Darnell snapped into sassy mode and shook his finger at Ricky. "Don't be hatin'. Drag queens are an important part of our culture."

Ted said to Bryan, "Don't mind him. To him, a gay cinematic classic would be *Powertool*."

Ricky replied, "Damn right. It is a classic of its genre."

Bryan asked, "What's *Powertool*?"

Darnell replied, "Use your imagination, dear. There's a time and a place for movies of that nature, but this is neither."

Ted added, "You can watch that one alone in your room sometime."

A New Man
Monday, October 15, 2007

Bryan had purchased an inexpensive but sufficiently presentable black suit for this occasion, along with a white dress shirt, a blue and purple striped tie, and a pair of shiny black dress shoes. Hal assured him that anything nicer than shorts or jeans and a T-shirt would have been acceptable, but he had never appeared before a judge and he wanted to make a good impression. Besides, today was a special day and there would be other occasions when he would need a suit. Hal wore one of his more expensive suits, but such attire would be expected of an attorney.

They allowed plenty of time for traffic and finding parking, and arrived at the courtroom at 9:45 for their 10:00 appointment. Bryan had visualized the judge as a gray-haired, older, serious-looking man, but the judge turned out to be a professional-looking, non-threatening woman in her mid to late 30s. She was business-like but pleasant. This wasn't a murder trial, after all. Hal handed her the paperwork he had prepared. She asked Bryan why he wanted to change his name. She asked if he had a criminal record or any current legal actions against him, and Hal answered no. Then she granted his name change, and that was that. Compared to courtroom dramas Ryan had seen on TV, it seemed too simple and anti-climactic.

As they left the courtroom, Ryan was walking on air. The moment he had been anticipating for three months had finally come to pass! And it went off without a hitch.

Next, Hal drove Ryan to the Social Security office, where, after a half-hour wait, they issued him a new card that read Ryan Brandon Robertson. After stopping for a bite to eat, which Ryan insisted on paying for, they spent an hour at the Department of Motor Vehicles getting a new driver's license for Ryan. His picture turned out great – he looked splendid in his suit and he was grinning like a kid on Christmas morning.

***

At the Bauer home in Prairie Village, Brenda located Detective Sue Wagner's card and gave her a call.

"Detective Wagner speaking."

"Good morning, Detective. This is Brenda Bauer calling. As I'm sure you remember, our son Bryan went missing back in July."

"Yes, of course."

"I haven't heard anything from you in a while, so I thought I'd call to see if there are any updates."

"Let me pull up his file… hmm… No, I don't see anything new."

"Isn't there anything else you can do?"

"I'm afraid we've done all we can with the limited information we have to go on. Do you have any new information for us?"

"Sadly, no. But… is anybody actively working on this?"

"I check for updates with the National Center for Missing and Exploited Children and the Kansas Bureau of Investigation about once a week. They're supposed to alert me if there's something new."

"Is that all?"

"Yes. Mrs. Bauer, that's all we can do. This is a small city, and we have a small police force with limited resources. Our scope is enforcing the laws and protecting the people of Prairie Village. We don't have the resources to search across the entire country, especially with so few leads. Anything outside of Prairie Village is out of our jurisdiction anyway. That's why we network with the NCMEC and the KBI. The KBI interfaces with the FBI as needed."

"So my child is missing, and you just sit there and check for updates now and then."

"It's not like this is the only case I have to work on. I need to investigate burglaries and homicides that happen here in Prairie Village. Remember, Mrs. Bauer – your son left voluntarily. He wasn't kidnapped or abducted, and we have no reason to believe he's in danger. And as I said, we have nothing else to go on. If he had escaped by car and we had a license plate number, that would help, but we don't even have that. I know you must be distraught over your son's disappearance, and I can certainly empathize with you on that. I'd feel the same way if it was one of my kids. But there's nothing else we can do. I'm sorry."

"Well, thank you for saying that, and I apologize for getting upset with you. Yesterday was his birthday, so of course, that made me think about him even more than usual. So I thought I'd give you a call just in case. Hope springs eternal, I guess."

"Yes, well… since you mentioned it, I see that he turned 18 yesterday."

"That's correct."

"In that case, he's an adult now. He's no longer a missing child. As an adult, he's free to go wherever he wants. Even if we were to locate him, we couldn't force him to return home."

"So, what happens now?"

"Well, I expect the NCMEC will close his case in their database."

Brenda let out a long sigh. "It seems more hopeless now than ever. Are there any other options?"

"The only option I can think of would be to hire a private investigator. That might cost a lot of money, and with so little information to go on, he or she would have a hard time finding anything. But at least a PI would be able to devote more time and focus to it."

"Alright, well, thank you very much."

"You're welcome. And I hope you are reunited with him someday, sooner rather than later."

Since Monday was Brad's day off, he was working in his home office upstairs. He was reading through the draft manuscript for his first book that he had just received from his ghostwriter.

Brenda entered the office. "Sorry for interrupting. I just got off the phone with Detective Wagner from the police department. She said they have nothing new on Bryan. I don't think they've done much – she as much as said so. But now that he's 18, they're not going to do any more. Since he's an adult now, he's free to live wherever he wants. They couldn't force him to return home even if they found him."

Brad was mildly annoyed. He wanted to be diving into his new book, not dealing with this. But after yesterday's incident, he knew he needed to make nice and treat her gently. "Yeah, I guess they're right. He's an adult now. Even if he hadn't run away back in July, he could decide to walk out the door today and there would be nothing we could do about it."

"Well, there is something else we could do about it. We could hire a private investigator."

"Oh, dear God, Brenda! That would cost a small fortune!"

"Not nearly as much as a very public divorce and years of alimony and child support payments." Brenda glared at Brad, and he could tell she was serious. "So, what's more important to you? Money or our son? Answer carefully."

"Our son, of course, but like you said, a PI couldn't force him to come home."

"Yes, but wouldn't it at least be nice to know where he is? To know that he's safe? To be in touch with him? I know we'll probably never get him to come back home again, but wouldn't you rather be in contact with him than not?"

"Well, yes, of course."

"So I want to at least check into who's available and what they would charge and what they might be able to do."

"Did that detective refer you to anyone?"

"No, but I didn't ask. I wanted to check with you first. I'll call her back."

Brenda called Detective Wagner again. "Good afternoon, Detective. It's Brenda Bauer again. Say, I was wondering if you have any private investigators you could recommend?"

"Good afternoon, Mrs. Bauer. I have some names and numbers I can give you. However, I am not permitted to give recommendations or indicate preferences. I would be happy to provide those to you, but honestly, it's highly unlikely that Bryan is still in Kansas. Remember, we know that he boarded a westbound bus on the night of his disappearance. We don't know where he got off or where he's gone since then."

"I understand that, but…"

"Mrs. Bauer, private investigators are licensed by the state. Anyone you hire here can't legally work outside of Kansas. If you were to discover what state he's in, you could hire a PI in that state."

"Oh, I see."

"I'm sorry. I guess I didn't make that clear when we were talking earlier."

"Well, okay. Goodbye."

***

On Tuesday, Ryan brought his court order into school with him. He stopped in the principal's office. "Hello, Mrs. Rodriguez?"

"Why, hello Bryan – I mean Ryan. How are you?"

"I'm terrific! Thanks. And about the name change… Yesterday, it finally happened! I am now officially Ryan Robertson. Here's the court order." He handed the document across the desk to Mrs. Rodriguez.

"Well, alright! I'll get this information entered into the system. I'll notify your teachers since your name will now be different on their rosters. Can you stop back around lunch and pick it up?"

"Sure thing! Thank you very much."

***

After school, Ryan hurried home to change into his Pure Foods shirt. He left for work early so he'd have time to stop by Banktopia and get his name changed there.

As he approached, he remembered Skyler. He never did call or email him after the mini-date they had at the coffee shop the day Ryan opened his account. Of course, Skyler hadn't called him either. Oh well, there was nothing he could do about it now. Ryan figured he would be pleasant with him – if he was even in the office today – and take it from there.

When he entered the bank, another employee whom he hadn't encountered on previous visits was staffing the concierge desk. Ryan asked, "Is Skyler in today? I've dealt with him in the past. If not, anyone who can help me with a name change on an account would be fine."

"Please wait here. Let me see if he's available."

Skyler's head popped up above the cubicle wall. When he saw that it was Ryan, he said, "Yes, Skyler is definitely available!" He was just as perky and overtly friendly as before, which reassured Ryan that he wasn't upset with him.

Once they were seated in Skyler's cubicle, he said, "It's nice to see you again. I wondered if you had been abducted or something. How have you been?"

Ryan replied, "Fine – and very busy. Between work and school and marching band, I've been swamped. Sorry I didn't call. I barely have five free minutes."

"Oh, no worries… Anyway, what can I do for you today?" Skyler sat upright in his seat and leaned forward slightly.

Skyler seemed so eager to provide best-in-class customer service with a smile. Ryan suspected that if he replied, 'Give me a blowjob,' Skyler would have happily done it. He was committed to good customer service, after all.

Ryan said, "Remember when I was in here before I said I was going to change my name?" Skyler nodded. "Well, it's happened! It's legal now. I have the court order." Ryan reached into his backpack and produced the document for Skyler.

"Congratulations! Here, let me take care of that for you."

Skyler placed the document on the tray of his scanner and scanned it. Then he spent several minutes focused on his PC screen, navigating around the various forms and typing all sorts of information. Ryan assumed he could just type over the Name field, but apparently it was a lot more complicated than that.

Finally, Skyler turned back toward Ryan and handed him the court order.

"All set! Would you like me to order you a new batch of checks?"

"Yeah, sure."

Skyler unleashed another flurry of keystrokes. "And you'll receive new debit and credit cards in the mail in five to ten business days. You can still use your old ones in the meantime. The numbers will be the same."

"Okay! Well, thank you very much!"

"My pleasure." Skyler reached over to his business card holder, retrieved a card, and wrote his personal cell phone number on the back. Then he handed it to Ryan. "And please feel welcome to contact me any time." His smile and direct eye contact left no doubt that he was still interested in getting together.

Ryan took the card and said, "Thanks. I'd really like to, but I barely have any free time. About the only free time I have is Saturday morning and early afternoon. I don't have to be at work until 3:00."

"Well, then, let's get together for brunch. This Saturday at 11:00?"

"Yeah, I guess. Where?"

"There's this cute little place a few blocks from here called Eggstravagance. It's on Gayley, just before you get to Wilshire. How about that?"

"Okay, sure."

Skyler escorted Ryan to the bank entrance, and they smiled and waved goodbye. Ryan was still trying to figure out gay protocol, but he figured it was too soon and perhaps not the right place for a hug.

Ryan hustled into Pure Foods, barely making it on time. He showed his court order to Veronica Masters, and she took care of changing his name in their payroll system. He would visit the cell phone store tomorrow.

Where Were You?

Thursday, October 18, 2007

Ryan debated whether he wanted to remain part of the Gay-Straight Alliance after all the other members had abandoned him and LaTanya at the booth last week. *Who needs fair-weather friends? Are they allies or not?* He decided to go, if only to one more meeting. They needed to have a conversation about what happened and why.

Ryan was the first student to enter the room. Mr. Perez was already there since it was his classroom. Ryan said, "I wonder how many kids will show up today."

"What do you mean?"

"Well, they didn't show up at the table last week."

"True. But they did contribute material for the display."

"Yeah, but you don't have to show your face in front of the whole student body to do that."

LaTanya walked in. A minute later, Mike Nguyen, the other self-identified gay person, showed up. Just when it was starting to look like nobody else would arrive, Amber, Allyson, and Monique walked in carrying to-go meals from the cafeteria. There was a palpable chill in the room. No one said hi to any of the others.

Mr. Perez began. "Hello, everyone. How has your week been so far? Who wants to start?"

For a moment, no one spoke. LaTanya broke the silence. "Well, this week's been pretty quiet so far. Not nearly as eventful as last week."

No one responded to that.

Ryan said, "Okay, I'm just going to put this right out there. I'm disappointed. I'm angry. And I feel less safe and less accepted than I did before last week. But it's not just what happened to the bulletin board that makes me feel this way, although that was bad enough. No. I'm angry and disappointed in *you*! Yes, *you*. Everybody in this room except LaTanya and Mr. Perez." Ryan glared at each person in the room, in turn. No one made eye contact with him. They averted their eyes and looked down at their lunches. "You made a commitment to show up and staff that table, and every one of you abandoned LaTanya and me. Silly me! I thought if we did this Ally sticker thing, we'd get more people to support us. Turns out, I can't even count on the few people who I thought supported me now! So yeah. I feel just about as alone and insecure as I did the first day I walked in the door."

The silence was deafening and uncomfortable.

Finally, Amber said, "Well, it's not like you needed more people there. Nobody went up to the table."

Ryan replied, "That is *so* not the point. You said you would be there, and you didn't show up. Maybe if people saw that other straight kids were stepping up to be our allies, they would have too."

LaTanya said, "Yeah. You could have been role models for straight people supporting their gay friends, but you didn't."

Mike said, "I'm sorry I wasn't there. I was sick. I didn't even come to school that day. I was so nervous about doing this I threw up my breakfast. I was a wreck. I guess I'm just not ready to be out to the whole school yet. I worry about getting picked on as it is."

Ryan said, "Well, okay, but–"

Mike continued. "And then when I came in on Friday and saw what they did to the display case, that kind of confirmed my fears."

Monique said, "And then there's this. You're always saying that for gay people, coming out is a journey. Give them space until they're ready to come out. People shouldn't be forced out of the closet until they're ready. Well, what about us? Maybe being a straight ally is a journey, too. Maybe we're not ready to come out to the world as straight allies yet, either."

Ryan wasn't sure whether to give credibility to that or if it was just a feeble excuse. "Well, okay, but if that's the case, you should have said, 'I'm sorry, I'm not comfortable doing this.' But you said you would, then you didn't show up."

"Maybe you just assumed we were all going to be there. I didn't actually say that. Besides, how many people do you really need to hand out stickers?"

LaTanya said, "Having enough people to hand out stickers isn't the point. Having people who will visibly support us is the point. We needed as many people as we could get."

Allyson said, "Besides, how would people know we're straight allies and not, you know, lesbians?"

LaTanya said, "And there you have it. Right there."

Allyson looked perplexed. "What?"

Ryan said, "Yeah. That pretty much sums it up. You say you're willing to support LGBT people, but only if you can do it in secret, or only if it's perfectly clear that you're straight."

LaTanya added, "And if there was really nothing wrong with being lesbian or gay, then you wouldn't care if someone mistook you for a lesbian. But nooo...! We can't risk that, can we?"

Ryan and LaTanya looked at each other and silently reached the same conclusion. They stood up.

LaTanya said, "I am outta here. I ain't got no time for this bullshit."

Ryan said, "With friends like these, who needs enemies?"

Amber said, "Okay, that was harsh."

As Ryan and LaTanya were almost out the door, Mr. Perez called out, "Please! Can we talk about this some more?"

Any further discussion was not going to include Ryan and LaTanya.

Over Easy with Skyler
Saturday, October 20, 2007

On Saturday morning at around 10:40, Ryan got on his bike and pedaled the mile and a half to Eggstravagance. He arrived early, but better to be early than late.

A few minutes before 11:00, Skyler arrived. He was smartly dressed in a stylish short-sleeved shirt with a floral pattern that fit him perfectly. It was just loose enough to hang comfortably on his lean torso. His pants fit him perfectly too, like the pants he wore the day Ryan met him at Banktopia. They showed off his bubble butt to nice advantage, but they weren't close-fitting enough to reveal anything in front.

Ryan realized that he was the more plainly dressed of the two. He wore a solid polo shirt and a pair of plain jeans that were about a year old. They looked neither new nor tattered, but they looked like they had been worn for a while already. Gay fashion was another thing Ryan was still clueless about. Of course, he didn't have a lot of extra money to spend on clothes anyway.

The hostess seated them at a table and handed them menus. A few minutes later, a slender waiter with a man bun approached the table. "Hi, I'm Christopher, and I'll be taking care of you this morning. May I start you off with something to drink?" Skyler ordered coffee. Ryan said, "I'll have the orange juice and a glass of water."

"Sparkling?"

Ryan looked puzzled. Then he remembered the overpriced bottles of sparkling water they sold at Pure Foods and figured it would probably be even more expensive here. "Can I just have, like, tap water?" He hoped there wouldn't be a charge for that. There never was back in Kansas.

"Sure." Christopher turned and left in a manner that seemed a little dismissive.

Ryan asked, "So, what's good here?"

"Pretty much everything. The crepes are to die for. And the huevos rancheros is good too if you're looking for something heartier."

Ryan had no idea what either of those things was. He decided on an omelet with a side of bacon. Christopher returned with their beverages and they placed their orders. Skyler ordered the crepes, so at least Ryan would find out what the heck that was.

After Christopher departed, Skyler said, "So… you've been here three months now. Bring me up-to-date."

"Well, let's see. I started school back in August. We had two weeks of band camp before that. I'm in marching band, wind ensemble, and jazz ensemble."

"How do you like it?"

"It's okay. It's a lot different from the school I went to last year in Kansas."

"In what ways?"

"Well, for one thing, it's a lot more diverse. And that's fine, it's just different. It's mostly Latino kids, some Asians, and a few African-Americans. The school's probably only about ten percent White."

"Yeah, well that's LA. How's the band?"

"It's okay. It's not as good as the music program at my last school. But I'm thankful to have someplace to play."

"What instrument do you play?"

"Trumpet. Do you plan an instrument?"

"I play the skin flute." Skyler acted like he had just said the wittiest thing ever. Ryan smiled to be polite, but he didn't think it was funny. But it did confirm that Skyler was, in fact, gay.

"How about you? What's happened in your life over the past three months?"

"Nothing. Still working at the bank. Still living at home. Pretty boring."

"So, what do you like to do?"

Skyler paused for a moment to decide whether there was any innuendo attached to that question. He decided there wasn't.

"Oh, I don't know. Go to the movies, watch TV. How about you?"

"Well, I don't have much time to do anything. When I'm not in school or at band practice, I'm working at Pure Foods. The guys I live with always get together on Sunday night for dinner. Then after that, we either watch a movie or play some kind of game. It's kind of like a family night, even though it's not my family – well, not my biological family. In a way, they are my family."

"So, you said you were staying with friends."

"Yeah. They're the best friends I have. Well, them and this girl at school named LaTanya."

"So… did you know these guys before you moved out here?"

"Nope." Ryan realized they were heading toward an explanation of why he left Kansas and come out here by himself.

At that moment, Christopher arrived with the food. He scurried away and returned with a coffee pot and a water pitcher and topped off Skyler's cup and Ryan's water glass. He turned to Ryan. "Would you like another orange juice?" Ryan considered how much the first one had cost and said, "No, I'll stick with water from here on."

They took a few moments to taste their food. The omelet was delicious. It was also about fifty percent larger than Ryan envisioned it would be. It was accompanied by four pieces of diagonally-sliced toast, a mound of diced potatoes, and the side order of bacon. The crepes looked like little thin pancakes that were folded over, topped with some fruit, and dusted with powdered sugar. It was certainly a lighter meal, but Ryan was happy with what he had ordered. It would probably take him about twice as long to eat, but maybe that would allow Skyler to do more of the talking.

Ryan asked, "Do you have any siblings?"

"Yeah, two brothers. They're eight and ten years older than me, so it's not like I'm all that close to them. My mom and their dad got divorced, then she married my dad. So that explains the age gap. Anyway, they've been out of the house for a long time. One of them is married and they have a couple of little kids. The other one has a girlfriend he's been with for like five years."

"So, are you out to your family?"

Skyler feigned a look of shock. "Oh! What… What made you think

I'm gay?"

Ryan looked mortified. How could he have misread all the signals? How could he possibly recover from this blunder?

Skyler milked the moment, then laughed. "Yes, of course, I'm gay. What could possibly have tipped you off?"

"Well, the skin flute comment was a pretty good clue."

"Yes, I suppose that would give it away. Anyway, yes. I've been gay since the day I popped out. I finally told my mother when I was around 12 or 13, and she said she knew by the time I was five. And she and my dad had talked about it, so it was no surprise to him either. My brothers know, and they don't care. As I said, they're off living their own lives. What about you?"

"Well… My parents found out back in June. They're really religious and conservative and stuff, so let's just say it didn't go over very well."

"Any brothers or sisters?"

"Just a younger brother. He's eight years younger than me."

"So, do you have a boyfriend?"

"Well, not anymore. He's still back in Kansas. So yeah, we're not together anymore. It's kind of complicated."

"Oh, well, that's too bad. So, tell me about this house you live in."

"Well, when I arrived in Los Angeles, I went to the LGBT Youth Project. While I was there, I met this guy named Hal who's an attorney. He owns this house several blocks west of UCLA and rents several bedrooms out to gay guys – usually guys who are going to UCLA. He had an opening and offered it to me, so I took it. It's pretty rad. It's got a pool and a hot tub and everything. And the other guys are all really nice. So yeah, it's a pretty good living situation. I'm very fortunate."

"Sounds amazing! You think I could see it sometime?"

"Yeah, I guess. It's still about three hours before I have to go to work, so if you want I can take you there after we eat."

"That would be awesome!"

They finished their meal and paid the check. Ryan wrote his address and directions on the back of his credit card receipt and gave it to Skyler. "I rode my bike here, so it will take me about 15 minutes to get home.

Just wait in your car until I get there."

"Sounds like a plan."

***

Fifteen minutes later, Ryan was showing Skyler around the house. When they got to the kitchen and Skyler saw the upgraded appliances and the nice décor, he muttered, "Nice." But when Ryan led him out into the backyard, Skyler's jaw dropped. "Oh my god… This is incredible! It's like some kind of tropical resort back here!"

"Yeah, it's pretty sweet. Every so often, when it's a beautiful day and I have some free time, I float on a raft and soak up the sun. It's very relaxing. And one time, one of the other guys and I came out here late at night when the stars were out and it was peaceful. We just talked and sipped wine. It was really nice."

"Maybe we could do that sometime, or get in the hot tub."

"Yeah."

"I'll bet you could have some great parties out here."

Ryan thought back to the time he came home and they were filming an orgy here, with Ricky in it. "Yeah, probably so."

Ryan led Skyler back inside and led him to his room. "And here's where I stay. So, now you've seen where I live. If I get accepted at UCLA, this will be my home for four more years."

"Sweet." Skyler stepped closer to Ryan. "And speaking of sweet, I think you're adorable." Skyler placed his hands on Ryan's sides, raised himself up on his toes, and stretched his neck upward. At 5' 8", he had a ten-inch height difference to deal with. He planted a gentle kiss on the side of Ryan's neck. Then he gazed upward into Ryan's startled eyes with a look that said, 'Now how about on the lips?' He placed his right hand on the back of Ryan's head and drew him closer.

Skyler pressed his lips against Ryan's, and Ryan's lips instinctively puckered. As they continued kissing, Ryan's thoughts began spinning out of control. *Isn't it a little soon for kissing? I so wasn't expecting this. Should I be kissing him? I mean, he's cute and kinda nice, but… I guess there's nothing wrong with kissing. But what else does he want? Where is this going to lead? What am I comfortable with doing? I'm not sure I'm comfortable with even this. But it does feel good. It feels nice to kiss another man. Why not enjoy it?*

The kisses were growing more intense. Skyler pressed his tongue into Ryan's mouth, and Ryan allowed it in. Skyler's left arm pulled their bodies closer together. Ryan placed his hands on Skyler's sides. *This feels good. It's actually kind of hot. But what does he have in mind? Where is this heading?*

Skyler pulled back a few inches from Ryan's face and said, "I'm getting tired of standing on my tip-toes. Why don't we lie down on your bed?" Without waiting for an answer, Skyler kicked his shoes off and climbed onto Ryan's bed. He laid on his right side and beckoned with his eyes for Ryan to join him.

Ryan couldn't bring himself to say no, and he wasn't sure he wanted to. He said, "Yeah, sometimes being tall has its disadvantages. My boyfriend – well, my former boyfriend – was around six feet tall, so we were a few inches closer." He took his shoes off and laid down next to Skyler.

Skyler said softly, "Sometimes a few inches makes a big difference." As he said it, he rubbed Ryan's crotch with his left hand. "Mmmm…!" He scooted closer, wrapped his left hand around Ryan's back, and began passionately kissing him.

Ryan decided not to feel Skyler's crotch, and instead draped his right arm around Skyler's back. He was still wondering how much farther he should continue down this path. His growing erection was making a strong case for proceeding.

Skyler scooted a couple of inches closer. With their bodies pressed against each other, there was no mistaking the fact that both of them were hard. Skyler nudged Ryan onto his back and rolled with him, putting him on top. His left leg now rested between Ryan's legs and directly over his mound. Skyler's relentless kisses were driving the temperature higher and higher.

Skyler shifted his left leg to Ryan's side, so he was now straddling

Ryan at his waist. After a couple more minutes of deep tongue exploration, Skyler raised himself upright, peeled his shirt off, and tossed it aside. He worked his fingers under the bottom edge of Ryan's polo shirt. "Let's get this thing off you." Ryan lifted himself slightly and raised his arms. Skyler pushed the shirt upward until it cleared Ryan's head and arms. Ryan dropped onto his back and Skyler lowered himself down on top of him. The sensation of Skyler's warm, naked chest pressed against his led Ryan to shed whatever inhibitions remained.

Skyler kissed Ryan several times around his neck, then lowered his mouth to Ryan's nipples. Skyler's hands caressed Ryan's chest and torso, while Ryan ran his hands up and down Skyler's back. Skyler worked his way down to Ryan's navel and treasure trail. Now kneeling between Ryan's legs, he unbuckled his belt buckle and unzipped his pants. Ryan arched his back to raise his hips a few inches, and Skyler tugged Ryan's pants and underwear down just enough to release his cock. Now freed, it quickly surged to full erection. Skyler stared at the flagpole before him and muttered, "Jesus Christ! Dude…!" Gradual, prolonged foreplay was no longer an option. Skyler stroked Ryan's cock a few times. Then he lowered his mouth down onto it, devouring it like a starving child at a buffet.

Waves of sensation washed over Ryan. He gazed down at Skyler, who was voraciously servicing him with laser-sharp focus. Ryan admired his technique. Skyler had acquired a lot of expertise at this skill, and Ryan hoped he could at least perform adequately when his turn came. But for now, Ryan wasn't sure how much longer he would be able to hold back.

Suddenly, Skyler stopped blowing Ryan and jumped off the bed. Within seconds, his pants fell to his ankles and he stepped out of them. "I've got to sit on that thing *right now*!" He grabbed the ends of Ryan's pantlegs and pulled his pants off. "Where are your condoms?"

"Uh… well… I don't have any."

Everything ground to a screeching halt.

"Dude… you don't use condoms???" Skyler looked incredulous.

"Well, I… uh… I wasn't expecting that we would be doing this. I thought we were just having breakfast."

"But, you don't even have any around? Do you bareback other guys?"

"Bareback…?"

"Fuck without condoms."

"Well, I've only done it once before, and that was with my boyfriend. And it was his first time, too. I guess we didn't think about it. I mean, it's not like we could get each other pregnant."

"Yeah, but haven't you ever heard of HIV? And AIDS? Didn't they teach you about safe sex in school?"

"No. I went to this little private Christian school up through eighth grade. They never talked about any of that stuff."

"Not even in high school?"

"No."

"Well, you're from Kansas, so I guess that doesn't surprise me. It's probably illegal to teach that stuff there."

"Even so, I didn't expect to be having sex until I found my next boyfriend."

"And yet, here we are. Okay, so I'll be your sex-ed teacher. If you're going to be having sex with guys, you need to use a condom. Every single time. Don't ever fuck a guy or let him fuck you without one. Don't believe him if he tells you he'll pull out. He may say he's negative, and maybe he is, but he may not know for sure. Or he may be lying – you just don't know. Don't fuck a guy without a condom even if he asks you to. Believe it or not, some guys will. Just be responsible and use it. Insist upon it every time, or no go. Got it?"

"Yeah."

"Okay, schoolboy, here's your homework assignment. You need to buy a box of condoms and a bottle of lube. Make sure it's water-soluble, not Vaseline or something else with any kind of petroleum ingredient in it. It will say 'water-soluble' on the label – if it doesn't, don't buy it. Any questions?"

"What about oral sex?"

"That's pretty safe. Your saliva can kill HIV. So, unless you've got bleeding gums or a sore in your mouth, you can suck a guy without a condom."

Skyler started putting his pants back on.

Ryan said, "Well, can't we at least do oral?"

Skyler thought for a second. Both of their cocks had gone soft. "No, I think the mood has passed for today. But after you've got your condoms and lube, give me a call, okay? I want to finish what we started. That dick is amazing, and I need to have it inside me."

Both of them finished putting their clothes back on, then Ryan escorted Skyler to the door. Skyler gave Ryan a quick kiss and said, "Until next time." He winked at Ryan and headed out the door.

Men Are Pigs
Sunday, October 21, 2007

All day Saturday and Sunday, Ryan kept replaying what happened with Skyler. So many questions swirled through his mind.

Was Skyler only interested in me for sex?

Do gay men often have sex on their first date?

Did I lead him on? Was I unknowingly sending the wrong signals?

Is Skyler boyfriend material?

Do I even want a boyfriend now?

Am I attracted to Skyler, or do I just want a friend?

If we had a condom, should I have had sex with him? How would I be feeling now if I had?

At what point during the dating process should I start having sex?

Do gay men have sex just for fun, when they have no intention of dating or forming a relationship?

Am I okay with having sex just for fun, if I don't really have feelings for the guy?

How can I tell if someone is really interested in me or just wants sex?

Am I just desperate for a guy to be with?

Ryan thought about Ted, and how he has sex with men for pay. 'Escorting,' he calls it.

He thought about Ricky, who has sex in porn movies – another way to get paid for having sex.

This whole sex-for-money thing seems so cheap and so… wrong. But apparently, there are plenty of people who do it, including two of my friends. Other than that, these guys are good people. So, is it really wrong? If everyone involved is willingly participating and nobody is being harmed, then is it okay?

And what Skyler did… let's face it, he pushed me into having sex without really asking. Although I didn't stop him. If I had said no and he continued, that would have been wrong, for sure. But he didn't ask, he just assumed. So, was that right? It doesn't feel like it.

What's really right?

The more he pondered all these questions, the less he knew any of the answers.

***

On Sunday evening, everyone gathered for family night dinner, as usual. Hal made pizza, which was delicious as always. Ted offered Ryan a beer. He was about to decline but he changed his mind and accepted. It might relax him a little bit for the conversation he wanted to have with his housemates, who often served as his unofficial advisory council.

Several of the others talked about what was going on in their lives. Then about halfway through the meal, there was a natural pause in the conversation.

Darnell turned to Ryan and said, "You've been quiet. It looks like you may have a lot on your mind."

Ryan replied, "Yeah, I do. I'd like to ask you guys for your advice on something."

He took a swig of beer. Everyone was watching him with anticipation.

"Okay, so yesterday I had a late breakfast – I guess you could call it brunch – with this guy who works at Banktopia. He was the rep I met when I opened my account. He's cute and perky and friendly, and like, he was all flirty and stuff. Back when I opened my account, he had a break coming up, so he and I went to this coffee shop across the street. It was only for like 15 minutes, so I don't know whether that counts as a date or not, but–"

"And…?" Darnell said, hoping it would prompt Ryan to get to the point.

"Okay, so anyway, when I went in on Tuesday to change the name on my account, I saw him again and we agreed to meet for breakfast yesterday."

Darnell cut in. "Okay, so now I have to ask, who asked who?"

Ryan replayed their dialog in his mind. "I'm pretty sure it was him who asked me."

Darnell clasped his hands in front of his chest and gushed, "Oh, my! Our new adult just went out on a date!"

"Yeah, well, so we met at this place called Eggstravagance on Gayley–"

Ricky jumped in. "Yeah, that place is gayly, alright."

"Anyway, the brunch went okay, and at one point he asked me about where I live. So, I told him all about this place and how cool it is and how nice you guys are, and he asked if he could come over and see it. And I thought, well, I had a couple of hours before I had to be at work, so I said 'sure.' So, I showed him around the place and we ended up in my bedroom. And like almost immediately he started kissing me. Next thing you know we're lying on the bed and he's taking off our shirts, and like two minutes later, he's unbuckling my pants and going down on me."

Ryan had everyone's rapt attention.

"Then he wanted to have sex. You know, go all the way. And all this time I'm like, 'What's happening here? Should I be doing this?' And then he said, 'Where are your condoms?' And like I don't have any, 'cause, you know, I never expected any of this to happen. I just thought we were going out for brunch. So anyway, he stopped and put his clothes back on and left. But he said as soon as I get some condoms, we can pick up where we left off."

Ricky asked, "Okay, so what's the problem here?"

Ted said, "At least he insisted on using condoms."

Darnell said, "Honey, if you needed a condom, you could have gone into my room and taken one of mine."

"Well, I didn't want to enter your room and go looking through your stuff without your permission. Anyway, that's not the point. Even if I did have a condom, it's like I couldn't believe he was expecting that we'd have sex right away. I mean, it was our first date. We aren't even boyfriends yet or anything. It's like he didn't even ask, he just assumed it was okay and went for it."

Hal asked, "Did you tell him no?"

"No, and that's the thing. I thought about it, but I couldn't. I couldn't think straight – er, I mean clearly. It's like part of me didn't think it was right and the other part of me didn't want it to stop."

Ricky said, "Oh, I've been there before."

Darnell cast him some side-eye and said, "You have…?"

Ricky replied, "Bitch. You don't know what goes on in my head."

"That's for sure."

Hal said, "But back to Ryan. So okay, all this happened. What's bothering you?"

"I guess I'm trying to figure out what's right and what's normal. I'm still trying to get used to this whole gay thing. I mean like, do gay guys always expect sex when they go out on a date?"

Ted said, "Not always, but sometimes. But yeah, I get what you're saying. It's hard to tell whether a guy is interested in dating and maybe having that turn into a relationship, or he just wants to hook up for sex."

"Yeah. Exactly."

Darnell said, "Well, here's the thing. If you're out at a bar or something – and I know you're not old enough for that yet but it could happen anywhere – and a guy says, 'Hey, you wanna go home together?' that's a hookup. It's just for sex. Asking someone out for coffee or a meal is usually a date. At least that's what I think."

Ricky said, "Yeah, but you know, some guys are like if they think you might be boyfriend material they still want to have sex right away. A, because they're horny, but B, because they figure if you're lousy in bed or you're not sexually compatible, like if you're both bottoms or you give bad head or something like that, then why waste any more time on the relationship?"

Ryan thought about that for a moment. "Yeah, but in that case, it seems like sex is more important to them than anything else about the relationship, like whether you love each other."

Hal said, "Yeah, some guys are like that. And those are the ones that can't make a relationship last more than six months. As soon as the hot sex cools down, they realize there's not much else there."

Ryan said, "I guess what I'm trying to figure out is, what should I have done in that situation? I mean, let's say I had a condom. Should I have gone ahead and fucked him? Is that the way I want to be? Or do I want to hold off until we get to some point in the relationship when sex seems appropriate? What do other guys do? I guess I never received any training on this gay sex and dating thing."

Ted said, "There's no one answer. It's up to you to determine what's right for you and what you're comfortable with. You don't have to compromise your values because you think that's what all the other gay guys do. The other gay guys are all over the place on this. You do what's right for you. And you have to think about that ahead of time and decide what your values are when you can think about it objectively, not when you're in the heat of passion with some hot guy."

Ricky said, "I don't know. I've never regretted a decision I made when I was in the heat of passion with some hot guy."

Darnell replied, "Yeah, gurrrl, that's 'cause you a ho'."

"I prefer to think of myself as hospitable, and 'ho' is short for hospitable."

Ryan continued. "And the other thing I'm trying to figure out is, was this guy really interested in me or did he just want me for sex? And how can I tell?"

Darnell said, "Well, maybe he was interested in you, but your irresistible sexiness and charm drove him insane and he just couldn't help himself."

"Yeah, right."

"No, I'm serious. Honey, you are young, cute, and a very wholesome-looking young man. You're going to get a lot of attention."

Ricky said, "I get a lot of attention too, for exactly the same reasons."

Ted said, "Dude, he said 'wholesome' – not 'some hole.'"

Ricky feigned indignation and replied, "Ugh! That comment did not come from a loving place. A little jealous, are we?"

"Whatever."

Darnell continued. "And a lot of guys have a thing for tall men. And because you're tall and slender, they may assume you have a big dick. A lot of guys with your body type do – or so I'm told."

"So, you're saying that some guys may be interested in me just because they think I have a big dick?"

Hal said, "Yep. There are a lot of size queens out there."

Ricky said, "And there's only two types of gay men: size queens … and liars."

Darnell said, "Ain't that the truth."

Ryan looked discouraged. This whole thing was depressing and confusing.

Darnell reached across the table and placed his hand on top of Ryan's hand. "Honey, men are pigs." He paused for emphasis. "But we *looove* bacon, don't we?"

Income Opportunities

Saturday, November 3, 2007

On Saturday morning, Ryan knocked on Hal's door. Hal replied, "Come in!"

Ryan said, "Hi, Hal. Here's the $500 for November." He handed Hal a check.

"Great. Thanks. So how is everything?"

"Pretty good, overall, but I've got something I'd like to talk about if you have a few minutes."

"Sure, now's a good time."

"So, I'm starting to apply for scholarships for next year."

"Fun, isn't it? I remember when I went through all that. There are a hell of a lot of forms to fill out. They all want so much information, and it's all different."

"Yeah, it's pretty intimidating. Like if I don't fill everything out just right I might miss something, and that might cost me the scholarship."

"Well, let me know if you need help with anything. I'd be happy to look over your applications before you submit them."

"Thanks. But I guess what I'm really concerned about is this. I won't know how much I'll get until later, and I should be able to get some money but maybe not a full ride. So that means I'll need to come up with at least some of the money to pay for college. And if I totally strike out, I'm going to have to pay for all of it. I had around $3,000 when I came here, and I've already worked through some of that. Like changing my name ended up costing me around $600. It was totally worth it, but still, there went 20 percent of my money.

"So anyway, I'm working all the hours I can at Pure Foods, but I'm still just earning enough to barely get by. I have no idea how I'm going to be able to pay for college, even with some scholarship money."

Hal said, "I understand your predicament. I was in the same place you are. Remember, my parents kicked me out and disowned me after they found out I was gay. And let's face it, you're not going to be able to save up any money with a job that pays minimum wage or something close to it. People can barely get by on that. You sure won't get ahead."

Ryan said, "So, what did you do? How did you put yourself through college? Plus, you went to law school too."

"Well…" Hal paused. "I did porn."

Ryan was stunned. "Really?"

"Yes. I didn't have many other choices. If I tried to get a full-time job with just a high school degree, it wouldn't have paid very well. Most of my money would have gone toward living expenses. It would have taken me years to save up enough for college. Or I could have gone into the military like Ted did. That would have made me eligible for the GI Bill. But I really didn't want to, and if they found out I was gay they would have kicked me out. I could have taken out student loans, but then I would have graduated with a lot of debt. So, I needed something that paid well, that I could do while I was going to school."

"Does it really pay that well?"

"Yep. Back then, in the 80s, I could easily get at least a thousand dollars, sometimes more. Nowadays, a guy like you could get at least two or three thousand. Even more, once you start getting better known. Some guys do escorting too, because if you're a porn star that makes you a lot more marketable as an escort. And there's photoshoots and personal appearances."

"I dunno. That doesn't seem right to me. I talked to Ricky after I found out he was doing that, and he didn't seem to have any problem with it. But I don't think it's something I would be comfortable with."

"I understand. I had a lot of trepidation going into it as well. But I adjusted to it pretty quickly, especially when the money started rolling in. As the saying goes, 'it only seems kinky the first time.'"

Ryan wondered who actually said that, but whatever. He asked, "Would they even be interested in me? I mean, I've only gone all the way once, with my boyfriend last summer."

"It's not a difficult skill to learn. That time you had sex with your boyfriend – didn't you figure out what to do? It's pretty instinctive. Besides, on the set, the director is going to tell you what he wants you to do."

"Okay, but like with any other kind of job, they'll want to know what kind of experience or qualifications I have."

"This isn't like most other jobs. And let me assure you, you are extremely well qualified for the job." Hal smiled at Ryan knowingly.

Ryan looked puzzled.

"Look. They're only interested in three things: a nice face, a great body, and a big dick. If you have two out of the three, you'll be successful. If you have all three, you'll be able to get all the work you want. You're cute. You've got an innocent-looking, boyish face. You definitely fit the 'boy next door' type. Your body isn't muscular, but it is lean and slender. And that's fine for a young guy. If you get a little more definition, that will help as you get older. But really, the most important thing is a big dick. They want either guys who have 'em or guys who can take 'em – or both. And…" Hal paused. "Okay, one day when you were in the pool floating on a raft, I happened to glance out my window and… well, let's just say you're an extraordinary young man. They will be *very* interested in you."

Ryan recalled the time last summer he and Chris had gone to the track team party at Trevor Zimmerman's house. For some reason, Rocket Crockett, the most popular guy on the team, convinced Trevor to put on one of his dad's porn videos. While they were watching the video, Rocket said, "You should have that schlong of yours in porn. You'd make a fortune!" That was only five months ago, but it seemed like a lifetime.

Ryan asked, "So, you said earlier I could earn two or three thousand dollars."

"Easily."

"Is that, like, per month?"

"Per scene."

"Wait. You mean every time I have sex with a guy on camera, I'd get two or three thousand dollars?"

"Yep."

"How does that even work? Who has that kind of money?"

"The porn business is a multi-billion dollar a year industry, and the vast majority of it is made in the San Fernando Valley, just north of here. It's extremely lucrative. The amount of money they pay the performers is a small percentage of the overall picture."

"So if people can make two or three thousand dollars every time they screw, why isn't everyone doing it?"

"Well, remember the three qualifications: a nice face, a great body, and a big dick – or the ability to take one. Most people don't have those qualifications. Most people probably don't know that you can make that much money. And most people don't want to."

"And so that's how you paid for college and law school."

"Yep. And paid for food, clothing, and a place to live."

"Is that how you were able to afford this house?"

"No. I stopped doing porn when I graduated from law school and started working. I had a job at one of the big prestigious law firms downtown. Things were fine for the first couple of years, but then people started finding out that I'm gay. There were clients of this firm who told them they didn't want me on their contract. Pretty soon I noticed that I was being given the shittiest assignments and passed over for promotions. Guys who came along after me were getting better opportunities and bigger raises. So finally, I talked to one of the partners about it. He came right out and said that my potential for advancement within the firm was extremely limited due to my 'lifestyle choices.' That's exactly how he put it. I said, 'you mean because I'm gay,' and he said, 'yep.' So I sued them, because employment discrimination based on sexual orientation is illegal in California. A partner at a law firm should have known that. Anyway, I won a judgment for 2 million dollars, and I bought this house with some of that money. But that also made it hard for me to find a job with another big law firm. So, I ended up practicing law in the adult entertainment industry. I already had a lot of contacts from my years of performing."

"Okay, well… Thanks for sharing all that with me. I'll have to think about it."

"If you decide to move forward with it, let me know. I can introduce you to the right people."

Ryan walked back to his room. He thought about his conversation with Ricky after he learned that he starred in porn. He remembered some of the things Ricky said.

"I do it for the money – the same reason anybody else does it."

"There's making love and there's having sex. You and your boyfriend were making love. All we're doing is having sex. We're giving them something they can get off to."

"I don't think there's anything wrong with it. If I did, I wouldn't do it."

He thought of Ted. He had done porn and didn't have any regrets about it. And he didn't have any issues with being paid to have sex with people as an escort.

Still, it seemed to go against his upbringing. But so did being gay. He had already rejected his father's dogma – intellectually, anyway. But the prospect of doing porn still didn't sit well with him.

He walked out to the family room. He thought he remembered seeing some videos on the shelves that looked like they might be gay porn. Sure enough, there were. He chose a couple of DVDs that looked like they might be interesting and carried them back to his room. He could play them from the disc drive on his laptop. That would be a lot less awkward than watching them in the family room and having one of the other guys walk in.

It Only Seems Kinky The First Time
Saturday, November 24, 2007

Ryan woke up at 6:15 a.m. He needed to be at the studio in Chatsworth at 10:00 a.m., so he had set his alarm for 8:00. He tried to get back to sleep, but he couldn't stop thinking about what was going to happen in a few hours.

What would it be like to have sex with a stranger, with a director telling me how to do it and in what positions, with cameramen and who knows who else in the room? What if there were camerawomen? What will my partner be like? What if I have trouble maintaining an erection? There's a first time for everything. What if I come too soon?

Should I even be doing this? Will other people still like me if they find out? Who might see my movies someday? Will I regret it for the rest of my life?

But on the other hand, I need the money to pay for college. I can't think of any other way to earn so much money so quickly. Then I'll have more time for homework and music, and maybe I can have a social life.

At 7:00, Ryan gave up trying to go back to sleep and got up. He took a long shower and fixed himself breakfast. Since it was Thanksgiving weekend, he had more time on his hands than usual. He straightened up his room. He checked his email and deleted a bunch of old emails. He visited a couple of news websites to catch up on what was going on in the world. But all he could think about was what was about to happen.

At 9:00, he knocked on Ted's door. "You about ready?"

"Yeah."

Ted had agreed to give Ryan a ride up to the studio in Chatsworth. He couldn't give him a ride home, since he had an appointment with an escort client. That would have been too much to ask, anyway. Plus, Ryan didn't know how long shooting this scene would last. So, he planned to ride the bus home. It would take two or three hours, but he didn't have anything else to do today. Ryan realized that if he was going to continue in this business, he would need a car – which would mean some of his earnings would have to go toward that.

***

At 9:45, Ted turned the car into the parking lot of a non-descript building with few windows and no signage other than the street address number. He pulled into a parking spot near the front door and said, "I'll wait here until you're sure this is the right place."

"Okay, thanks for the ride. I owe you one."

"Good luck."

"I'll need it."

"You'll do fine. You can tell me all about it later – if you want to."

"Okay, bye."

Ryan left the car and entered the front door. There was a small waiting room with no one in it. Ryan stepped through the door at the far end of the room into a larger warehouse-type space where some makeshift walls divided the space into smaller rooms. He saw a couple of people walking around and said, "Hello?"

One of them, a cheerful 30-ish man, smiled and hurried up to him. "Hi, I'm Reed, the production assistant. May I help you?"

"I'm Ryan Robertson. I'm here for a shoot."

"Oh, yes. Good. Glad you're here. Let me take you to meet the director."

"Okay, but I need to let my ride know he can go."

"No problem. I'll wait here."

Ryan walked back to the front door, leaned out, and gave Ted a thumbs-up.

Reed led Ryan down a hallway and into a studio where a living room set had been constructed. It looked like a typical living room, except for the lack of a ceiling and a fourth wall, an array of stage lights positioned above the set, and a couple of boom mics. A few people were adjusting the lighting and testing the sound.

Reed introduced Ryan to Bill Wiggins, the director.

"Nice to meet you, Ryan. So... you live in Hal's house, I

understand."

"Yes, sir. I really like it. And Hal's great."

"Yeah, Hal and I have known each other for years. And when he sends talent my way, I know I'm getting someone good. He's never let me down."

"Well, I'll do my best, sir. Although I'm a bit nervous."

"Everyone is, their first time. Just relax and you'll do fine."

"Yes, sir."

"Remember, we may or may not use this scene. This is just to see how you do on camera and under the lights. It's kind of a training exercise, so you learn how this is done and get used to having sex for the camera. If it's a little awkward or clumsy, that's okay. This is where we work that stuff out. And doing this isn't for everybody. If it's not for you, we'll figure that out today. So, no pressure."

Yeah, right, Ryan thought. *They'll be evaluating how good I am at having sex with a stranger on camera. My future in this business rests on this. My ability to earn money for college rests on this. No pressure at all.* He let out a nervous laugh. "Okay."

Reed led Ryan to a room that had a small kitchen, with a refrigerator, sink, a small counter with a few cupboards, a microwave, a table with six chairs, and a couple of couches and easy chairs. "This is the green room. I don't know why they call it that, since they usually aren't green, but anyway… You can hang out here until we're ready for you. There's water and soda in the fridge, and help yourself to the food if you're hungry." There was an assortment of small bags of chips, some cookies, and a couple of pizza boxes with half-eaten pizzas. Not quite the spread Ryan remembered from the orgy that took place in his backyard a couple of months ago, but not nearly as many people to feed, either. Today was obviously lower budget.

As Reed turned to leave, another young man entered the green room. Reed said, "Hey, Steve, glad you're here. Thanks for coming in on short notice."

"Sure, no problem. Always happy to help."

Reed said, "Steve, meet Ryan. Ryan, meet Steve. Or as he's known on-screen, Brady Kensington. He's one of our most reliable actors. Very easy to work with. We use him for a lot of our audition videos for just that reason."

Ryan took a couple of steps toward Steve and they shook hands. Steve was short – probably around 5' 4", Ryan guessed. He appeared to be in his mid-20s. He had a clean-cut appearance, with short, straight blond hair, a lean, compact frame with slightly pumped chest and arms, and no tattoos or piercings that Ryan could see. He fit the young, cute, boy-next-door type – definitely someone Ryan could imagine making out with, at least based on his appearance.

Reed asked, "Ryan, what's your porn name?"

"Uh… I haven't decided yet. My housemates and I were brainstorming names yesterday, and one they came up with is Luke Loadstar."

Reed paused for a moment, then said, "Yeah, I like that. I think that'll work, especially after seeing your pictures. I'll see what Bill thinks, and we can finalize that later. Anyway, I need to get to work. You boys hang out here and get to know each other. If you need to take a shower or get cleaned up, Steve can show you where that is." Then Reed left the green room and headed back to the set.

Steve plopped down on one of the couches. Ryan walked over to the fridge and looked inside. Fortunately, they had Dr Pepper. "You want anything?"

"Water's fine."

Ryan grabbed a Dr Pepper and a water bottle and walked to the couch. He handed Steve the water and sat down on the other end of the couch, angled toward Steve.

Steve didn't seem stand-offish, but neither was he taking the initiative to start a conversation. Ryan said, "So, this is my first time. How long have you been doing this?"

"Oh, a couple of years now."

"Do you always work for Bill?"

"Not always, but I've done a lot of work for him. Whenever he calls, I say yes if at all possible."

Ryan paused for a moment to see if Steve would continue the conversation. He didn't. Ryan had another question he wanted to ask. "So… what advice would you give to a newbie?"

Steve thought for a moment. "Just go with the flow. He'll tell you what he wants you to do. Don't look at the cameras. Try to forget they're there and just focus on what you're doing with me. That said, you always have to be mindful of camera angles. The cameras have to be able to see what you're doing, especially the close-ups. The positions Bill will put us in are all about the camera angles."

"Okay…"

"And remember, the most important thing is the cum shot. The bigger load you can shoot, and the farther, the better. He'll tell you when he wants you to cum, and where – like on my face or my chest or my ass or whatever. Try your best not to cum until he tells you. If you feel like you're starting to get close, stop, and we'll take a break until it subsides. If it comes on fast and there's no turning back, say something like, 'Oh my god, I'm gonna cum!' so the cameras can get ready for it. I know, sounds intelligent, right? Anyway, they can usually edit that and move it to the end of the scene, but try not to cum too soon if you can help it."

"I had no idea it was so complicated."

"Yeah, well, that's why not everybody makes it as a porn star. When you see the final edited product, it looks easy. But you have to be able to keep it hard, cum on command, and act like you're really getting into whoever and whatever you're doing, even if you're not. And most of the time, you're not."

"Okay. Well, thanks for all the info." Ryan slumped back onto the couch, feeling overwhelmed by all this advice. The confidence and optimism he was trying to maintain were fading fast.

Steve leaned forward and put his hand on Ryan's knee. "Hey. Don't worry about it. That's the worst thing you can do. Just roll with it and try to get into it. You'll do fine."

"Thanks. I hope so." Ryan was warming up to Steve. Steve was good-looking – hot, even. And he seemed like a nice guy – someone

Ryan might want to be friends with or even date in real life. Steve seemed to be opening up to him, too.

Reed stuck his head in the door. "Okay, let's head on over to make-up."

They stood up from the couch and headed out the door. Ryan looked at Steve and whispered, "We have to wear make-up?"

Steve's initial expression conveyed, 'Yes, of course, dummy,' but then he remembered this was Ryan's first time. "Yeah. It's not like what women wear, but they dust a little on your face to make sure there's no glare. If you have any blemishes anywhere, they'll cover them up."

After they were through with make-up, Reed led them onto the set. Bill motioned for Ryan and Steve to sit down on the couch. The rest of the crew gathered around. "Okay, this one's going to be pretty basic. Nothing out of the ordinary, just your basic sucking and fucking. Ryan, here, is with us for the first time, so this is just sort of a screen test. Okay, so we're going to start with the two of you sitting on the couch like you're watching a football game. And you're rooting for different teams. Oh, and Reed? Go get one of the pizza boxes with a couple of slices left in it and set it on the coffee table. So you guys start by talking some trash, you know, 'your team sucks,' 'no, *you* suck' – stuff like that. I'll feed you some dialog. Then you make a bet that whichever team loses, that guy has to give the other guy a blowjob, and you shake hands. When Steve's team loses, Ryan, you stand up and whip your dick out and tell him to pay up. Steve, you start with 'I thought we were just kidding, do I really have to?' But then, of course, you suck his dick, then he sucks yours, and you're gradually throwing off clothing, then you 69 each other on the couch, then Ryan fucks Steve. Or, I should say, Luke fucks Brady. Got it?"

Steve and the crew nodded, and the crew got in their positions. Ryan looked overwhelmed. Steve whispered, "Don't worry, we'll take it one step at a time."

***

Four hours later, it was over. Yes, four hours. Even though Ricky and Hal told Ryan it would take several hours to shoot a 15- to 20-minute scene, he had to experience it to believe it. There were frequent breaks to adjust the lighting to eliminate glare and shadows, re-takes for multiple camera angles, re-takes for the dialog at the beginning, breaks for nature calls and lunch, and breaks to regain erections. Ryan's first moments of complete nudity and arousal in front of the small crew had been extremely embarrassing and uncomfortable, but in less than ten minutes, he became accustomed to it. He soon realized it was a non-event for everyone else – they were used to seeing this every time they shot a scene. Another day, another dick.

For all the discomfort, nervousness, and uncertainty Ryan felt earlier in the day, he felt remarkably nonchalant afterward. Actually, he wasn't sure what he felt. He didn't feel anything, good or bad. He and Steve didn't say much as they took a quick shower and put on their clothes. Then Ryan asked Steve, "So, how do you think it went?"

"Fine. I'm pretty sure Bill got what he wanted."

"Did I do okay?" Ryan felt silly after he said it, like he was some kind of insecure kid wanting validation.

"Yeah, you did fine – especially for the first time."

Ryan was about to ask, 'Was it good for you?' but thought better of it. Instead, he said, "Uh… I hope I didn't hurt you."

"Nah… it was alright. I'm used to it."

Steve didn't seem to be very interested in doing a post-mortem on what had just happened. Ryan let it drop. After all, it was Ryan's first time, but Steve had been at this for two years. To him, it was just another day on the job.

Ryan's mood improved considerably when Reed handed him a check that was larger than any check he had ever received in his life. As he was heading toward the door, Bill called after him. "Hey, Ryan?" Ryan turned and took a few steps toward the director. "Just wanted to let you know, you did a fantastic job. So, after having experienced what it's like to do this kind of work, are you interested in continuing?"

Ryan's thoughts up to this point had been focused on replaying everything that had taken place. He hadn't had time to consider this question for himself yet. But then, he did need the money. "Yeah, sure. I'd like that."

"Good. I've got a new project coming up that I think you'd be an excellent fit for. It will be a series called 'Men on a Mission,' about a bunch of Mormon missionaries. It calls for some fresh-faced, cute, young guys, just like you."

Ryan nodded. "Okay."

"I'll be in touch soon."

"Okay. And thanks. I was really nervous about doing this."

"Yeah, I could tell. That's to be expected. But you did pretty well, and you'll gain more confidence as you go along. If I didn't think so, I wouldn't be talking about bringing you back."

"Thanks!" Ryan smiled and turned to go.

"Oh, and Ryan?" Ryan turned back. Bill looked him straight in the eye. "You have everything you need for a very successful career in this business if you choose to do so." Bill winked at Ryan, then he turned and walked back into the studio.

Ryan left the building, turned right, and walked down the street. He arrived at the bus stop, then reached into his backpack to find his iPod and earbuds. A white Honda Civic passed. The driver looked like it might have been Steve. A couple of minutes later, the same white Honda Civic approached and paused in front of the bus stop. Steve rolled down the passenger window. "Where are you headed?"

"Westwood."

"Hop in."

Ryan thought, *Sure, why not? It's not like he's a stranger. We just shared an intimate act, after all. And it will sure beat spending three hours on a bus.* He said, "It's not going to be out of your way, is it?"

"No, it's fine. Get in."

Ryan got in the car. "Thanks."

Steve smiled. "That's a long way to go on a bus."

"Well, I don't have a car, so I don't have much choice. A bus or a cab, I guess. One of my friends drove me here, but he couldn't pick me up."

"Yeah, you really need a car to get around out here. Especially in this business."

"I know, right? Part of the money I'm gonna make from doing this is going to go toward buying a car."

"It's like you need to have a car to get to work, but the money you make from working just goes into your car."

"Yeah. And Chatsworth is so far away. I wonder why they don't have their studios closer in."

"It probably gets more expensive the closer you get into town. Especially around Hollywood and Beverly Hills. And Westwood, for that matter. But even if it was somewhere closer, you would still need a car. Most of the shoots aren't at the studio."

"Really?"

"Yeah, a lot of times they do scenes outdoors or in people's houses, especially if there's a pool involved."

"Funny you should say that. A couple of months ago I walked into my house after being at work all day, and they were shooting an orgy out by our pool."

"You're kidding!!! What??? Wait a minute… your parents let them shoot an orgy at your house???"

Ryan laughed. "No, no… I don't live with my parents. I live at this house near UCLA. The guy who owns the place rents several rooms out to gay guys who go to UCLA."

"Do you go to UCLA?"

"Not yet. I'm still in high school. But I hope to go there next year."

"You're still in high school?"

"Yeah, I just turned 18 last month."

"Man… you don't waste any time, do you?"

"Well, I kinda need the money. I'm going to need a lot more for college than I have saved up now, plus I've gotta get by, you know?"

"Oh, I hear you." Steve took a moment to process the information he had just received. "So… okay, this is none of my business, but… you're in high school but you're renting a room in a house. Why aren't you living with your parents?"

"Well, it's a long story, but let's just say they aren't cool with me being gay. My dad's the pastor of this big mega-church in the Midwest, so having a gay kid didn't exactly fit into his world. I kinda had to leave. But anyway, that's why I laughed so hard when you asked if my parents let them shoot an orgy at their house. Like, my dad and pornography? And orgies? That would so never happen."

Steve chuckled, then turned more serious. "So, you're out on your own?"

"Yeah, but it's cool. I'm getting by pretty well. The house I stay in is super nice, and the guys I live with are cool. They're kinda like my brothers now. I have a job at a grocery store, and now this. Bill said he's going to cast me to be in some new project he has coming up. Something about Mormon missionaries."

"Ha! I'm going to be in that too. Who knows, maybe we'll work together again. Anyway, I'm glad it's working out for you. That must have been tough to get kicked out of your home."

Ryan decided to leave it at that and not dive deeper into the story. "So what about you? What do you do when you're not shooting porn?"

"I'm going to school up at Cal State Northridge. Trying to finish up a degree in Business Management."

"How do you like it?"

"What, the school or business management?"

"Either, but I meant the school."

"It's pretty good. It's not well-known like UCLA or USC, but the campus is nice and it's a pretty good school. And it's closer to home, so the commute's easier."

"Cool. I need to keep my options open in case I don't get accepted at UCLA."

"Yeah. It's also a lot cheaper – like half as much as UCLA."

"I'll keep that in mind. A lot depends on whether I can get a scholarship or financial aid."

"So, back to something we were talking about earlier. The guy who owns your house rented it out for a shoot?"

"Yeah, I guess he does it a couple of times a year. One of my housemates was in the scene. That's how I found out he does porn. I came home and looked out back and saw him getting pounded by some guys on camera."

Steve laughed. "That's funny. What's his name?"

"Ricky Montez."

"Is that his real name or his porn name?"

"His real name. I don't know his porn name. Do you know him?"

"I may have done a group scene with him once. So is he the one that got you into porn?"

"No, actually that was my landlord. He did porn when he was younger, but now he's an attorney. He works in the business."

"What's his name?"

"Hal Morris."

"Oh, yeah. I've met him a couple of times."

"Oh, by the way, you need to get off at the next exit."

Steve flashed his turn signal and started moving over to the right lane.

Ryan said, "Hey, I've enjoyed talking with you. You wanna hang out sometime?"

Steve paused while he chose his words. "Well … I mean, you seem like a nice guy and everything, but between going to school and doing shoots and taking care of my little girl while my wife works her job, I don't have any extra time for hanging out."

"Wait. *What???* You have a wife and a little girl?"

"Yep."

"So… you're straight?"

"Yep."

"But…"

"Yeah, I know. I'm straight, but I star in gay porn movies and get fucked in the ass. It's a job, and we need the money."

"Turn left, then left onto Sunset. But couldn't you do straight porn?"

"I auditioned with a couple of companies, but according to them, I'm not quite the type they're looking for. Plus, my dick's not all that big. But the last guy I talked to suggested that I could probably get hired for bottoming in gay porn. And he was right."

"How does that even work? With your wife, I mean."

"She's okay with it. In fact, she's a lot more comfortable with me doing gay porn. She feels a lot better knowing that she'll be the only woman I sleep with. She knows I'm only doing it for the money."

"Turn right at the next street, then left, then right. So… you're not gay, but you have sex with guys. Doesn't that make you at least bi?"

"No, I'm straight. I desire women. One in particular. I mean, I have nothing against gay people – I'm very supportive. I've met some nice gay guys, including you. But no, I'm straight. You'd be surprised how many straight guys do gay porn."

"Why? Can't they find enough gay guys? Oh, and that's my house up there on the right, with the BMW in front."

"I don't know. All I know is that I can make two thousand dollars for getting fucked in the ass for a couple of hours, and they seem to be pleased with my work because they keep calling me."

"Wait a minute. They paid you two thousand dollars? I only got one thousand."

Steve pulled over to the curb behind Ted's BMW. He left the car running but shifted it into Park. "Wait a minute. That's your house? The one on the right?"

"Yeah."

"I was there for a shoot a couple of months ago. You were talking about coming home and finding an orgy being shot around your pool? And your roommate was in it?"

"Yeah…"

"So was I. And now I remember who your roommate is. Ricky. I think he goes by Juan Knight. Small world, huh? Anyway, you did well to get a thousand. Remember, this was an audition. They weren't counting on getting usable footage, although I'll bet they end up using that. But from now on, don't work for anything less than two thousand dollars. And once you get more experienced and you become better known, you can ask for more. You're young and cute and you have a huge dick. Having your name and face on the box will sell a lot of movies for them, and they should pay you for that."

"Thanks. And thanks for the ride. That was nice of you. So, where do you live?"

"Up in North Hills. It's just a straight shot up the freeway."

"That's not even close to here! You really went out of your way! At least let me give you some money for gas."

"Nope. I don't mind at all. I couldn't see you taking a bus from Chatsworth to here."

"Now I feel really bad."

"Don't. And besides, I enjoyed getting to know you." Steve turned slightly in his seat toward Ryan. "You know, if I was gay and I had the time, I'd definitely hang out with you." Steve leaned over and gave Ryan a quick kiss, which caught Ryan completely off-guard. "I gotta run. Take care, man. Maybe we'll work together again sometime."

Ryan got out of the car. "I hope so. Thanks again." He closed the car door. Steve backed up a few feet, then steered the car around Ted's BMW and took off down the street. Ryan waved, in case Steve was looking in the rear-view mirror.

Family Night Gets Real
Sunday, November 25, 2007

On Sunday evening, as usual, the men of Hal's house sat down to dinner. Hal usually cooked, but this time he brought in Chinese take-out. "I did enough cooking for Thanksgiving dinner. I wanted a break from the kitchen." No one could argue.

Everyone filled their plates at the cafeteria-style spread on the kitchen island, then sat down to eat. Nobody said much of anything. Ryan sensed a hint of anticipation, like there was an elephant in the room but nobody wanted to be the first one to bring it up.

Finally, Darnell said, "Well, we're a quiet bunch. Surely somebody must have something they'd like to talk about."

Ryan looked up from his food. Everyone was looking at him and smiling.

"Well, okay, I'll start. So, yesterday I did my first shoot."

Immediately, the tension vanished and the room came to life.

Hal tried to sound nonchalant as he said, "Oh, yeah, that's right. How did it go?"

All eyes were on Ryan. No one was eating their food.

"Well, pretty good, I guess. I mean, I got through it."

Darnell asked, "Did they pair you up with a hottie?"

"Actually, yes. That really helped. I kinda got into having sex with him."

Ricky said, "Yeah, that's great when you get someone you'd actually fuck in real life. But it won't always be that way. Sometimes you take one look at the guy and you think 'Ewww...', but then you have to do it anyway."

"Still, it was pretty weird. First, it was weird being naked around a bunch of people I didn't know. And then it was even weirder having sex with some stranger with all those other people looking at me. But after like 15 minutes or so, somehow I got over that and it didn't bother me anymore. I just focused on the other guy and tried to block out everyone else. Except for Bill, the director, who would keep telling us what to do next and how he wanted it done. And then we'd stop like every minute and change positions or something."

Hal said, "Yeah, that's the way it works. People see the finished product and think the people in the video just got together and screwed and it was all over in 15 minutes."

Darnell said, "It's the same thing with music. You hear the final song, but you have no idea how many takes they had to do and how much editing and overdubbing was involved."

Ted asked, "So, now that you've done it, how do you feel about it? I know you had a lot of hesitation going in."

"I don't know. That's the part that's the weirdest. I don't know how I feel about it. I mean, once we got going, it didn't even seem like it was me that was doing it. It's like I checked out and my body ran on auto-pilot. You know how people talk about having an out-of-body experience? Maybe that's what it was. It was like it wasn't actually me fucking that guy, it was just my body doing it."

Ricky said, "It's like you became your character. That's what actors do."

"Yeah, but it was weird. I mean, is it that way for you?"

"Not really, but for me, I think it's different. See, I've never had any issues with doing porn, so it doesn't bother me. I know you were struggling with whether you should do this."

Hal said, "There's a name for that phenomenon. It's called dissociation. It's sort of a coping mechanism for your soul. Usually, that happens in more traumatic situations, but that could be what happened to you."

Ryan said, "I didn't feel traumatized, but I guess I don't know what that would feel like."

Hal said, "I think it's more like you were pretty far out of your comfort zone. This was outside the boundaries of what you would normally do. Sexual intimacy can reach pretty deep into your psyche."

Ryan recalled those two times he had been intimate with Chris, and the vulnerability and deep emotional connection he felt.

Ted asked, "So, do you think you'll keep doing it?"

"Yeah, probably. When I was getting ready to leave, the director asked me that. I said yes, without really thinking about it. He said he had a project coming up that I'd be a good fit for."

Hal said, "Well, that means he was happy with you."

"Yeah, I guess. Anyway, here's the other thing that was weird about yesterday. The guy I was doing the scene with? Turns out, he's straight! I mean, it blew my mind that a straight guy would have gay sex – even though I know it's only for the money. And he said he's always the bottom."

Hal said, "We call them 'gay for pay.'"

Ricky said, "There's a lot of straight men in gay porn – tops and bottoms. And besides, I think a lot of straight men would enjoy getting fucked in the ass if they would just open themselves up to it."

Darnell said, "Literally! It's like they get all hung up about 'if I like this, does that mean I'm gay?' Either that or 'what if there's shit?' But we all know how good it is."

Ricky said, "Like that guy who was going to move in here this year, but then he lost his scholarship and had to go back home. He said he was straight, but I have it on good authority that he liked to get it in the ass."

"Mmmmpf!" Darnell almost spat out his drink. "He's straight alright. Straight to bed!"

Ted said, "Wait a minute. You fucked him? I thought you were a total bottom."

Ricky said, "I'm versatile! I only play a bottom onscreen. Anyway, he was here for a party one night, and he had a few in him–"

Darnell cut in. "Literally?"

Ted said, "Yes, literally."

Darnell said, "Ooooo! You nailed him too?" and high-fived Ted.

Ricky said, "As I was saying…! Anyway, we were talking about me doing porn and he said, 'So what's it like to get fucked in the ass?' and I said, 'Wanna find out?' and as it turns out, he did."

Hal said, "So, wait a minute. All three of you fucked him? That explains why he was hanging around here so much. No wonder he wanted to live here."

Ryan's mind was blown. *Chris's older brother Tyler has been fucked by three of my housemates? Is he really gay? Or is he straight but likes anal sex? It hardly matters, but still... Wow. Just wow. Someday, when I'm back in touch with Chris, should I tell him? I guess it depends...*

Ted said, "I wonder how he's doing."

Darnell said, "I'm friends with him on Facebook. He doesn't post very often, but he seems to be doing okay. I posted that picture of us at the table on Thanksgiving, so he'll probably comment on that, or at least give it a 'like.'"

Ryan immediately tensed up. "Uh… which photo did you post, the one where I was behind the camera or the one where you were? Or both?"

Darnell replied, "I used my expert Photoshop skills to splice the two pictures together, so it looks like we're all in it."

Oh my god, Ryan thought. *Tyler will see that picture and show it to Chris and... who knows who else will see it?*

When they finished dinner and were carrying their plates over to the sink, Ryan pulled Darnell aside and asked, "May I ask a favor? Would you please take down that picture with me in it? You can use the picture I took that I'm not in."

Darnell looked at him quizzically. "Why?"

"Tyler lives in Prairie Village, right? I don't know who he knows or who else he's friends with on Facebook. I don't want anyone from back home to recognize me and figure out where I am."

"Are you serious?"

"Yes. Please. It's very important to me."

Darnell sighed. "Alright. I will honor your request. But let me tell you something, sugar. You can't live your entire life hiding from your past. Someday, they're going to find you. Sooner or later, your past is going to catch up with you, and you're gonna have to deal with it. And now that you're getting into the porn business, someday people are going to find out about that, too. So don't be doin' things you have to hide from others. You need to be proud of yourself and what you do, or else maybe you shouldn't be doing it. Having to keep parts of your life hidden is no way to live. People can tell when you're hiding stuff from them. You need to be honest about yourself and not worry about what other people think."

Darnell turned and walked back to his bedroom, and swapped the pictures on his Facebook page.

Season's Greetings
Saturday, December 15, 2007

As Christmas approached, Ryan couldn't help thinking about his past Christmases in Kansas.

Christmas in Kansas usually meant freezing temperatures and snow. Here in Los Angeles, the daily high was usually around 70 degrees, while at night it dropped down to 50. Bryan loved the warmer weather, but it didn't seem like Christmas.

He thought of the bands at Prairie Village High School and all his friends. He wondered what songs they would be playing in their concerts during the coming week.

Most of all, he thought of his family. This would be his first Christmas without them, and their first Christmas without him. Of course, even if he hadn't left, he would be living on his own after he graduated from college anyway. Who knows whether he would have returned to the Kansas City area to pursue his career or where else he might have ended up? Maybe he would have traveled to Prairie Village to spend Christmas with his family, or maybe not – depending on his circumstances. But all that was just idle speculation. His life was on a new course now – irreversibly altered forever.

It hurt that he wouldn't see Brandon at Christmas. He wished he could give him a present. He longed to be able to see the joy on his young face as he opened his presents. He was always such a bundle of happiness and energy. He lit up the room every bit as much as their Christmas tree. Ryan wanted so badly to hug him right now.

And then there was Chris. Chris had broken up with Ryan, but he only did that because it seemed at the time like they would be separated for their last year in high school. When Ryan's father found out he was gay, he grounded Ryan indefinitely and forbid him from ever seeing Chris again. He was going to send Ryan to a small Christian high school. But if none of that had happened, they'd still be together – attending school and playing in band together, hanging out together, and making love whenever they could find a private moment. They'd still be building their relationship and planning where they'd go to college together. They'd still be sitting in a car at Slush Fun drinking slushies, eating junk food, joking, and talking about life together.

Ryan wondered if Chris ever thought about him. Surely, he must. But more to the point, Ryan wondered *what* Chris thought about him. Chris had broken up with him after all. Did he regret it, or had he gotten over Ryan and moved on? Maybe he was dating someone else now. Maybe he was offended that Ryan had disappeared without saying goodbye. Ryan had no idea where he stood with Chris, but he knew that he wanted more than ever to be able to hold him again.

It occurred to Ryan that neither Chris, Brandon, nor his parents even knew for sure whether he was alive. He didn't care so much about his parents, but he wanted Brandon to know. Now that he was over 18, he wondered whether it was time to come out of hiding. He had no desire to deal with his parents. And the whole business with Tyler's gay exploits involving his housemates made getting in touch with Chris more complicated.

Ryan left the house a half-hour earlier than usual so he would have time before work to shop for a couple of Christmas cards. They had cards for parents, grandparents, kids, husbands, wives, and plenty of general-purpose cards, but nothing for brothers. Finally, he settled on a whimsical card that showed Santa with a toy sack so full he got stuck in the chimney. Inside it said, 'You must have been extra good this year. Merry Christmas!' Ryan knew that Brandon would get a kick out of that.

Then he looked for a card for Chris. They had a few boyfriend cards, but they weren't boyfriends anymore. He perused the entire selection of cards until he realized he had five minutes to make it to work. He selected a card with a picture of a warm, homey scene showing a fireplace with stockings and a beautifully decorated Christmas tree surrounded by presents. On the front it said, 'I'll be home for Christmas,' and inside, '...if only in my dreams. Wishing we could be together this Christmas.' It was rather bittersweet, but it was the best they had to offer.

At work, he was able to perform most of his duties on auto-pilot. He could think of little else besides what he would write in each of the Christmas cards.

When he got home, he addressed one envelope to Brandon and the other to Chris. He affixed a stamp to each envelope but wrote no return address.

Inside Brandon's card, he wrote, 'To the best little brother in the world. I think about you every day. Love, Bryan.'

Inside Chris's card, he wrote, 'Just wanted to let you know I'm alive and well. I miss you every day and I cherish the time we had. Someday, we'll reconnect and I will tell you everything, but the time isn't right yet. Have a wonderful Christmas. Love, Bryan.'

He inserted both cards into their envelopes and sealed them.

***

The next day, he saw Darnell and asked, "When are you flying to Macon to visit your folks?"

"Friday. I didn't want to miss your concert on Thursday night."

"Awww… that's really sweet! May I ask a favor?"

"You may ask…"

Ryan handed Darnell the two cards. "Would you please mail these once you get there?"

Darnell looked puzzled.

"Just drop them in any mailbox."

"Well… okay. That's not too much to ask."

"Thanks! I really appreciate it."

Ryan figured if Darnell mailed them on Saturday, December 22nd, they might arrive by the 24th. Even if they arrived a day or two late, at least Brandon and Chris would get them. He also realized that his parents might see the card for Brandon and wonder why he was receiving a card postmarked in Macon, Georgia with no return address. They would examine it and see who it came from. But there was nothing he could do about that. He still wanted Brandon to get the card.

The Show Must Go On
Thursday, December 20, 2007

The Westwood High School Music Department's end-of-semester concerts took place during the last week of school before Christmas break. The wind ensemble concert on Wednesday evening had gone well. The jazz ensemble was eagerly awaiting their performance on Thursday evening. The guitar class students performed first, followed by the full choir. There was an intermission, during which the choir risers were collapsed and wheeled offstage and the chairs and music stands for the jazz ensemble were set up. The second half opened with the 12-voice jazz choir, accompanied by the jazz ensemble's rhythm section. The jazz ensemble held the honor of bringing the show to an energetic climax, although many of the choir kids and their parents had departed during intermission. Ted, Darnell, Ricky, and Hal had come to hear Ryan play.

Due to the multi-cultural demographics of Westwood's student body, this wasn't specifically a Christmas concert. There would be some Christmas tunes included in the various ensembles' repertoire, but plenty of secular music as well.

Ryan and his bandmates waited quietly offstage in the wings, where they could hear the jazz choir and catch a partial side view of the performers on stage. Ryan and LaTanya had positioned themselves in a good spot and were enjoying the performance. The jazz choir was talented and they were in particularly good form tonight. The audience was responding enthusiastically. The excitement was building among the jazz ensemble, knowing that the jazz choir had primed the audience for them.

As the jazz choir began their final number, Julio, the third trumpet player, stepped away from Jordan and a couple of the sax players and walked over to Ryan. He whispered, "Hey, Ryan, can I ask you a question?"

"Sure."

"Let's go out into the hallway for a second. The light's better, and they won't hear us onstage."

Julio opened the side door quietly and they stepped into the hall. Julio was carrying his trumpet and his part for one of the songs.

"So, on 'Santa's Swingin' Christmas' I have this place after letter B where I have to go back and forth between a low D, first and third valves, and F-sharp, second. This always screws me up. I can't move my fingers up and down in opposite directions that fast without flubbing it up." He fingered the notes on the valves to demonstrate. "Do you have any suggestions?"

"Yeah. There's an alternate fingering for the F-sharp. You can play it with all three valves down. That way, you can leave first and third down and just move second up and down."

Julio tried playing that passage softly using Ryan's suggestion. It was so much easier.

"Yeah, that works. Thanks, man! I knew you would have the answer!"

Ryan smiled, although he wondered why Julio had waited until moments before the concert to ask him this. They opened the door carefully and re-entered the backstage area. A few moments later, the jazz choir finished their last number and the audience burst into applause. As they filed offstage, the jazz ensemble members gave them fist bumps and whispered "great job!" Ryan retrieved his trumpet, mutes, and music folder from the spot where he had left them backstage. With the jazz choir now offstage, Ryan and his bandmates entered the stage and took their places.

As soon as they were set, Mr. Scales entered the stage to polite applause, then turned to the band. He opened the score to the first piece. As Ryan held his trumpet, he engaged in his subconscious habit of fingering his valves a few times.

To his horror, when he pressed down on the valves they slowly oozed their way back up, taking two or three seconds to return to their full open state. Ryan pressed a valve again, and it struggled to raise itself back up. What the…???

"Shit!" Ryan uttered in a loud whisper. A couple of the trombonists in front of him, Stan and Raul, glanced back to see what was wrong. Mr. Scales abruptly stopped counting off the opening tune.

Ryan bolted offstage and back to his case. He pulled out his cleaning cloth and unscrewed one of the valves. The entire valve was coated with some kind of gooey slime. He furiously wiped off the valve with the cloth, but the goo was so thick it was difficult to remove. He applied a few drops of valve oil and inserted the valve back into its casing, but it still didn't work. Ryan realized that the inside of the valve casing was coated with goo, too. And the other two valves were similarly coated.

Onstage, Mr. Scales looked puzzled and desperate. In a voice just loud enough for the band to hear, he asked, "What's happening?"

Jordan answered in a stage whisper, "Something's wrong with his trumpet. Go on – I can cover his part for now."

For a few seconds, Mr. Scales contemplated what he should do. He decided he couldn't have the band sit there doing nothing, not knowing how long this was going to take. The show must go on! Hopefully, Ryan would be back on stage before the end of the first number.

Ryan realized that his cleaning cloth alone would not be sufficient to clean up this gooey mess. With his trumpet and valve oil in hand, he exited through the backstage door and ran down the hallway to the nearest restroom. He grabbed a handful of paper towels, then unscrewed all three valves. He held one of the valves under the running water in the sink and tried to scrub the goo off with a paper towel. The nozzle filter which dispersed the water in dozens of tiny sprays to enable hand-washing made this task painfully inefficient. It took him nearly five minutes to sufficiently scrub all three valves. Then there was the question of how to clean out the casings. Ryan unscrewed the bottoms of each casing and set the springs aside. He tried to run water through the casings, but his trumpet was larger than the sink and he couldn't get it far enough into the sink to get the open casings under the spigot. The nozzle filter made this nearly impossible anyway.

He grabbed some more paper towels and rolled them into a cylinder, soaked it with water, and tried to shove it down into one of the casings.

But the wet paper towels went limp. He tried dry paper towels and discovered they worked much better. Still, it was difficult to get all the gunk removed. He struggled to clean his valve casings for another ten minutes.

Finally, he got his trumpet clean enough that the valves could operate reasonably well. He coated the valves with valve oil and fingered them quickly. It wasn't perfect, but it would have to do. He grabbed a few more paper towels and wiped off the remaining water from the exterior of the trumpet.

He ran back to the auditorium and re-entered through the stage door. The band was already playing their final number, and Jordan was playing the trumpet solo that was supposed to be his.

Ryan broke down in tears. Up until now, he had focused entirely on fixing his trumpet. Now, it became clear who had done this and why. Julio pulling him aside to ask about fingerings was just a ruse to get him away from his trumpet for a few minutes. The fact that he missed the entire performance was bad enough. That someone would intentionally inflict such a dastardly act of cruelty upon him was unbearably painful. Tears streamed down his face.

There was no way Ryan could return to the stage at this point. The last song was more than half over. He didn't want anyone to see him crying like this. He put his trumpet back in its case and hurried out the stage door. He ran down the hallway to a door at the back of the school and walked out into the night. He trudged across the football field. As the events of the last half hour sank in, the hurt and loss compounded inside him. He walked behind the bleachers on the far side of the field, sat down, and cried some more.

Ten minutes later, his phone vibrated in his pocket. Fuck it. He didn't want to have anything to do with anyone.

A couple of minutes later it vibrated again. Might as well at least see who it is. It was a text message from Ted. *What happened? Where are you?*

He typed a message in response. *Just go home without me.*

The first buzz had been a call, and the caller left a voicemail. It was

LaTanya. "Hey. Give me a call as soon as you get this."

Ryan thought, *Why should I call? The concert is over. What can they do about it now? Summon everyone to return and do it all again? No, what's done is done, and there's nothing anyone can do that will restore what has been stolen from me. I'm defeated. He won, I lost. Why fucking bother?*

He knew LaTanya would try to console him, but he was beyond consolation. There was nothing anyone could say or do that would make this any less painful. Still, she was his friend. He couldn't just ignore her. She would start getting worried about where he was.

He called her back. "Hey. I got your message."

"Where are you?"

"I'm alone. I just want to be by myself."

"Yeah, I get it. But hey. You know when Julio pulled you away for a few minutes? I saw Jordan go over by your trumpet. I couldn't see what he was doing, and I didn't think much of it at the time. But then when I saw you dash offstage with your trumpet, I thought, 'What the fuck?' and I wondered if maybe he had done something. So during that Count Basie tune, 'Li'l Darlin',' that I don't play on I went offstage and looked around. And you know what I found in his trumpet case? A jar of Vaseline. Yeah. So I took a picture of it, and I showed it to Mr. Scales afterward and told him what I saw. He's mad as shit."

"Well, thanks for doing all that, but it doesn't make a damn bit of difference now. It's not like they're gonna do the concert over."

"I know, but something's gotta get done."

"Maybe, but what's the point? Whatever they do can't make up for this. I'll never get this night back. I'm just going to quit."

"Whaaaat??? That's bullshit. You can't just roll over and play dead. You can't let him win like that."

"Yes, I can. It's not worth it. You know, I play music because it brings me enjoyment. But instead, it brought me this. If it stops bringing me enjoyment, I should stop doing it. Besides, now every time I see that little fucker, I'm going to be reminded of this."

"Well, whatever. But are you gonna be alright?"

"Probably not. Oh, but hey. I just thought of this. Can you still get into the auditorium? I just realized I left my mutes onstage."

"I got 'em."

"Thanks. At least there's that."

"Are you still near the school?"

"Yeah."

"Can you come back in? Mr. Scales wants to talk with you."

"I'm really not in the mood."

"Will you at least talk to him on the phone?"

"Yeah, I guess."

"Let me go get him."

He could hear LaTanya walk about a dozen steps across the floor. She put her hand over the phone, and although she was muffled he could hear her say, "He won't come in, but he says he'll talk to you."

Mr. Scales took the phone from LaTanya and said, "Ryan? Listen, I'm really sorry about what happened. I promise you we'll get to the bottom of this."

"Well, thanks, but it's not going to bring back tonight."

"I know, but… well, we'll come up with something. I'm going to speak to Mrs. Rodriguez first thing tomorrow and make her aware of the situation. We'll talk about how to proceed from there."

"Thanks, but don't bother. I've decided I'm going to quit."

"Oh, no… please don't do that!"

"It's just not worth it. And I don't want to be anywhere near Jordan if I can help it."

"Look, none of this was your fault. We'll come up with some sort of resolution to this issue. But don't make a final decision now when you're still hurting from what happened. Let the holidays pass, then we can talk some more about it after the first of the year. I really want you to stay in the band."

"Well okay, I'll think about it." Ryan realized that this incident would probably be the only thing he thought about for days to come. Merry fucking Christmas.

"Okay, well again, I'm very sorry about what happened tonight. We will do something about it. You take care. And happy holidays."

"You too."

"Okay, I'm going to give the phone back to LaTanya."

LaTanya came back on. "Okay, now… Do you have a way home?"

"Nah, I sent my housemates on without me. I'll just walk."

"It's what – three miles? Bullshit. My folks can drop you off."

"Thanks, but I'd rather walk and have some time alone."

"Alrighty, then. I'll just leave you alone to be a martyr and drown in your self-pity."

"Oh, alright. Where should I meet you?"

"At our car in the parking lot. It's probably the only car left."

"Okay. See you in a few minutes. Oh, and hey… Thanks for being such a good friend."

***

As the Harringtons drove home in their Mercedes, Mrs. Harrington turned to Jordan and said, "I'm very proud of you, son. You played extremely well tonight."

Mr. Harrington added, "Yeah, you definitely belong in first chair. I'm glad your director came around and saw it that way, too."

Mrs. Harrington asked, "What happened to that tall kid beside you, who ran off stage just as you were getting started?"

Jordan replied, "I don't know. He was really nervous before we went on. Maybe he had to throw up or he crapped his pants or something."

***

As Ryan rode home with the Sheridans, Mrs. Sheridan asked, "So, what went on this evening? How come you had to run off stage so fast?"

Ryan sighed. He didn't want to talk about it, but the Sheridans were being kind to him and they seemed to be genuinely concerned. Besides, LaTanya was the best friend he had at school. "Well, first there's some background. At the beginning of the year, Mr. Scales auditioned everyone and put me in first chair. The guy standing next to me, Jordan, who played all the solos? He thought he deserved to be in first chair. His dad, who I guess is the president of the band boosters and donates a lot of money to the band, came in and tried to pressure Mr. Scales into putting Jordan in first chair, but Mr. Scales refused. So tonight, right before we went on, this other guy who's friends with Jordan pulled me out in the hallway and asked me this question about alternate fingerings so he could play his part better. And I'm pretty sure he did that just to divert me, because while I was out there, somebody, probably Jordan, put Vaseline on my valves. That gummed them all up so they couldn't go up and down quickly, which made it impossible to play. So, I ran to the restroom to try to clean it all off, but it was hard to get it off and it took me over 15 minutes. So basically I missed the entire performance. That meant Jordan got to play the lead trumpet part and all the solos."

Mrs. Sheridan said, "Oh, my word! What a horrible thing to do! All that because he didn't get first chair?"

"Yeah, that and it might have something to do with the fact that I'm gay. He and a bunch of the other guys pick on me all the time about that."

Mr. Sheridan said, "Seriously, man? That's messed up."

LaTanya said, "Yeah, they get on me about that, too. I just let it roll right off, but I shouldn't have to deal with it."

"Damn right."

Ryan said, "Yeah, they're all a bunch of jerks. Like when LaTanya first joined the band playing percussion, Jordan and a few of the other guys called it 'the jungle beat.'"

Mr. Sheridan got even more upset. "Oh, now that shit's gotta stop." He turned to his wife. "Honey, I think it's time for us to pay a visit to the principal."

Ryan said, "Actually, Mrs. Rodriguez is very committed to diversity and making the school a safe place for everybody. But she and the teachers can't monitor everything all the time."

"Still, she needs to know that this is going on. She can't do anything about it unless she knows about it."

They pulled up in front of Ryan's home. Mr. Sheridan said, "Hang in there, young man. They're small-minded people and you're bigger than that. We'll get something done."

"Thanks, Mr. and Mrs. Sheridan. I appreciate your support. It was nice to meet you, and thanks for the ride."

Mrs. Sheridan said, "Our pleasure. And Merry Christmas, or however you celebrate."

"Merry Christmas to you too." Ryan and LaTanya fist-bumped, and Ryan got out of the car.

***

When Ryan passed the family room on the way to his bedroom, his housemates were all gathered there waiting for him. Hal said, "Welcome home."

"Hey." Ryan stepped into the family room. He didn't want to go through the whole thing again, but he knew he should. After all, his housemates had come to the concert to support him, and they didn't get to see him play. They deserved some sort of explanation.

Hal asked, "So what the hell happened?"

Ryan recounted the evening's events as he had just done for the Sheridans, including the underlying homophobia.

Darnell asked, "Who was that girl playing percussion? Man, that sista had it goin' on!"

"That's my friend LaTanya. Her parents drove me home. She's about the only real friend I have at school. And she's a lesbian, so between being Black, a woman, and a lesbian, she gets it from all sides. Like Jordan and his friends call her 'LezTonya' or 'LaTongue-ya.' She's really strong and she says she just ignores it and she doesn't care what other people think, but I know it has to hurt deep inside."

"No kidding, man, they call her that shit?"

"Yeah."

"Man, that's pretty fucked up."

Hal said, "The whole thing sucks. You know, I hear about how kids today are so much more open-minded, and how being gay isn't an issue for them anymore. But then I hear stuff like this, and it sounds as bad as it was when I went to school."

Ted said, "And that Jordan guy sounds like a real tool."

Ryan said, "Yeah, he thinks he's entitled because his dad's the head of the band boosters and he donates a lot of money. And who knows? His dad might be putting pressure on him to be the first chair."

Darnell said, "Like it's really that important?"

Ryan said, "It must be, or he wouldn't have done what he did."

Ricky said, "Sounds like I need to round up a few of my homies and go fuck his ass up."

Ryan said, "Thanks, but there's no need for violence. That's not going to solve anything."

Hal said, "When I saw him, I thought he'd probably enjoy getting his ass fucked."

Ted said, "Maybe that explains why he's so homophobic toward you and LaTanya. Sometimes the closeted ones are the biggest homophobes."

Ryan said, "Well, whatever. I've had a shitty night and I'd rather not keep reliving it. Thanks for coming to the concert. I'm sorry you didn't get to hear me. And thanks for your support."

Everyone got up and hugged Ryan, then went back to their rooms.

The Morning After

Friday, December 21, 2007

When Ryan's alarm went off at 6:30 a.m. on Friday, he punched the snooze bar. He needed at least nine minutes to think about how he wanted to handle today.

He replayed last night's disaster in his mind and ended up with the same conclusion. *I am finished with music – at least at Westwood High. It's not as much fun as it was in Kansas, the bands aren't as good, and it isn't worth putting up with the shit. Maybe there will be a band I can join at UCLA – if I even have time.*

Back at Prairie Village High School, all of my friends were in band. Now, there's just LaTanya and Mike. Some of the other kids are okay, but they aren't close friends like the kids in Kansas were. But then there's Jordan and Julio and several of the others who are douchebags. I didn't care much for them even before last night, and I know they don't like me for whatever reason – probably because I'm gay. Most days they are tolerable, but shouldn't it be better than merely tolerable? They'll never be friends. I'm not going to major in music, so I'm in band for enjoyment. And I'm not enjoying it.

I just can't deal with it today. Mr. Scales said he was going to talk to Mrs. Rodriguez, but so what if he does? It's the last day of school before Christmas break, and they won't get anything done. Everyone's looking forward to being off for two weeks. In two weeks, everyone else will have forgotten about this. Everyone will be focused on starting the new semester. Everyone else will go on with their life.

There's no point in going in today. Nothing of importance is going to happen in any of my classes on the last day before break. What will they do in band, since the concert is over? Listen to the recording of the concert? Sightread something? And I can't even with Jordan. I wish I could never see him again, but certainly not today. I don't even want to see the school building or the band room or any of the kids. I just can't.

The alarm went off again. He shut it off and rolled over. He tried to fall back asleep, but he couldn't. His mind was awake now, shifting between anger, hopelessness, and wallowing in self-pity.

***

As soon as the bell rang and first period classes started, Mr. Scales walked into Mrs. Rodriguez's office. She attended the concert and, like many others in the audience, wondered why the tall kid left the stage so abruptly and didn't return. Mr. Scales told her all about it.

She listened to everything he told her with an alarmed look on her face. "So, you're telling me that Jordan Harrington purposely put Vaseline on Ryan's valves so his trumpet wouldn't work right, just so he could play the solos? Why would he do such a thing?"

"Well, there's some backstory. At the beginning of the year, when I auditioned the kids for seating in the wind ensemble and the jazz ensemble, Ryan was clearly the best player. He's new here this year. Jordan came into his senior year expecting that first chair would be his. Then this new kid came on the scene and beat him for the part."

"Is it that big a deal?"

"For some kids, it is. Once Jordan found out he got second chair, his father came in and told me that there must have been some mistake and I should re-audition the kids."

"So Jordan's father pressured you to put him in first chair."

"Right. And he happens to be the president of the band boosters club. He donates a lot of money to the band program."

"Did he threaten to withhold future donations?"

"Not in as many words, but that was clearly implied. He's a department head at UCLA, so he's used to telling teachers what to do and getting his way. He's kind of obnoxious."

"Sounds like it."

"Anyway, I wasn't going to give in to that pressure. If he doesn't donate anymore, so be it. We'll have to make do with whatever we get. But I'm not about to play favorites with the kids of the parents who donate. A lot of these kids' parents don't have money to donate. Ryan is the better trumpet player and he earned first chair. He's a real good kid."

"Yes, he is. I got to know him when he came in to enroll before the school year began."

"So, what can we do about this?"

"Well, first we need to bring Jordan in and hear his side of the story. I want to hear directly from Ryan, and from LaTanya about what exactly she saw. And Julio, the one who called Ryan out into the hallway – obviously he was in on it. Do you think other kids in the band might know something?"

"Probably."

"Okay, then. Let's start bringing them in, one at a time. Let's hear from Ryan first, then LaTanya, Julio, and Jordan – in that order. Then we can decide if we need to talk to any of the other students based on what we've heard. How does that sound?"

"Sounds good."

"I'll have my secretary start bringing them in." Mrs. Rodriguez jotted the four students' names on a piece of paper, got up from her chair, and walked to the outer office. A few seconds later she returned. "Ryan should be here in a few minutes. Carolyn is going to call him out of his class now."

A few minutes later, Carolyn stepped into Mrs. Rodriguez's office. "Ryan isn't in school today. Should I proceed with summoning LaTanya Sheridan?"

"Yes, please."

Mrs. Rodriguez wrote a sticky note to herself to remind her to call Ryan's home.

A few minutes later, Carolyn ushered LaTanya into Mrs. Rodriguez's office. "Good morning, LaTanya. Sorry to pull you out of your class."

"No problem. It's the last day, so nothing important is going on. And we need to deal with this."

"Okay, so please tell us what you saw. Go into as much detail as you can recall."

"Well, Ryan and I and several of the others were backstage, just behind the curtains on the right side, watching the jazz choir perform. When the last number started, Julio came up to Ryan and tapped him on the shoulder, and pulled him away like he had a question he wanted to ask him. He led Ryan out into the hallway. I didn't know what that was about at the time, but it seemed a little strange. Anyway, as soon as they were out in the hallway, I saw Jordan walk over to the table where his case was, but I couldn't see what he was doing. And something didn't seem right. So I went closer, and I saw him holding a trumpet and doing something with it. And it wasn't his, because his trumpet was still laying on top of his case.

"So anyway, then the jazz choir finished and started coming off stage. I went back over to the side of the stage so I'd be ready to go on. And I saw Ryan and Julio come back in from the hallway. Then Ryan walked over to where Jordan had just been, and he picked up his trumpet and came around to the side of the stage with the rest of us.

"Then we went on stage. Mr. Scales started counting off the first song, and I heard Ryan go, 'Shit!' and run off stage. And Mr. Scales was like, 'What's going on here?' Jordan said something was wrong with Ryan's trumpet. He said just go on, and he'll cover the part. So then a couple of songs go by and Ryan hasn't come back yet. Then we got to this song that I don't play on, 'cause like it doesn't need percussion, so I walked offstage. And I kept thinking, what was it that Jordan got out of his case, and what was he doing over by Ryan's trumpet? So I looked in his case, and there was a jar of Vaseline in it. And I thought that was strange, so I took a picture of it. After the concert was over and Ryan never came back, I went up to Mr. Scales and told him I saw Jordan doing something to Ryan's trumpet, and I showed him the picture of the jar of Vaseline. Here, let me show you." LaTanya got out her phone and showed Mrs. Rodriguez the picture.

Mrs. Rodriguez asked, "So did you actually see Jordan putting Vaseline on the valves of Ryan's trumpet?"

"No, I couldn't quite make out what he was doing. He had his back to me, and it was dark back there."

"So then, at what point did you talk to Ryan?"

"After I talked to Mr. Scales, I tried calling him. I left him a voicemail message. About ten minutes later, he called me back. I don't know where he was, but he went off somewhere to be by himself. And he was like really hurt and feeling all hopeless, and he was saying stuff like he's going to quit and he doesn't want to deal with it anymore. I asked him to come back in and talk to Mr. Scales, but he didn't want to. But at least he talked to him on the phone. Anyway, after that, he said he was going to walk home, and I said, 'No way!' 'cause it's like three miles. So I talked him into letting my parents drop him off."

"Well, thank you for looking out for him and being concerned for his welfare."

"It's what friends do."

"So, why do you think Jordan would do such a thing?"

"Cause he's an entitled little prick."

Mrs. Rodriguez looked taken aback by this response.

"Seriously, he thinks just 'cause he's a senior and he's popular and he's white and his dad's some bigshot at UCLA who's the president of the band boosters, he should just be given first chair. Like he's entitled to it. And then there's this. So, Ryan's gay, you know? And they make fun of him behind his back, like they get limp wrists and act swishy like they're mocking him. Even though he isn't like that at all. And they call him Ryan Robert-thun, like they're lisping the S. As if gay people really talk like that."

"So you suspect there might also be some homophobia involved?"

"It's obvious. I mean, they call me LezTanya an' shit like that… oh, sorry."

"That's okay."

"All that started after we had that table at the cafeteria on National Coming Out Day. Ryan and I were the only ones in the GSA that showed up to staff the table. All the other kids made lame-ass excuses."

Mrs. Rodriguez turned to Mr. Scales. "Have you ever witnessed this sort of behavior?"

Mr. Scales replied, "Well, no, but you know they're only going to do it when the teacher isn't looking."

Mrs. Rodriguez asked, "LaTanya, thanks for everything you've shared with us so far. Is there anything else you can think of?"

"Yeah. Ryan was talking about quitting band. After what happened last night, I'm afraid he won't come back. And that's like totally not fair. It's not his fault. I can see how he wouldn't want to be around Jordan after what he did. I mean, you can't just go on as if nothing happened. But it doesn't seem right that he should have to keep suffering for it when it wasn't his fault in the first place."

Mrs. Rodriguez replied, "I understand your concern. Thank you."

"So now that you know all of this, what are you going to do about it?"

"We don't know yet. We're going to talk to Jordan and Julio and maybe some others. But I can promise you that we will do everything we can to address this properly and make things right again. And I want to do something about the homophobia, too."

"Yeah, well, good luck with that."

"Have you seen or talked to Ryan this morning?"

"No, why?"

"He's not in school today."

"I'll give him a call in a minute."

"Okay. And I was planning to call him, too."

A few seconds passed and the three of them said nothing. Mrs. Rodriguez said, "Thank you for your input, LaTanya. You may return to your class now."

LaTanya got up and left. Mrs. Rodriguez followed her into the outer office. She saw Julio slouching in a chair, doing something on his phone. "Julio, would you please come into my office now?"

He finished what he was doing on his phone, slowly got up, and sauntered toward Mrs. Rodriguez's office, clearly communicating that there was an infinite number of things he would rather be doing at this moment.

***

As soon as LaTanya left the office, she pulled her phone out and called Ryan. She got his voicemail.

"Hey, man, it's LaTanya. You've gotta come in today. I just got through talking with Mrs. Rodriguez and Mr. Scales. And Julio's in there now and they're gonna talk to Jordan next. So shit's gettin' real. You need to get in here and tell your story. Anyway, I gotta go back to class now, but call me. And come in, okay? Stay strong, brother."

***

Once they were in the office with the door closed, Mrs. Rodriguez said, "Good morning, Julio."

"G'mornin'."

"I attended your concert last night. The band sounded very good. But I couldn't help but wonder why one of your fellow trumpeters ran off stage and didn't return. You were standing next to him, right?"

"Yes, ma'am."

"Would you please tell us what happened, from your vantage point of being right next to him?"

"Well, we all walked on stage, and then Mr. Scales came out, and like people clapped and stuff. Then he was about to count off the first song, and suddenly I hear Ryan go, 'Shit!' Uh… sorry, but that's what he said. And then he ran off the stage."

"Do you know what happened?"

"I guess there was something wrong with his trumpet."

"Do you know what it was? Could you see anything wrong?"

"No, ma'am."

"Did you have any other contact with Ryan last night?"

"Not really. We might've said Hi. I didn't see him after the concert."

"Anything else you can think of? What about before the concert?"

Julio paused. "Oh yeah. I asked him a question about fingerings for this one part I was having a little trouble with."

"Tell me more about that."

"Well, it's kind of a trumpet thing, so you might not understand. But there was this one place where I have to go back and forth between playing a note that you play with first-and-third and a note that you play with second, and it's like you have to move your fingers up and down in opposite directions real fast. So I asked him if he knew any other way to play that."

"And when did you ask him this?"

"Right before we went on."

"Where were you when you asked him this?"

Julio was getting nervous. "We were backstage, so I asked him to go out into the hall so we wouldn't interrupt the concert."

Mr. Scales spoke up. "So, I'm curious. We've been rehearsing that music for four months. Why did you wait until the last minute to ask for help on that?"

"I don't know… I guess I thought that if I practiced it enough I could work it out."

"Did you ask anyone else?"

"No. I figured if anyone knew, it would be Ryan."

"What song was that in?"

"I think it was 'Santa's Swingin' Christmas.'"

Mrs. Rodriguez asked, "So, how would you describe the social dynamics in the band? And in particular, the trumpet section."

"What do you mean?"

"Are there any personality clashes? Any disagreements? Any underlying tension?"

"No… I can't think of anything."

"Can you think of anyone who might have wanted to get back at Ryan for something, or play a trick on him? Someone who was mad at him for some reason, or was holding a grudge?"

Julio paused just long enough to give the impression that he was pondering the question. "Umm… No… I'm not aware of anything."

"Did you see anything unusual going on backstage before your band went on? Anything at all."

"No, ma'am. But remember, I was out in the hall."

"Who would you say are your best friends in the band?"

"Oh, I don't know… I guess I hang out with a few of guys in the trombone and the sax sections sometimes."

"Who?"

"Uh… Miguel. Stan. Raul."

"How about the other trumpets?"

"Yeah, maybe Jordan."

"How about Ryan?"

Julio paused for a moment, like he was trying to decide what to say. "He's pretty quiet and shy. We don't have that much in common."

"Is there anything else you saw or heard last night that might shed some light on what happened to Ryan's trumpet? Anything at all?"

Again, Julio paused just long enough to give the impression that he was thinking about it. "No, ma'am, I can't think of anything."

Mrs. Rodriguez gave him a stern look to let him know that she didn't believe him. "Well, if you think of anything, please come back and let me know. You may return to your class."

Julio got up and left.

Mr. Scales got up and closed the door. Then he said, "Well, that wasn't very productive."

"He knows. But he's not going to tell us anything."

"That business about asking about the note fingerings seems a little bit fishy. I never noticed him having trouble playing his part on that song."

"Yeah, and there's something else. Did you catch how, when I asked if he had seen anything unusual backstage, he made it a point to mention that he was out in the hall with Ryan?"

"Yeah…"

"It's like he knew that was when something was going to happen."

"We can't prove anything, though."

"No, but let's hear what Jordan Harrington has to say."

Mrs. Rodriguez stepped out of her door, into the outer office. "Jordan, would you come into my office, please?"

Jordan entered and sat down, and Mrs. Rodriguez closed the door.

"Good morning, Jordan. Do you know why I called you into my office this morning?"

Jordan hesitated. "Well, since Mr. Scales is here, it might have something to do with last night."

"What happened last night?"

"We had our holiday concert."

"Yes, I was there. And something unusual happened right next to where you were standing. Why don't you tell us exactly what you saw?"

"Well, Mr. Scales was getting ready to count off the first song and I heard Ryan, the guy next to me, say a curse word. Then he ran off stage."

"Why would he do that? What happened?"

"I don't know. I was focused on the song we were about to start playing."

"Did you look at him when he said that?"

"When I looked he was already running off stage."

"So you have no idea why he suddenly ran off stage."

"No, ma'am."

Mr. Scales said, "That's odd, because last night when I asked what was going on, you said there was something wrong with his trumpet."

"Oh, yeah, that's right."

"Like what?"

"I think he might have been having trouble with his valves."

Mr. Scales and Mrs. Rodriguez exchanged glances.

Mrs. Rodriguez said, "Let's switch gears. Where were you before you went on stage?"

"I was just hangin' around backstage."

"With whom?"

"A few of my buds – Raul, Stan…"

"Julio?"

"Yeah, he was there."

"Did you see Ryan?"

"I think he was standing in the wings with a few of the others, watching the jazz choir."

"Did he have his trumpet with him?"

"I don't remember."

"Were you watching the jazz choir?"

"No, but I could hear them pretty well."

"At any point, did you see Julio interact with Ryan?"

"Yeah. He wanted to ask Ryan something about alternate fingerings for a couple of notes."

"While you were backstage before you went on, did you see anything unusual? Maybe someone who didn't belong there?"

"No, ma'am."

"Can you think of any reason why someone would do something to mess with Ryan's trumpet?"

"No, ma'am."

"Can you think of anyone who might have wanted to get back at Ryan for something, or play a trick on him? Someone who was mad at him for some reason, or was holding a grudge?"

"No."

"Is there anything else you saw or heard last night that might shed some light on what happened to Ryan's trumpet? Anything at all?"

"No."

Mrs. Rodriguez looked Jordan straight in the eye and paused until he had made eye contact with her. "Is there anything else you'd care to tell us about last night?"

"No, ma'am."

"Well, if you think of anything, please don't hesitate to come back and let me know." She turned to Mr. Scales. "Anything else?"

He shook his head.

"In that case, you're free to return to your class."

Jordan stood up to leave.

Suddenly, Mr. Scales said, "Wait a minute. You're an excellent trumpet player. How do you play an F-sharp?"

"Which one?"

"First space on the staff."

"Second valve."

"Any other way?"

"Well… you could play it with all three valves down."

"Good. Thank you. You may go."

Jordan looked puzzled as to why he was just asked that question, but whatever. He was glad the interrogation was over. He hurried out.

Mr. Scales closed the door and sat back down. He sighed. "Okay, so where are we?"

"Well, I think we caught Jordan in a couple of lies. First, he said he never looked at Ryan and couldn't tell what the problem was, but then he knew it had to do with his valves. Is there any other way he could have known that?"

"Not unless LaTanya or I told him."

"And he seemed to know that Julio asked Ryan about that fingering thing, but Julio said he went right to Ryan. How would Jordan know what Julio asked Ryan about?"

"Yeah. And Julio and Jordan hang out together. They don't hang with Ryan – in fact, according to LaTanya, they make fun of him. So if Julio really wanted to know about the fingering, he would have asked Jordan first. That's why I asked Jordan that question. He knows the answer, so he would have told Julio and Julio wouldn't have had to go to Ryan."

"So the whole thing was a ruse to distract Ryan so Jordan could put Vaseline on his valves right before they went on."

"That's sure what it looks like. And that's why Julio took him out into the hall, rather than asking him backstage. He could have whispered and it wouldn't have carried out into the audience."

"So do you think Jordan sabotaged Ryan so he could play the first trumpet part and the solos, just so his dad would think he was back in first chair?"

"Given what I know of his dad, and Jordan for that matter, that seems like a plausible motive."

Mrs. Rodriguez shook her head. "I'm shocked that someone would do something like that. Anyway, we need to hear from Ryan. Let me give him a call."

Mrs. Rodriguez turned to her computer and pulled up Ryan's

information. She picked up the phone and dialed.

The landline phone in the kitchen rang. After a few rings, Ricky picked up. "Bernie's Bar and Billiards. Who in the hall do you want?"

"Who? What? Uh… I'm trying to reach Ryan Robertson. Is this the correct number?"

"Oh, yeah. Hold on. I'll see if he's here." Ricky took a couple of steps toward Ryan's room, then turned back. "May I tell him who's calling?"

"It's Mrs. Rodriguez, the principal of his school."

"Okay. Hang on."

Ricky knocked on Ryan's door. He was still lying in his bed awake. "Yeah?"

Ricky opened the door and stepped in. "Dude, it's your principal. Are you skippin' school today?"

"Yeah." Ryan pulled the cover back and pivoted to a sitting position. Since Ryan slept naked, Ricky was treated to a full view.

"Dude!"

"Later." Ryan shooed Ricky away, and he left. Ryan found a pair of running shorts, stepped into them, then walked out to the kitchen.

"Ryan speaking."

"Ryan, it's Mrs. Rodriguez. Are you alright?"

"Not really. I'm sorry, I didn't feel up to coming to school today. Something bad happened last night."

"Yes, I know. Mr. Scales and I have been working on it all morning. It would really help if you could come in. We want to hear the story from your mouth."

"Do I have to?"

"Yes."

"Can't we just talk on the phone?"

"It would be much better if you came in."

Ryan sighed. "Okay. But do I have to stay the rest of the day?"

"You should, but we can talk more about that when you get here."

"Alright. Well, it will take me 30 or 40 minutes to get there."

"That's fine. We'll be here. When you get here, please come straight to the office."

"Okay, bye."

Ryan took a shower and put some clothes on. He was torn between hurrying and taking his sweet time. He wanted to eat breakfast – to stall for more time as much as anything – but he told them 30 to 40 minutes. He decided he should keep his word.

***

When Ryan arrived at Mrs. Rodriguez's office, she ushered him in and texted Mr. Scales to let him know Ryan had arrived. Ryan sat down in one of the chairs across from her desk. She could tell that this was not the upbeat, optimistic kid who visited her office before school started to enroll. Ryan looked defeated, dejected, and broken.

"Ryan, I am so sorry about what happened last night. Mr. Scales and I have interviewed several other students and we're starting to put the pieces together. I want to assure you that the actions that happened last night have no place at Westwood High School. We will do everything we can to identify the perpetrators and deal with them appropriately. As a side note, I am also saddened to learn that we seem to have a homophobia problem. I want to explore some ways to deal with that, too."

Those were all the right words, but Ryan's demeanor didn't improve. Mrs. Rodriguez shifted from her business-like principal persona to her maternal, nurturing side. "Most of all, I want you to know that you are valued and accepted just as you are. I want to do everything in my power to make this school a welcoming place for you and every other student." Ryan looked up and saw empathy in her eyes.

Mr. Scales entered the office, closed the door behind him, and sat down in the other guest chair next to Ryan. He said, "Ryan, I am so sorry about what happened last night – and also very upset. I promise something is going to be done about it. Please tell us everything that happened last night, from your perspective."

Ryan signed. "Well… I was standing offstage with several of the other kids, watching the jazz choir. Then Julio came up and tapped me on the shoulder and said he wanted to ask me something. He led me out into the hall 'cause he said he didn't want us to make any noise that might disturb the concert. Then when he had me out there, he asked me if I had any suggestions for how to play this one part where he has to go back and forth between two notes, and it's kind of awkward fingering. So I suggested an alternate fingering. He tried it out, and it worked, so he thanked me. Then we went back into the backstage area."

Mr. Scales asked, "Did you have your trumpet with you?"

"No, it was backstage next to my case, on my trumpet stand."

"Do you remember seeing anyone else backstage near where your trumpet was?"

"Yeah. Jordan was back there. His case was next to mine."

"Anyone else?"

"Raul, one of the trombone players, was back there, but he wasn't that close. I think most of the others were watching the jazz choir."

"And did you think there was anything strange about what Julio was asking you?"

"Not at the time. I mean, it was a reasonable question. I wondered why he waited so long to ask about it."

Mrs. Rodriguez said, "You said, 'not at the time.' Do you think differently about it now?"

"Oh, yeah. He just wanted to distract me and get me away from my trumpet so somebody else could mess with it. That's what I think. But I can't prove it."

"Okay, then what happened?"

"So then the jazz choir came offstage and I went back and got my trumpet and walked onstage. Then, when I was getting ready to play, I pushed my valves down and they stuck. I mean, they just oozed up real slowly. So I panicked. I ran offstage and went back to my case to get my cleaning rag. And I pulled out one of the valves and there was this gooey slime all over it. Same with the other two valves. And I knew I wasn't going to be able to get it off with just the rag, so I ran down to the bathroom to try to wash it out. And it took me like 15 minutes 'cause that stuff was really hard to get off. Plus, it was all over the inside of the valve casings, too, so I had to roll up little tubes of paper towels to stuff down into the casings to try to clean them out. Anyway, it was really frustrating and it took me a long time to get it all out. Then when I finally made it back to the backstage area, the band was already halfway through the last song. And I started to cry, and I didn't want anyone to see me like that and I just wanted to get outta there, so I put my trumpet away and ran out the door."

Mr. Scales asked, "Can you describe what the substance looked like?"

"Well, it was kinda creamy and thick and gooey."

"What color was it?"

"Kinda yellowish."

"Was it like anything else you have ever seen?"

"I wondered if it might be Vaseline or something like that."

Mrs. Rodriguez asked, "Do you have any idea who might have done this, and why?"

"It was probably Jordan. I mean, I saw him back there, but I didn't actually see him do anything."

"And why would he have done that?"

"He's always been upset that I got first chair. And earlier in the year, I heard that his dad came in and confronted Mr. Scales about it."

"And do you think Julio was in on it?"

"Yeah, him taking me out into the hall to ask me that question was probably part of the plan."

"How does Jordan treat you, on a day-to-day basis?"

"Well, it's not like we're friends. I mean, he has his own group of friends. It's like I'm just kinda there, you know? And he probably wishes I wasn't."

"Does he ever tease you or give you a hard time?"

"Not to my face, but I suspect he says or does stuff behind my back. I think he makes fun of me because I'm gay. But I don't know."

"How about the other kids?"

"I'm good friends with LaTanya and Mike. He's the piano player.

We're both in the GSA too. Some of the other kids are okay. Several of the ones Jordan hangs out with probably make fun of me behind my back too."

"And who are they?"

"Julio, Connor, Raul, Stan… they're the main ones."

"Okay, well thank you for sharing all that with us. I know it's probably unpleasant to have to keep thinking about it. Can you think of anything else?"

"No, I don't think so."

Mr. Scales said, "So last night on the phone, you were talking about quitting. And I really don't want that. I want you to stay in the band. None of this was your fault, and you shouldn't be deprived of enjoying band. I know how much music means to you – especially jazz. And you're so talented!"

"Well, thanks. Music does mean a lot to me. It means everything. It's probably my favorite thing in the world. Music has gotten me through a lot of hard times this year. But all that changed last night. If I stay, I'll have to see Jordan every day and sit right next to him. Every day, I'll be reminded of what he did to me. Every day, I'll have to fight off the urge to punch him out, or grab his trumpet and throw it on the floor and stomp on it. There's no way I'm going to enjoy band for the rest of the year. So I'd rather quit."

Mrs. Rodriguez asked, "Is he in some of your classes?"

"Yeah, there's that too. That's kinda why I wanted to stay home today, so I wouldn't have to face him. Plus, I just feel like crap. But I guess I can't avoid seeing him forever. At least in our other classes, we're not playing music together. I don't have to sit next to him or interact with him."

"Okay, well, given the circumstances, if you want to go back home after this, you can. I'm not supposed to say that, because you're only supposed to miss school if you're sick, but in this case, I'll make an exception."

"Thanks."

Mrs. Rodriguez turned to Mr. Scales. "Do you have anything else you'd like to ask Ryan?"

"No, I don't believe so."

"Okay then, will you excuse us, please?"

"Sure." He stood up, but before he left, he turned to Ryan. "Believe me, we'll get this resolved, and we'll come up with the best solution we can for the rest of the year. Happy holidays, Ryan."

"Happy holidays to you too, sir."

After Mr. Scales left, Mrs. Rodriguez asked, "Ryan, if you don't mind me asking, how is your home life?"

"It's okay. I'm really busy with the band, my homework, and my job. I hardly have any time. I guess if I'm not in band anymore, that will lighten my load quite a bit and I'll have more time to study."

"Okay, well this is none of my business, but I care about the welfare of my students. Um… are you living in a bar?"

Ryan looked puzzled. "No… why do you say that?"

"When I called you this morning, some guy answered and said it was something like Bernie's Bar and Billiards."

It took Ryan a moment, but then he remembered it was Ricky who answered the phone. "Oh, no… that was one of my housemates. Nobody ever calls on our landline, so when the phone rings, he figures it's a wrong number or a sales call or something like that, so he makes something up. He thinks he's being funny."

"Do you have a cell phone?"

"Yes, ma'am."

"May I update my records with your number?" He gave her his number and she typed it into the computer. "But your living situation is okay."

"Yeah, it's fine. I'm very lucky. My housemates are like brothers. In fact, they came to the concert last night to hear me, but of course, they didn't get to."

"I'm very sorry about that. So, is there anything else you would like to talk about?"

Ryan thought for a moment. "Yeah. You were asking me earlier about how I was treated by other kids. Well, remember on National

Coming Out Day, when we had that table by the cafeteria that LaTanya and I were at? So now a lot of kids know I'm gay and it's like most of them don't want to deal with it. Like I don't get called fag or queer or anything, at least not to my face. Most of the time I just get ignored, like I'm ostracized or something. I mean, I've learned to deal with it and I've gotten used to it. I've got a couple of friends here, but I guess I'll never really fit in."

"And you think that's because you're gay, and more people know about it now?"

"I'm pretty sure. And seeing how LaTanya and I get treated makes a few of the other kids in the GSA who are still closeted even more hesitant to come out. We've had a few people quit."

"I guess we still have a lot of work to do to rid our school of homophobia."

"I guess so."

"Okay, Ryan. I hope your day gets better and you're able to enjoy your holidays. Do you have any plans?"

"Not really. A couple of the guys in my house are going home to their families. The rest of us will probably exchange a few little presents, but that's about it. It will be my first Christmas since I've been out on my own, but I'll find something to do."

"Maybe you'll have a little time to relax."

"Yeah."

"Okay, well you take care. And I might call you later this afternoon."

"Okay, thanks. Bye."

***

When Ryan left the office, he passed Raul, one of the trombone players in the jazz ensemble. Ryan was focused on getting out of the building as quickly as possible, so he barely noticed him as he passed.

"Hey, Ryan!"

Until today, Raul rarely acknowledged Ryan with anything more than a nod when they passed in the halls. He was one of Jordan's buddies, after all. Ryan considered forging ahead as if he hadn't heard. But he decided that would be rude, so he turned and took a couple of steps back toward Raul. They stepped to the side to move out of the traffic flow.

Raul glanced down at the floor, then looked back up at Ryan. "Hey, man. Ummm… Look, I'm sorry about what happened last night."

"Thanks." Ryan forced a weak smile, then started turning to go.

"No, really, man. I mean, Jordan's one of my friends and everything, but that was just wrong."

Wait a minute. Raul was essentially telling him that he knew that Jordan did it.

"How do you know what happened, or that Jordan did it?"

"Well, um, I was backstage the whole time. I mean, I was like 10 or 15 feet away, and it was dark and I couldn't see everything. But I saw Jordan and Julio standing there next to each other and they were talking about something. I couldn't hear what it was, but I could tell something was up. They weren't just standing there hangin' out. Then Jordan nodded his head, and Julio took off and went over to you, and I saw him take you out into the hallway. Then I saw Jordan get something out of his case and he went over to your trumpet and did something. I couldn't really see, because it was dark and he had his back turned. Then he put whatever it was back in his case and grabbed his trumpet and walked away, right before you got back. I didn't know what to make of it until we were on stage and I heard you go, 'Shit!' I turned around and you were freaking out and your valves looked like they were stuck halfway down. And then you had to miss the whole concert. I couldn't figure it all out, but then when you didn't come back and he tried to play all your solos – he didn't do nearly as good as you, by the way – it slowly dawned on me. And then after the concert, Jordan and Julio were back there laughing and congratulating themselves. And I was close enough to hear Julio say something to Jordan about having a fag-free band."

Most of Raul's story confirmed what Ryan suspected. But that part at the end hurt.

Raul said, "Anyway, I just wanted to tell you that I think what they did sucked. And I feel really bad for you."

Ryan said, "So, uh, would you do me a big favor?"

"Yeah, what?"

"Would you go tell all that to Mrs. Rodriguez? I just came from talking with her about it. She and Mr. Scales are trying to figure out who did it, and why."

"I don't know, man. You're asking me to rat on my homies."

"Well, was what they did wrong or not? Do you really feel bad about what happened, or were you just saying that?"

Raul stood there looking consternated.

Ryan said, "They've been talking with several others, too. So it's not just you. Jordan and Julio won't know that you talked to them."

Raul still looked unsure, and a bit scared.

"Well, I'll leave it up to you. You do what you think is right. But it would mean a lot to me." Then Ryan turned and left.

Raul resumed walking down the hall. When he passed the door to the principal's office, he stopped. He stood there for about ten seconds, then walked in. He told Carolyn, "I'd like to speak to Mrs. Rodriguez, please."

***

At around 3:00 in the afternoon, Mrs. Rodriguez called Ryan.

"Hello, Ryan. How are you?"

"Okay, I guess. And you?"

"It's been quite a day. Not how I would have expected to spend the last day before the holiday break. But when things come up you just have to deal with them. Anyway, I wanted to call and give you an update. So, we had another person come forward. That person provided some information that corroborated what we had gathered up to that point, about who put Vaseline on your trumpet valves, and why. So we felt we had enough substantial proof to move forward with a resolution. Jordan and Julio have been suspended from school for a week. That will take place during the first week of the new year. Further, they have been expelled from the band for the remainder of the year."

"Just the jazz ensemble, or the wind ensemble too?"

"All bands. Mr. Scales and I agreed that it would be uncomfortable for you to have to sit next to them and be reminded of this incident every day for the rest of the year. You shouldn't be deprived of the opportunity to enjoy band because of something that wasn't your fault."

"That's great. Thank you for doing that."

"Now, will you reconsider your decision to quit the band?"

"Yes, of course."

"Oh, and one more thing. Mr. Scales and I talked about how we might find a way to do something that might partially make up for the fact that you didn't get to play in the concert. Here's what we came up with. We were already planning to have an assembly in February for Black History Month. Well, since jazz owes so much of its history to African Americans, we are going to have the jazz ensemble perform during the assembly. They can play the non-holiday songs they played last night, and then Mr. Scales said he's going to find a piece by someone like Miles Davis or Louis Armstrong, and feature you on it. I know that still won't undo what happened last night, but how does that sound?"

"Really? You'd do that for me? Yes! That sounds awesome!"

"Well, good. I believe it's the right thing to do, and it's the best we could come up with."

"That's really great. Thank you so much, Mrs. Rodriguez!"

"You're welcome. I hope you have a Merry Christmas and a Happy New Year."

"Now, I will. You have a Merry Christmas and a Happy New Year, too!"

Christmas Eve
Monday, December 24, 2007

On Christmas eve, Ryan worked a full day at Pure Foods, from 9:00 a.m. to 6:00 p.m. The store closed at 6:00 so the employees could spend time with their families and perhaps attend a Christmas eve service. Ryan would be doing neither.

He walked around Westwood Village and considered his options for dinner. Unfortunately, most restaurants were also closed for Christmas eve. So he trudged home and resigned himself to celebrating Christmas Eve with a frozen entrée.

When he got home, he knocked on Ted's door. No answer. He tried Hal's door. No answer there either. Darnell and Ricky had traveled to enjoy Christmas with their families. The house was painfully quiet. Even the Christmas tree and the decorations around the house seemed forlorn, having nobody to entertain or cheer up. The tree had only a few presents underneath, including the ones he had bought for the others. There was nothing under the tree for him yet.

Ryan's mood was sinking by the minute. He selected one of his entrées and popped it into the microwave. While his dinner was being nuked, the front door opened and Hal and Ted entered. They were both in an upbeat, cheerful mood, which unfortunately wasn't contagious enough to spread to Ryan.

Ryan said, "Hey guys."

Hal said, "Hey Ryan!" as he hurried to his room, as if he had something he didn't want Ryan to see.

Ryan asked Ted, "Have you had dinner yet?"

Ted answered, "Yeah. We were out doing a little shopping and we grabbed something to eat while we were out. Sorry."

"That's okay." Ryan turned to go to his room to grab a can of Dr Pepper to go with his Christmas Eve feast.

"Hey. You wanna get in the hot tub later?"

That perked Ryan up a little. "Yeah, sure. What time?"

"Say around ten?"

"Sure. Thanks."

Ryan retrieved his soda and arrived back in the kitchen just as the microwave bell dinged. He sat down at the table and started digging into his Salisbury steak, mashed potatoes, and green beans. The portion-controlled, factory-produced food was sufficiently good, yet still depressing.

This evening and tomorrow would be the most downtime Ryan had since school started. His fall had been a whirlwind of attending school, marching band rehearsals and performances, working at Pure Foods, and somehow finding time for homework.

He was already getting calls to do porn gigs, so he had informed his manager that December 31 would be his last day. She seemed genuinely sorry to receive this news. He hoped his last semester of high school would be a bit less frenetic. Maybe he could have some sort of social life, and maybe even date someone. Of course, he had no idea who. Aside from Mike Nguyen and LaTanya, his hope that he would be able to meet some gay people in the GSA had gone bust. Mike was nice, smart, musically talented, and attractive. But where romantic interest was concerned, nothing clicked. He was still mostly closeted anyway.

Ryan finished his meal, such as it was, and returned to his room. Maybe playing some Christmas music would help, or playing his trumpet. But when he pulled his trumpet out of its case, the whole episode with Jordan came flooding back. He just couldn't.

Ryan opened his laptop and visited the websites of several music vendors. He scanned their catalogs for big band arrangements that had featured trumpet solos. He found a few, then searched on YouTube for videos of bands playing them. Mr. Scales could probably find something good for his feature in the jazz ensemble's upcoming performance for Black History Month. But Ryan figured he might be open to suggestions.

Being sucked down the YouTube rabbit hole helped Ryan's mood improve and made the time pass quickly. After what seemed like only an hour or so, he glanced down at the time on the lower right corner of his screen. It was 10:08 already.

Ryan shut down his computer, hurriedly stripped off his clothes, and wrapped a towel around his waist. He grabbed a can of Dr Pepper and practically sprinted out to the hot tub.

Ted was already in, with a bottle of wine and two clear plastic wine glasses on the side shelf.

"Sorry I'm late. I let the time get away from me."

"No problem. It's not like we're on a strict schedule."

"Yeah, but I didn't want you to think I blew you off."

Ted smiled. Ryan quickly recognized the double entendre in his choice of words. *As if!* he thought. He decided it would be best to let it go.

Ted said, "Would you prefer your Dr Pepper or a nice oaky Chardonnay?"

"The Chardonnay. I just didn't want to make any assumptions."

Ted poured each of them a glass. "Cheers! To spending Christmas Eve in a hot tub!"

"Cheers!" *To spending Christmas Eve in a hot tub with a hunky naked man*, Ryan thought. "It's hard to believe this is December. I don't think I ever want to live in a place where it gets cold again."

"Yeah, I know what you mean. That 'White Christmas' stuff is highly overrated."

"Still, it doesn't seem like Christmas, you know? I mean, people put lights on their houses and you see Christmas trees and decorations and stuff, but… I dunno, it's not quite the same."

"I've gotten used to it. And Christmas isn't a big deal to me, anyway."

"Really? How come?"

"Well, for one thing, I'm not religious. And it's not like when we were kids and it was your big annual day to get toys. I'm single and I'm not in close contact with my Mom and her family. I sent her and her wife a card and I'll call her tomorrow at some point. Here, we exchange little gifts with each other. But this year Ricky and Darnell are gone, so it's just you and me and Hal, and Hal's Jewish. So it will be pretty low-key."

Ryan took a couple more sips of wine. He stared up at the stars and thought about what Ted said. *Is this how Christmas is going to be from now on?*

After a few minutes of silence, Ted asked, "So how are you doing?"

"Not very well. I miss my family. And if I were back at home now, we'd be at the Christmas Eve service at the church. I'm not that big into the religion thing either. But still, it was kinda special, with all the music and the decorations and stuff. It was joyful. And most of all, I miss Brandon. I'll miss seeing him get all excited about opening his presents. And every year, he would make me a homemade Christmas card out of construction paper, magazine clippings, and colored markers. It was priceless. I really love that little guy. We had a special relationship."

Ryan felt like he might start crying at any moment. Ted reached over and put his arm around Ryan's shoulder.

"I'm gonna be thinking about all that stuff tomorrow. And this year, at least I had my holiday concert to look forward to, and that fucking Jordan took that way. So yeah, Christmas pretty much sucks ass this year."

Despite his best efforts, a few tears escaped from Ryan's eyes. He gently splashed his face with water, then looked away. *C'mon, Ryan, hold it together. Don't turn into a blubbering baby in front of Ted.*

Ted took a moment to consider what he could say that might help. Then he said, "You know, I tend to think of Christmas more as a season than as a single day. It's festive with all the lights and decorations and stuff. There are parties and concerts. People are happier. Overall, it's uplifting. I try to focus more on the joy of the season than what's supposed to happen on Christmas day. Like I said, when you're a kid it's all about the toys you get. But that kind of goes away when you become an adult. Now, Christmas day is just a day to relax. It's like forced downtime because everything is closed. I usually go for a hike or a walk on the beach or something, or maybe I'll read a book or watch a movie. I do whatever I feel like doing without being concerned about anything else I *should* be doing. It's a 'me day.'"

Ryan thought about that. *It seemed kind of like taking lemons and making lemonade, but sometimes that's what you've got to do. Anything would be better than being sad and mopey all day.*

"So what are you going to do tomorrow?"

"I don't know. I'll see what I feel like tomorrow. Maybe drive out to Santa Barbara. Maybe go hiking in Topanga State Park or the Santa Monica Mountains. It might be nice to get out in nature for a while."

Ryan so wanted to go along, but he wasn't sure if he should ask. If Ted considered it a 'me day,' he might prefer to be alone.

Ted picked up the three-quarters-empty bottle of Chardonnay. "A little more?"

Ryan nodded. Ted divided the rest between the two of them.

"Thanks."

They spent the next few minutes in silence. Ryan gazed into the night sky. He wondered, *What will Christmas be like for Brandon and his mom and dad? How's Chris and his family, and how has Chris been getting along for the past half year? What had his former band played at their Christmas concert, and how were his friends in the band? Ah, those were the good old days. At the time, I never thought about what it would be like to not have those days anymore. But then again, those days would have come to an end sooner or later anyway.*

He glanced over at Ted. Ted's eyes were closed, and his face looked peaceful. Who knows where his thoughts had wandered? He was probably just enjoying the moment.

The jet cycle ended and Ted opened his eyes. "Had enough?"

"Yeah, I guess."

They climbed out, dried off, and walked back into the house. When they reached the space between their bedroom doors, they turned and faced each other.

Ted could tell that Ryan was still sad and depressed about his situation. "Hey. Hang in there. I know Christmas kinda sucks for you this year, but I think tomorrow's going to turn out okay. And there will be happier Christmases to come." He stepped up to Ryan and wrapped his arms around him. They remained embraced for at least ten seconds.

After the first few weeks of living in the house, Ryan had accepted the fact that nothing romantic or sexual was going to happen with Ted. Still, the pleasure of feeling Ted's muscular, warm, and moist body pressed tightly against his was therapeutic – and a little exciting. Most of all, it was comforting.

Ryan spoke softly into Ted's ear. "Thanks for being like a big brother to me." He paused. They squeezed a little tighter and gently rocked. They remained in each other's arms for a few more seconds, up to the point where it could start becoming awkward. They released each other. Ted's hands remained on Ryan's forearms a second or two longer. Their eyes met, and for a second, Ryan felt he could see into Ted. He saw a complex combination of emptiness, loneliness, concern, caring – and love. Ted gave Ryan a quick kiss. "Good night."

"G'night. And Merry Christmas." There was more he wanted to say, but it was too risky. Too potentially awkward. Too open to misinterpretation.

Ted turned and disappeared into his room.

Ryan took a couple of steps toward his room but decided to make one last trip to the family room. He dropped to his knees and looked under the Christmas tree. Still nothing for him.

Christmas for Grown-ups
Tuesday, December 25, 2007

Ryan didn't set an alarm.

When he was a kid, he never needed to. He would always wake up by 6:00 a.m. at the latest, motivated by the eager anticipation of what might have magically appeared under the tree overnight. He recalled one year – he must have been 8 or 9 – when he got up at 4:00 and tore into all of his presents before his parents got up. He was gently admonished for that and told that in the future, he was not to get up until at least 6:00 and he could not start opening his presents until everyone else was up.

This year, none of that applied. He had no parents to place such arbitrary restrictions upon him. Besides, as of last night, there was nothing under the tree for him anyway.

He figured he would get up whenever he felt like it, and do whatever he felt like doing. Ted's idea of treating Christmas as a 'me day' had a lot of appeal.

By 9:00, he was awake. He realized he wasn't going to go back to sleep, so he climbed out of bed, threw on his robe, and headed for the bathroom.

When he opened his bedroom door, the tantalizing smell of bacon immediately lifted his mood. He followed the aroma into the kitchen and found Ted at the stove frying the bacon and scrambling some eggs in a bowl. Hal was setting the table. Hal looked up, saw Ryan, and smiled. "It lives! Good morning, Sleepyhead."

"Good morning!"

Ted said, "Hurry up and throw some clothes on. Brunch will be ready in five minutes."

Ryan went back to his room and changed into sweatpants and a long-sleeved T-shirt, like Ted and Hal were wearing. He could shower later. He ran his comb through his hair. Thankfully, he didn't have a bad case of bed hair this morning.

When he returned to the kitchen, Ted was stirring the eggs in a skillet. A couple slices of toast were browning in the toaster. Ted stopped stirring the eggs long enough to transfer the sizzling bacon from the skillet onto a bed of paper towels.

Hal asked, "I assume you wouldn't object to a Mimosa?"

"What's that?"

"Champagne and orange juice."

"Sure. Why not?" Christmas morning never included alcohol at the Bauer home in Prairie Village, Kansas. Maybe Christmas for grown-ups wouldn't be so bad.

In a few minutes, Hal, Ted, and Ryan were seated at the table. Hal and Ted raised their glasses, and by now Ryan knew the routine. Hal said, "Cheers – to excessive consumerism at its finest." Ted smirked. They clinked their glasses and took a sip. It took Ryan a moment to process that. Before this year, extreme Christianity was the norm in Ryan's world. He never thought about how non-Christian people dealt with a holiday that was so forcibly thrust upon them despite having no significance to them.

Ryan said, "So, sorry if this sounds naïve, but how do you deal with Christmas, since you're Jewish?"

Hal replied, "Well, obviously it's not a holiday to us, but it's impossible to avoid it. I mean, it's everywhere you look, starting in October – or even earlier. I try to enjoy the good parts and ignore the rest. I like some of the music, the lights and decorations, and getting to see friends at parties, stuff like that. And of course, we get a day off from work like everyone else."

"So what do you usually do on Christmas day?"

"Well, the stereotype is that Jewish families see a movie in the afternoon then go to a Chinese restaurant for dinner. Because, of course, most Chinese don't celebrate Christmas either. There's probably a lot of truth to that stereotype. Anyway, I get together with a bunch of guys in my gay Jewish group, and we go see a movie and then eat dinner at a Chinese buffet."

"I didn't know you belonged to a gay Jewish group."

"Yeah. I'm not real observant, as you can tell." Hal paused to take a bite of thick-sliced peppered bacon. "I don't go to synagogue every week or anything like that. I only observe the major holidays. Like for Passover, I'll get together with my group for seder. I light candles for Hannukah in my room. I might fast for Yom Kippur. That's about it."

"This brunch is delicious. Thanks for including me."

Ted said, "Yeah, no problem. We figured we'd wait until 9:00. We were getting ready to go on without you. We didn't want to wake you up."

"Sorry, I didn't know. You could have woken me up. Anyway, next year I'll get up earlier."

They finished brunch, cleared the table, then gathered in the family room. Ryan noticed a small box with a big ribbon and bow that wasn't there the night before. *Maybe I'll get something after all*, he thought.

Hal donned a Santa hat, then reached under the tree, selected a present, glanced at the label, and handed it to Ted. It was the present from Ryan. Ted ripped off the paper, opened the box, and pulled out a fancy wine bottle opener. "Now, whatever gave you the idea that I might have a use for this?"

Hal and Ryan laughed.

Ryan said, "There's more."

Ted looked in the box again and retrieved a $50 gift card for Wally's Wine World.

Ryan said, "You're always sharing your wine with me, but I'm too young to buy wine so I figured that would be the next best thing. Besides, then you get to pick what you want. I'm still learning what's good."

Ted said, "Thank you! This is great. Very thoughtful. I'm sure I'll put it to good use."

Hal added, "Tomorrow."

Ted replied, "*What* are you saying?"

Everyone laughed. Hal picked another box. This one had his name on it. It was from Darnell. He opened it.

Hal continued to distribute the presents that were for him or Ted. He set the gifts for Darnell and Ricky aside. They would open their gifts when they returned home from visiting their families. Hal seemed to like his present from Ryan – a Queer As Folk DVD box set.

Finally, Hal said, "Well, there's just one more to go." He reached down and retrieved the small box and handed it to Ryan. "It's from all of us."

Ryan carefully unwrapped the present, neatly undoing the paper folds at the ends. The box was slightly larger than a deck of cards. He removed the paper, and a white glossy box with a familiar logo in the center came into view.

"OMIGOD! OMIGOD! OMIGOD! OMIGOD! What…? An iPhone??? You guys gave me an iPhone?!?!?" Ryan was on the verge of tears.

Hal said, "I think that's the last one in the entire LA metro area. We called all over the place. Finally, that one turned up. We had to drive to Moreno Valley yesterday to get it."

"You guys… OMIGOD! But… But… These are expensive! I can't believe you did this."

Ted said, "We can afford it and you're worth it. After the year you've had–"

Hal interjected, "And after what that little snot did to you a few days ago–"

Ted continued, "We wanted to do something nice for you. Darnell and Ricky pitched in for it, too."

Ryan still couldn't quite believe it, even as he held the phone in his hands. "Guys, thank you, thank you, thank you. I mean, really… This was so nice of you."

Hal said, "Well, I'm glad you like it. Of course, you're going to have to go into the store tomorrow and get it put on your plan. We couldn't do that."

"Yes, of course. Guys, I… I just don't have the words."

Ted said, "No words necessary. The look on your face says it all."

"Yeah, but… I mean, the phone is great and everything, but it isn't just the phone. It's that you guys thought enough of me to get it for me.

And you went to so much trouble to get it."

Ted said, "Well, we figured with this being your first Christmas away from home, and the circumstances and everything, we thought it might be kinda rough for you. So we wanted to do something a little special."

Hal added, "And we think the world of you. You're a strong young man with great character. We're proud of you."

Ted said, "Not many kids could have dealt with everything that's been thrown at you, but you've handled it well. You have no idea how much you've grown in the past five months. It's been amazing to watch."

Hal said, "Normally, I wouldn't have a minor living here. It's legally risky and usually they're not mature enough yet. But when I met you, I sensed that you were special and it would work out okay. And I was right. We're glad you're here and part of our little family."

Ryan said, "And so am I. You have no idea."

Ryan hugged Hal, and then Ted. "Thanks, guys. Merry Christmas!"

Hal said, "Merry Christmas. From the Jewish guy."

Ted said, "Merry Christmas. Now, if you'll excuse me, I'm going to go call my mom. It's three hours later there."

Hal said, "I'm going to change, then go out and meet up with my friends."

They each retreated to their rooms.

Ted didn't say what he was going to do with the rest of his day. Ryan didn't feel right about bringing it up and trying to force an invitation to come along. He decided to wait around in his room for a while. He could write an email to Russ Simonton, or perhaps call him. Or look through the videos in the family room and pick something to watch. Or go out for a run later.

About half an hour later, Ted knocked on Ryan's door. "Hey. I was thinking about going for a hike over at Topanga. Wanna come along?"

"Yeah, sure. Maybe we can grab some Chinese food after that."

A New Year, A Fresh Start
Monday, January 7, 2008

Ryan walked into the main entrance of Westwood High School on the first school day of the new year with a renewed sense of optimism. He hoped his final semester would go a little better than the previous one had. If nothing else, in five months it would all be over.

The time off for the holidays had been a relief. The last semester had been stressful not only socially, but also logistically. He had no time for himself. The last two weeks afforded him plenty of time to listen to music, spend time with his housemates, and chill.

The horrific incident caused by Jordan and Julio still lingered in his mind, but he was pleased that justice had been served. It brought some level of closure to the event. He felt relieved that he wouldn't have to face them in school for the first week and in band for the rest of the semester.

At the beginning of the wind ensemble rehearsal, Mr. Scales made a carefully worded announcement. "Before we get started, I need to briefly address an unfortunate incident which took place at our jazz ensemble concert. Those of you who were present noticed that Ryan was unable to perform in the concert at the last minute. That was the result of a deplorable act of vandalism which rendered his trumpet unplayable. An investigation the next day revealed that this act had been perpetrated by Jordan Harrington, with help from Julio Garcia. As a result, Jordan and Julio have been suspended from school for a week and banned from participating in any bands for the rest of the school year. Such acts will not be tolerated in this band or this school. So, everyone in the trumpet section who was seated behind Jordan and Julio can slide up two chairs. We can re-balance the parts."

And with that, Mr. Scales led the band through their warm-up exercises. Then they sight-read the new arrangements they would be playing for their next concert.

Two of the remaining trumpet players were recruited to join the jazz ensemble. At their first rehearsal, Mr. Scales announced, "I have some exciting news. The jazz ensemble will perform in the school assembly that's taking place on Friday, February 15 to commemorate Black History Month. We'll be performing the two non-holiday songs we performed at the holiday concert, as well as two new tunes that we need to get ready in six weeks. One of them will feature Ryan as a soloist. So, let's get busy!"

After the jazz ensemble rehearsal, Raul caught up with Ryan. "Hey, man. It's great that we're going to get to play for the school. I'm glad you're going to get a solo. It sorta makes up for what happened."

"Yeah, thanks. I'm kinda nervous about it, but it'll be cool."

"So, uh… I went and talked to Mrs. Rodriguez. You were right. I needed to do the right thing."

"Thanks, man, I really appreciate it. Mrs. Rodriguez called me that Friday afternoon to let me know what they were going to do, so I kinda figured you had."

"I have your back, bro." Raul patted Ryan on the back of his shoulder.

Ryan smiled.

Raul continued. "Hey, I have something else to ask you. So, uh… are you still in that gay-straight group they have?"

"Nah. I went to a few meetings, but LaTanya and I stopped going in October. We got kind of disappointed with it."

"Oh." Raul looked disappointed.

"Why? What's up?"

"My sister, Angelica, came out to our family over Christmas. I thought if she joined the group and went to a few meetings, she might make some friends and get some support. I told her I'd go with her, you know, as a straight ally."

Ryan said, "Okay. Well, it's a new year. Maybe I'll start going again. And I'll talk to LaTanya."

"That would be awesome, man. Thanks."

"So how did your folks take the news?"

"Eh… it was kind of rough. They're pretty religious. The Catholic church is a pretty big part of their lives, especially for my mom. They're talking about sending her somewhere to get counseling."

"You mean to try to make her straight?"

Raul nodded.

"Oh, no, man. That's bad news. My parents tried doing that to me. The guy they sent me to was a real creep. A real whack-job. Then they were going to send me to this secret gay conversion therapy place in Alabama, and… well, I ended up running away from home. That's how I ended up here."

Raul gasped. "Really, man? You had to run away?"

"Yep."

"Do they know where you are?"

"Nope."

"Aw, man… So you're out on your own?"

Ryan nodded.

"Oh, wow, man. That really sucks."

"Yeah. Christmas was kinda weird. But overall, I'm doing okay."

Raul thought for a moment. "Would you be willing to come over and talk to my parents? Maybe tell them your story?"

"Yeah, I guess… If they'd be open to it."

"I'll talk to them. In our culture, family is more important than anything else. We stick together no matter what. They're kinda stunned now 'cause it caught them off-guard, but they just need some help dealing with it. I think it will end up being okay."

"Okay, well let me know."

"Thanks, man." Raul stepped up and gave Ryan a quick bro hug.

***

The next day, Ryan passed LaTanya in the hallway between classes. "Hey, girl, wassup?"

"Not much. How you doin'?"

"Pretty good, actually. Hey, I think we should give the GSA another try."

"How come?"

"You know Raul, the trombone player in the jazz ensemble? He said his sister came out to their family over Christmas. He asked me if I was still going. He was thinking she might want to go, and he said he would go too, to support her."

LaTanya thought about it for a second. "Yeah, sure. Let's give it another shot."

"Okay, I'll talk to Mr. Perez and make sure they're still meeting. If not, maybe they can start up again."

"Cool. Text me when you find out."

"K. Bye."

Later that day, Ryan stopped by Mr. Perez's room between classes. "Hi, Mr. Perez. You got a second?"

"Sure. What's up?"

"Is the GSA still meeting?"

"No, it kind of ran out of gas after you and LaTanya left."

"Do you think we could try starting it up again? I think we may have a couple of new members."

"Funny you should say that. I've had a few other kids ask about it too. So yeah, let's give it a go."

"This Thursday or next Thursday?"

"Let's go for next Thursday, so there's more time to get the word out. I have a feeling we'll get a little more interest between now and then."

"Cool. Thanks." Ryan turned to go.

"Oh, and Ryan? I heard all about what happened at the jazz concert. That was awful. Do you think what he did was driven by homophobia?"

"I don't know. The guy who did it has been kinda cold to me since the beginning of the year, because I got first chair and not him. But on the other hand, after the concert one of his friends said something about how it was now a 'fag-free band.' So yeah, that might have been part of it."

"Seems pretty obvious."

"Apparently they don't know about Mike. Anyway, the guy who

heard that is one of the kids who is interested in joining. His sister came out over the holidays. He's being pretty nice to me now."

"Well, that's good."

"Yeah. Anyway, I gotta run. See you next Thursday!"

GSA 2.0: Week 1

Thursday, January 17, 2008

At lunchtime on Thursday, students began filing into Mr. Perez's classroom. He had prepared for the meeting by moving 15 of the desks near the front of the room into an oval. Amber, Allyson, and Monique returned, as did Mike, LaTanya, and Ryan. A couple of the other kids who had come to the first meeting at the beginning of the school year also returned. Six new kids trickled in, so by the time Raul and Angelica arrived, all the desks in the circle were filled. A few of the kids closest to the door scooted their desks back so a couple more desks could be squeezed into the circle.

The new kids, especially Angelica, seemed hesitant and curious about what would happen at a Gay-Straight Alliance meeting. Mr. Perez and the returning members were excited to see so many new people.

After Raul and Angelica were seated, Mr. Perez launched the meeting. "Hello, everybody, and welcome to the Westwood High GSA's first meeting of 2008. I'm thrilled to see so many new faces. And, of course, I'm thrilled to see the returning faces as well. I'd like to start by reminding everyone about our ground rules. First, you don't have to identify yourself as LGBT or straight or anything else, unless you want to. Second, please respect the fact that not everyone is ready to be out to the entire school yet. So there should be no talk outside of this room about who's gay and who isn't, or about any of the discussions we have here. This room is a safe space. What happens in this room stays in this room. Does everyone understand?"

He looked around the room and everyone nodded.

"Okay, then. Since we have so many new people, I'd like to start by having everyone introduce themselves. If you want to use only your first name, that's okay. And remember, you don't have to disclose your orientation unless you want to. So please tell us your name and something interesting about yourself. I'll start. I'm Mr. Perez. I teach history and sociology. I'm a straight ally, but I have a brother who's gay. I'm a strong supporter of the LGBT community because of him. I serve as your faculty advisor because I want to do whatever I can to make this school – and the world – a more accepting place for all of you. Ryan, would you please go next?"

"Hi everyone, I'm Ryan Robertson. I'm a senior, I'm gay, and I play trumpet in our wind ensemble and our jazz band."

One of the new kids said, "Aren't you the guy who couldn't play in the concert because Jordan Harrington did something to mess up your trumpet?"

"Yeah, that's me."

"That sucks. That was, like, totally wrong."

Ryan looked around. A few of the other kids looked shocked at what they had just heard. A few of the others were nodding. "Yeah, thanks."

LaTanya went next. "I'm LaTanya Sheridan. I'm a junior, and an out and proud Lesbian. I write poetry and I play percussion in the jazz ensemble, thanks to Ryan who got me in the door."

A couple of the other kids introduced themselves as straight allies. Then it was Raul's turn.

"I'm Raul Hernandez. I'm a senior. I play the trombone. I'm also in the wind ensemble and the jazz ensemble. I'm straight, but I'm here to support my friends, Ryan, Mike, LaTanya, and my sister Angelica. I'll let her take it from here." He put his arm around his sister's shoulder and jostled her affectionately, then dropped his arm to his side.

Angelica seemed shy and extremely uncomfortable. She looked down at the floor, paused, then said in a soft voice. "I'm Angelica Hernandez. I'm a sophomore. He's my big brother…" She gestured toward Raul. "And… uh… I just came out as a lesbian to my family a couple of weeks ago. Anyway, uh… I'm glad you're all here."

LaTanya started a round of applause, and most of the other kids joined in. Mr. Perez said, "We're glad you're here, too. Congratulations on taking this big step. That took courage."

Angelica meekly smiled and nodded, grateful that she had survived this moment.

The rest of the kids introduced themselves. Aside from Mike, none of the others specifically stated they were gay or lesbian, but several kids didn't say they were straight, either.

One of the other new kids asked, "So, what do you do in a gay-straight club?"

Mr. Perez answered, "Sometimes we talk about what's going on in our lives. You can ask questions if you have something on your mind. If there's a current event that concerns the LGBT community, we can discuss that – like same-sex marriage, for example."

Ryan said, "Last semester, we did a couple of projects, like putting up a display on the bulletin board about famous gay and lesbian people and trying to start an LGBT Ally campaign."

LaTanya added, "Those didn't go so well."

Mr. Perez replied, "Yeah, but sometimes you have to be patient. Sometimes one event can be a catalyst, but the change takes place over time. For example, nobody came up to the table we set up outside the cafeteria to ask for an Ally sticker. But I had some students stop by the classroom later to ask me for some. And I've had more interest in the past two weeks. And look at how many new members we have."

Ryan said, "I had a couple of people ask me for one."

Monique said, "I think what happened to Ryan at the concert is going to change things. That's all everyone's talking about now."

Amber said, "But did that have anything to do with him being gay? I mean, that was awful and everything, but was it homophobic?"

Raul said, "That was part of it. After it happened, I overheard Jordan and a couple of others talking about having a fag-free band."

LaTanya said, "Like they didn't even think about me."

Mike added, "Or know about me."

Raul said, "When Angelica came out to us, I remembered what they said. And I realized this is the kind of world she's going to have to live in. So that's when I decided I needed to do something to help change things."

Ryan said, "Thanks, man. That's great that you're stepping up to help your sister."

Raul said, "Not just her. You too. And everyone else. What they did to you made me sick."

Ryan said, "So here's a question I'd like to ask. I'd like to ask each person to tell us what brought you to this room today. Why are you here? What do you hope to get out of being in this group? Any answer is fine. Or no answer. I'll start. I was new here last August, so I just wanted to make some friends – either gay friends or straight friends who were okay with gay people. I dropped out for a while, but I came back when Raul told me about Angelica. I want kids who are just coming out to have a safe place to come, and they won't have that if nobody shows up."

Allyson said, "I'm here because I have a couple of gay friends. They're so scared to have anyone find out about them, they won't even come here. I want to learn more about what it's like to be gay so I can relate to them. Maybe they'll come with me someday."

Amber said, "Same here."

Mike said, "I'm not out to very many people. And after seeing the bulletin board defaced and seeing what they did to Ryan, I'm not sure I want to be out. But I know I should, 'cause if people don't start coming out, nothing's going to change. I'm pretty much here for the support. And to make friends."

Payton, one of the new kids, hadn't said anything up to this point other than introducing himself. Ryan recognized him from a couple of his classes, but he hadn't had any interaction with him up to this point. Payton said, "Okay, well, I came here because… You know how Allyson said she's here because she has some gay friends who are scared to have anyone find out about them? Well… one of them is me."

The room fell silent. Everyone wanted to say something encouraging, but nobody knew exactly what words to use. After a few long seconds, LaTanya realized that if she started a round of applause when Angelica announced that she had come out to her family, the same response was appropriate now. She started clapping, and everyone else joined in.

When the applause died down, LaTanya said, "Well, you came to the right place, Payton. You now have 15 new friends who are cool with you being gay."

Mike said, "Yeah. You're safe and welcome here."

Raul said, "Hey, that took guts, man. Congratulations!"

Allyson, who was sitting next to Payton, reached for his hand and said, "I'm so proud of you!"

Payton smiled. "Thanks, everyone. That was easier than I thought it would be."

Monique said, "So do your parents know yet?"

Payton replied, "Oh, no. I'm not sure I want to tell them."

Ryan said, "Well, take your time. You don't have to tell them until you're ready to."

Mr. Perez said, "That's right. I suggest that you wait until you're more comfortable with being gay yourself. If they sense that you're still tentative or anxious about it, they may not react so well. If they see that you're comfortable with it, they won't worry so much."

Payton said, "I just don't know how they'll react."

LaTanya said, "Nobody does. And they might surprise you either way. You might expect that they'll be upset about it, then you tell them and they're totally cool with it. Or you may expect them to be fine with it and they totally lose their shit. ... Oh, sorry. But even if they react badly at first, they'll get used to it and they'll come around. My parents had a real hard time with it at first. See, they're with the God Squad. They got all Jesus on me back then, but now they support me."

Mr. Perez said, "That's right. Remember, it's taken you a while to get to the place where you can accept that you're gay. They might need some time to work through their issues before they get to a place where they can accept it."

Amber said, "They may not be happy about it, but they still love you. It's not like they're going to throw you out or anything."

Ryan said, "Uh, reality check here. I hate to break it to you, but yes. A lot of parents throw their kids out."

Amber looked shocked. "Are you serious? No way…"

"Way. It's not as bad as it used to be, but it still happens sometimes. There's this place called the Los Angeles LGBT Youth Project over in

West Hollywood. Homeless kids show up there every day, from all over the country. Either their parents kicked them out or they had to run away to escape from a terrible situation at home. So yeah, it happens all the time."

Amber asked, "How do you know all this?"

"Because that's the first place I went when I got to LA after I had to leave home."

The room fell silent.

Then Amber said, "Wow, that's harsh. I'm sorry. I didn't know."

Ryan said, "That's okay. I don't go announcing it everywhere. I'd actually prefer that most people don't know, 'cause I just want to be like any other kid. But back to Payton. I agree with Mr. Perez that you should wait until you're ready to tell them. But you need to think about what you'll say if they ask you tomorrow or if they find out before you want them to like mine did."

Payton said, "How did your parents find out?"

Ryan said "It's a long story, but a policeman caught me and my boyfriend kissing in a car, and he told my parents. And, uh… let's just say they weren't amused. And so, here I am. Another story for another time. Anyway, hope for the best, but prepare for the worst."

Everyone had been upbeat a few minutes ago, but Ryan looked around and saw nothing but sad, stunned faces. "Sorry, I didn't mean to be a buzzkill."

Nobody knew what to say. Thankfully, Mr. Perez came to the rescue. "No, that's okay. One of the reasons we have this club is so it can be a place for us to share our experiences and get support from each other. Anyway, we're almost out of time. I'd like to ask everybody to think about what you'd like to see the club do this semester, and come to our next meeting in two weeks with some ideas. Thanks for coming, everyone. I hope to see you all back here in two weeks!"

Raul said, "Mr. Perez, do you have some more of those Ally stickers?"

"Yes, I do."

"I'd like one. And at the next meeting, maybe we can talk about how we can get more of these things out there."

"Sounds good."

The bell rang, and the kids got up and rearranged their desks back into their original rows. Payton came up to Ryan. "Thanks for your support, and for everything you said to me."

"Sure, no problem."

"Can we have lunch sometime? I'd like to get to know you a little more."

"Yeah, sure. Several of us, like LaTanya and Mike and me, usually sit together. You're welcome to join us."

"Okay." Sitting with a group wasn't quite what Payton had in mind, but he could start with that.

After the meeting, Ryan and LaTanya walked down the hallway together.

Ryan said, "I've never seen you so upbeat and outgoing. You were positively ebullient!"

LaTanya gave him side-eye and said, "Ebullient? What the hell kind of word is that? Sounds like e-bullshit to me."

"Ebullient – overflowing with enthusiasm or excitement. There you have it – your word of the day."

"Oh, no, honey. The word of the day … is *Angelica*!" LaTanya lit up just saying it.

"Oooo, girl, sounds like someone is in love! …Or in lust. Or maybe both."

"Angelica – a beautiful, angelic female sent down from heaven and into my arms. Now *that's* a word of the day!"

"Word."

"Seriously. Did you catch how beautiful she is? Her hair! Her eyes!"

"Her nice boobs."

"You got that right. Wait a minute! You're not supposed to notice those things. Are you sure you're not straight?"

"I am 100 percent not straight. I'm not blind, either. But no question, she's beautiful."

"Just thinking about her makes me moist."

"Ewww…!"

"Oh, please. That ain't any worse than you saying Raul makes you hard."

"Yeah, but I didn't say that."

"Not out loud."

"Besides, Raul's straight."

"Doesn't mean he couldn't make you hard."

They reached Ryan's next class and stopped outside the door.

"Whatever. But he *is* a nice guy. He's the one who witnessed what Jordan did, and he went and told Mrs. Rodriguez about it. That gave them the proof they needed. He said he has my back. He's on my side."

"He has your backside?"

"Shut up! But he's like the first straight-guy friend I've made here. And look at how he's helping his sister. He said he's going to see about having me meet with their parents to talk them out of sending her to counseling."

"Ooo! Can I come along?"

"There you go, being ebullient again. I think it might be a little early to have them meet her first girlfriend, considering you and she haven't even had your first date yet."

"Oh, I'll be takin' care of that."

"Yeah, well, go slowly. She just came out. She's still new to this. She might not be ready for dating yet."

"I know that!"

"Don't pounce on her, is all I'm sayin'."

"*Pounce*? Who do you think you're talking to? What, you think I'm gonna hit her over the head with a club and drag her back to my cave?"

"I don't know how you lesbians work."

"Oh, I heard that. You're still tryin' to figure out how gays work."

That brought the playful bantering to an abrupt halt. "Ouch."

"Sorry."

"It's true though."

The bell rang. LaTanya said, "Catch you later," and scurried down the hall to her next class.

GSA 2.0: Week 2

Thursday, January 31, 2008

The second GSA meeting of the new year was as well attended as the first; in fact, a couple of new kids joined. The positive energy in the room was contagious. A few of the newer kids were still a bit nervous about being there, but most of the kids were excited about sharing ideas and planning for what they would do during the spring semester.

Monique said, "I want to see if we can do something to get more kids on board with the Ally campaign."

LaTanya and Ryan cast wary looks at each other. LaTanya said, "Not unless we get a more solid commitment from our straight allies to actually show up."

Allyson said, "Yeah, we shouldn't have skipped out on you. But I think it's different now. There's more interest. There's more momentum. I think more people will be willing to say they're supportive."

Raul said, "Yeah. I'm totally on board. I could get some of my buds to do it."

Ryan said, "Well, okay, but this time, I want to see you straight folks take the lead on this."

Mike said, "Here's another idea. I've been thinking a lot about what Ryan said about homeless gay kids and the Los Angeles LGBT Youth Project. I'd like to learn more about what they do. Maybe there's some way we can help them."

Amber said, "That's a great idea! Like maybe we can do something with the kids there."

Monique said, "Maybe we can raise money for them."

Mr. Perez stepped in. "These are all great ideas, and I know your hearts are in the right place. But we need to tread carefully here. There are guidelines and restrictions surrounding what official school groups can raise money for. And the Youth Project probably has some policies about who can interact with their kids, especially if there are both minors and adults involved."

Raul said, "I think we need to learn more about the organization and what kinds of support they need."

Ryan said, "The guy who owns the house I live in volunteers with them. He's an attorney, and he helps kids if they need legal services. I think he used to serve on their board. Anyway, he knows the people who run the organization, and he could ask one of them if they'd come here and talk to us."

Mr. Perez said, "That's a great idea. I'd have to get approval to have an external speaker come in, but that's usually not a problem. If nothing else, we can learn more about the scope of the issue and what the organization does."

Ryan said, "Okay, I'll ask Hal about that."

Monique said, "But back to raising money for them. Couldn't we do something on our own, like outside of school? Like have a car wash or something."

Mr. Perez said, "As long as you don't say that it's the Westwood High School Gay-Straight Alliance that's holding the car wash and you don't do it on school property, that should be no problem."

Monique said, "Well, okay then, who wants to do this?"

Most of the kids raised their hands.

Mike said, "That's great, but I'd still like to see if we can get someone from the organization to come in."

Monique said, "Well, who's in favor of that?"

All the kids raised their hands.

Allyson said, "You know what else? I think it would be nice if we had some sort of social event at some point. You know, a party. That way we could all get to know each other a little better."

Ryan thought Hal would probably let him have it at their house, but he didn't want to say anything until he asked.

Amber said, "Funny you should say that. The Super Bowl is this Sunday. My parents have a party every year, and they said I could invite some of my friends from school. So I'm inviting all of you to my house this Sunday. The game starts at 3:30, so you can start arriving at around

3:00."

Raul said, "Cool! Do they want us to bring anything?"

Amber replied, "No, they always have way too much food. We don't need anything else."

Ryan said, "You know what else? I think it would be great if, near the end of the year, we had our own dance. Kind of like a mini-prom."

LaTanya said, "Why should we do that? Why don't we just go to the prom like everyone else?"

Mike said, "I don't know… I'm not sure I'd feel safe there. Or at least not very comfortable."

Payton added, "And some kids who aren't out yet might be willing to go if it was only their gay friends – and allies, too – but they probably wouldn't go to the real prom."

LaTanya said, "I hear that. But you know, I'm not goin' for separate but equal. They tried that with the schools, and we all know how that turned out. I'm goin' for full inclusion. Yeah, it might be uncomfortable at first. And if we make some people uncomfortable, you know what? Tough. If anyone can't handle two guys or two girls dancing together, they need to deal with it and get over it."

Monique said, "Maybe if we make good progress with getting more kids to be straight allies, that will help pave the way."

Mr. Perez said, "You know, I read something that Representative Tammy Baldwin of Wisconsin said not too long ago. She's one of the few openly lesbian or gay representatives in Congress. She said, and I'm paraphrasing here, 'If you want to live in a world where you can walk down the street holding your partner's hand, then walk down the street holding your partner's hand. Then you'll be living in that world.' There was more to it than that, but you get the idea. I'll see if I can find the whole quote and bring it in."

Mike said, "Yeah, that's great until a bunch of thugs come along and beat you up. Or worse. Remember Matthew Shepard?"

LaTanya said, "Well, sometimes you've got to be brave and risk that. Otherwise, we live in fear and hiding our entire lives."

Ryan said, "Well, we have several months to think about that. But

I'm leaning toward going to the prom, just like everyone else."

Mr. Perez said, "We're almost out of time. So, Ryan, you're going to see about getting a speaker from the Los Angeles LGBT Youth Project. Who wants to be on a committee to re-launch promoting the Ally stickers? Okay, Monique, Amber, Allyson, Raul, and Angelica. For the car wash idea, let's wait until after we hear the speaker. And don't forget Amber's invitation to the Super Bowl party at her house this Sunday at 3:00. Amber, what's your address?"

Amber gave her address and most of the kids jotted it down.

"Okay, good meeting! See you in two weeks."

The Super Bowl Party
Sunday, February 3, 2008

Thanks to his earnings from two porn shoots he did in January, Ryan was now the proud owner of a used but well-maintained Toyota Corolla. It had over 120,000 miles on it, but Hal advised Ryan that with Toyota's reputation for longevity, he could easily drive another 100,000 miles on it if he was diligent with the routine maintenance.

When Ryan turned the corner onto Amber's street at around 3:15, it was already lined with cars. He found a spot a block away. He knocked on the door and Amber's mother invited him in. He realized that he was among the last to arrive.

Amber's mother led him through the living room into the kitchen. Some of the kids were already gathering around a large flat-screen TV with plates full of party food. Ryan waved and several of them said hi. The kitchen island was loaded with chicken wings, vegetable trays, sliced sandwich wraps, potato chips, brownies, colorful cupcakes decorated with the Giants' logo and little footballs, and much more. Mrs. Stevens said, "Help yourself! There are sodas and water in the coolers out on the patio."

A dozen adults were claiming their seats around an even larger TV screen in the family room across from the kitchen. Ryan guessed it had to be at least 60 inches. He loaded up a plate with food, grabbed a soda, and headed back to the living room. All the cushioned seats on the sofa and side chairs had been claimed, so Ryan sat down on one of the last remaining folding patio chairs that had been added to the room for the occasion.

The kids watched the opening hoopla and listened to Jordin Sparks sing "The Star-Spangled Banner."

"Who's she?" Ryan asked.

The girls looked at him like he had just arrived from Mars. Allyson said, "Only, like, one of the hottest singers in America today. She won American Idol last year."

Amber added, "Her debut album is already platinum. She's been nominated for a Grammy." Implied but left unsaid was, 'Duh… I can't believe you don't know this stuff.'

"Oh. Okay." Ryan decided he should probably remain quiet on matters of current pop culture.

They watched the coin-toss and the kick-off. Once the game got underway, interest in the game waned. The kids started chatting in small groups and wandering into the kitchen for more food.

Ryan walked up to Raul. Raul turned to him and smiled. "Hey, man, who're you rooting for?"

"I don't know. I don't follow football. How 'bout you?"

"Giants all the way, man. I hate the Patriots. They're probably going to win, though. They're undefeated this year."

"Ah. Well, I'll cheer for the Giants too. Gotta root for the California teams!"

Raul looked at him funny. "Uh… the Giants are in New York."

"Really? I thought it was the San Francisco Giants."

Raul laughed. "That's baseball, man."

Ryan tried to shrug it off. "Oh, right. As I said, I don't follow football." *Pop culture, and now football. That makes two topics I need to shut up about, which is especially inconvenient since everyone is here to watch a football game. And whose brilliant idea was it to give teams in different cities the same name? Seems like the cities should decide on one mascot they'll use for everything and stick with it.*

Meanwhile, Payton was chatting with Mike. Neither of them was particularly interested in the football game. Payton said, "So, how well do you know Ryan?"

"Kinda well. We play in the jazz ensemble together. We have a couple of classes together. We've hung out a couple of times to listen to music."

"What kind of music does he like?"

"Jazz. All jazz, all the time."

"Oh." Payton knew nothing about jazz. "What's he like?"

"I don't know… he's nice. He's real smart. And very talented. He's a great trumpet player. He's kinda guarded, though. He doesn't share much about himself."

"Is he seeing anyone?"

"I don't know. I don't think so. Why don't you go ask him yourself?" Mike was tired of being interrogated about Ryan, but Payton didn't seem to take the hint.

"I dunno… I'm kinda scared."

"Scared of what? He's not going to bite you."

"I know, but…"

"Well, if you'll excuse me, I'm gonna go take a leak."

Payton wandered over to where Allyson was chatting with Amber and Monique. He hung around on the periphery and gradually inserted himself into their conversational group.

Allyson was saying, "Yeah, like they should totally get Justin Timberlake to sing the national anthem."

Amber said, "I don't know. He's already been part of the halftime show. Remember when he was part of that 'wardrobe malfunction' thing with Janet Jackson?"

Allyson said, "Do you think that was planned or not?"

Monique replied, "Probably. Look at all the publicity it got her."

Amber said, "How come they've never had Whitney Houston?"

Monique added, "Or Jennifer Lopez?"

Payton saw an opening. "I think they should get Lady Gaga."

Allyson laughed. "I can only imagine what kind of outfit she would wear."

There was a brief lull in their conversation. Payton whispered in Allyson's ear, "Can I talk to you for a sec?"

She glanced at her friends as if to say, 'I'll only be a moment.' Then she and Payton walked out onto the back patio. A couple of the men were out there drinking beers and talking football stuff.

Allyson said, "So what's up?" Her look said, 'make it quick.'

"Well, uh… So what do you think of Ryan?"

"I don't know. Band geek. Smart. Kinda nerdy. Kinda makes a big deal about being gay. But I dunno… He's alright, I guess. Why?"

"I kinda like him."

"Well, alrighty then. You're gay, he's gay, see what happens."

"Yeah, but how do you go about letting a guy know you're interested in him?"

"I don't know. Just make eye contact with him and smile. Hang around him and see if he notices you. Then go up and talk to him."

"About what?"

"Anything. It doesn't have to be important. In fact, it's better if it's not. Just make small talk. You'll be able to tell whether he's interested in keeping the conversation going. Don't put pressure on yourself. You'll get nervous and it'll be awkward."

"I don't know. I'm pretty nervous already."

"Then now's not a good time. Try not to worry about it. If it happens, it happens. If it doesn't, it doesn't. You can try again another time. And there are lots of other men."

"Yeah, but not very many other gay men."

"Yeah, I guess. Well, I need to get back to the party."

"Thanks."

Everyone returned to their seats as the first quarter came to a close, so they could watch the multi-million-dollar commercials that debuted as part of the Super Bowl spectacle. Once the second quarter got underway, most of the people dissociated themselves from the game and returned to socializing and grazing.

Ryan wandered out to the kitchen to get some more wings and mozzarella cheese sticks. They were cold by now, but they still tasted okay. They brought back memories of sitting in the car with Chris at Slush Fun. Ryan shook it off and walked out to the patio for another soda. He opened the cooler with the sodas and fished around in the icy water until he found a Dr Pepper.

He looked up and saw that Payton had followed him out to the cooler. "Hey, you want anything?"

"Yeah, another Dr Pepper if you can find one. Or else Coke."

Ryan found another Dr Pepper and handed it to Payton.

"Thanks. So…"

Ryan stood up, and now towered nine inches over Payton. "So…?"

Payton fought the urge to turn and run, and uttered the only thing he could think of. "Hi."

"Hi."

"So, uh, are you enjoying the game?"

"It's okay. I'm not really into football. As my band director at my last school used to say, they need to have football games to entertain the crowd before and after the marching band show."

Payton looked puzzled. "Yeah… uh… heh heh."

"Do you play an instrument?"

"No, uh… So, since you're so tall, do you play basketball?"

"Nah… I'm pretty much a klutz at anything involving a ball. I was on the track team at my last school, though."

"Oh, really?"

"Yeah. I can run pretty fast. And my long legs gave me an advantage when it came to the hurdles and the long jump."

"Yeah, I guess so."

"I won first place in the 300-meter hurdles at the state championship meet last year."

"Really? Wow!" Payton wasn't quite sure what 'the hurdles' were, but he wasn't about to let on. Whatever it was, first place in the state was pretty impressive.

"So… what are you into?"

"What do you mean?"

"What are you interested in? What do you do outside of school?"

"Well, I work in a grocery store. Other than that, I don't know. Video games, I guess."

"What store?"

"Fred's. The one on Wilshire Boulevard, near the school."

"Ah. I used to work at the Pure Foods in Westwood Village."

"What do you do now?"

"Well, uh… I'm working in the film industry."

"Oh, cool. What do you do?"

"Whatever they need me to do, I guess. I'm just getting started.

Well, hey, let's go back inside and join the others."

Mike had been watching this exchange take place from his vantage point in the kitchen. When he saw Ryan and Payton heading back inside, he took a few steps down the hallway toward the bathroom. After Ryan and Payton were back in the living room, he ducked out onto the patio and quietly let himself out through the gate at the side of the house.

The second quarter was almost over, and people were claiming seats to watch the halftime show. LaTanya and Angelica had been sitting on the sofa next to each other, watching the game with more interest than the other kids. Raul and Monique walked up to the sofa, and Raul said, "Hey, we can fit four on here. Can you scoot over a little bit?"

LaTanya was more than happy to oblige. Angelica scooted left a couple of inches until she was pressed up against the armrest, and LaTanya scooted in closer to Angelica. Their hips and thighs were now touching. Monique plopped down next to LaTanya, and Raul filled in the remaining space between Monique and the other armrest. He nonchalantly flung his left arm over the back of the sofa, not quite touching Monique – yet.

"Does anybody know who they're having for the halftime show this year?" asked Allyson.

LaTanya replied, "Some band called Tim Petty and the Heartaches, or something like that."

"Who are they?" asked Angelica.

Amber replied, "Some seventies band. I think my dad has some of their albums – you know, from back in the old days when they used to make vinyl records."

Monique asked, "Are they even relevant?"

Allyson took a couple of steps into the family room and came back. "Well, they're relevant to the older folks in the other room."

Ryan said, "What? Aren't they going to have a marching band?"

Everyone looked at Ryan like he had three heads.

Raul said, "Dude. They don't have marching bands at the Super Bowl."

"*What*?!?!? You can't have a football game without marching bands! It's just not proper."

For a moment, nobody said anything. Then Raul said, "Man, you're weird."

"It's un-American," Ryan said.

Everyone sat through the halftime performance, disappointed that one of their current popular stars wasn't performing. At least there were the commercials.

When the game got back underway, most of the people stayed in the living room and watched. No one was hungry anymore, and the game was still close. The undefeated Patriots were expected to make easy work of the 10-6 Giants, who had somehow managed to get into the playoffs as a wild card team and earn their way to the big game. But the Giants were keeping the game close. People were paying attention to the game. At one point, LaTanya slid her hand over a few inches and placed it on top of Angelica's. Angelica turned her hand over, palm side up, and they interlocked fingers. Raul's arm somehow found its way onto Monique's shoulder.

With less than three minutes to go, the Patriots were leading 14-10 when the Giants took over the ball on their own 17-yard line. Quarterback Eli Manning threw a pass to David Tyree, who leaped into the air and caught the ball between his hand and his helmet.

Both the living room and the family room erupted. Everyone leaped to their feet. Raul shouted, "Holy shit! Did you see that? Damn!" People relished every replay of that spectacular catch. The mood remained electric while the Giants completed their drive and scored the go-ahead touchdown with 35 seconds remaining. Even Ryan and Payton got caught up in the excitement and remained riveted to the screen during the final minutes.

After the game, things started winding down. Some people discussed their favorite commercials or their favorite plays of the game. Ryan looked around and noticed that Mike wasn't there. He was going to go look in the kitchen or the family room to see if he might be there, but Payton came up to him and asked, "So, where do you like to eat?"

"Oh, I'm not too picky. There's a place I like in Westwood called

My Gyro. It's Mediterranean food. But I like almost anything."

"You wanna go get something?"

"Now? Seriously? I'm stuffed."

"You wanna just get a soda at McDonald's or something?"

"Nah, I've had plenty of soda too. Maybe we can do something next weekend."

"Yeah. Okay."

"Or come sit with us at lunch."

Payton nodded.

Ryan said, "Okay, well, I'm gonna say my goodbyes and be on my way."

"Okay, well… bye. It was nice talking to you."

They looked at each other for a few seconds. Payton didn't move. He looked up at Ryan with a hopeful look in his eyes. Ryan bent down and gave him a quick hug. Payton smiled. Ryan turned to go find Amber's parents to thank them for the party.

Good News
Sunday, March 2, 2008

It was family night, and Ryan and his housemates were enjoying a delicious dinner of chili and jalapeno cornbread – one of the most consistently satisfying dishes in Hal's repertoire. As was customary, each of the men took a couple of minutes to update the others on what was going on in his life.

Ryan started. "Guys, I have some great news. I just got accepted into UCLA!"

Everyone put their forks down and applauded.

"Of course, I still don't know how I'm going to pay for it. I'm still waiting to hear about my scholarship and financial aid applications."

Ricky said, "Don't worry. When your videos start coming out, you'll start getting lots more calls. You'll have all the work you can handle."

Hal said, "I'm sure you'll figure it out. I'm thrilled that everything is working out for you. I know it's been your dream to go there."

Ted said, "And speaking of which, I just got accepted into the Master's program for International Business! So it will be two more years of school for me."

Ted basked in another round of applause.

Ryan said, "That's awesome, man. Congratulations! Does that mean you'll continue to live here?"

"I hope so. Unless you guys kick me out to make room for some hot young twink."

Darnell replied, "That's okay, we already have one of those."

Ricky added, "But you can never have enough."

Ted replied, "That certainly seems to be your motto."

"And your point is…?"

Hal said, "Okay, okay. Ted, of course you can stay. I don't think I've ever had a grad student living here before."

That made Ryan happy.

Then Darnell spoke up. "But wait! There's more! My dears, I have a special announcement to make!"

Everyone put their forks down. They were accustomed to Darnell's flair for the dramatic, but tonight Darnell was beaming with pride. Something special was about to happen. Everyone looked at Darnell with anticipation.

"It is with great pleasure that I announce that Miss Whitney Austin has been selected to perform at the prestigious annual gala benefitting the Los Angeles LGBTDQ Youth Project!"

All the other guys showered Darnell with applause.

Ryan said, "Wait a minute. Did you just say LGBT*DQ*?"

"That's right, dear. Lesbian, Gay, Bisexual, Transgender, and Drag Queen!"

Ted said, "Good thing you clarified. I thought you meant Drama Queen."

Darnell placed the back of his hand against his forehead and let out a loud sigh of mock exasperation. "Oh, the indignities I must suffer at the hands of my entourage!"

Ted said, "But seriously, that's fantastic. I know Whitney will bring the house down!"

Hal said, "That segues nicely into what I have to say. This year, the gala is on Saturday, May 17th. As always, I have purchased a table for ten, so of course, you're all invited. Let me know in the next couple of days if you can or can't go and if you'd like to bring a guest."

Darnell turned to Ricky and said, "Hopefully you can dig up something better than that skank you brought along last year."

Ricky rolled his eyes.

Ryan said, "I assume there's a story."

Darnell slipped into his catty queen persona. "I'll say. Miss Thang here showed up with some banger from the barrio he probably met when he was dancing on some pole and… well, let's just say he was nice to look at and he had the good sense to keep his mouth shut most of the time. But as people started leaving, he went around to the empty tables and finished off all the drinks people left behind."

Ricky buried his head in his hands.

Ted said to Ricky, "I bet you danced on his pole later that night."

Ricky glanced dismissively at Ted and said, "I plead the fifth."

Hal said, "Girls, girls! Retract the claws, please."

Ryan said, "This is great! Now I'll finally get to see you perform."

Darnell corrected him. "You'll get to see *Whitney* perform. But yes. It will be a condensed version since I'll only have twenty minutes instead of my usual hour. But you'll get the general idea."

"Cool. So, what's this banquet like?"

Hal replied, "It's a pretty high-class affair. There will be around two hundred tables, so about two thousand people. A lot of wealthy, influential people in the community – both LGBT and otherwise – will be there. There will be a few speeches by dignitaries and they'll give out some awards. And they have entertainment such as the now internationally-famous Whitney Austin. But the real purpose, of course, is to raise money for the Youth Project."

Darnell said, "You neglected to mention the best part – a sumptuous gourmet chicken dinner, prepared by world-famous French chefs just for you – and 2,000 of your closest friends."

Ryan got wide-eyed. "Really???"

"No, silly. Rubber chicken prepared by the hotel staff. But it's elegantly presented with frou-frou garnishes and table decorations to die for!"

Hal said, "The meal isn't the point. The point is to raise money. Also to see and be seen, which reminds me – we'll need to take you out and get you a nice suit to wear."

Darnell added, "And you'll need to go someplace nicer than Cross Dress for Less."

Ted said, "Something tells me you're familiar with that place."

Darnell put a finger to his lip. "Shhhhh…"

Ryan said, "I think I might have someone to come along. I'll have to ask him to be sure."

Everyone stopped eating. Darnell said, "Oh, really? And who might this be?"

Ryan said, "Well… I've been kinda seeing this guy in my GSA group at school for the past month or so."

Darnell asked, "Do tell! Does he have a name?"

"Payton."

"As in Peyton Place or Payton Manning?"

Ryan looked puzzled.

"Never mind, dear. I'm happy for you!"

Ricky asked, "So have you sampled the merchandise yet?"

Ryan feigned indignation. "Please! He's not merchandise. Besides, he's still dealing with coming out. I don't think he'll be ready for that for a while."

"OOOooo! Maybe you can be the one to pop his ass-cherry!"

"Really? Do you ever think of anything besides sex?"

"Hmmm…" Ricky paused for a moment. "No."

Hal said, "Well, let me know within a week or so, okay? So I'll know how many other people to invite."

"Okay, thanks."

The Truth Will Set You Free
Sunday, May 4, 2008

Saturday, May 3, marked exactly three months since Ryan and Payton had started dating. Payton seemed more eager than usual to get together with Ryan on that day. Ryan had a shoot scheduled for Saturday, so he told Payton he had to work, but he could get together on Sunday.

They started the day with brunch at Eggstravagance. Ryan half expected to see Skyler there, which could have been awkward – but he wasn't. Still, Ryan recalled that brunch and how they had ended up in Ryan's bedroom afterward. He remembered how Skyler had pressured him into having sex, only to have it screech to an abrupt halt when Ryan didn't have condoms. After that day, Ryan bought a box of condoms and kept them in his nightstand drawer. They had yet to be used, and Ryan wasn't sure he wanted today to be the day that would change.

While they waited for their food, Payton asked, "Is everything okay?"

"Yeah. Why?"

"It seems like your mind is off somewhere else."

"Yeah, it kinda is. Sorry."

"What were you thinking about?"

"The last time I was in here. It was sometime in October. I was having brunch with this guy I met at my bank – the guy who opened my account. He acted really friendly to me and he wanted to get together, so we came here. It's funny… when we walked in the door, I wondered if I would see him in here."

"Is he here?"

"No. It was pretty unlikely, but you never know."

"So what happened with him?"

"Nothing. I mean, he was friendly and cute, but we didn't have that much in common. Later I figured out that he was more interested in hooking up than dating."

"You mean, like, for sex?"

"That's what I mean."

"So did you?"

"We went part of the way, but then we stopped. It was way too fast. I mean, it was the first date. Well, we had gotten together one other time for coffee. But that was only for like 15 minutes, so that didn't really count as a date."

The waiter delivered their food and they dug in. After a couple of minutes, Payton asked, "So have you done it?"

"Done what?"

"You know."

"Uh, we're in a restaurant. There are people around."

"Nobody's paying any attention. We'll keep our voices down."

"Well, yes. I had a boyfriend last summer, back where I used to live. We went all the way once."

"How was it?"

"Unbelievable. It's hard to describe. I mean, I had no idea it would be so intense. When you're with the right person, at the right time, it's incredible."

"So how come you only did it once?"

"I had to run away, remember? When my parents found out I was gay and we were boyfriends, they grounded me and I couldn't see him anymore."

"Oh, that's right. Sorry."

He had to bring that up.

After a moment passed, Payton asked, "So what about us?"

"What about us?"

"That's what I asked. We've been together for three months now. Actually, it was three months yesterday."

"Oh, yeah, that's right. We kinda got started at that Super Bowl party."

"Yeah. Anyway, I really like you. And we have fun hanging out together."

"And we're going to the prom next weekend!"

"Yeah. I'm still kinda nervous about that."

"It'll be okay."

"Do we have to dance?"

"We can play it by ear. We'll see what the vibe is like."

"Okay. But anyway, getting back to us. I was thinking maybe we could start, uh, getting a little more serious. You know, start taking things a little farther."

"You mean going beyond kissing."

"Yeah."

Ryan paused. He knew this topic was going to come up. But now, right here in a restaurant? It wasn't so much that he didn't want to have sex with Payton, but he dreaded having to disclose the related information. And he didn't want anyone at school to find out, including Payton.

"Can we talk about this more when we get back to my place?"

"Okay."

"So what are you going to do this summer?"

"Probably just try to get more hours at the store. What about you?"

"I'm going to stay with what I'm doing now. I want to try to get out and see some stuff around town, too. It's like I've lived here for almost a year, but I've been so busy with school and band and work, I haven't had time for anything."

"Yeah, we can do stuff when we have days off together."

"I'd really like to go to Disneyland. I've wanted to go to Disneyland all my life."

"Well, it's packed in the summer. That's when the tourists from everywhere else come to see it – that and over Christmas. The best times to go are in the spring and fall. Same thing with Universal and Magic Mountain and Knott's Berry Farm."

"So what's good to do during the summer?"

"I dunno. Hangin' out in your pool would be fun. We can get in naked, right?"

"Yeah, if you don't mind any of the other guys seeing you if they happen to come out."

"They're all gay, right?"

"Yeah." Ryan wanted to go see things around town, not stay home.

The waiter came and cleared their table and left the check. They figured out how to split it, paid, and left.

When they got back to the house, Ryan said, "You want to take a walk around the neighborhood or campus?"

"I'd rather hang out in your room."

"Okay." As Ryan led Payton back to his room, he could tell Payton was getting excited about what might happen next.

Once they were in the room with the door closed, Payton stepped up to Ryan and placed his arms around him. "Three months! I think that's something to celebrate!" He stretched upward toward Ryan's face and started kissing him on the side of his neck. Ryan leaned down so their lips could meet and they kissed some more. Payton hugged him tighter as their tongues explored each other's mouths.

After a minute, Payton started working his hand inside Ryan's polo shirt, pushing it upward. "It's getting warm in here. I think it might get hotter."

Ryan and Payton had kissed on several occasions in the past, but this was the first time clothes started to come off. Payton unfastened Ryan's belt. When he reached down inside Ryan's pants, he let out a gasp. "Uh… is that for real?"

"Yep." Ryan hated these 'My God, you've got a huge dick' moments. That was usually communicated silently via stares in the locker room or occasionally in the eyes of a co-star he had been paired with. *Yes, it's that big. It's what I was born with. Now can we move on?* On the other hand, it was helping him finance his college education.

Payton lowered himself to his knees and slid Ryan's underwear and pants down simultaneously. Ryan's rapidly hardening cock sprang out and smacked Payton's chin.

"My God, you've got a huge dick!"

"Yeah, I guess so."

Payton stared at Ryan's manhood growing larger in front of his eyes. He started stroking it. "Wow. That's amazing."

Ryan was used to that kind of commentary on the set, but there it was said for the sake of the audio track. In this scenario, it seemed decidedly unromantic. Ryan gently placed his hand on the back of Payton's head. He took the hint. Ryan figured he wouldn't be able to talk with his mouth full.

Soon, they were lying on the bed completely naked, sixty-nining. Inevitably, the moment of truth arrived.

Payton said, "I'm not sure I'm going to be able to take all that."

"You don't have to put it all in. Just do what's comfortable. Or you can fuck me."

"Yeah, but I want to at least try it."

Ryan reached for the drawer in his nightstand and pulled out the box of condoms, lube, and a hand towel.

Payton asked, "Do we need to use those? It's not like you're going to get me pregnant."

"Yes, we really should. To prevent the spread of HIV."

Payton looked alarmed. "Do you have HIV?"

"No, in fact, I got tested last week. Negative."

"Well, it's my first time, so I don't have it. So we don't need to use them. It'll feel a lot better without them."

"I'd still feel more comfortable if we did."

Payton was starting to get suspicious. "So, you said you and your boyfriend did it last summer. Did you use condoms?"

"No, actually, we didn't. But we probably should have."

"So has there been anybody else?"

"Yeah, there have been a few others."

"Well, okay, but at least that's in the past." Payton leaned in and kissed Ryan on the cheek. He gazed into Ryan's eyes and whispered, "Will you promise me that I'll be the only one from now on?"

Ryan took a deep breath. *Here goes.* "No, I can't make that promise."

Payton sat upright. "Why not? Are you seeing other guys too?"

"Not as in dating."

"What do you mean?"

"Okay, look. We need to talk." Ryan got up, pulled his desk chair closer to the side of the bed, and sat down on it. He pointed to the side of the bed and said, "You sit here." Payton looked confused and a bit angry. "Okay, so I know I've been kind of vague about the kind of work I do in the film industry. The truth is, I star in adult films."

"You mean, like, R-rated? Stuff that's not for children?"

"I mean porn. Gay porn, to be specific."

"You mean, you like take your clothes off–"

"I fuck other guys. On camera. For X-rated videos that they sell in adult bookstores and by mail and online."

"They actually pay people to do that?"

"Yes, a lot. A hell of a lot. It's how I'm going to pay for college. That's the only reason I'm doing it."

"So every time you say you have to work–"

"I'm going somewhere to shoot a scene for a video in which I fuck another guy."

"So, like yesterday–"

"Yes, I fucked a guy just yesterday. Two, in fact. It's what I need to do to support myself. Remember, I don't have parents. I'm out on my own. I have to cover all my expenses and save money for college. I can't quit my porn career just because we're dating."

"Can't you get a regular job?"

"Not one that pays well enough. I worked at Pure Foods last fall. I worked all the hours I could get. I found out that I could barely scrape by with a part-time job that pays $10 an hour, and I sure couldn't save money for college. Or afford a car, for that matter."

Payton stared down at the floor, frowning. Then he stood up and started putting his clothes back on as fast as he could.

"I can't believe you did this to me."

"Did what to you?"

"You lied to me. You led me on. I thought we were a couple. I thought you were only interested in me."

"I never once lied to you. And I am only interested in you. I'm not interested in those guys I have sex with. I don't even know them."

"Why didn't you tell me until now?"

"We weren't doing anything together. You didn't need to know until now. Besides, I don't want it to get around school. I want to keep my work and school separate."

"Well, maybe you didn't lie to me, but you sure didn't tell me the truth. How can I ever trust you again?"

"It's just a job. We're just bodies doing things for other people's fantasies. It doesn't mean anything."

"It means something to me. It means you're a whore. A cheap, dirty whore."

"Now wait a minute…"

"No. You get paid for having sex. With strangers. Last time I checked, someone who gets paid for having sex is a whore. Well, I'm not interested in dating a whore."

By this time, Payton was fully dressed. He stormed toward the door. He turned back toward Ryan and said, "You're a cheap, disgusting, filthy whore!" He slammed the door behind him, ran to the front door, let himself out, and slammed it too.

"I guess that means we won't be going to the prom," Ryan said to no one.

***

After Ryan stopped crying, he decided that perhaps floating on a raft in the pool might put him in a better mood. It was a beautiful day, and the fresh air and cool water would be good.

As he passed through the kitchen on the way to the pool, he saw Ricky.

Ricky said, "Hey, man, what was that all about?"

Ryan sighed. "I just got called a whore by my now ex-boyfriend when he found out I do porn."

"Aw, man, that sucks. Well, some people just can't deal with it. That's their problem. Fuck him."

"I didn't get to. We were about to, then he found out."

"Sorry."

"So, how do you deal with this? How do you handle dating?"

"I guess I'm not really into dating. I'm having too much fun just playin' around. But anyway, I don't hide what I do. Pretty much everyone knows what I do, and whenever I meet someone new, they find out pretty quickly. And they're either okay with it or they're not, and that's their choice. It's not my problem."

"Yeah, okay. Thanks." *That wasn't too helpful. What am I supposed to do? I can't imagine introducing myself by saying, 'Hi, I'm Ryan, and I'm a porn star.'*

Ryan opened the sliding glass door, stepped out, and turned around to close it. Ricky called out, "Forget about him. He wasn't the one. Don't worry, the right one is out there for you somewhere. Just keep lookin'."

The right one is back in Prairie Village, but is there any hope for that?

He selected a raft, threw it in the pool, and lowered himself in. He climbed up on the raft and closed his eyes.

Payton wasn't Mr. Right. He was just Mr. Right Now. But at least he was someone, and someone was better than no one. But now, I'm back to no one.

Salacious Gossip

Monday, May 5, 2008

Monday morning at school, something seemed strange, although Ryan couldn't quite tell what it was. As he walked through the hallways between classes, it seemed like everyone was looking at him. He decided he was probably imagining things.

But at lunch, as he was making his way through the cafeteria to the table where he and his friends usually sat, he heard someone call out, "Lookout! It's Dongzilla!" A couple of other voices let out 'OOOooo…'s and he heard several fake gasps of panic. Others were giggling or laughing out loud.

He thought, *What the heck? Dongzilla? What's that about? Is it about me?*

Then he passed another table, and someone called out, "Lights! Camera! ACTION!" which was followed by more laughter. *Payton. Payton's been telling everyone about yesterday. That little shit. Who else could it be?*

He made it to his table and sat down. His friends could see the anger and embarrassment on his face.

LaTanya said, "What was that all about?"

Ryan sighed. He took a few moments to regain his composure and figure out how he was going to explain this to his friends. He took a deep breath. "Okay, so first of all, Payton and I are no longer an item. We got together yesterday to celebrate three months together. We were having brunch at Eggstravagance. And then right there in the restaurant, he starts talking about maybe it's time we, you know, took things to the next level. You know, physically. So anyway, we went to my place after that, and he started coming on to me. And we started gettin' into it, y'know, and then when we got naked and he saw my… well, let's just say it's kinda big. So that kinda surprised him, but we went on. And then right when it got to the point where we're about to go all the way, he said, 'Will you promise I'll be the only one?'"

Ryan looked around the table. He held everyone's rapt attention. He glanced around at the nearby tables to make sure other people weren't eavesdropping. Then he lowered his voice and said, "Anyway, there's something else I need to tell you. So, you know last fall I was working at Pure Foods? And I was putting in all these hours, but I wasn't making that much money. And I need to save for college and everything, so I needed to find something that would make me more money." He paused and took a breath. Here goes. "So, I starting doing porn."

LaTanya, Angelica, and Mike looked stunned and said nothing. Raul exclaimed, "Dude!" and raised his hand to high-five Ryan. That wasn't what Ryan wanted to high-five someone for, but he half-heartedly raised his hand and lightly slapped Raul's hand.

"Yeah, so anyway, obviously I couldn't promise Payton that he'll be the only one. So things pretty much went off the rails at that point. I mean, he totally lost his shit. Then he said some pretty mean things to me and stormed out the door. Now it looks like he's told half the school about it."

LaTanya said, "Well, I'm no fan of pornography, but that was a shitty thing for him to do." Everyone nodded in agreement.

Raul said, "So what's it like?"

Ryan said, "It's a job. It's work. It's not all about getting laid. It's not really fun."

LaTanya said, "I'm still tryin' to wrap my head around this. That doesn't seem like something you would do."

"Yeah, I didn't think it was something I would do, either. I went back and forth on it a lot. Finally, it came down to this: I need the money for college. I mean, I'll be getting some financial aid, but that'll only cover about half of it. Or I could get a student loan, but then I'd graduate being like $30,000 in debt. Or I could go to a community college, which would cost a lot less, but I'd still have to make more money than I was making at Pure Foods. So yeah, I'm only doing it for the money."

Mike asked, "Does it really pay that well?"

"You'd be surprised. It's how I was able to buy my car. I've already saved enough to cover my first semester. Anyway, now I get to look forward to being called names and getting a lot of attention for something I'd rather not get attention for."

LaTanya said, "Just let it go in one ear and out the other. Hell, I get called names all the time. LezTanya, Latrina, Lasagna…"

"Lasagna?"

"Yeah, I heard that one last week. I'm like, whatever. If they have to call me names, I guess being called a tasty pasta dish is a lot better than the other stuff."

Angelica said, "Maybe they could call you LaTanya."

"I know, right? But anyway, you can't stop 'em, but you can ignore 'em. I just let it slide right off. They're really putting themselves down, not me."

Ryan said, "Yeah, I guess so. But it still hurts. It's like why should I have to deal with this?"

"I refuse to let mean people ruin my day. Anyway, I'm sorry about you and Payton."

"Thanks. It's okay. I mean, it probably wasn't going to last anyway. We'll be going off in different directions next year and we didn't have that much in common."

Everyone was finished with their lunch and the bell would ring in a couple of minutes. So they got up and took their trays to the conveyor that would transport their dirty dishes through a small opening into obscurity.

Mike and Ryan were in the same class next, so they walked down the hall together.

Ryan said, "I know this is kinda short notice, but since Payton and I are over, you want to go to the prom with me this Saturday? I already bought the tickets."

"You mean like be your date?"

"Yeah. I mean, we'd just be going as friends, but yeah. LaTanya and Angelica are going, and so are Raul and Monique, so you'll have your friends there. It'll be fun. And we're going to dinner beforehand."

"Let me think about it."

"Okay. I know, now that I'm Dongzilla the porn star, you may not want to be seen with me."

"It's not that. You're my friend. Those idiots are not."

"Thanks. I really appreciate that."

"I'm just not sure I'm ready to be out to the whole school yet."

"I get it. Well, remember, we only have a month to go. After that, you'll be off to Stanford and you won't have to deal with these low-lifes anymore. Does it matter much at this point?"

"I guess not. But let me think about it. And I have to ask my parents."

"Okay, cool. And if you're not comfortable with it, I understand."

"I'll let you know tomorrow."

***

The next day, Mike informed Ryan that, yes, he would go with him to the prom.

May I Have This Dance?
Saturday, May 10, 2008

At 5:30, Ryan drove to Mike's house to pick him up for dinner before the prom. At the same time, Raul was driving his sister Angelica to pick up LaTanya and Monique. The two cars arrived at Al Fresco's Italian Ristorante about ten minutes before their 6:00 reservation.

Arriving at a consensus on where to eat among six people with varying tastes, diets, and budgets had been a challenge, but the group was able to agree on Italian. Al Fresco's had a lovely outdoor dining area in the back, adorned with bougainvillea and roses and illuminated with overhead light strings and tastefully placed colored accent lights. Hal had recommended this place to Ryan. The others looked at the menu and pictures on the restaurant's website, but none of them had ever been here before. For the lower-middle-class kids at the table, this was their first time in a restaurant this nice. Their nervousness about seeming out of place was offset by their anticipation of what they hoped would be a special, memorable evening.

Mike was especially nervous, for another reason. With a hushed voice, he asked, "Do you think we'll be okay here? I mean, everyone else looks so... straight. And older."

Ryan said, "We'll be fine. There are three girls and three guys. Nobody will know how we're paired up. Besides, we're the nicest dressed people in here."

At a few minutes before six, they were seated at a round table in the back garden. Once they had ordered and started enjoying their salads and the freshly baked Italian bread dipped in oil, their nervousness and apprehension faded and the dinner took on a more celebratory mood. For Ryan, Mike, LaTanya, and Angelica, the opportunity to enjoy a special evening with a same-sex companion was liberating. They felt like they could finally have a place in the world and enjoy the same niceties as their straight counterparts.

After a busboy cleared away their salad plates, their waiter and another server delivered their entrées. The presentation was perfect and everything looked delicious. An instant before the eager, hungry teens started digging into their food, Ryan said, "Wait! Let's get a picture!"

He stood up and summoned their waiter, then fished his smartphone out of his pocket. "Would you take a picture of us?"

The waiter, being accustomed to such requests, agreed. The softer lighting of the early evening was ideal for a good photo.

The prom began at eight, and the group arrived moments after the doors opened. As they entered, a few of the parent chaperones looked surprised. The kids who were already there noticed their arrival and frowned. The upbeat, relaxed vibe they had enjoyed at dinner evaporated and was replaced by an uncomfortable sense of foreboding. Mike leaned toward Ryan and said, "I'm not sure if this was such a good idea."

Ryan felt self-conscious and insecure himself, but said, "Well, let's give it some time and see how it goes."

LaTanya, who always claimed that she would proudly do her own thing without caring about what other people thought, seemed uncharacteristically nervous. "Let's go hang out over at the far end until more people get here."

As more people arrived, there was less focus on the two guys and two girls standing off to the side. Mike and Ryan weren't a couple, just good friends, but they were still each other's date to the prom. They stood a foot or so apart because it seemed more comfortable. LaTanya and Angelica avoided holding hands and any other gestures that might signal they were a couple. Raul and Monique were circulating among some of their other friends.

Ryan glanced at the entrance and saw Jordan, Julio, and Connor enter. Apparently, none of them were able to secure dates for the evening. Under his breath, Ryan uttered, "Shit."

Mike looked over at him. "What?"

Ryan sighed. "Nothing." *I'm not going to let them ruin this evening.*

As the crowd approached critical mass, more people started dancing. For the first hour, Ryan, Mike, LaTanya, and Angelica circulated around the perimeter, sometimes chatting with others for a few moments. They were still apprehensive about venturing out onto the dance floor for fear of causing a scene.

At one point, Ryan excused himself to go to the restroom. When he entered, Miguel, Amber's date, was standing at the first urinal. Ryan left the customary one-urinal gap and stepped up to the third urinal.

Seconds later, Julio and Connor entered the restroom snickering. Ryan immediately tensed up. They stepped up to the second and fourth urinals.

Ryan glanced at them warily. "What's up with you guys? Get the sudden urge to pee?"

Connor grinned and said, "We were hoping we could get a look at that *big dick*!" He and Julio leaned their heads slightly over the barely sufficient dividers. Ryan hadn't started peeing yet, so he reeled his dick back into his pants as quickly as he could and zipped up. As he walked toward one of the stalls, he said, "If you want to see my big dick, buy my movies." He closed the stall door and latched it behind him.

Julio entered the stall next to Ryan, got down on his knees, and started to poke his head underneath the stall wall.

Ryan said, "Don't even think about it. If I see your head under there, I'll piss on it."

Miguel called out, "C'mon guys, leave him alone." Julio got up and backed out of the stall. Miguel said, "Down on your knees in a bathroom stall? Really? How gay is *that*?"

Connor, Julio, and Miguel left the restroom. When Ryan finished and exited, Miguel was hanging around outside the door. Ryan said, "Hey, thanks, man."

"No problem, man. Those guys are assholes." Miguel stepped a little closer to Ryan and whispered, "Hey uh… if you ever need a bro to … y'know … help ya out…" he winked and glanced down at Ryan's crotch, "hit me up, okay?"

It took a moment for Ryan to contemplate how he should respond. He settled on, "Later, dude," and walked away. He found Mike, LaTanya, and Angelica over on the far side of the gym, where they had spent much of the evening.

Mike looked up at him. "What's wrong, man?"

"Nothing. I just had a couple of really bizarre encounters. I'll tell you later." Ryan hoped Mike would forget about it and he wouldn't have to tell him later.

Ten minutes later, Raul and Monique left the dance floor and walked over to where the four gay kids were standing. Raul asked, "Why aren't you out there dancing?"

They looked at each other, waiting for someone else to say something. Lady Gaga's "Just Dance" started playing, so Raul grabbed his sister's hand and motioned for her and LaTanya to come out on the dance floor. Monique looked at the two guys and said, "You can dance with me," and led them out onto the floor. At first, they looked uncomfortable and awkward, unsure if they should really be doing this. Monique said, "Come on! You heard what Lady Gaga said. Just dance!"

The DJ transitioned into Britney Spears' "Heaven on Earth," and the six of them continued to dance in a cluster. A couple of other kids without dates joined them, and then a couple more. Soon, it was just a big mixed group of kids dancing with no discernable pairings. Ryan, LaTanya, and Angelica got over their self-consciousness quickly. They smiled with the joy of finally getting to dance just like the other kids. It felt like heaven on earth. It took Mike a couple more songs to get over his apprehensiveness, but he gradually relaxed and started getting into it.

Then the DJ switched to David Archuleta's "Crush," a slow dance. About half of the kids left the floor, including the single kids and some of the couples who wanted a breather. The remaining dancers took their partners in their arms and began slow dancing. LaTanya and Angelica paused for a moment to consider what they would do next. LaTanya stepped closer to Angelica, took her in her arms, and began dancing with her. Although Ryan and Mike weren't a couple, Ryan didn't want to leave them alone on the floor at this critical moment. He grabbed Mike, and before Mike could protest, he pulled him close and started dancing with him. With a height difference of 16 inches, they made a comical sight. But the height difference wasn't what most of the other kids were staring at.

Ryan looked around. Most of the other couples who were still on the floor had stopped dancing and were staring in disbelief at the sight of two same-sex couples dancing together. LaTanya and Angelica were totally absorbed in each other and either didn't notice or didn't care. Either way, they were determined to have their moment. Mike stared straight into Ryan's chest to avoid having to see what was happening around him. He trembled in fear. Ryan felt the stares of hundreds of eyeballs, but he kept dancing. Nobody said anything or approached the two couples, but everyone was anxiously waiting to see what might happen next.

Allyson and Amber glanced at each other and nodded. They separated from their dates, walked to an open spot within a few feet of the two couples, and started dancing with each other. Their dates were initially perplexed, but then they realized this was a show of support. They awkwardly stepped into each other's arms and began dancing. Then several other kids paired up into same-sex couples and joined them. Many of the other opposite-sex couples who had stopped to witness this scene went back to dancing together as if nothing was wrong.

Raul and Monique took a break so she and a couple of her friends could visit the restroom. While he waited, Raul walked up to Jordan, Julio, and Connor and said hi. Jordan was fuming. "Jesus fucking Christ. It was bad enough that they crashed the prom in the first place, but now they're turning it into a fucking gay pride dance!"

Raul frowned at him. "Dude, that's my sister you're talking about. And it's their prom too. They should be able to enjoy it like everyone else."

Julio said, "I think lesbians are hot. But two guys doin' it? That's just wrong."

"Chill, dude. They're just dancing. They're not fucking."

Jordan said, "So you're on their side now? What, are you turning queer too?"

"There's no need for sides. And I'll stick with Monique. But as a matter of fact, we had dinner with them earlier this evening. We had a great time. They're really nice."

"Yeah, well if they're gonna be queer, they can at least keep it to themselves. Why do they have to come here and ruin it for the rest of us? I mean, two guys dancing together? That's fucking disgusting."

With his right hand, Raul grabbed Jordan's left wrist and yanked him a few steps out onto the dance floor. Jordan sputtered, "Dude! What're you tryin' to do, man?"

Raul turned and faced Jordan and adjusted his firm hold on his wrist. With his left hand, he grabbed Jordan's right wrist and extended it out like they were dancing.

"No way, man! No way I'm dancing with a dude."

Raul replied, "Hmmm… actually, it would appear that you are."

Raul was bigger and stronger than Jordan and his grip on Jordan's wrists was so tight that Jordan realized he couldn't escape. Jordan planted his feet on the floor, but Raul swayed back and forth in front of him in an attempt to dance. "Dude, you dance like shit. No wonder you couldn't get a date for tonight."

"Let go, mother fucker!" Jordan suddenly shook himself in an attempt to break free, but Raul gripped him even harder. "Ouch! Man, that hurts."

Raul said, "Man up, dude. It's just one dance. It's not gonna make you gay."

"Yeah. Sorry to disappoint you."

Raul stared into Jordan's face and said, "Listen, asswipe. You've done some shitty things to Ryan. Why don't you try being nice to him for a change?"

Jordan stood there and stewed. He glanced over at Julio and Connor, who were laughing at him and taking pictures.

The song ended, and Raul let go of Jordan's wrists. Jordan started to throw a punch at him, but Raul intercepted it, grabbed Jordan's wrist again, and twisted it. Jordan winced in pain. Raul said, "I'd think twice if I were you." He let go.

Jordan glared at Raul, then turned and stormed off the dance floor.

Monique had returned from the restroom. She witnessed most of the scene that had just taken place. She walked up to Raul, planted a big kiss on his cheek, and smiled. Raul took her hand and led her out to the center of the floor to dance with the others.

Jordan retreated like a scolded puppy with its tail between its legs to the spot where he had been hanging out with his buds for most of the evening. Julio and Connor were grinning from ear to ear and trying their hardest not to crack up.

For one awkward moment, nobody said anything.

Then Connor said, "Did he ask for your phone number?"

Julio and Connor started laughing and Jordan's face turned redder.

Julio stopped laughing long enough to ask, "And did you give it to him?" They high-fived.

"Very funny, douchenozzles."

Connor turned to Julio and said, "I dunno. I think he kinda liked it. That Raul is so manly! So strong and forceful."

Julio said to Jordan, "I didn't know you liked it rough." Connor and Julio snickered some more.

"Fuck you!" Jordan snarled. "Fuck you both. And if any of those pictures show up anywhere on the internet, I will literally kill you."

Connor said, "Oh, calm down. At least you got to dance with someone."

Jordan replied, "Which is more than I can say for you two losers. C'mon, let's get out of here. This dance is lame."

Ryan, Mike, LaTanya, Angelica, Raul, Monique, and several of their other friends danced for the rest of the evening, feeling liberated now that the barrier of opposite-sex-only dancing had been broken and most people didn't seem to care. It was the first time all year Ryan felt like a normal high school kid like everyone else.

The last dance ended and the lights came on. Students started making their way to the door, sometimes stopping for quick photos with their friends. Ryan, Mike, LaTanya, Angelica, Raul, and Monique all took pictures of each other in varying combinations. They found someone else to take a few pictures of all six of them. Tired but elated, they were among the last to head out the door and to the parking lot.

After hugs and goodbyes, LaTanya, Angelica, Raul, and Monique approached Raul's car as he clicked the Unlock button on the remote. Ryan and Mike walked past their car to Ryan's car, which was parked a few spaces beyond Raul's.

Ryan and Mike froze when his car came into view. Someone had scratched 'FAG' on his car doors with a key.

The Children Are Our Future
Saturday, May 17, 2008

On the day of the banquet, Ryan showered and put on his suit. He took a moment to admire himself in his full-length mirror and made a mental note to ask one of his buddies to take his picture. He fidgeted with his tie knot until it looked just right, then ran a couple of fingers through his hair to give it that tousled-just-right look.

He texted Mike to ask if he was ready. He was, so Ryan made the quick trip to pick Mike up and bring him back to the house.

Ryan and Mike entered through the front door and walked into the family room. They were greeted by whistles and catcalls from his housemates and several of Hal's friends who would be joining them at the banquet. Everyone was enjoying a pre-banquet cocktail. Hal offered Ryan and Mike a lemon drop martini, which Ryan gladly accepted and Mike politely declined.

Mike whispered to Ryan, "They let you drink?"

"Yeah, now and then, like once a month or so."

Ryan introduced Mike to his housemates and the guests. Hal introduced his friends to everyone.

Ted strolled up to Ryan. "Well, you clean up nicely."

Ryan smiled. "You look quite handsome yourself. Dignified, even!"

"Oh, I wouldn't go that far."

Ryan pulled his phone out of his pocket. "I would. Can I take your picture?"

"Sure." Ted smiled, and Ryan captured a good photo. It was nice to see Ted smile. He usually looks so serious and a little sad.

Then Ryan asked, "Would you mind taking a few pictures of me?"

Ted took the phone, then took a few steps back and attempted to fit all of Ryan's 6'6" body into the frame. "Can you take a couple more steps back, please? … Okay."

"With or without the drink?"

"With. Or how about one each way." Click, click. "Okay, now a headshot." He moved in closer and snapped a nice headshot. "Now, how about a couple with Mike." Mike stepped up next to Ryan. Their height difference of over a foot looked a little awkward, so Ryan leaned down so his head was next to Mike's. Ted took a couple of close-ups, then handed the phone back to Ryan.

Ryan handed the phone to Mike. "Would you take a couple pictures of Ted and me?" Ryan stood close enough to Ted that their heads were only a few inches apart. They both smiled beautifully. Mike gave the phone back to Ryan, and Ryan reviewed the photos in the camera roll. Perfect – especially the ones with him and Ted.

Ricky walked past. "That's probably the most pictures you've ever had taken with your clothes on."

"Bitch! But even though I hate you, let me take your picture."

Ricky posed. Ryan counted, "3… 2… 1…" At the moment Ryan pushed the button, Ricky puckered his lips and blew Ryan an air kiss.

"How sweet. Now, just smile."

Ricky smiled and Ryan took another picture.

Mike wasn't quite sure what to make of the rapport between Ryan and his housemates, but he decided to just go with it.

They mingled with the guests for fifteen minutes or so, then Hal called out, "The limo is here. All aboard!"

Everyone finished their drinks, then filed outside and into the limo. Ryan had never seen the inside of a limo before, let alone ridden in one. There was a mini-bar inside, with glasses and a selection of bottled water, sodas, mixers, wine, and several liquors. The passengers kept the party going as the limo made its way to a swanky hotel in Beverly Hills.

The hotel was only a few miles away. Ryan could have ridden in the limo for the rest of the evening.

***

The limo turned into the hotel entrance. It cruised past the drive-up entrance to the registration lobby and drove to the ballroom complex farther back. Everyone in the limo sped up their drinking tempo to finish their drinks in the next 30 seconds without looking like they were chugging. The limo glided to a stop in front of the main entrance doors. People were mingling outside, enjoying the beautiful evening, greeting their friends, and maximizing the opportunity to see and be seen. Some were standing off to the side, sucking in the last cigarette they would be able to smoke for the next three or four hours.

Many of the other people seemed to be right at home in this environment. Ryan figured they probably attended this banquet every year, as well as banquets for other causes throughout the year. But he and Mike felt a bit overwhelmed by the entire spectacle. Every detail of the luxurious, expansive hotel had been painstakingly perfected by some designer to convey dignified opulence. The wealthy, upper-class people were dressed to the nines in either traditional formalwear or festive over-the-top outfits befitting fabulous gay men. Ryan's tasteful but understated suit seemed plain and conservative in comparison. Ryan realized that, as a high school kid from Kansas who had to do porn to save for college, he was far out of his element. But the glances and smiles he was receiving as they passed through the crowd reassured him that a tall, blond, and cute young man was a welcome addition to the evening.

Hal knew some of the people in attendance. He stopped every few steps to greet and hug some friend or acquaintance. Most of them seemed to know that his entourage of trailing young men were probably those who lived in his house. Ryan whispered to Ted, "Do you think these are all people he knows from the adult entertainment business?"

"I don't know. Probably some of them. But he's lived here for years. They could be board members of the Project, other people he's met in the community over the years, or friends he's met at parties. He has a pretty big network."

Ryan had never thought of Hal as a networker or a social butterfly. But he had attended a bunch of parties during the past holiday season and hosted one of his own. Hal was clearly adept at mingling, remembering names, and initiating brief conversations. The social Hal was a sharp contrast to the man Ryan was accustomed to seeing at home, where he was usually sequestered in his office working in solitude.

Since Ryan, Ted, and Mike knew no one outside of their party, they wandered around the silent auction tables filled with gift baskets, art and crafts, and gift certificates for spa treatments or weekends in a cabin. A few minutes before the banquet was due to start, Hal led the group into the banquet hall. The enormous room was crammed full of round tables with elegant place settings and fabulous floral centerpieces. Ryan estimated that there must be between 180 and 200 tables, which would mean between 1,800 and 2,000 attendees. At $100 a seat, that would mean the Project stood to raise between $180,000 and $200,000, minus expenses. As he looked around and took it all in, he wondered how much this extravagant affair cost to put on.

A broad stage bathed in festive lighting, with a fancy backdrop and some perfectly-placed flowering plants spanned one side of the room. A table held several large acrylic award plaques which were etched with lettering Ryan couldn't read from a distance. Two large video screens bookended the stage.

As the salad course got underway, some singers from the gay men's chorus entertained the crowd, followed by an all-male troupe of square dancers clad in cowboy garb. Ryan and Mike were among the few people in the crowd paying much attention. To most others who were engaging in conversations at their tables, they were a sideshow.

As the main course was served, a pair of MCs, a man and a woman, stepped up to the dais and welcomed the crowd. Their opening remarks had been tightly scripted to alternate their lines so that the man and the woman would receive equal time. They introduced a lengthy roster of local dignitaries including the mayor, several city council members, and a few state representatives and senators. Each received polite applause. Ryan realized that he would be doing a lot of clapping throughout the evening.

When the main course had concluded, the MCs returned to the stage and introduced Jean Holloway, the Executive Director of the LGBT Youth Project. She rose from her seat at a table in front and climbed the five steps up to the stage to appreciative applause. She was beaming with so much enthusiasm that Ryan wondered whether she had some sort of surprise or special announcement in store.

Jean began speaking. "Tonight, I am filled with gratitude. As I look out across this sea of two thousand beautiful faces, I marvel at the broad community support of our mission. I'm amazed at how far we have come in thirty years. This organization began as a support group for gay teens, meeting one night a week in a church basement. We held bake sales to raise funds. In thirty years, we've grown from bake sales to banquets. We've moved from that tiny room in the church basement to our own building. We are open 365 days a year to serve the needs of our youth. For twenty-two of those years, it has been my privilege and honor to serve as Executive Director. The journey hasn't always been easy. It has taken an army of volunteers, an active and committed Board, and the financial support of our community to do the amazing things we've been able to do. But there's one person in particular who has always been there behind the scenes, out of the spotlight, supporting me every step of the way. Of course, I'm referring to my partner of 25 years, Sue Jacobs. She's my rock. She's the wind beneath my wings. Tonight, I would like to thank her for always being right there at my side, through thick and thin. Sweetheart, would you please join me up here on stage?"

The crowd clapped enthusiastically as a shy, self-conscious woman climbed the steps and walked to the side of her partner.

"Now, as you know, two days ago the California Supreme Court ruled in favor of the right of same-sex couples to marry."

The crowd burst into applause, punctuated by a variety of whoops and hollers.

"Now, we're not quite there yet. There's been a request for a rehearing." Several people booed. "Our journey to this historic point has been filled with progress and setbacks, from legislative victories to Governor Schwarzenegger's vetoes to appeals court rulings. But now, I believe we are finally on the verge of achieving that goal many of us have only dreamed about for years."

Most of the crowd was giddy with excitement and anticipation. They sensed that something was about to happen. But Hal was visibly irritated. He turned toward Ted, Ryan, and Mike and whispered, "What the hell is she doing? She's taking all the focus off of the event! This is about the kids, not gay marriage!"

Ted replied, "I don't know, but it's getting the crowd whipped up. Maybe they'll donate more."

Ryan wondered if Hal wasn't in favor of same-sex marriage.

They turned their attention back to the stage and the Executive Director. She had refocused her remarks onto her partner at her side. "I often feel like I haven't been able to adequately thank you for your endless love and support. I've struggled to find a way to show my appreciation for everything you do and how much you mean to me. So tonight, in front of 2,000 of our closest friends, I have one question for you." She dropped to one knee. "Will you marry me?"

The crowd exploded. The applause continued while Jean stood up and the two women held each other in a long embrace. The female MC had returned to the stage with an enormous bouquet for Sue. Cameras snapped. Once the roar died down, Jean said, "You probably couldn't hear it, but she said yes!"

Finally, the crowd settled down and took their seats. Sue left the stage carrying her bouquet and returned to her seat, grateful to be out of the spotlight. Ryan wondered how Darnell would be able to follow a show-stopping moment like that.

Jean presented awards to an assortment of people and companies who had made valuable contributions to the Project or the LGBT+ community. Each recipient was featured in a brief video that highlighted their contributions. Ryan marveled at how much time and effort went into organizing and producing each video – all for the person's five minutes of fame at this gathering.

After six such awards, the crowd was ready for something a bit more entertaining. Not a moment too soon, the MCs returned and introduced one of the evening's featured entertainers. The male MC announced, "Our next performer has delighted audiences from Los Angeles to Provincetown to the Mediterranean."

Not missing a beat, the female MC continued. "With her amazing voice, her incisive comedy, and her fabulous outfits, she is winning the hearts of fans worldwide."

The male MC added, "She has performed in clubs and on Pride stages across the country. She performed on last summer's gay Mediterranean cruise. And tonight, she is here on our stage!"

The female MC concluded, "Ladies and gentlemen, please welcome the one, the only, the *fabulous* Whitney Austin!"

Ryan leaned over to Mike and said, "The guy in the gown is Darnell. He lives with us."

Immediately, an attention-grabbing big band track began playing. Whitney Austin walked confidently onto the stage, waving at the crowd and flashing an ear-to-ear smile. "Hello, Los Angeles!" She then launched into a fun, rollicking rendition of "I Can Cook Too," from the musical *On the Town*. She owned the song, and she owned the stage. The audience roared with applause.

When the applause died down, Whitney delivered several marriage jokes she had inserted into her act for this occasion. Then, she bemoaned her single status as a perfect segue into "Saving All My Love for You."

Next, Whitney delivered a brief comedy routine about her forays into online dating. She concluded with the advice that you need to love yourself before you can love someone else. Then she said, "This is my very favorite song, and I end every show with it. But tonight, since we are here to raise money to help our LGBT youth, the lyrics to this song take on a special meaning." On cue, the background track started and Whitney Austin launched into an emotional performance of "The Greatest Love of All."

Ryan was amazed at Darnell's talent. His voice was truly remarkable. It was difficult for Ryan to tell when Darnell's natural tenor slid seamlessly into his soaring falsetto, but the impact was visceral. But his voice was only half of the equation. Darnell was pouring his heart into every word he sang. Darnell's performance as Whitney connected with Ryan in a way he had rarely felt before in his life. Tears welled up in his eyes. He scanned the room. Nobody was taking a drink of water, checking their phone, or whispering to the person next to them. Every pair of eyes was focused on Whitney Austin, and most of those eyes were moist. Ryan glanced over at Ted. There were tears in his eyes, too. Ryan reached over and placed his hand on Ted's lap, and Ted held it.

When the song reached its emotional conclusion, everyone in the house rose to their feet with thunderous applause. Whitney bowed several times. Someone came up and gave her flowers.

When the applause died down and people took their seats again, Whitney took several steps forward to the edge of the stage and paused. She took a couple of deep breaths, then spoke.

"Thank you so much for all the love you have just shown me. It's a great privilege for me to be here this evening on this stage. You see, for me, this isn't just any gig. Tonight means more to me than any performance I have given in my life up to this point."

Darnell reached up and pulled his wig off. Some people in the audience gasped.

"Those of you who have seen me before know that this is not part of my act. But tonight, I would like to speak to you, not as Whitney Austin, singing sensation and queen diva…" Darnell paused while some in the audience chuckled, "…but as Darnell Jones.

"You see, just four years ago, I was a young black man, barely 18, from Macon, Georgia. When my daddy found out I was gay and I liked to dress up as a woman and try to sing like the divas I worshiped, well, let's just say it didn't go down very well. He didn't exactly kick me out, but he said to me, 'Son, there's no place for a boy like you here in Macon. There may be a place for you in some big city where all the faggots and freaks and weirdos go to live, but not here in these parts.' And then he told me he would pay for a bus ticket so I could go live in one of those big cities and be with my kind. And I got on that bus and rode it until it reached Los Angeles. When I got off that bus, I didn't know where I was. I didn't know anybody, I had no money, and I had no idea what I was going to do. For a few nights, I slept on the street or under a bridge or on a park bench. I begged on street corners so I could eat. And let me tell you, I was scared. Because I knew that if the wrong people figured out who I was… well, I don't want to think about what might have happened to me.

"But one day, I saw a billboard that said something about an LGBT Youth Project in Hollywood. Now, I was somewhere in downtown LA at the time, and I had no idea where Hollywood was or how I was going to get there. So, I started asking people, 'How do I get to Hollywood?' One guy said, 'Get an agent.'" Several people chuckled. "Another guy said, 'You don't belong in Hollywood, you belong in Compton.' But finally, someone said, 'It's up northwest of here.'

"So, I stood on the street corner begging until I had scraped up enough money to get on a bus. And somehow by the grace of God I made it to Hollywood and found my way to the Los Angeles LGBT Youth Project. And when I got there, someone smiled at me and said hello, like I was a real human being worth caring about. And they had food and a shower and a bed I could sleep on for the next few nights. And they helped me get a job and they found some people I could live with for a little while until I could get on my feet.

"Since that time, I got my GED and now I am studying to become a nurse practitioner. I make enough money to support myself. I live in a loving home with several other gay guys who are my family of choice. And I created Whitney Austin! I've been able to perform all across the country and on a gay cruise. I am achieving my goals and fulfilling my dreams. All because the Los Angeles LGBT Youth Project was there to pick me up when I was at the lowest, most hopeless point in my life. They gave me love, support, and hope. I am not exaggerating when I tell you that the Los Angeles LGBT Youth Project saved my life. I believe that with all my heart.

"My friends, the sad truth is that every day, several little Darnell or Darnella Joneses arrive in Los Angeles with no hope and no place to go. They may come from Mobile, Alabama or Wheeling, West Virginia or Pocatello, Idaho or Kalamazoo, Michigan. But they end up here. And those children, whose families just threw them away, become *our* children.

"Now, as I look around this room, I see that many of you are successful, affluent, and comfortable. And I know you've struggled, and you have worked hard for it, and you deserve it. I know that many of you have fought homophobia and prejudice to get where you are today. But somewhere along the way, someone gave you an opportunity. Someone gave you a hand. Someone showed you some love.

"Think about me, just four years ago. Think about those kids who just got off the bus today. Remember the words I just sang. Those children are our future. Tonight, I am asking you to open your mind, open your heart, and open your wallet. Will you do that for me?"

Some people applauded.

Darnell spoke louder. "I said, will you do that for me?"

The applause escalated.

"Thank you. I love you. Now, I'd like to sing the song I always sing as an encore. It's by the wonderful Patti Austin – she's the other half of my name – and she did it as a fundraiser for AIDS research. It's called 'We're All in This Together' – because we are."

The background track started, and a wigless Whitney Austin sang her heart out.

Jean Holloway returned to the stage. "Let's hear it for Whitney Austin!" The crowd rose to its feet and roared. Whitney took several graceful curtsies, waved goodbye to the crowd, and sashayed off the stage.

Jean continued. "Well, I had some prepared remarks, but I don't think I can say anything more heartfelt and passionate than what Darnell said just moments ago. Our volunteers are circulating among the tables now with pledge cards and envelopes. You'll find some pens near the center of each table. I'd like to humbly ask each of you to look deep into your heart. Remember what Darnell said about how there are kids who arrive here every day from all over the country, with no home and no hope. Please give what you can, so the LGBT Youth Project can continue to expand and thrive and provide a place to stay and resources so these kids can have a fresh start. Those children are now our children. They are our future."

Ryan recalled the day he arrived in LA by bus and had taken a cab to the LGBT Youth Project. He remembered his intake interview with a friendly, caring woman named Cynthia, who made him feel like he mattered and things would be okay. He remembered her saying, 'So many kids who arrive here have no place to go. We have some beds here, but often there aren't enough and kids end up sleeping on the street. They come from all over the country. It's tragic how many parents kick their kids out and how many kids come here to escape bad living situations. We have a lot of resources to help runaway and homeless kids, but it never seems to be quite enough.'

He knew he was lucky – he never had to live on the street. Through some kind of miracle, Hal came along at the right time and happened to have a room available in his house. Ryan reflected on his good fortune. It could have been so much worse.

Ryan knew his first priority was saving for school. But now, thanks to his new career, he was pulling in $8,000 to $10,000 a month. He owned a car. Paying for college now seemed assured, not hopeless. He could afford to give a little to help other kids who were in the same predicament he had been in just ten months ago. He filled out the pledge card and gave $2,500 – the usual amount he was making for shooting a porn scene these days. With his earnings from only one shoot, he could help some disowned, cast-away homeless kids have a better life. That was something he could give a fuck about – literally.

He wondered if he should give more, then decided this was enough for now. He could donate more at any time. He decided that supporting an organization such as the LGBT Youth Project that helped queer kids in need would be something he would do for the rest of his life, just like Hal was doing.

The banquet dragged on for two more hours with a live auction for some extravagant prizes, another entertainer, and a keynote speaker. Everyone in the room was growing tired. People trickled out into the lobby. Some ordered yet another drink and continued to mingle, while others queued up for the valets to retrieve their cars. Ryan got the feeling that a few people in the crowd recognized him since videos starring him were now being released. Hal introduced him to several people he knew in 'the business.' including a photographer who expressed an interest in doing a nude photoshoot with Ryan for potential submission to a gay magazine or a gay calendar. He gave Ryan his card and took Ryan's contact info. Ryan said he'd think about it.

After about 15 minutes, Darnell arrived in plain clothes, carrying his garment bag and a small rolling suitcase that contained his high heels, his wig, and all his make-up accessories. Ryan gave Darnell a big hug and said, "Honey, you were *fabulous*! You just killed. There wasn't a dry eye in the house!"

Darnell was still riding the high from his smashing performance, and still partially in character. He turned his head to one side so Ryan could place a dainty kiss on his cheek.

Ryan introduced Darnell to Mike.

Ted said, "That was awesome. You did great. And I know you brought in a lot of money for the Project."

Darnell replied, "And that's what really counts."

Other people started flocking around Darnell. Several people who seemed a bit more purposeful chatted with him and handed him business cards.

After Hal and Darnell circulated a bit longer, Hal texted the limo driver. A few minutes later, they were piling back into the limo. The ball was over. The clock was about to strike midnight.

Catharsis

Saturday, May 17, 2008

After the limo dropped everyone off at Hal's house, Ryan and Mike climbed into Ryan's car so he could drive Mike home. Mike hadn't said much during the evening. Ryan asked, "So what did you think? Did you have a good time?"

"Oh, man. It was awesome. And eye-opening. The whole thing was kinda overwhelming. I've never been in a room with so many other gay people in my life."

"Totally. I just experienced a part of gay society I never knew existed."

"Yeah. Hey, could we pull over for a few minutes and talk?"

"Sure." Ryan pulled into the parking lot of a grocery store and parked in a space near the street.

Mike continued. "I'm still trying to process it all. I mean, that was like 300 times more gay people than I've ever been around before."

"I know, right? And it's like, this is the first time I've ever been in a situation where gays were the majority. Everybody could be themselves without worrying about whether they fit in. Like being gay was the norm."

"Yeah. And it was kinda nice to see gay people who are successful and affluent and comfortable with who they are."

"I hear ya. It gave me hope. I mean, we'll both be going to good universities. We'll come out with engineering degrees and get well-paying jobs. That will be us in ten years."

"I dunno. I've never thought of myself as being – I don't know – high society and fabulous like that."

"Me neither. That was totally unlike anything I ever saw in Kansas. Or even imagined."

There was a brief pause in the conversation. Ryan was about to start the car up again. But then Mike said, "So anyway, I had a great time with you tonight. Thanks for bringing me along."

"Yeah. I'm really glad you could come."

"And last weekend too, at the prom. I have to admit, I was pretty scared for most of the evening. But in hindsight, I realize I didn't have anything to be scared of. Now that I look back on it, it was fun."

"Yeah, it was. Well, except for getting my car keyed."

"And again, thanks for asking me to come with you." Mike paused. "I really like you. I'm going to miss you next year."

"I like you too. But don't worry, there will be lots of new kids for you to meet at Stanford. And plenty of gay kids. I'm sure they have a gay group there. And you won't be living with your parents, so you can be more open if you want to."

"Yeah, but I'll still miss you." Mike paused again. "I'm kind of kicking myself right now. I wish I hadn't been so scared all year."

"Scared? Scared of what?"

"Of being gay. Of having the other kids find out. Of letting you know I like you, let alone asking you out. I was scared of actually falling in love with a guy."

Ryan glanced over at Mike. A few tears were running down his cheeks. Ryan had no idea what to say at this moment. He reached over and took Mike's hand.

Mike continued, "And then I saw you and Payton getting together, and I knew I had missed my chance."

Ryan thought, *Shit. Stupid, naïve me – I had no idea. I would have rather dated Mike than Payton any day.*

Ryan said, "Well, we still have this summer. I'd love to hang out together. We can go hiking or go to the beach or go to some concerts. Maybe go to Disneyland. We can go swimming at my house. And we can get together whenever you come home on breaks."

"Yeah, but it won't be the same as seeing you every day like we did at school."

"True, but that would have ended when we both went off to college anyway."

"I guess. Still, I wish we had those few months."

"Me too. Anyway, we can still be friends. We can stay in touch."

Mike didn't say anything. He just sniffled and wiped away his tears.

Ryan said, "You're a really sweet guy." He leaned over and kissed him. It was just a friendly, affectionate kiss. Mike smiled. They kissed again. And again. Then Mike put his hand on the back of Ryan's head and held him close while he pressed his open lips against Ryan's.

Ryan flashed back to that night last June when he and Chris were kissing in the car and the cop busted them. He suddenly started panicking and pushed Mike away. "I'm sorry. We can't do this out here in this parking lot."

"Why not?"

Ryan started sobbing. "Because when I did this with my boyfriend Chris, we got caught by a cop, and that's how my parents found out I'm gay. And because of that, I had to run away from home, and I now may never see Chris or my little brother Brandon again." Tears were streaming down Ryan's cheeks. He folded his arms on the steering wheel and buried his head in them while his sobs grew louder.

Mike didn't understand how that had anything to do with them kissing. He didn't know how to handle seeing strong, confident Ryan breaking down like this. He had no idea what to say.

Ryan was trembling and tears were streaming down his face. He picked his head up and stared out the windshield. He started blurting stuff out with no filters. "You have no idea what it's been like to have to run away from home because your parents hate you because you're gay. To constantly have to watch everything you say for fear someone will turn you in and then you'll get sent back. To fall in love with the guy you want to spend the rest of your life with, and then have to leave him behind and not even let him know where you are or what happened. To not know when you'll ever see your little brother again. To have to leave your high school and all your friends and come out here to this place where everything's second-rate and a lot of the kids are shitheads. To have people tease me because I have a big dick. Hell, I didn't choose that, I was born that way. I had to celebrate Thanksgiving and Christmas without my family, and now they're not going to see me graduate. I'm all alone in the world. I mean, the guys at the house have been great to me, and I try to be thankful. I know I'm better off than most of the runaway kids who end up here. But it still sucks, goddammit. And then I have to do fucking porn to make enough money to survive and pay for college, and then people give me shit about that! IT'S NOT FAIR, AND IT SUCKS, AND I FUCKING HATE IT!!!" Ryan pounded his fists on the steering wheel.

Mike had no idea how to respond. He reached for the door handle. "Hey, uh, I'd better be going. Don't worry, it's not far. I can walk from here." Mike stepped out of the car, shut the door, and took off running across the parking lot. *Shit,* he thought. *I finally got to kiss a boy – a boy I really like. I finally got up the nerve to tell him I like him. And he pushed me away, and he broke down and started crying. Am I really that gross? Just ... Fuck my life.*

Ryan stayed in the car with his head buried in his arms, resting on the steering wheel. He cried his eyes out.

After about ten minutes, his phone buzzed. It was a text from Ted. *Everything okay?*

He texted back. *No.*

Where are you? Do you need help?

No, I'm safe. I'll be home soon.

Ryan took a couple of minutes to calm down and compose himself, then he drove back home. He hoped his housemates had gone to bed and the other people who went to the banquet weren't still there partying. He wanted to go straight to his room and not have anybody see him like this.

He almost made it, but Ted heard him come in. He stepped out of his bedroom and saw the pain in Ryan's eyes and the dried tears staining his cheeks. He wrapped his arms around Ryan. "What happened?"

"I don't know. I was taking Mike home, and we parked the car just to talk. But then we started kissing, and that trigged me 'cause it made me think of that time Chris and I were kissing in the car and we got caught by that cop. Then I totally lost it. I started crying and saying all kinds of shit about how terrible my life has been. Then Mike got out of the car and ran away. I totally lost my shit."

"I'm sorry." Ted kept hugging him. He heard Ryan sniffle. "Sounds like you had a lot of stuff bottled up inside, and it finally got out. Maybe you needed some catharsis."

"Maybe. But right now I just want to go to bed, okay? We can talk about it tomorrow if I feel like it."

Ted released Ryan. "Okay. Goodnight."

The Valedictorian Speaks
Thursday, June 5, 2008

Tonight was Ryan's high school graduation – the ceremonial culmination of twelve years of school. Ryan couldn't stop thinking about the Valedictorian speech he would give this evening. He ran through it over and over in his head. He sat down at his laptop every 15 or 20 minutes and tweaked the wording. He did so many run-throughs standing in front of his full-length mirror that he practically had the speech memorized.

At 5:30, he eagerly chomped down a microwaved chicken pesto entrée. After the ceremony, his housemates were going to take him to Burger Betty's in WeHo to celebrate, so he just needed enough to tide him over until then. He hoped he wouldn't belch or fart or get an upset stomach, given his nervous anticipation.

At 5:45, he changed into a white dress shirt, dark blue tie, black pants, and black shoes. He printed a final copy of his speech, grabbed the plastic bag which held his cap and gown, and headed for the door.

At 6:15, he arrived at the high school gymnasium. The seniors lined up in the proper order for their march out to the ceremony. Mrs. Rodriguez emphasized that they needed to stay in the correct order, so they would receive the correct diploma. She reviewed the route they should take from their seats to the right side of the stage, across the stage, down the left side, and back to the same row. As Valedictorian, Ryan would be seated on stage, along with Mrs. Rodriguez, the assistant principal, a representative from the school board, and several faculty members.

The kids were so giddy with excitement they were barely paying attention. Ryan was completely preoccupied with his speech. It was the first time he had ever spoken in front of a gathering of hundreds of people, and he wanted it to be perfect. He thought of Brad, his biological father, who spoke to hundreds of people every week on the gigantic stage of the Eternal Savior Christian Church. While the subject matter was entirely different, Ryan hoped he could project some of the poise and confidence Brad had mastered.

At 7:00 sharp, the gymnasium doors opened. The juniors and sophomores from the wind ensemble began playing "Pomp and Circumstance." All the alphabetically-sequenced seniors processed in a line out to the football field.

Rows of folding white chairs were set up between the 35-yard lines, facing the center of the field. A portable stage had been set up with a lectern, a sound system, and several folding tables with stacks of diplomas. The grandstand was filled with the proud families of the soon-to-be graduates. It was a far cry from the marching band rehearsals and Friday night football games of the previous autumn. It seemed almost surreal.

After everyone had filed into their places, the band played "The Star-Spangled Banner." Mrs. Rodriguez welcomed everyone and introduced the various dignitaries on stage. She then introduced the class president, who gave a brief speech. Ryan didn't glean much substance from it. He wondered if she used a speech she found on the internet.

The speech ended with polite applause. Then Mrs. Rodriguez stepped up to the microphone and announced, "Ladies and gentlemen, our class Valedictorian, Ryan Robertson." There was scattered applause. Since Ryan had spent only his senior year at Westwood High School, he didn't know most kids as well as he might have if he had spent four years there. Most of the kids were probably wondering, 'who is this guy?'

Ryan stepped up to the lectern and scanned the crowd. For a brief moment, the fact that he was standing on stage commanding the attention of almost a thousand people filled him with both pride and fear. For a few brief minutes, this was his time to be heard. He took a deep breath, forced a smile, and told himself, *You've got this.*

"Good evening fellow students, faculty, administration, parents, families, friends, and distinguished guests. In other words, everyone who's here tonight." A few people chuckled.

"It seems hard to believe that our journey through primary and secondary school is finally coming to an end. Throughout the past twelve-plus years, there were probably many times when you thought school would never end. Each year seemed to go on forever. But now, here we are. It has come to an end. But tonight is more than just an occasion to celebrate. It's an occasion to look back and reflect upon some of the most memorable moments that have taken place along the way – both the good and the bad – for they have made us the people we are today. It's an occasion to remember our teachers and our fellow students, for they each taught us something.

"For many of us, school was not easy. It certainly wasn't easy for me. Sometimes it was quite difficult, both academically and in other ways. There may have been times when calculus or chemistry or medieval history kicked your butt. And there may have been times when a bully or a group of mean kids kicked your butt – figuratively or literally. But if school was always easy and we just sailed right through it, we wouldn't have learned nearly as much. We wouldn't have grown. Each of those butt-kickings was an opportunity to learn, grow, work harder, overcome an obstacle, and become better. Each of those challenges, setbacks, and defeats was temporary, but the knowledge, growth, and strength we gained from them will carry us forward throughout our lives and help us meet each new challenge.

"Your life after today won't be easy, either. Chances are good that at some point, you'll get fired. You'll be discriminated against, and maybe physically harmed. You'll be cheated and have things stolen from you. Your heart will get broken. There will be times when you struggle to make ends meet. For those of us who are going on to college, the classes will get harder, not easier. But remember, each of those challenges, setbacks, and defeats will be temporary, and they will be an opportunity for you to grow stronger and improve.

"The world we now enter as high school graduates is an imperfect place. Of course, you all know that. But it's also a beautiful place. Always try to see the beauty in each sunset and flower; the beauty in art, music, and literature; and the beauty in each person you encounter. With some people, you might have to look hard for it, but believe me, it's there, somewhere." More chuckles.

"As you go out into the world, you have a choice. You can look at the pollution, the political corruption, the wars, and all the intolerance and hatred that exists, and you can give in to it. You can allow yourself to become cynical, hopeless, and mean. You can become part of the problem. Or you can look at everything that's wrong with the world and see it as an opportunity to make it a little better. You might not discover the cure for cancer, but you can create a better way to do something or find a new solution to a problem. You may not be able to bring about world peace, but you can treat everyone you meet with kindness, compassion, and respect. You can try harder to understand and accept people who are different from you. You may not be able to end world hunger, but you can donate to or volunteer for an organization that helps homeless kids or other people in need.

"As we leave this place and venture out into the world, I wish every one of you happiness, good health, and success. I hope you find good jobs, make lots of money, find people to love, and have plenty of fun. I hope you live comfortably and enjoy your life. But in addition to whatever career success you might achieve and whatever material things you may acquire, I want to wish you this more than anything else: that you'll be a good person – a decent, honorable, loving, and tolerant human being. Come to someone's rescue. Comfort someone who's hurting. Stand up for what's right in the face of hatred and injustice. Always take the high road, even when it's the more difficult path. Be part of the solution, not part of the problem.

"Now, go out and make the world a better place, and have a blast doing it!"

The crowd rose to its feet and applauded enthusiastically. Ryan paused for a second to bask in the moment – all his classmates in their robes and square hats cheering, and him up on stage receiving their applause. He glanced over at Mrs. Rodriguez. She was smiling at him proudly. He gathered his notes and smiled as he stepped away from the lectern. It had been a difficult year, but at this moment, everything was okay.

After the ceremony concluded, the seniors sought out their friends, hugged and congratulated each other, and posed for pictures. The families filed out of the bleachers, and the two groups converged into a sea of people looking for their loved ones. Ryan spotted Hal, Ted, Darnell, and Ricky up in the stands during the ceremony, but he couldn't yet see where they were among the meandering crowd. As he scanned the crowd looking for them, he felt a tap on his shoulder. He turned around. It was Jordan. "Hey, Ryan."

"Hey."

"So, uh… that was a great speech you gave."

"Thanks." Ryan turned to go look for his chosen family again.

"Um, Ryan…"

Ryan turned back to face Jordan again.

"You know all that stuff you said about being a decent person? About being kind and tolerant and trying harder to understand and accept people who are different from you?"

Ryan nodded.

"Well…" Jordan paused. "I felt like you were talking directly to me. I know I said and did a lot of really bad things this past year, like putting Vaseline on your values and messing up that display. I said a lot of bad stuff about you and, well, I was pretty much a total jerk."

Ryan thought, *So it was you who defaced our GSA bulletin board display. I guess I shouldn't be surprised.*

"Anyway, some stuff happened at the prom and, uh, let's just say one of our mutual friends called me out on my shit. I've been thinking about it ever since. Now I realize that I did some terrible things, and I'm ashamed of them and, well, I've been a pretty shitty person. So I'm going to try to change my attitude. You know, be part of the solution, not part of the problem, like you said. All the stuff you talked about in your speech. And, uh, I'm sorry. I'm sorry for everything. What I did was wrong. I wish I could take it all back and do it over again, but I can't. Anyway, I just want to let you know I'm sorry, and I'm going to try to do better."

Ryan extended his hand and Jordan shook it. "Thanks. Apology accepted." Ryan turned to go.

"Oh, and… it was Julio who keyed your car. I didn't do it, and actually, I talked him out of slashing your tires. But I couldn't stop him from keying your car. How much did it cost to get it fixed?"

"Around $500. They didn't have to repaint the whole car, they just had to paint over the sections that got keyed. The paint matched up pretty well. You can't really tell."

"Okay, good, and … well … I want to pay for it."

"Why? You didn't do it."

"Yeah, but I want to pay for it anyway. Just to kind of make up for everything I've done to you."

"Nah, that's okay. Don't worry about it."

"No, man, I really want to. I want to do something nice for you – sort of a peace offering. It's important to me."

"Well, okay, but…"

"Can I send it to you by PayPal?"

"Yeah, I guess…"

"What's your email?"

Ryan gave it to him, even though he didn't want to have anything more to do with Jordan. He hoped he would never see him again.

"Okay, thanks. And great speech. I'll bet your parents are proud of you."

"Nope. I don't have parents anymore. I'm not in contact with them. See those guys over there? I live in a house with them. They're my family now."

Ryan turned and started walking toward his chosen family. Jordan followed. "Huh? I don't get it. What's the deal with your parents?"

This was the last thing Ryan wanted to think about right now, but he realized it could be a teaching moment. "They couldn't handle me being gay. They were going to send me to some isolated place that was going to try to force me to become straight. I had to run away."

"So… you're out on your own?"

"Yep."

"Wow. That sucks. I had no idea."

"Maybe if you had gotten to know me instead of hating on me, you would have known. Maybe things would have turned out different. But whatever. Too late now. Anyway, I have these guys. They love and support me. I'm very fortunate." Ryan was now a few steps away from the guys. "Well, good luck. Have a nice life."

"Yeah. You too." Jordan stood still, trying to absorb everything he had just heard. He watched as Hal, Ted, Darnell, and Ricky hugged Ryan and congratulated him. The camaraderie and affection they shared were obvious. Ryan looked genuinely happy as he and his housemates walked toward the parking lot, bantering back and forth.

Jordan's parents walked up to him. His mom hugged him and said, "Congratulations dear, we're so proud of you!"

Jordan's dad said, "Yeah, good job, son." He extended his hand and gave Jordan a manly handshake. They started walking toward the parking lot. "That guy you were talking to… the guy who gave the speech? I just saw him hugging a bunch of other guys. Is he queer or something?"

"He's gay."

"They're not gay, they're miserable. You shouldn't be hanging around with queers. They'll try to recruit you."

Jordan knew there was nothing he could say to his dad. He wished he would shut up about it, but he didn't.

"No wonder he was up there saying all that touchy-feely, kumbaya crap. I can't believe they let him speak. But I guess the schools have bought into all that liberal diversity shit now."

Jordan said, "He got to speak because he got the best grades in the class. That's what Valedictorian means."

"Do you think I'm stupid? I know what Valedictorian means. And I know it should have been you."

Jordan sighed. *I earned a 3.92 GPA. Wasn't that good enough?* "I thought it was a good speech."

Jordan's mother came to the rescue. "Let's not argue now. This is a special night. My son, my special man, is now a high school graduate!

I'm very proud of you, dear."

"Thanks, Mom."

"Are there any parties you want to go to?"

"Not really. Let's just go home." Jordan didn't have many friends left, and he realized he had made some poor choices in that regard. He was through with them. Fortunately, it was unlikely that any of them would be going to UCLA next year.

Afterword

Thank you for purchasing and reading this book. I hope you enjoyed it.

This is the second in a series of six books that follow Ryan as he finishes high school, goes to college, launches his career, forms relationships, and comes to terms with his past.

I invite you to subscribe to my newsletter. I'll keep you informed about my upcoming books and offer them to you at a discount. I'll share background information about the stories and the writing process. From time to time, I may solicit your input which will help make the books even better! To join, visit my website: AuthorDaveHughes.com.

To thank you for joining, I will send my short story, *Cruise Virgins*. In it, Ryan (as a young adult) and Ted experience their first gay cruise – and confront their feelings for one another.

Now, I have a small favor to ask.

As a new, self-published author, it's incredibly difficult to get my books noticed in a world in which hundreds, if not thousands, of new books are released every day. It's challenging to build an audience for my work. If you enjoyed this book, please consider posting something about it on your social media platform of choice. All it takes is something simple, like 'I just finished reading *Instant Adult*, by Dave Hughes. It was great! Check it out.' Also, please consider leaving an honest review on the website where you purchased this book.

Thanks! I truly appreciate it.

I would like to thank my beta readers who provided valuable feedback that helped me improve this book: Linda Magata, Jeff McKeehan, Russ Smith, and Michelle Taquino Alcina. Also, I would like to thank my launch team: Tom Bogardus, Gary Brenkman, Aaron Chavez, Jeff McKeehan, and Mike Triggs. And thanks to Chad Anderson for sharing his subject matter expertise.

Very special thanks to Mark McNease – friend, prolific author of LGBT-themed mysteries (check them out!), and promoter of all things positive about aging – for his generous and enthusiastic support of all my writing, from RetireFabulously.com and my three retirement lifestyle books to my current fiction projects.

Most importantly, I would like to thank my husband, Jeff McKeehan, who has supported and encouraged me every step of the way, provided great ideas and valuable feedback, and tolerated all those times when my mind was immersed in the world of my characters. Every spouse of an author knows exactly what I'm talking about.

Other Books by Dave Hughes

Fiction

Maybe Next Year
Open Books, Closed Sets
If I Seem Quiet...

Retirement Lifestyle

Design Your Dream Retirement
Smooth Sailing into Retirement
The Quest for Retirement Utopia

AuthorDaveHughes.com

About the Author

This is author Dave Hughes' second novel. It is the second of four published novels in the series "Gay Tales for the New Millennium," with two more scheduled for release in 2024.

Before writing fiction, Dave wrote three retirement lifestyle planning books, *Design Your Dream Retirement, Smooth Sailing Into Retirement,* and *The Quest for Retirement Utopia.* Dave created the website RetireFabulously.com, which enables readers to envision, plan for, and enjoy the best retirement possible. In addition to writing hundreds of articles for RetireFabulously.com, Dave's writing has appeared on US News & World Report, lgbtSr.com, Medium, Yahoo! Finance, CNN/Money, Next Avenue, Tiny Buddha, and others.

Aside from his writing, Dave is also a jazz musician. He plays trombone and steel pan in various bands in the Phoenix area. He owns an embarrassingly large collection of jazz, Brazilian, exotica, steel band, jazz/rock, and vocal ensemble CDs and videos.

Before retiring early at age 56, Dave was a software engineer for 34 years, working for companies such as Intel Corporation, Computer Sciences Corporation, McDonnell Douglas Space Systems, and NCR Corporation. Throughout his career, his assignments included software development, customer support, training, course development, and management.

Dave resides in Chandler, Arizona with his husband Jeff and their dog Maynard.

Dave is available for interviews, book readings/signings, speaking engagements, and panel discussions. You may contact Dave at dave@authordavehughes.com.

Visit AuthorDaveHughes.com to learn more and subscribe to his newsletter.